A

MIDNIGHT
SO
DEADLY

WREN HANDMAN

First published in November 2024

E-book ISBN: 978-1-956136-79-1

Paperback ISBN: 978-1-956136-80-7

PARLIAMENT HOUSE PRESS

www.parliamenthousepress.com

Cover by: Maria Spada

Edited by: Malorie Nilson and Sabrina Terry

1

MAEVE

When Maeve decided to record her dreams and post them online for everyone to see, she had imagined it all—the glitz of a rooftop party, VIPs turned out in style, the flash of cameras and the call of crowds. The thrill of baring your soul for the world and having them say, "Yes, yes! We feel the same, and we love you for it!"

What she *hadn't* imagined was spending three hours trying to edit together some semblance of entertainment from a surreal nightmare about giant slugs.

Rolling the footage back for the eighteenth time, she watched as her foot, with pale ankle skin peeking out above a bright yellow sneaker, came *shlucking* backward out of a pile of gleaming, gelatinous slug goop. It was disgusting. Hilarious, but disgusting—and definitely not on brand. *I really need to stop watching gardening shows before bed.*

She chuckled and cut that section, then leaned back to watch the clip she recorded the night before. It had been a weird one. In the dream, she and her best friend Josie had been kicked out of a bar only to discover that the world had been overrun with yellow gastropods the size of buses. The ridiculous scene culminated in an even more absurd game of chicken between a blue minivan and a slug, after which the narrative sort of fell apart. When she woke up the dream lingered, like cobwebs she couldn't get off her fingertips.

Maeve knew the footage wouldn't be that popular, but she could play it for laughs. She stopped editing to take a long pull from an energy drink, rubbing an itch on her ear as she did. Absent-mindedly, she scooped a spoonful of cereal into her mouth before spitting it out in disgust as the soggy mess reminded her of how long it had been sitting.

She leaned back in her chair and closed her eyes, then groaned as she kicked herself back into gear. *Just finish this and then you can go,* she promised herself. It would all be worth it someday, when her channel took off.

Maeve liked to joke that she'd become a dreamer because she loved the commute—right from the bed to the computer in her tiny bachelor basement suite. The truth was that she'd always felt like an artist, but with no particular talent. She loved to listen to music but couldn't sing in key. She could spend hours wandering through art galleries and maker spaces, but when it came time to put brush to canvas or hands to tools, she didn't have the skill to bring any of her half-formed ideas to life.

In high school, everyone called her dramatic, and she embraced it. A gifted kid with consistently good grades, Maeve wore printed scarves, quoted her favourite literature, and filled her electives with novel studies and art classes. Most of her friends were theatre kids, and she briefly toyed with the idea of being an actor. But she knew her chances of success were slim, didn't want a schedule where she worked eighteen hours a day, and hated the pressure of live performance.

That left her mired in the kind of deep existential crisis that only a teenager can truly appreciate. A life without a creative outlet felt like a prison sentence. There had to be *something* she could do, *something* she was good at! Then, a few years after she left university with a Bachelor of Communications and no real goal, the technology to record dreams was invented.

Suddenly, Maeve's fertile imagination and quirky attitude had a purpose. When she started to share her dreams with the world, she finally became the artist she always imagined herself to be. People actually liked her stories, and she felt like she was finally contributing something. When she died—hopefully on some far instance day—she would leave a real mark on the world. *If* she could crack the popularity code and make a name for herself in the saturated field of dreaming.

That meant putting in the work. Maeve tapped the air to navigate over to Zzz+ and uploaded the teaser trailer, reminded viewers to like and subscribe, then did the same on her other social media platforms. She would finish editing the whole story tomorrow, but for now she was done—and done in.

She rubbed her eyes again and checked the views on her last video. *Oof.* Her manager wasn't going to like that. Most of her content was highly narrative, but she had tried posting a surreal piece to draw in new viewers... with dismal results. Maeve was two years deep into her career, just six months into becoming a full-time streamer, and every day felt like a struggle to keep up with the mad pace of the industry.

A vibration at her wrist indicated a call was coming in, and Maeve flung her fingers up and forward to accept it through her computer. For a second, she thought she might have summoned Laura, her angry manager, just by thinking about her.

When the box appeared, it was Josie's laughing face that took over the screen instead, her silky black hair falling across her perfectly made-up face as she mugged at Maeve through the camera. Josie had the classic good looks of a 1930s film star. She should have been walking into an office in an expensive fur coat to fire a jaded private eye to solve her husband's murder, not going out for cheap beer on a Friday night. Maeve made sure the camera on her end was dead; she didn't want Josie to know she wasn't dressed yet.

"Womaaaaan! You better not still be at home!" the tall Filipina-Russian woman hollered. In the phone's awkwardly angled image Maeve could see that Josie was in a car; her boyfriend Jason, who was probably driving, wasn't visible, but there were three large and uncomfortable-looking men crammed into the back seat.

Maeve winced at her best friend's good-natured scolding. She had known Josie for a decade and had never been able to match her friend's punctuality. Josie had everything together, from her career as a massage therapist to her beautiful apartment and successful boyfriend. Maeve sometimes wondered how she put up with the chaos that defined Maeve's day-to-day, but the two friends might as well have been attached at the hip.

"I'm not! I'm on my way," Maeve promised. She moved the window on her screen out of the way with a flick of her wrist and logged into her bank account. The balance was almost as depressing as the outfit she picked out for tonight.

"You are such a liar. I can *see* you're in your apartment."

Maeve panic-checked her camera, saw it was definitely off, and then realized what Josie had done. "Stop using Find My Friend! That's for emergencies!" Maeve quickly transferred a few dollars from her savings to her checking account, biting her lip. Could she afford two drinks with Josie before she went out for her dinner date, or only one? And did she really want to go on a date with someone who thought ten p.m. was—

"Stop being a *liar* and *get your butt out here!*" Josie hollered.

"Okay, okay, I'm leaving!" Maeve gestured one finger in a 'come hither' crook, and the call seamlessly transferred from her computer to her watch. "Give me five minutes."

"You better be squeezing into some Spanx and putting on your shoes."

"Bitch, did you just say I need Spanx?" Maeve grabbed the deceased bowl of cereal and the empty energy drink can and ran them into the kitchen.

"No, obviously your curves are perfect and beautiful, and any man or woman would be lucky to have you, but we are literally pulling up now!" Josie turned the camera so that Maeve could see outside the car window, but it was so dark, and the image was so small Maeve had no idea what she was looking at. "You need to come here right now and save me from being the only woman in the group. You're already leaving early. You're not allowed to *also* be late!"

"I know, I know, I'm sorry!" Maeve ran into the bathroom, shrugging out of her white-woman-on-a-budget yoga pants, and grabbed the *Tetris*-print leggings she had set out earlier. She tugged a loose grey cable-knit sweater-dress over her tank top and grabbed the small, dangling rainbow earrings she had conveniently placed on the edge of the sink. *Thank you, Past Maeve.*

Critically, she examined the effect in the mirror. Her brown curls were thick and hung a few inches past her shoulders, and the remains of the eyeliner she applied yesterday added a pop of green that brought out hints of hazel in her deep brown eyes. The sweater would probably look better with a necklace, but it complimented her curves enough for a first date with a "maybe" swipe from a dating app. "Okay, I'm dressed, I'm peeing, and then I'm out the door!"

"Don't hang up on me!"

"What part of 'I'm peeing' did you not understand?" Maeve tapped her watch with three fingers, grinning as it disconnected. Josie may not have had the world's most well-established boundaries, but without her Maeve would *definitely* have been late. Later.

Maeve waved a hand over-dramatically through the air, almost shouting over the music and the noise of the other tables around her. "No, no, because abstract dreams don't *give* you anything! It's all on you to interpret and try to pull a story out of—"

"But that's what people *like* about it," Matt insisted, enjoying the argument. Matt was a young Chinese with broad, slightly rounded features and one dimple. He and Maeve had met at club week during university, bonded over their mutual love of board games, and quickly became friends. As a computer science major, his life had taken a different path than hers—a more successful one, some might argue. Despite that, their friendship stayed strong. "They're tired of being spoon-fed their entertainment! Watching a fic-dream is just watching a movie that isn't directed by—"

Maeve put down her glass of local craft beer mid-sip, shaking her head. "No no no, it's way more immersive! A movie is completely flat! With a dream—"

"Immersive? Without a VR rig, a dream is *literally just a movie*— but it's a movie with all this context you're not getting because you don't have access to the vocabulary of the dreamer!"

Matt, Josie, and Maeve were crowded around a small square bartop table at Brass Screw, a trendy brewery on Main Street. The walls were decorated with polished wood beams, and the exposed pipes along the ceiling did nothing to dampen the sound of forty-plus people enjoying a night of drink and conversation. The smell of hops and wheat easily overpowered any perfume or cologne the young crowd wore.

Jason and his three friends, who Maeve didn't know by name, were at an adjacent bar-top having a parallel conversation. They all looked oddly similar: white men in their late twenties, with expert fades and expensive smartwatches, wearing expensive jeans and bright sneakers paired with graphic T-shirts. Jason clearly spent some time in the gym, and his friends were the same, though none of them had the V-shape of dedicated bodybuilders.

With seven people drinking, there were beer glasses everywhere; Maeve had immediately forgotten she was only supposed to have one drink, but she hadn't yet done the mental calculus to decide how that would impact what she could afford to order for dinner later.

Josie, looking effortlessly beautiful in a cropped tank top and skinny jeans, leaned her chin on her hand and cut in. "I'm not sure I buy that you need VR for a dream to be immersive. Sure, if you wear a VR rig you can experience the dream first-person, just like the dreamer did. But not everyone likes that. It puts you in someone else's shoes, someone you might not identify with. If you watch a dream on a screen, like you would a movie, it can actually be *easier* to empathize, because that's the way we're used to consuming stories. Third-person."

"Let's not get off-track," Matt countered, running a hand through his buzzed black hair. "We're talking content, not medium. I'm saying that when you *have* a dream, you have context that's missing when you *watch* a dream."

"Like if the dreamer is in their childhood home, they recognize that fact and it colours the setting and adds emotions for them. But if you're watching the dream, on Zee Plus or through VR, you don't get that context?" Josie asked.

"Exactly!"

"Yeah, but both the dreamer and the characters featured in the dream know, and that comes through from the way they respond to the situations around them," Maeve countered. "It's subtext for the viewer, not context, but it enriches it."

"You talking about dreams?" the guy on her other side asked. Maeve turned to give him more of her attention, immediately distracted by the words "Download This" on his shirt, with an accompanying arrow pointing to his crotch. If the idiotic slogan was anything to go by, this wasn't going to be a promising detour in the conversation.

"Yeah—I'm a dreamer."

"Oh, cool! Have I heard of you?"

"Maybe—Maevericious?" she offered. He shook his head, unembarrassed, and Maeve shrugged with a "whatcha-gonna-do" smile. "I post mostly narrative stuff. Lots of fantasy adjacent with some action-adventure."

"That's so cool. I never remember my dreams," the guy said. "Except sometimes I dream that, like, I'm trying to get somewhere, but I never do."

"I've always had wild, intense dreams." Maeve drummed her finger against the tabletop, thinking about the way she felt when she was dreaming. Like she controlled the whole universe. Like she hadn't been wrong, all those years, to feel a little bit different. "I was so stoked when the tech came out to record them. It was like it was meant for me."

"Please don't tell me you believe that dreams are, like, prophecies of the future." The guy held up a hand like he was warding off bad energy, but smiled to take the sting out of it in case Maeve *was* into that.

"God, no," she assured him. "My dreams are amazing, but they're not giving some deep insight into my subconscious mind. They're my imagination unleashed. Sure, they're fed by input from the real world, but having a dream with a frog doesn't mean that I'm going to win the lottery. Dream interpretation is total fiction."

"Unless you see a lot of penises. We all know what *that* means." The guy waggled his eyebrows suggestively.

Maeve rolled her eyes and glanced at Jason as he hopped up from his seat and came to stand behind Josie, draping his arms possessively around her and taking over her conversation with Matt.

Unimpressed, Maeve drifted back to her own conversation and tried to shift the subject. "I just think it's cool that we can record brain activity and translate that into visuals. Next up—reading minds." Not that she needed mind-reading tech to know what this guy was thinking about. Good thing that *didn't* exist.

"You ever tried Blank?" He sounded genuinely curious.

Maeve laughed. "No way. If I'm gonna cook my brain, I'll do it with something that's been legal for decades and has all kinds of peer-reviewed studies. Like this beer!" She downed the last of the glass, toasting with the empty mug before she dropped it back on the table. She didn't mention that she was scared of what Blank could do to her. Her dreams were already so vivid, and waking up sometimes felt like she was struggling for the surface of an angry ocean. Taking Blank could turn that ocean into a tsunami.

"I just got some. I wanna see if I remember anything," Jason's friend explained. "The dreams you have when you're on it are supposed to be totally wild."

"All my dreams are wild," Maeve told him with a wink. "Check out my channel sometime."

"Oh my god, you're incorrigible!" Josie inserted herself into Maeve's conversation with a grin, half-pulling out of Jason's arms. He tried to whisper in her ear, but she waved him off.

"I'm an entertainer! I just want to share my creative vision with the world," Maeve said, unapologetic. She wasn't getting anything else out of a conversation with this guy. Why not at least get a view-bump?

"I don't think that's what most people are checking out on your channel." Jason's friend snorted and nodded at her chest, and Maeve's smile dripped off her lips and vanished.

"Just because you're a creep doesn't mean the rest of us are," Matt interjected, his easy smile taking some of the challenge out of the words and turning it into something closer to teasing. "I don't want to be on this guy's team. You want on my team?" He tapped the table to indicate another of Jason's friends, who was too busy flirting with the other guy at their end of the table to notice.

Maeve clutched her empty glass and breathed through her rage, grateful to Matt for stepping in. He had a way of challenging people on their shit without causing even more drama—unlike Maeve, who just ended up fanning the flames.

She turned to Josie to exchange a silent best-friend reaction, but

Josie wasn't listening. She had turned aside and was arguing quietly with Jason. Maeve couldn't hear what the fight was about, but she was instinctively on Josie's side. She hated how Jason pushed Josie around. Jason always managed to turn fights around, making himself into the victim so that Josie would end up apologizing, even if she had been the one who was angry to begin with.

Someone hit Maeve on the shoulder as they navigated through the packed brewery, and she fidgeted to get more comfortable on her tall wood stool. Turning her attention back to the table, she found that the conversation had moved on. Matt was distracting Douchebag McGee, and Jason's other two guy friends were making out in a drunken flurry that made Maeve feel like an accidental voyeur.

Maeve twisted her empty glass, thinking. She'd been hearing a lot about Blank. Dreamers that used it were exploding in popularity, even though the drug was illegal while it crawled through regulatory hell. She didn't want to hop on every bandwagon in a hunt for popularity... but what if Blank became industry standard? Did she want to be behind the curve?

Viewers had short attention spans. They wanted fresh takes, new experiences, new highs. They wanted to disappear into the story and live their lives in dreams. Maeve was still pretty new to the scene, but trying to stay abreast of the trends was hard. She wasn't sure how far she would run chasing success. Or how desperate she would have to get before she went too far.

Josie interrupted Maeve's reverie with a nudge. "We're heading out," she said, her voice thick with emotion that seemed to hover between anger and tears. Maeve's chest constricted in instant empathy. *What did that asshole say to you?*

"Is everything okay?" Maeve asked. Her eyes travelled to Jason's hand, tight around Josie's upper arm, then back up to Josie's face. Maeve narrowed her eyes, but Josie didn't respond to the unasked question.

"Jason's got an early day." Josie leaned in and kissed Maeve's cheek. She smelled like smoke and citrus, hidden just under the sharp tang of beer.

"I can get you home if he wants to take off," Maeve suggested, despite the cheek kiss that had clearly been a *goodbye-and-please-don't-make-it-a-thing*.

"Don't you have a date?" Jason asked, his bass voice sharp and clipped. He waved goodbye at his own friends, who seemed not to care much that they were being abandoned.

"Not for an hour! What am I supposed to do for an hour?" Maeve implored.

"What am I, chopped liver?" Matt asked.

"You smell like it," Maeve teased.

"That's my cologne—eau de man meat."

"Byyyyye," Josie inserted. Jason stepped between her and Matt, bringing her up short, and she aborted her lean-in with an awkward laugh, patting Jason's chest. Maeve and Matt both noticed and commented on the interaction with their eyes. Josie waved instead of hugging Matt, then she and Jason walked out, their hands tightly linked.

"Have I mentioned I hate that guy?" Maeve murmured once the pair were safely out of earshot, speaking low so that Jason's remaining friends wouldn't overhear.

"That's because, unlike your best friend, you have good taste," Matt answered, his own voice more indelicately pitched.

She swatted his arm, but she was smiling. "If that's true, how come the last guy I dated went full Boyle on me?"

Matt sipped his beer with a smile, refusing to be sucked in. "Josie said you're heading for a date, right? Do I know this one?"

"Nope, first date. She had a single picture in her profile, and I decided it was mysterious." Maeve tapped her watch to bring up the app and flicked through her messages.

Matt laughed. "Okay, I take it back, you do *not* have good instincts when it comes to dating."

"You didn't say I had good dating instincts, you said I had good taste in people." She showed him the photo.

"It's black and white!"

"So?" Maeve turned the watch to look at it better.

"It's in silhouette!"

"Yeah. Mysterious." It was an artsy picture, no question. She couldn't really see the woman's face, since it was half-turned away from the camera. And it was cropped pretty close, so she didn't know what the woman was wearing, or where the photo was taken. But it had *character*. Maeve swiped the app to close it and picked up her empty glass, holding it up in a toast. "To adventure."

Matt picked up his own glass. "To sitting through a thirty-minute diatribe about how water is sentient, and since you don't tell your water that you love it, you're not actually being hydrated." He clicked his empty glass against hers.

"Matt." Maeve clunked her glass down on the tabletop, rattling the empties. "Come on. What are the chances that that happens to me *twice?*"

2

PERI

Peri leaned back in their computer chair, facing the ring light they had ordered just for this interview with a prominent tech reporter. The light provided a soft, even glow that highlighted their high cheekbones, slim nose, and charcoal grey eyes. They let their hands tell a story as they sought just the right words.

They didn't want to explain the dry specifics of dreaming. They wanted to share how dreaming was as much a part of them as a heartbeat. While some people thought dreaming was just entertainment, or even a cheap thrill, Peri viewed it as a gift. Dreaming gave them the space to breathe. It was a whole world, one that sometimes felt more real than the daylight one they inhabited.

But could they find the words to share that ephemeral truth with Sheila now?

"There are so many cultures around the world who believed—or, sorry, who still believe—that dreams exist in a secondary realm, one that we make a sort of transitory visit to. Sometimes, that realm is a place where gods walk and can share their messages and wisdom."

One side of Peri's head was freshly shaved for the interview, the other side curly, purple, and a little wild. They didn't look the part of an academic, but Peri was okay with that. They *weren't* an academic, but that didn't undermine their experience. It had been a long road to getting comfortable in their body, but they were at the point where they didn't want to smash a screen just because their face was reflected in it.

"I find the idea of dreams as a transitory realm a little too distant, personally," Peri continued. "Obviously I have great respect for differences of belief and thought in this area, but my preferred interpretation is that the dream realm is a sort of shared public consciousness, a kind of all-mind of the world. Each of us contributes to it and each of us builds on it. We're visiting it but also creating it. Constantly. A shifting vortex of our own subconscious beliefs, hopes, fears, desires. In either philosophy, though—in any understanding of dreams-as-place—is it any wonder that we can visit and revisit the same worlds over and over? See the same people or experience the same altered reality? If you were a tourist, you wouldn't be surprised that Greece continued to exist after you got on the plane to head back home, that it has a reality separate from yourself. So why not apply the same logic to the world of dreams?"

"So, you really believe that dreams are a place?"

Peri smiled at the interviewer. "Not a physical place, not like Greece, but a shared experience—a shared creation? Something that has tangibility and presence? I think they could be, yeah. Just look at my dreams as an example. They linear, but they also recur. I go back to the same place over and over, I revisit plot threads and stories, I walk in the same world but in a new skin."

On the other side of the screen, the woman leaned toward her camera, her large brown eyes almost as intense as Peri's own. She didn't seem to notice the strand of hair that had fallen across her forehead. "Isn't the simplest explanation that dreams are a reflection of the dreamer? It's Occam's Razor. You go back to the same places over and over because *you're* the same, not because those places exist outside of you."

"But that's the beauty of the theory!" Peri's hands flew in front of them as they sketched ideas in their mind. "Both of those things could be true! A reflection and a place. *Of* us, built *by* us, incredibly personal and intimate and internal. At the same time universal, public. It's "both and" instead of "either or." It's infinite and bounded."

"And people who never return to the same dreams?" the tech reporter pressed. "What about them?"

Peri grinned. "Some people don't own passports. Maybe some people never leave their personal dreams to venture into the wider world available to them. But others do, and that echoes back into the dreams. I think those are the most interesting dreams to watch, because maybe you see or feel a bit of the echo of yourself in it."

"That's beautiful. Very well said." The woman smiled and Peri returned it, suddenly self-conscious.

They pressed their lips together, resisting the urge to wet them, and nodded. "Thank you. I obviously spend too much time thinking about this." Their laugh was self-deprecating, and the interviewer waved it away.

"No, definitely not! I love this stuff—we all do, that's why everyone is tuning in. I think a lot of people wish they could dream like you do. Do you have any advice for aspiring dreamers?"

Peri hesitated, torn between honesty and what they knew the viewers were hoping to hear. No one wanted to hear that the key to dreaming was to get more REM sleep, especially when that meant different things for different people. Peri had one friend who only dreamed after waking up and falling back asleep, and another who needed nine solid hours before they remembered a thing.

Peri settled on a blend of honesty and hopeful enthusiasm. "Personally, I try to read a lot, watch other streams, get my creative energy flowing. And don't put too much pressure on yourself if your dreams aren't narrative. It isn't a character flaw, we're all just built a little differently. If there's one thing we can't control, it's our dreams."

"Unless you're a proponent of lucid dreaming," the interviewer said with a wink. "But that would be a whole other episode. Thank you so much for joining us, Peri. If you're a fan of Peri's streams as DreamsAway—" Peri felt their smile become a little wooden as the interviewer rattled off a short bio of Peri's online life and where to find them, following up with a thank you to guests and a reminder to follow and like the interview. The interviewer waited a second, her own smile equally frozen, and then relaxed. "Okay, and I'll cut there. Thanks so much for that. You had a fascinating take."

"Thanks for having me. I love talking about this stuff," Peri admitted, their smile more natural now that the spotlight was off.

"I'll follow up and let you know when the interview is live, and if you can share it on your end, I'd love that."

"Oh, yeah. Totally. Of course. Looking forward to it!"

"So great to meet you. Bye!"

Peri's own farewell was cut off as the interviewer closed the video call on their end, and Peri sunk down into their gaming chair like a puppet with cut strings. They rubbed their palms against their jeans, fighting the pounding headache crawling up from just behind their eyes. They had no idea how other people did it—talked, laughed, put on a smile that didn't reach their eyes. It was *exhausting* trying to anticipate what other people expected from a conversation.

They had almost said no to the interview request. They hated talking to strangers, and PR was an awkward social interaction to the power of ten; but the show was one they watched, and they hadn't been able to resist the personal invitation.

A meow from below demanded their attention, and Peri reached down without looking to scratch Juniper on the head. The huge grey cat purred loudly before wandering away.

Peri considered getting up and following her, but their chair felt soft and comfortable, and the little den Peri had converted into an office felt cozy. Their desk was decorated with a handful of small plastic figurines from shows and games that Peri liked, and there were a handful of fidget toys discarded around the keyboard.

Getting up also meant braving cold toes: the condo's faux-wood floors were freezing. It wasn't quite winter in Vancouver, but the fall storms came with a vengeance, and the unappealing chill of the outside world seemed to seep inside and touch everything.

Peri glanced at their watch. The interview ate up a good chunk of the evening, but it was too early to go to sleep. Peri felt adrift. Their mind was on dreams, locked into that better world, and every instinct urged them to give in. To go to the bedroom and drift, not away, but *toward* something.

In the waking world they were... locked in. *I'm trapped by the real, the possible, the probable.* Not so in their dreams. In that world they were never too awkward, never too strange, never too different. They were completely free to be themselves, to adventure through possibility and become anyone, anything. The waking world was a prison of flesh, a prison of *true*.

When thoughts like that crowded their mind, Peri knew they were supposed to focus on what was good about the real. Their therapist, Jasmine, kept saying, "Find things that connect you to *this* world. When you're drawn to sleep, remember what makes being awake so much fun."

"Ice cream!" Peri announced to the empty room. "Ice cream is fun."

It was a weak argument, but it was all they had. Peri got up in a burst of motion. Avoiding the bedroom and its closed door, they hurried into the kitchen. Juniper immediately rushed after them, hoping a treat might be imminent.

"You're such a dog," Peri teased, petting the sleek grey cat with one socked foot while rooting through the freezer with both hands. Juniper happily meowed; she might not understand the words, but Peri's tone screamed that treats were nigh. Peri grabbed a small container of non-dairy ice cream and left it to defrost on the counter for a few minutes, then took a piece of freeze-dried salmon out of a bag and gave Juniper a treat of her own.

They wandered over to the window and looked out on the city. The Yaletown lights were bright against the coal-grey sky, and soft rain turned the night foggy and mysterious. Peri watched a couple weave along the street, laughing as they struggled to stay under a single shared umbrella.

Where are they going? Peri wondered. *How will their night end?* Peri pictured the pair pressed up together in the crush of a crowded bar, an intimate bubble in the chaos of shouted conversation. Or maybe they were heading to a concert and would find their friends holding their space in line, waving and shouting across the road as their eyes met across the string of cars.

Peri tried to replace their own face with one of those imagined friends, but couldn't. What was the point of being out there, in the city, engaged in any of the normal activities they knew they were supposed to care about? It was so hopelessly mundane... and their dreams were waiting.

Peri knew that most people didn't think of their skin as a prison. The endless expanse of sky outside didn't steal most people's breath, make them feel rootless and afraid. Most people didn't wander through humanity like a ghost—no, like an alien scientist determined to make sense of the pattern in the chaos.

And in their dreams, Peri didn't, either.

They went back into the kitchen, stubbornly refusing to check the time on the green stock-top clock, and scraped some still too-hard ice cream into a bowl. They collected the bowl and Juniper and went back to the living room. Curling up in a reclining wingback chair upholstered in fabric and decorated with ancient manuscript illuminations, Peri took a deep breath in and out.

Gently, they petted Juniper with one hand, settled her, and then lifted the spoon to their lips. The ice cream was soft and sweet against their lips and tongue, and they closed their eyes and tried to *be* in the moment. To taste the soft hint of coconut milk. To feel how it melted so quickly against the roof of their mouth and slid down their throat, shivery cool and—

With a sigh, they gave up and opened their eyes. *It's just ice cream, not the Notre Dame cathedral. This is too much pressure to put on salted caramel and chocolate.*

A woman's voice happily purred a "Ring, ring!" from the phone in Peri's pocket. The sound of the alarm usually made Peri laugh, but at night it made their blood sing. It signalled freedom.

"Time for bed!" Peri crowed happily, leaping to their feet. The sudden motion dislodged Juniper, who meowed grumpily before padding away to find a less impulsive place to sleep.

Peri absentmindedly licked the last melted dregs of their ice cream from the spoon, dumped it and the bowl into the dishwasher, then raced into the bathroom. They perfunctorily brushed and flossed their teeth, peed, and splashed water on their face. Then they were in the bedroom like a shot, tossing off their clothes and dropping them in the hamper. Grabbing a fresh pair of boxer briefs from the built-in shelves in the closet, they pulled them on while haphazardly retrieving their sleep shirt, with its adorable llama-print, from where they had tucked it under the pillow that morning.

They dropped their phone onto its charging pad, jumped enthusiastically up onto the bed, and finally dragged their large *Steven Universe* duvet up to their chin. All this had been done mostly in the dark, from the soft light leaching in through the half-closed bedroom door. Blackout curtains covered in small silver stars killed any light from the streetlamps outside, and their analog bedside clock let off no light.

Peri reached for the small electrodes that would record their dreams. The toonie-sized silver electroencephalogram nodes attached via suction to their temples. The sensors read the electrical signals in the brain and then wirelessly transmitted those signals to the computer in the other room. That was where the real scientific development happened: a program, running on Peri's computer, that could translate that basic EEG into the visual spectrum.

It was through this technology that Peri shared their dreams with the outside world, but that was a convenience, a way to pay rent and maintain their independence. Peri didn't care about ratings or market trends. Unlike what they'd stated in the interview, they didn't worry about what media they consumed during the day and how it might influence their slumbering mind.

Peri only cared about the dreams.

Jasmine said Peri had problems with avoidance. In dreams, there were no consequences. Why be anxious when no one could stop you? Why not be yourself, when no one was there to judge? Jasmine was probably right. The waking world felt stifling, and it was second nature for Peri to avoid uncomfortable feelings. It was something they were trying to work on, though, being more open. Making more friends. Leaving their condo...

But it was hard when the dreams kept calling.

Peri dreamed every night. In their teenage years, those nightly wanderings were frequently mundane. Often, the dreams drifted away when Peri awoke, fading faster the harder Peri tried to cling to them. Once or twice a week the dreams were fantastical narrative-driven adventures, and Peri remembered every detail. Sometimes they continued night after night, and Peri learned to linger in them, enjoying the thrill of a hidden world that few others seemed to have access to.

But in the last few years, something had changed. Peri had no idea what it was, but their dreams became more solid. They remembered every single one, every night. The world beyond their subconscious grew more and more engaging, and as it did, the appeal of the so-called "real" world faded in equal measure.

Who wanted anti-anxiety pills when you could befriend a dragon and ride the wind above a black mountain peak? Who wanted boring parties with friends of friends when you could host a ball and run through a hedge maze in a red dress, searching for your lost love amid the prickly holly?

Peri wasn't sure how much technology was to blame—or praise —for this new state of affairs. The dream-recording technology they used was fairly new, and there weren't a lot of peer-reviewed studies about it, but it was also incredibly simple. All it did was passively record the electrical signals of the dreamer and transmit those signals to a computer for interpretation.

Peri had done what research they could, and from everything they had read, they were convinced that the device they used to record their dreams couldn't have any effect on the dreamer. There was no way, scientifically, that the nodes could increase electrical brain activity. There were drugs that could, but Peri had no need to take them, and no friends to pressure them into trying, anyway, so that road was, as yet, untaken.

Peri was pretty sure whatever was causing their dream landscape to shift had to be internal. And Peri had a suspicion about what the cause might be. They were digging deeper into the dreams because Peri was looking for *her*.

For the last year or more, the same unknown woman had appeared in almost every one of Peri's dreams. Her name changed, so Peri had nothing to call her. She was sometimes a villain, but always a sympathetic one. Sometimes the love interest, sometimes the rival. But the heart of who she was never shifted. She was wild, and adventurous, and bold. She was everything Peri was not, and she was determined to draw Peri out and make them more than what they were. She was fiercely loyal but capable of small cruelties, and her mind moved too fast to follow, even for someone as smart as Peri.

Her costumes changed, and sometimes the cut and style of her hair, but her face was her own. She was tall, with straight black hair and piercing dark brown eyes. She had an aristocratic bearing no matter what character she played, and the hard but voluptuous curves of a woman who had a layer of hard muscle under gentle fat. She was beautiful in a demanding way, with clear knowledge of the power she wielded.

Peri knew how pathetic it was to feel this way about someone who wasn't, strictly, real. They had talked to Jasmine about it at length. Avoidance came up. Fear. It was hard to find partners who were asexual, or allo partners who were willing to find a way to make it work. Real relationships were full of so many pitfalls, so much compromise. Jasmine suggested that maybe Peri felt that this woman was safe.

But that didn't feel quite right to Peri. This woman didn't make them feel safe. This woman made them feel... alive.

And as Peri closed their eyes and drifted into sleep, it was this woman their mind called out to. The possibilities of what role she would play and who they would be to each other were endless and thrilling.

Between blinks, Peri's bedroom disappeared, and a futuristic room took its place. The lush carpet underfoot was patterned in red and black, reminiscent of an old library. On three sides, the walls were formed of sculpted, nearly seamless white plastic panels. The last wall was distant, and the lighting was such that it disappeared in shadows.

Huddled together in the illuminated section was a large group of scared, excited people. They ran the gamut in age, race, and gender. The only thing they had in common was their nervous expressions and their hair, which was all slicked back and, if the length permitted, tied in buns. They were dressed eclectically, in thick but form-fitting clothes in a variety of colours, patterns, and styles. One woman had a huge purple flower on her lapel; a man held an old-fashioned cane, leaning his entire weight confidently on its slender length.

Peri looked down; they were wearing a white uniform, just a few shades crisper than their sun-starved skin. There was a hollow in Peri's mind, a blank spot that obscured both their past and their present. Who were they, and who were these people? Where were they going?

They looked around the room, trying to remember where they were. Outside the windows, black space and burning bright stars tumbled past so fast Peri felt their stomach lurch. A ship. It wasn't a room at all

—it was a spaceship! As Peri had the thought, a sound alarm crashed through the background murmur of people, and yellow warning lights flared bright.

Peri kept turning, and they picked out a woman in the crowd, dressed in a similar uniform to Peri. Her hair was also pulled back into a severe bun, wet with gel or mousse, and her brown eyes flashed with rage as they made eye contact. Peri knew this woman was no stranger.

This woman held the keys to everything.

3

MAEVE

Maeve scooped up a forkful of saffron rice and studied the woman in front of her. At first glance, she had a lot of appeal. She was a little younger than Maeve, but only by a few years, and her chestnut curls were downright adorable. She was wearing a graphic T-shirt, with a dinosaur in the Obama "Hope" style, and a thin braided bracelet.

She looked fun. She looked nerdy. She looked like someone Maeve would stop at a party to chat up. And yet here they were, ten minutes into the date, and they had barely managed to exchange a few pleasantries about the weather before the conversation *fully* dried up.

Maeve prided herself on being good at chatting. She never asked someone what they did for a living; she asked them what they were passionate about. She didn't ask where they grew up; she asked where they could live if money was no object.

She was giving everything she had, but the other woman— whose username was K, but whose real name Maeve had already forgotten—was a closed door. She answered each question in short, direct sentences that left no room for follow-up questions and provoked no return questions.

Maeve was deeply regretting breaking her rule that first dates should only ever be coffee. When K suggested Sweet Cherub for their first date, Maeve just couldn't turn it down. It was a little hole-in-the-wall Indian restaurant on Commercial Drive, with wood-panelled walls covered in huge mirrors and an attached grocery store. Everything about it was warm, from the art on the walls to the smell of turmeric and cardamom. Maeve loved their food—and their prices. At least if the date went badly, she had figured, she could soothe her pain with curry.

Desperate to fill the silence, Maeve asked, "Seen any good movies lately?"

"Hmm?" the woman asked, looking up from her own plate.

"I just asked what kind of movies you like," Maeve repeated, struggling for patience. So the conversation wasn't flowing yet. That was okay. This could still be salvageable.

"I don't really watch movies," the woman admitted. "I don't have a TV."

"Oh, no worries." Maeve was a bit of a couch potato herself, but not owning a TV wasn't a deal-breaker. "Are you into books, then?"

The woman scraped her fork across her plate. "Not really."

There was another long, awkward silence. Maeve glanced around the restaurant, more as a distraction than because there was anything interesting to look at. It was a popular spot, but this late at night there were only a handful of people eating. Maeve saw a lot of dyed hair, linen shirts, and facial piercings. Her crowd.

The other woman had requested the oddly timed date, and Maeve had been excited. She wasn't really one for schedules. Left to her own devices—which she generally was, given her job—Maeve often stayed up until sunrise and slept well into the afternoon. It was hard, at her age, to find someone who hadn't fallen into the regular nine to five. That had caused some friction in past relationships, especially given that schedules and being on time weren't exactly her strong suit.

Thoughts of her job and the odd schedule it promoted gave Maeve the idea that maybe this K lady didn't watch TV or read books because she was into more modern media. Maeve had heard some kids thought 2D media was all a waste of time.

"Are you more into VR? Dreams?" Maeve asked.

The woman shovelled curry into her mouth and shook her head.

At least she swallowed before answering. "I don't have a headset either."

Maeve stared, aghast. Was this seriously happening? If the woman had read Maeve's profile at all, she knew Maeve was a dreamer. *You could at least pretend to have an interest in my career! Why did you say yes to this date at all?*

Maeve felt her shoulders slump as defeat drained away the last of her energy. No matter how many bad dates she went on, she couldn't stop herself from getting excited every time she went on a new one. She tried to keep her expectations low, tried not to get invested until date two or three, but that wasn't her. She ran into every new encounter at top speed, thrilled and excited by the possibility that this one, finally, would be *the* one.

It wasn't that she didn't like being single. Not exactly. She loved the independence that came with having no obligations to anyone. And she wasn't lonely—she had a great circle of friends and a close-knit family. She was happy in her own skin, and proud of the life she'd built. She didn't need anyone to complete her.

That didn't stop her from *wanting* someone, though. She hated the expression that love found you when you stopped looking. As if a partner would just fall into her lap if she deleted all the apps. That wasn't how life worked. Getting what you wanted took effort, whether it was a romantic partner or the job of your dreams.

Maeve scarfed down curry as fast as she could without choking. She couldn't leave before her food was done, so she dug around for a question that would hopefully inspire some conversation. "Oh! Computer games. What kind of games are you into?"

"I don't really play games," the woman said. Her voice and tone were as bland as the content of her incredibly short answers.

Maeve started to bite her own hand in frustration but managed to cover it up by pretending to yawn into her fist. *Is that any better?* she wondered belatedly, then decided that she was beyond caring. "But your profile said you were working on making your own game."

"Oh, yeah. I just wanted to see if I could." The woman shrugged.

"You don't play them at all?" Maeve couldn't keep the disbelief out of her voice.

"Nope."

"Cool. Great. Sure." Maeve stuffed the rest of her food into her mouth at breakneck speed, barely avoiding choking on a piece of potato as she chewed half as much as she should have. She pushed her empty metal plate away as she huffed out a satisfied noise. At least the food tasted good. "Well, I should really get going. It's pretty late."

"Oh. Yeah. Okay." The woman didn't seem surprised that Maeve was leaving barely fifteen minutes into a dinner date. Of course, she didn't seem much of anything.

Maeve fought down a shiver. Was she being too judgmental, or was this whole thing as creepy as she felt it was? It was one thing not to read books or not to watch dreams. But who didn't consume media *at all?* Stories made life worth living. They inspired the imagination, created entire worlds for the span of their consumption. Without stories, life was... emptiness.

"It was... nice to meet you," Maeve lied. Thanking whatever was watching over her that she had paid at the counter and didn't need to wait for a bill, Maeve shoved her chair back with a violent screech and booked it out of the restaurant. The cool autumn air woke her up with a slap, and she hurried down the Drive, passing packed sports bars, trendier restaurants that were still busy, and even a record store that was open late on the weekend.

What the hell was that? She wasn't sure whether to laugh or cry. It was by far the worst date she had ever been on, but on the plus side, a woman who seemed allergic to stories at least made for a good one. Maeve would probably be telling this one for years to come.

Chewing a pen with her nose scrunched up, Maeve tapped out a quick response to yet another social media post. She wished there was a world where she could be a creative who *didn't* have to do her own marketing, but if there was, it wasn't the one she lived in. This was the price she paid for being a dreamer. She wouldn't hate it as much if she knew it was guaranteed to work, but sometimes it felt like playing Russian roulette. She couldn't *make* people watch her streams. She couldn't just *decide* to be successful and make it so. It was all so—so arbitrary.

Maeve re-read the comment she had just written to make sure it captured her voice. Not trying too hard to be casual, a little self-deprecating, clever without being cute. It was hard to hit all of those points on, "Glad you liked it! If I dream one more sheep, I think I'm going to stab my eyes out, lol," but Laura said there was no point in engaging if you weren't engaging right. Maeve even heard the words in her manager's deadpan baritone.

Laura probably got the line from some seminar run by a woman in a too-bold power suit, proclaiming the secrets to marketing success behind a dingy podium on hotel carpet twenty years out of date. But Laura was all Maeve could afford.

Maeve glanced over her checklist for the day. She was trying to get more organized about the tasks she hated doing—otherwise, she ended up avoiding them so long it stopped being procrastination and turned into full-on ball-dropping. So far, she had responded to all her positive comments, made a few jokes on the bad ones, and blocked four creeps. She commented on twenty-six fellow streamers (and watched videos from at least four of them) and scheduled four previews for the new stream. That only left...

"Do I have to?" she asked the empty apartment.

She clicked over to her email, but there was nothing outstanding that she had to deal with. She logged out of her work account and into her personal one, but social media was quiet. There was one message from Josie, but it was just a meme Maeve had already seen. In the image, a shaggy white dog was hanging out with a bunch of sheep, pretending to be one of them.

Maeve answered like it was new anyway, not wanting to pour cold water on her friend's fun.

> Lol, love that! Baaaaa ba ba!

Swiping back to her work browser, she looked at her to-do list and saw there was still one task that she was putting off. Cringing internally, she took a deep, cleansing breath and called Laura on her watch.

"Slugs? Really?" Laura asked immediately after the call connected.

"So, no bites?" Maeve let her head fall back as she spun around in her chair.

"Stop it, I can hear you spinning," Laura said.

"You cannot."

"Are you spinning?"

Maeve stopped. "No."

"No one wants a thirty-minute dream about giant slugs chasing you and your drunk friend through the city."

"The slugs weren't chasing us. The *car* was chasing us. The slugs were more like... an environmental condition." Maeve pushed her chair away from her computer desk, but it immediately bumped into the rug behind her and stopped.

"Oh, god, really? Well, that changes everything." The eye roll was clear in Laura's voice. "You've got to stop watching nature documentaries before bed."

"They're relaxing," Maeve muttered. And it wasn't like what she watched *actually* controlled what she dreamed about. That was out of her hands. She picked up the pen and started to chew again, letting her chair drift more slowly—and quietly—in a circle.

"Eat some edibles and watch porn or something."

"I'm not watching porn! I mean, obviously, I watch porn." Maeve's voice turned thoughtful as she finished her rotation and dropped her feet back to the ground to pause the chair. "Porn doesn't give me those sorts of dreams, though. I think I'm all worn out by the end of it. I usually only have sex dreams when I'm really frustrated. Give me a good Austen or something, you know, with all the unsatisfied yearning—"

"Thank you for that wildly unnecessary information," Laura interrupted, her voice dry and crisp.

"You asked." Maeve craned her neck to look outside. The windows were so high up she couldn't see out of them when she was sitting down, but she was pretty sure the lack of view helped her focus. Right now, she could see a tiny bit of grey sky.

"I really didn't."

"So, you don't think you can sell it?" Maeve picked up the necklace she kept on her desk and used as a worry toy. It was a long band of segmented silver pieces that she could twist into a ton of shapes.

"Sorry, kid. There just isn't a market. But it'll get you some ad revenue at least."

"Yeah. Okay." Maeve sighed and dropped her head onto the desk.

"You're doing your social media stuff?"

"Yeah," she mumbled.

"And the teasers?"

"Yeah."

"It'll happen."

"I know." She sat up and started to spin again. "I just... hate all the work around the work, and not even knowing if it will work, if anyone will care. If I could just edit and dream and upload!"

"If you don't like it, try working a real job."

"I just love how warm and fuzzy you are." Maeve snorted.

"Stop spinning. And buy some Austen."

"Ew. You're such a capitalist."

"Thank you."

"Not a compliment!" Maeve yelled, but Laura had already hung up.

Maeve scrunched her nose up at the blank screen of her watch. Sometimes she worried that Laura didn't get it. Maeve didn't want to make videos just to be popular. She wanted to create beautiful stories. She wanted to show off the inside of her brain and say, "This was always there. You just never saw it before." Sometimes it felt impossible to express how much more there was beneath the surface of who she was. Like a plant whose roots went deep into the earth, bringing back everything she needed to truly *live*.

Dreams were the only way to connect with that other part of her, the only way to express the fullness of her spirit. And to do *that*, to keep doing that, she had to be commercially successful.

Not that she would turn her nose up at fame and riches, either. She wouldn't mind being like one of those Hollywood stars who did the big franchise movie to get the money so they could work on whatever indie flick they wanted. If Maeve did what Laura said, and found her way to success, she would make an easier life for herself. And within that easier life, she could make any kind of art she dreamed of.

But it wasn't as easy as just doing what Laura said. Dreams came or they didn't. They were exciting or they weren't. She couldn't *control* that, but everyone acted like she could. Just eat some edibles! Just read some Austen! Just comment, like, and subscribe! If it was so easy, everyone would be doing it.

Maeve got up, padding across the tiny so-called living room, and stared into her fridge. She couldn't remember if she'd eaten lunch, but the expired milk in the door reminded her that she had definitely skipped breakfast.

"I have no foooooood," she whined out loud. "Only ingredients." She opened a few cupboard doors, hopefully, as if food might miraculously appear where there had been none a moment before. But dry cereal held zero appeal, and the box of granola bars was empty. "Shit. I don't even have ingredients."

She tapped her watch to make another call. "He-ey, Mom," she said, drawing out the "ey" a little suspiciously.

Maeve's mother was a middle-class white lady who knew her lane and stuck to it, raising Maeve to be as kind and empathic as she knew how. Speaking to her made Maeve smile, and she was suddenly glad to have called even beyond her imminent need for sustenance.

"Hi, honey! How was your date last night?" her mother said, clearly not picking up Maeve's ulterior motives.

"Awful, Mom. Like, the worst date you could imagine in the history of dates. Except not actually that because that would be— never mind. The point is, she was as boring as wet cement."

"I lost a shoe in wet cement once," her mom said.

"What?"

"I'm just saying, it was pretty exciting. What was wrong with this one?"

"She doesn't watch TV!"

"Well, that's—"

"Or read books," Maeve interrupted before her mother could come to her date's defence. "Or watch dreams, or play dreams, or play games."

"So—what does she do?" her mother asked, bewildered.

"I have no idea! Not engage in normal human conversation, apparently."

"Oh, yeah, no. People without hobbies are best to be avoided," her mother said.

Maeve couldn't help but laugh. "Right?"

"You'll get the next one, honey."

"Thanks, Mom. I swear—I almost considered dating her just in case I ever get insomnia," Maeve said, and was rewarded with her mother's warm laugh. "Hey," she continued. "Can I help you with anything around the house, or..."

"Why are you being helpful?" her mother asked suspiciously.

"I'm out of groceries."

"Maeve! You really need to get more organized."

"I didn't forget to shop! I'm just... sort of waiting for my next royalty cheque and please don't freak out I'm getting it on the fifteenth and I am *fine*. I don't need money, but I would really appreciate it if you would feed me," Maeve admitted.

"Honey. You know you never need to ask if you can come over for dinner! But I *am* going to put you to work on that tree in our yard that's making your dad crazy. If you don't come and do it, he's going to get up that ladder himself."

Maeve laughed. She hated to admit that she needed the meal— she knew her mother worried about her too much already—but it would be nice to hang out with the family and forget about work for a few hours. "I will bring my gardening gloves."

"You don't own gardening gloves."

"I do too! You gave me some when I lived in that basement suite off Arbutus." Maeve grabbed her sneakers, put them on, then hunted for her jacket.

"When you were in school? Do you still have them?"

"I don't throw anything away. The only reason I'm not a hoarder is because my place is too small."

"I don't think that stops hoarders, honey. That's kind of their whole thing."

"Yeah, that was a bad example," Maeve acknowledged, shrugging into a jean jacket. "But I definitely have gardening gloves. I just have to find them."

"You can just use mine. Are you coming over now?"

"Now-ish, yeah."

"I can pick you up from the train."

"It's a ten-minute bus."

"Are you sure?"

"Love you." Maeve hung up, cutting any argument about a ride short. Work might not be going exactly as she wanted it to, but she could always count on her mom to make her feel more at ease. And hopefully to foist enough leftovers at her that she wouldn't need to shop again until her royalty cheque came through.

Maeve turned around, narrowly avoided banging her head on a cupboard door she'd left open, and went in search of her gardening gloves. She just kind of wanted to prove she still had them. That, at least, was something she had control over.

4

PERI

The yellow warning lights pulsed on and off. Everything they touched turned two-dimensional, hollowed out and not quite real. At the back of the room, where shadows had previously hidden them from view, the lights bounced off ceiling-tall tubes of glass. Within each tube a monster slept, almost but not quite human. Some had greyish skin and missing limbs. The faces of others were distorted in rictus grins, revealing broken and jagged fangs. With every flash of the lights the monsters within seemed to come to life for a moment and then faded into sleep once more.

The passengers were still huddled close, a nervous knot of twenty or so people shifting in tiny swells like waves lapping on the ocean shore. Peri stood at a small distance from them, close to the window and its field of tiny stars.

"Why are they in stasis? Why didn't the government destroy them?" a woman whispered. No one knew.

Peri took this in, processed it in a daze. They still had no idea who they were, but every time they gained new information it awoke a memory, like bubbles popping on the surface of their mind. The ship had recently left Mars, full to bursting with these zombies in stasis. They were en route back to Earth using Hohmann transfer orbits, and no one else seemed to be suffering from amnesia—so Peri was playing it cool, pretending they, too, understood their role on the ship.

"Are we even still heading to Earth?" a man in a starched uniform asked. With alarm, Peri saw that his question was directed their way.

"I—" They took a step closer to the crowd but hesitated, realizing they had no answer.

"Don't you know?" the first woman asked, her voice rising to a panicked squeak. "You're the damn pilot!"

A rush of memories hit Peri, the sensation physical enough that their legs buckled. They saw a pilot's uniform in a dingy mirror. The bridge of a ship and the sound of their laughter during training. On this very craft, the day it took off, determined and sure. With the memories came skills; they flicked their fingers and activated a panel, and the flight trajectory appeared in glowing blue against the white wall. Yes, they were on target to reach Earth in three days.

"We're on track," Peri assured the terrified group. However, though they now knew what they were, they still had no idea who they were.

Peri turned to survey the space, but their attention was split, eyes drifting back again and again to *her*. Though she clearly held some animosity toward Peri, she also didn't seem to be able to take her eyes off them. She had been watching them since Peri became aware of their surroundings on the observation deck, and for the entirety of the walk down to the storage bay. Now, as everyone trooped back upstairs, Peri manoeuvred back in line with her.

"You're angry with me," Peri said.

The woman crossed her arms protectively over her chest. "I don't even know you," she said, and somehow Peri knew the words were a lie. They reached out and ran three fingers lightly down the woman's arm and saw a shiver of recognition run through her.

"You know me," Peri said.

She turned those intense brown eyes on Peri. "I know you're a liar," she said.

Memories drifted through Peri, less intense this time: little lies, the kind everyone tells. *Oh, yeah, I read that article. I can't get together on Tuesday, I've got a thing. I love jazz!* Nothing worse materialized in the soup of their thoughts. "I'm not," they said, sure of their answer.

The group had reached the observation deck again. Stars glittered outside curved white windows. The furniture, white and blue leather in pleasing ergonomic shapes, was scattered artfully throughout the room, more akin to an upscale salon than any spaceship Peri had seen before. This was clearly a ship intended for the rich.

"Why not tell them the truth?" the woman demanded. Faces turned toward them, curiously drawn into what everyone had been treating, until then, as a private dispute.

"I haven't told them a lie," Peri snapped back. They were on the defensive now, not sure what they had done but terrified that the woman's anger was justified. But a quiet voice whispered that she was wrong, that they meant something to each other, and there was some comfort in that.

"You're nothing but—a finger!" the woman proclaimed, her own finger raised in accusatory determination.

Peri gasped and stumbled back under the force of the accusation. Around them, the passengers gasped and murmured to each other, sounding like nothing so much as a bunch of extras on a cheesy movie whispering "rutabaga" over and over.

With mounting horror, Peri remembered. The woman was right. Peri was a sentient finger. They had become separated from their body—cut off. Adrift, they wandered the universe alone, dying slowly, seeking a host to save them.

As those painful memories of disillusionment and isolation returned, so did their memories of the woman. They had been right! The woman was no stranger. The woman had taken Peri in, made them part of her when no one else would.

"I'm a finger," Peri admitted, and the crowd's shock crashed over them like ocean waves. "But you only know that... because I'm yours!"

The woman touched her hand, unsure, and her eyes flickered. Peri realized she was experiencing memories as they came up, just like Peri was. It seemed they were all suffering from this strange amnesia.

"You've forgotten me," Peri whispered. "But I'm right here. All you have to do is remember."

"I remember. I remember that you left me, too," the woman whispered back. Her voice was cracked, painful, full of rage and regret and... was that—could it be... love?

Peri shook their head, the memories falling into place to show the lie in the words. They had never wanted to leave her. They had rather wanted to be their own person, someone who could stand beside her instead of always to her side, always a forgotten piece. They didn't leave. They individuated.

"Talk to me," Peri said. They reached out a hand, hopeful, and watched the woman staring at that hand, considering. She reached out...

~

Peri turned over in bed, slowly coming awake. The dream was still sharp, for now, but the edges were beginning to fade, the connective tissue growing soft and malleable. *Sentient fingers?* Peri laughed and snuggled back into the pillow, tapping the electrodes on their forehead to make sure they were still firmly attached. Some people glued them down or wore crown attachments to make sure they stayed on all night, but Peri had never been a restless sleeper. It was just an abundance of caution that made them tap the nodes to check they were secure.

The woman had been there, as Peri knew she would be. Once again, they were drawn to each other, across dreams, across realities. Peri desperately wanted to know who the woman was. If she existed somewhere in the waking world, Peri would do anything to track her down. It wasn't just loneliness, though that was part of it. It was something in the way the woman looked at Peri. As if she saw more than what was there. Peri would give anything to feel that, to be made real through another's eyes.

Peri yawned and snuggled deeper into their pillows. Maybe if they were lucky, they could drop back into the same dream. It didn't happen often, but there was no better drug than hope.

Hope that was apparently misguided. They couldn't manage to get back to the dream, even after drifting back into sleep. By the time they woke up for good, the details of the dream were muddy. But they remembered the sensation of memories flooding in, the way their hand tingled as they held it out so hopefully, and the perfect brown of the mystery woman's eyes.

Peri checked their computer and confirmed that the EEG had worked. The machine registered three hours of dreams, with a core hour of uninterrupted footage. Peri set it to process and got ready for the day, but by the time they had showered, changed, fed Juniper, and eaten breakfast, it still wasn't done.

Reading a book distracted them for a few minutes, but their mind kept drifting. They couldn't concentrate on anything but the dream. Watching a dream let them take in details they hadn't noticed the first time and reminded them of everything that had gone fuzzy with sleep. It was their favourite part of the day, and it couldn't come soon enough.

Peri needed to do something proactive to ease the antsy waiting. Without pausing to grab their wallet or bag, Peri locked their door behind them and hit the sidewalk.

Peri hated walking. Jasmine said it was important to get exercise —hell, *everyone* said it was important to get exercise—but walking with no destination always felt so pointless. And downtown had an energy that always felt restless. Everyone was focused on getting where they were going, eyes and minds locked on the path. Wandering among them felt even more isolating.

Taking out their cell phone, Peri opened Discord. They had a few friends they gamed with online, people scattered all around the world. Despite their different time zones everyone kept such random schedules that there was always someone online, and Peri could use the distraction. Plus, if they walked while they talked, they were still taking Jasmine's advice and unplugging.

> Had the weirdest dream last night! How do you feel about sentient fingers?

Peri typed out meticulous grammar with ease of familiarity. They loathed the idea of a typo leading to an uncomfortable miscommunication. It was hard enough to understand and antici-pate people's reactions online without adding ambiguity from bad grammar to the mix.

> **Noodles**
> Like, your fingers are sentient?

Noodles was a gamer from the UK who didn't seem to have a consistent schedule. They were *always* online.

Like I was a finger who had escaped from my hand.

Noodles
RAD! Love the weird ones.

Peri blew warm air on their hands clutching the phone, wishing they had brought their credit card so they could at least stop for some bubble tea or a macaron at the patisserie that looked like an Instagram ad. At least then the effort of the walk wouldn't feel wasted. Instead, they hunched their shoulders a little higher, fighting the damp cold that ate slowly through their inadequate sweater, and directed their feet toward the ocean.

It was overcast, and early enough in the day that the breeze off the water hit like a knife. But nothing could stop the hordes of people, both tourists and locals, from enjoying Sunset Beach. Peri walked across the park's wide lawn and down to the water, only half-aware of the people all around them. Teenagers sat on blankets and took photos in the muddy light. Old ladies power walked tiny dogs wearing matching sweaters. Life went on, all around them.

Ross
I don't know how you can share your dreams.

Ross was in Australia, a computer programmer with a farm that took most of his time. He was almost never around just to chat; he must have been having a rare bout of insomnia.

I'd be scared for people to look inside my brain.

They're just stories. They aren't me.

Their steps had taken them off the beach and back toward the city, paying only enough attention to the world to make sure they didn't get hit by a car or wander too far away from their condo.

> Feels like a gift I'm just sharing.

Noodles
You're soooooo touchy-feely.

> Literally not.

Ross
They just want to find the mystery woman.

> Maybe. Maybe someone will recognize her.

The more Peri shared their dreams, the greater their reach grew. If they got famous enough, maybe someone would see the mystery woman and recognize her. Or maybe the woman would even see herself and reach out. Peri couldn't shake the feeling that she had to be someone they knew—someone Peri had met before but didn't consciously remember. A missed connection, maybe. A middle school crush who had faded from Peri's conscious memories. A face on a bus whizzing past. *Someone.*

Noodles
Maybe she's just like This Man and you never really saw her.

Ross
This man?

Noodles dropped a link, but Peri was already familiar with the story: thousands of people claimed the same man appeared in their dreams despite the dreamers not knowing him or each other. It was proven to be a virtual marketing stunt. Human minds are incredibly suggestible. As soon as people started claiming to have seen him, other people thought they had, too. They weren't lying, exactly. They honestly believed it to be true.

> Not the same, NO ONE ELSE has seen her. So where would the suggested implant have come from?

Noodles
Good point.

Ross
Hope you find her.

Peri wasn't so sure. If they did find her, what then? The real-life version of the woman would probably be nothing like the person Peri had constructed in their mind. She would want the kind of relationship that Peri couldn't give. Or wouldn't want Peri at all...

There were so few places where Peri *fit*, where the sum of who they were didn't come out to the wrong number. Then again, what if their awkward decimals added up to a whole? It was possible, Peri knew it was, that the feelings in the dream could survive into the waking world.

Thanks.

Peri felt a small smile tug at the edges of their mouth. They couldn't help hoping. Though Peri didn't believe in magic, a little voice in the back of their mind whispered, *Maybe*, and Peri couldn't help but listen.

And anyway, posting as DreamsAway paid the bills. If they were going to spend their whole life doing it, they might as well be able to afford a nice apartment with no roommates and the good, organic cat food Juniper loved so much.

It was the little things, as Jasmine always reminded them. The little things.

Wanna play a game later?

As they typed, they headed back for the apartment.

~

Turning on the TV, Peri scratched the sleeping Juniper under the chin and connected the TV to their drive. They had spent an hour building houses with Ross and Noodles while they waited for the footage to finish loading. Now they had two hours set aside to watch the dream, rewatch the best parts, and obsess over it a little bit (which meant rewatching it five more times) before they got down to the real work of editing.

They made microwave popcorn and a cup of tea, then queued the footage on the computer. Juniper snuffled and objected to the pillows shifting on the couch but otherwise ignored Peri as they got comfortable, dragging a throw blanket over their lap.

"Okay. Sentient finger here I come." They flicked two fingers to activate the TV's gesture controls and then clicked once to start the footage.

The dream began to play, and Peri settled happily down into the cushions. This was always their favourite part of any stream—when it was both alien and familiar. They remembered some parts of the dream in vivid detail, but others felt like distant memories brought back by a familiar smell. It would be as if a stranger spoke, but the words would almost appear in their mind as the small, recorded Peri spoke them on the screen, like lemon juice turning invisible ink black again. A return to memory, a fulfillment of scattered pieces. There was no feeling like it in all the world.

The ship was mostly as they remembered, though details had blurred: the strange silver stitching on their white pants, the buffed military shine of their shoes. They couldn't help but sigh wistfully when the mysterious woman appeared. Seeing her felt like catching a glimpse of the divine. Something rare and poorly understood that nonetheless filled their heart with a transcendent lightness. The yellow warning lights flared in the depths of her brown eyes, and Peri fought the urge to stop the stream and rewind to watch her appear again. They liked to watch the dream all the way through the first time, so they could experience it the same way they had when it happened. But it took effort to lean back against the cushions, to stick their hands under their thighs and just be in the moment.

"You've forgotten me," Peri whispered from the screen, and in the present moment, they mouthed along. "But I'm right here. All you have to do is remember."

"I remember. I remember that you left me, too," the woman whispered back. This time Peri was sure there was love beneath it.

What a strange and powerful dream it was. Peri couldn't help but wonder where it might have gone from there. They still hoped they might return to the narrative tonight, or maybe the night after. They wanted to know what happened to the finger, separated from its host but still connected to her, still loving her even while it craved independence.

"Talk to me," the Peri onscreen said. They reached out a hand, hopeful, and watched the woman staring at that hand, considering. She reached out, and then...

The dream didn't end.

"I don't know," the woman said, tears in her eyes as her hand hovered, inches away from Peri's fingers. "Something is wrong, I— this isn't right. This isn't the way it's supposed to be."

"I didn't want to leave you," the Peri onscreen promised. On the couch, Peri sat forward, eager and surprised, popcorn spilling out of their hand and across the couch. They had been so sure the dream ended when they had reached out a hand! Peri had never forgotten so much of a dream before. Their memories occasionally went cloudy or lost focus, but never vanished. It was something that set Peri apart from other dreamers.

"I don't mean that." The woman bridged the gap, suddenly and ferociously, grabbing the dream Peri's proffered hand in what looked like a painful grip.

Back in the waking world Peri watched in a daze, touching their own fingers and imagining the imprint of her fingers just *there*, and just *there*.

"I'm being pulled in too many directions," the woman whispered, her bright red lips just inches from dream Peri's ear. "Forced into roles I don't know how to play. I'm scared, Peri. What if I have to become something I don't like? Someone I don't recognize?"

Peri shivered in delight and their tea splashed everywhere. Hearing the name *Peri* on the woman's lips felt like a benediction. *Peri*, not whatever name the finger held in this narrative. *Peri*. Was it the first time the woman had said their name? Peri only chose it a few years ago, and it hadn't fully filtered into their subconscious. Though Peri often dreamed of themselves as they were, other people rarely said their name. *Peri*.

How was it possible that they didn't remember a word of this?

The memory of hearing their name on her lips should have seared into their hippocampus, a permanent new pathway in the brain's synapses. Losing entire minutes of a dream was strange, but losing minutes this significant was more than that. It was eerie.

"I don't understand, but I'll help you. Whatever you need, I'll help you," dream Peri answered.

"I'm sorry," the woman said. She was tender as she laid a hand against Peri's smooth chest. "I shouldn't have said anything. I shouldn't have brought you into this. But it's okay. You won't remember this in the morning."

As both Peris watched with wide eyes and breathless countenance, the woman leaned in, so soft. So slow. She pressed her forehead against Peri's, and both versions of them exhaled, one sinking into the motion, the other swaying on their feet, panic and shock fighting for room in their lungs.

The file ended abruptly, returning to a screenshot of the opening image, and Peri collapsed to the ground, unseeing eyes scanning the room around them.

What. What! No. What? Peri reached up, tapped the air, and played the clip again. They scanned through the footage, impatient, and stopped when they saw their own hand reaching out.

By the time it played for the second time they were lightheaded. They played it a third time, a fourth, a fifth, hardly breathing, feeling their heart beating faster and faster. Nothing changed. The same words were passed between them. No memory of any of it flickered in their mind. The woman had declared that Peri would have no memory of what had passed between them, and it came true.

Peri felt unmoored, adrift, as if the world of dreams was no longer the tangible, immutable place they knew and loved. For everyone else dreams were abstract, shifting, illogical. Not for Peri. Not until now. The hole in their memories was a whirlpool, threatening to drag them to its depths.

They knew they were spiralling, but Peri couldn't stop watching it again and again and again.

It was only when Juniper meowed quietly and placed a paw on Peri's thigh that Peri was able to recognize they were panicking. They scrambled to their feet, considered going to the bathroom to get an anti-anxiety pill, then changed their mind and stumbled to the bedroom to get their weed instead. Holding down the button on their vape pen to warm it up, Peri wandered back into the living room, trapped in the haze of brain fog that comes after too many racing and intrusive thoughts battle for attention.

Peri took a long drag on the pen, closing their eyes as they breathed slowly in and then out again. They directed their outward breath up, toward the ceiling, and then took another long breath in, this time of air. A count of five, another pull, another breath. It wasn't a panic attack, not really. It was just panic.

And with good reason. The image on the screen stared out at them, her lips open in the act of whispering, "You won't remember this in the morning." And Peri hadn't.

"Who are you?" Peri whispered. "Who the hell are you?"

The afternoon passed in a blur of simmering anxiety. Peri felt disconnected, as if they were watching their life from a great distance. They cleaned up the dream's audio and posted it online to their DreamsAway account, managed their socials, even answered some questions on Discord. But they were moving on autopilot, checking the boxes that had to be checked. It was only when Juniper jumped in their lap and demanded dinner with furious purrs that Peri realized they had been sitting at their computer for at least half an hour, staring at nothing at all.

When Peri's alarm went off that night, Peri hesitated to rise and head to the bedroom. The world of dreams was waiting, but Peri had no idea what it might hold. What might be waiting the next time they saw the mysterious woman? They felt that something had changed, but they had no idea what it meant for their dreaming life. They couldn't stand the idea of becoming just like every other dreamer, a tourist who never truly became part of the world they visited at night.

Peri had no desire to give up the world they loved so much. Dreams were a haven. They were another life, lived without expectations or fear, without boundaries. The world could be so... heavy. It pressed down and dragged out, cloying and endless. Not so with dreams. In dreams Peri knew the freedom to select a body based on their mood for the day, stepping into the masculine or feminine as they desired. They could experiment, try on new versions of life without ever closing a door. They could create entire worlds and live within them, never feeling alone on the outside. And they could skip all the boring bits in between. No dream ever featured walking thirty blocks in a downpour, or waiting forty minutes for a bus that never came. Dreams were powerful and fanciful. Dreams were...

Terrifying.

It was the first time Peri ever had the thought. They were in unknown territory, and there were few things Peri hated more than the unknown. They craved order in their life. Because it was impossible to sort and catalogue the unknown, there was nothing worse to Peri than a mystery. So much of the world felt opaque so much of the time. Everyone else seemed to understand, intrinsically and with casual ease, but couldn't explain the rules when Peri asked.

Peri had once thought about being a scientist because they longed to dissect the world and understand it, but they had quickly realized they had no patience for algorithms or formulas; minutiae were not their passion. They had gone into sociology with a drive to change the world, but had given that up after it became clear they couldn't handle the conflict with their teachers about when it became clear that the textbooks were still pushing outdated theory, and that while their professors were open to discussions in class about colonial trauma and other modern academic thought, they still expected essays and test answers that stuck to the old, worn, often damaging assumptions. Peri had never been able to back down when their knowledge pointed to an inaccuracy or injustice, and that had led to a lot of bad test grades.

They had made the switch to archaeology because the mysteries of the past had seemed so much more conquerable than the pain of the present. Control, again. Knowledge.

Then, in fourth year, the dream technology had been released, and Peri dropped out and made dreaming their career. It had been four years, and Peri liked to joke that they now had a degree in dream theory. Of course, it also meant they had given up their part in the ongoing raging academic fight against the West's outdated views of the past. That was convenient for Peri, who hated conflict and had spent most of university with their flight-or-fight system in overdrive, but it left them with a lingering sense of dissatisfaction and failure. If only they had been stronger, they might have changed the world like they always imagined they would.

Instead, they had ended up here, a dreamer with a unique relationship to dreams. They became someone who lived their fullest life when their eyes were closed, someone who trusted in a world without rules that still somehow afforded Peri the order and structure they desired. Chaos without containment. Freedom within bounds. A sandbox to play in that never rebounded and hurt Peri in strange or startling ways.

Unless the rules were changing, and the world Peri had relied on could no longer be trusted.

Peri went through their nighttime ritual reluctantly. Things Peri usually did hastily, or avoided altogether so they could get to bed as quickly as possible, were now urgently necessary, demanding more time than ever. Washing their face, clipping their nails, taking out their many earrings to disinfect and then return to their places, all became a deeply consuming task of avoidance. They even swapped out both of Juniper's water bowls for fresh ones. Finally, there was nothing to do but go to bed.

Still, Peri hesitated, waffling with a hand poised over the electrodes that would record their dreams of the night. Then the moment passed, and Peri knew without doubt that they were diving back in. Despite the panic and the fear of what was ahead, the woman was calling. And Peri couldn't fathom giving her up.

5

MAEVE

Maeve woke up, heart pounding, deeply disoriented as she clawed out of her dream and toward waking. What was this room? Did she live here? Groggily, she separated the details of her dream from reality. She was in her bed. Of course she was. She wasn't a witch, studying potions at an ivy-covered school. She was Maeve. This was her home.

As reality clarified the dream faded, but Maeve remembered enough to know it had been intense and deeply narrative. *Holy shit! That was a real-ass honest to God story. And it was good!* She stumbled out of bed, wincing as she yanked the electrodes off her forehead without first breaking the suction.

Rubbing her hand over her sore scalp, Maeve dashed through her apartment to the computer desk on the far wall, dancing back and forth in her unbridled excitement. The program was busily processing the electrical signal from the nodes, which now registered blank static, signifying it wasn't picking up anything at all. The signal history showed four spikes in activity, each indicating a different dream. One click was enough to export the activity spikes into video format.

Maeve grinned and did a little shimmy in her living room,

punching the air. Four files! Four different dreams. She didn't remember the first three, and the fourth was already starting to fade, but it had something to do with witches and an evil magic school. Something about having to evade the eyes of teachers while secretly concocting a potion to go back in time and connect with a past version of herself to do... something epic.

She couldn't remember what, exactly, but she was fairly sure that the whole arc had finished before she woke up. She hoped so, at least. There was nothing her audience hated more than a narrative dream with no ending. She didn't mind them when she was watching—it was fun to imagine what the end would be, become a director in the story. Unfortunately, her followers were less experimental. If she posted a dream that just trailed off, it meant wading through a sea of angry comments.

Shaking the thought off, she squealed again. *Witches* and *time travel! They'll eat this shit up. Laura might even be able to sell it to a big streamer!* If *it has an ending.* A network sale would mean big things for Maeve. Enough money to pay off her debts and get on solid footing, yes. More importantly, it would open up her whole catalogue to a wider audience. She was just waiting for that one break to jump-start her career.

Happily, Maeve ran back across the room, bounced onto the bed, and face-planted into her pillow. She considered trying to get another hour of sleep, but after all of thirty seconds the adrenalin rushing through her system had her turning over, eyes open and grin back in place.

She got up instead, shivering at the autumnal air on her bare butt, and headed for the bathroom. A quick shower killed a few minutes, and by the time she was dressed and back in front of her computer, the program had processed the first two files. It was still chugging through the third one, but she knew that would be another hour at least.

The first file opened to her quick tap, and Maeve fast-forwarded through it at quadruple speed to get an idea of what it was about. It looked like she was renting a giant car and freaking out because she wouldn't be able to drive it. Standard anxiety dream, and *no one* wanted to watch those. She labelled it and filed it away—she liked to keep all her old footage in case she needed to splice anything in to patch a plot hole in a better dream, fabricate an ending, or even create joke footage for ad content.

Some people hated it when they learned that dreamers spliced footage. Purists argued it ruined the magic that set dreams apart from films, with their directors and writers and team of studio executives trying to write to an algorithm. Maeve was of the opposing camp. Dreams were a product of her mind and her imagination. Editing dreams was just taking more active control over that product. It still came from her, and it made a way better story if she could eliminate some of the more confusing moments of dream logic.

When she opened the second dream it looked promising: she was running through dark hallways in some kind of castle, and every time she passed a doorway it flared with light. She never stopped to peer into any of the rooms, though. There was clearly some inner monologue stuff going on that the program hadn't quite been able to capture. There were limitations to dream recording, after all. It was an audio-visual medium, while dreams existed for all five senses, and then some. Inner thoughts, context, the way silk on your skin made you feel fancy and rich—none of that was recorded.

Suddenly, the dream morphed from the long hallways to a classroom, and then an air hanger, before the dream fizzed back into darkness. Might be good for background imagery if she wanted to splice something fancy together, but no use for a stream.

Please don't suck please don't suck please don't suck, she thought really hard at the two remaining still-processing files.

She got up, grabbed some leftovers from her mom's casserole for breakfast, and then sat back down to do some work while she waited for the other files to process. By the time she was done with the busy work of maintaining her accounts, conversion on the last two files was complete.

"Let's do this, brain," she told her computer, and clicked to open the third file. She grinned when she saw the timestamp—*twenty minutes, bay-beee!* She wondered how long the dream had lasted in real life, versus how long the video would be to watch. Most dreams were roughly equivalent—a five-minute dream was five minutes of recorded time—but sometimes, time in dreams did very strange things. She once dreamed an entire school day only to wake up and discover that just ten minutes of unprocessed brain signals had become nearly six hours of processed video.

Maeve opened the video and sat back in her chair, knees up and pinned between her body and the desk. An image resolved itself: an intersection of four castle hallways, stone worn to a polish by the passage of the years. The hallways met in a central chamber with arrow-slit windows and tiny gargoyles peeking out from the stone carvings along the top of the high ceilings. In the heart of the room, a basin of smooth marble stood on a slightly raised platform. Three women in sumptuous gowns stood around the basin, drawn up in poses of extreme readiness. It was clear violence could break out any second. One of the three women looked a little like the love child of Maeve and a red-headed Irish lad—and she recognized them immediately as the main character from her half-remembered dream.

"Oh my god it's third person!" Maeve screamed, abandoning her comfortable position to leap to her feet. She danced around in front of the screen, fist pumping the air as she jumped up and down. "Yes, yes yes yes *yes!*" She could usually remember if a dream was first-person or third-person, but if a dream was particularly fuzzy, she didn't always remember. Here was the proof, though, as incontrovertible as a paternity DNA test.

Third-person dreams were rare. Usually, the viewer was in the place of the main character, the dreamer. It was just like looking out of someone's eyes, without the nose that our brains naturally removed from our vision. You could see the character's hands, and sometimes their body, but never their face. With a third-person dream, there wasn't always just one main character. If there was, it was sometimes the dreamer and sometimes someone completely different. Or in this case a blending of reality and fiction with a younger, cuter, Maeve taking the leading role.

First-person content was popular online and help build a dreamer's career, but it was nearly impossible to sell the licensing rights to traditional streamers. The old guard considered dreams a fad and argued that the more content drifted away from standard movie visuals, the worse it sold. Whether it was true or not, it meant the sale of first-person dreams was limited to VR companies. In those dreams, viewers watched content through a headset as if they were the main character. That presented some awkwardness if the viewer didn't want to put themselves into the role of whoever was having the dream.

With third-person content, on the other hand, programmers could extrapolate the dream file into a 3D environment, and the player could walk around it as they pleased, a passive observer to the show. It wasn't interactive, so it wasn't quite as popular as regular non-dream VR, but there was a solid market for it and royalties were good.

But the *really* great part of third-person dreams was that standard 2D streaming services would buy third-person dreams and turn them into movies. It was the biggest moneymaker in the dream world and a huge source of revenue for the dreamer. It paid significantly less than the full budget of a standard movie, but still in the millions. That kind of money could completely change Maeve's life. She could hire a team to manage her accounts for her and only post content she was proud of. She could be an artist first and a businesswoman second, instead of the two roles constantly fighting for dominance.

As Maeve climbed back into her chair and watched the dream, her brain filled in the half-forgotten bits she remembered and expanded on things she had almost forgotten. Her memory of the dream blended with the experience of watching it until she didn't know which was which. She had read somewhere that memory wasn't set; every time a person revisited a memory it got rewritten a little bit, until what remained could be a complete fabrication. She certainly felt that way watching a dream of hers. It was like the visuals crept into her memory and repopulated it, until she felt like she must have woken up with the dream preserved in her mind like a flower in resin.

It was as good as she had felt it was upon waking. It wasn't only an evil magic school—it had the dreamy magic of a twelfth-century Scottish castle, all crumbling stone, red-peaked roofs, and angry clouds showing through the windows above. The students wore gorgeous gowns and embroidered suits in a hodgepodge of styles that spoke of Maeve's disregard for historical accuracy. The characters were all young adults, mid-twenties or so, and each one more gorgeous than the last. The time travel storyline had a great reveal, and there was even a plucky best friend with her own love story.

But just as Maeve's dream-alternate brought out the potion that would destroy the evil headmaster once and for all—a potion she had tricked him into brewing for her—the dream dropped to static.

"No! No, no, no! Come on, you're killing me!" Maeve gasped. She clicked back through the file and forward again, as if she could somehow make an ending appear. "No! You can't do this to me, world. Just give me one fucking break!" she screamed. Moaning, she dropped her head onto the desk. This was supposed to be fun. This was supposed to be her dream job! Why was everything so *hard* all the time?

Blinking back furious tears, she lifted her head and gave the computer the finger.

The act brought her eyes back to the screen, and she suddenly remembered the final file. She opened the dream processing program, located the file, and brought it up breathlessly. "Oh, please, come on," she whispered as she pressed play.

Her dream-face wavered into existence. "But how will we return to our own time now that the potion has done its work?"

Maeve dropped her head on the desk and groaned. The whole confrontation with the headmaster was missing. She had submerged back into the dream, but her brain knew where the plot was leading and decided she didn't need to dwell there. That happened sometimes; as you drifted in and out of REM sleep, your brain would sometimes come back to the same dream, but it wasn't always linear. Sometimes it would pick up earlier, retreading the same beats before then finishing. Other times, like now, it skipped some time.

The missing content meant there was no way the dream would get picked up by a streaming service. They only paid for dreams that were complete and linear—as close to a movie as a dream could get. So much for her golden ticket.

Pushing through her disappointment, Maeve watched the rest of the shorter clip, then went back to the original file and watched it again. If she stitched the two together, she might be able to add some rapid cuts and a voiceover to fill in the missing content. Her online audience would love it, and while the payouts there weren't as lucrative, they paid her rent.

Opening the larger file in her editing suite, Maeve got to work. She wanted to clean up the colours and put in a few rapid cuts to make the later transition feel more natural, and there was a bit of gibberish in the middle where she would have to record new dialogue. She loved doing ADR, since she was pretty good at acting, and no one had yet called her out on it. Some streamers did *terrible* voice-overs and the fans hated it. They claimed they wanted unedited dreams, but of course what they really wanted was dreams edited so professionally they couldn't *tell* they had been edited, which wasn't at all the same.

This was work that Maeve really enjoyed. It felt good to take the pieces her mind had conjured and slide them into place, like she was constructing a building based on the architectural designs she herself had sketched out. She had never been able to do that when she drew or painted. She had such beautiful images in her head, but the reality on the page came out flat. The spark was missing. It was the same when she tried to write. She loved coming up with stories, but writing them down was as painful as Hercules wrestling the Nemean lion. She had an antagonistic relationship with her work.

Editing dreams, on the other hand, was a dance that her body finally understood. She was an explorer, coming aground on a distant shore to find that she understood every word the locals spoke, knew all their legends and stories.

Maeve was most of the way through editing the first clip when her phone rang. She glanced at the caller ID, saw it was Josie, and tapped her watch to take it on speaker. "Who's dead? Why are you calling me?" she joked.

Most of her friends were horrified to get a phone call, but she hadn't been able to train Josie out of it. Not that Josie didn't also text, but if she had something quick to say (and since she knew from experience that Maeve would forget to check her phone and not see the text for hours...), she resorted to phone calls. That didn't stop Maeve from teasing her about it, of course.

But this time Josie's voice was full of tears. "I need you to come over and help me get my stuff and get the hell out of here before I change my mind," she blurted.

"Holy shit. What? Are you okay? I'm on my way." Maeve launched herself out of her chair, stumbling in blind panic. On the panic's heels came adrenalin, surging through her and clarifying her thoughts. Had Jason done something? She would kill him. She would tear his throat out with her teeth.

"I just—I just need to get out of here. Can you come?"

"I'm calling a car," Maeve promised. She grabbed her phone, opened her favourite rideshare app, and paid a rush fee to jump the queue. She was terrified that if she didn't arrive in time, Josie's courage would collapse like a house of cards. "I can bring my suit- case. Are you *leaving* leaving?"

"Yeah." Josie sniffed, and when she spoke again her voice was clearer. "I'm so fucking tired of this shit, you know? We've been fighting for *two days* about me paying too much attention to Matt at the brewery. *Matt!*"

"That is so messed up," Maeve agreed, her thoughts already racing ahead. If they couldn't take everything in Josie's car, Maeve could go back later with a few friends, get whatever they had to leave behind. Shit, this was really happening.

"Right? Like, when have I ever shown interest in Matt? And you know what, even if he was a 'roided out jock with his dick hanging out, I don't care! I can't talk to my fucking friends?" All of the energy drained out of her voice, and Maeve could imagine her slumping down at the table or sinking down into the couch. "I'm just... really tired. And the way he gets when he's angry, Maeve, I..."

"I love you and I've got you and you're staying here. ETA on the car is nine minutes," Maeve said as she stuffed her feet into worn- out black flats and ran into the bedroom to grab her suitcase. She had a giant one that she'd got second hand for a trip to Hawaii, and stuffed inside it was a duffel bag and a big backpack she used for weekend trips.

"Are you sure? I don't want to—"

"If you say, 'be in the way,' I will smack you," Maeve inter- rupted, and then immediately regretted her choice of words. Her breath hitched. She needed to know that Josie was okay. Whether the fight had been... But how could she ask that? *Should* she ask? She needed Josie to be okay.

"You're never in the way," Maeve said, regretting that she couldn't find the words to say how scared she was, how much she loved Josie, that she would do anything to keep her safe. "I've got the suitcase. Should I bring some bags, too? I'll bring some bags."

"Thanks," Josie said. There was a moment of quiet as Maeve manoeuvred the suitcase into the hall. "Nine minutes?"

"Seven now," Maeve said. She ran into the kitchen and grabbed cloth bags from wherever she haphazardly stuffed them around the room. She really needed a storage bag like Josie had. Her friend was so much more together than Maeve was. Josie always seemed to know exactly what she was doing and where she was going. How had she found herself mixed up with a guy like Jason?

All these questions were secondary to what Maeve was *really* avoiding: why hadn't she said anything sooner? She knew that she couldn't make her friend *do* anything, but she couldn't help asking herself why she hadn't fought to make Josie see how bad Jason really was. The truth was that she had been too scared of losing her —scared that Josie would pick Jason over her. She could never undo that cowardice. "Stay on the phone," Maeve told her. "Is Jason gone?"

"Yeah, he just left for work."

"Good." Jason was a programmer for some tech-douche crypto startup that made NFTs of people's butts. He often worked weird hours, sometimes from home and sometimes at the office, but if he had just left, he wasn't likely to come back for at least five or six hours. "I'm going to go outside and wait for the car. Do you want me to bring anything else?"

"No, I—I'm okay."

"I'm coming," Maeve promised.

"Thanks."

Josie opened the door and Maeve gave her friend a huge hug, burrowing her face momentarily into Josie's shoulder. Josie looked like she hadn't slept. Her long black hair was pulled back into a messy ponytail with an uneven part, and her eyes were red from crying. She held the hug a little longer than Maeve and squeezed her arm as they pulled away from each other, taking strength from Maeve being there.

"I've got a suitcase, a duffel bag, another suitcase, a bunch of bags, and doughnuts." Maeve handed off the doughnuts first, then started pulling bags out of her coat pockets like a magician with scarves. She dropped them on the ground, looking around the apartment. "Have you started?"

Josie shook her head, fighting between embarrassment, fear, and grief as she looked around the room. "I don't—I just couldn't... I don't know where to start."

"That's okay. We can come back later if you forget anything. I'll bring my mom," Maeve said with a gentle smile, and Josie laughed, sounding a little bit like her old self.

Josie covered her face with her hands and let out a short, sharp yell. "Why is this so hard? I made the decision! That was the hard part!"

"It's hard because you've been together for a year and a half and he's wormed his way into your life like a tapeworm, and now that you're pulling away it feels cold and wrong, even though you know it's right. It's like getting out of a hot tub. It feels like shit at first, but if you stay in there you will literally boil to death."

Josie laughed, but when she pulled her hands away from her face she was crying. "Hot tubs don't boil you alive."

"Maybe I'm thinking of lobsters." Maeve shrugged and wheeled the suitcase into the bedroom, and Josie followed. "Do you have a suitcase? Grab it and fill it with your shirts, then go into the living room, get any knickknacks you want to keep, and wrap them in the shirts. I'll get your other clothes."

"Are you some kind of spy? Why are you so adept at moving out in a hurry?" Josie did as instructed, pulling a small suitcase out from under the bed and unzipping it.

"No, I'm just painfully disorganized. One time I had six friends come over to help me move and when they got there—with the moving truck—I had only packed the kitchen. I had to do the rest of the apartment in the time it took them to move a couch, a chair, and three boxes of dishes."

Josie laughed. "What? Why wasn't I there?"

"Good question. Were you in Greece?"

"Ohhh, yeah, after graduation?"

"Yeah, when I moved out of the place on Eleventh."

Josie dumped a handful of shirts into her bag and moved into the living room to pack up. From the other room, she yelled, "Why weren't you packed yet?"

"What do you mean?" Maeve yelled back. She knew she should probably be rolling clothes to make more room, or something, but stuffing them in was faster and time was of the essence. She grabbed a drawer of socks and dumped it into the large suitcase.

"Why weren't you ready for the movers? Did you get the day wrong?" Josie yell talked.

"Oh, sweet summer child! You think I need a reason to be that disorganized?" Maeve called back.

Together the two friends made quick work of the living room and bedroom. They filled all the suitcases they had brought and a few of the canvas bags, leaving dusty imprints of glass bottles and picture frames on shelves around the house. As Josie grabbed her stuff from the bathroom, Maeve wandered the rest of the small apartment.

"Anything from the kitchen?" Maeve asked, looking through cupboards doubtfully. She had no idea how they were going to take anything else with them.

"No. It's mostly his anyway, and I don't want to have to come back and fight over who owns what."

Maeve joined Josie in the living room, where she was putting down a final canvas bag to join the small pile. The streamer put an arm around her best friend. "Furniture?"

"How am I going to take furniture? Where would I put it?"

"I don't know, we'll figure it out."

Josie dropped her head on Maeve's shoulder. "Thank you, but no. I don't want any of it. I don't want to fight about any of it. I just want to go."

"It just... doesn't seem fair. What about the sheets? Or your towels?"

"It's just stuff."

"Isn't that TV yours?" Maeve pointed out. It was a flat screen, not particularly new and impressive but big.

"Yeah, I can just see us staggering down the hall carrying that TV," Josie said with a laugh.

Maeve wrinkled her nose and sighed. "Yeah. I guess it wouldn't fit in the car."

Together, they carried the bags down to Josie's car, which took two trips. On the second trip they piled everything into the hall, and then Josie took a last walk around the apartment to see if there was anything she'd missed. She grabbed the toaster, changed her mind and put it back, then picked it up again.

"You want it, honey, you take it."

"It's just stuff," Josie said, echoing her own words from earlier but sadder now. "I don't care about the things. You know what I want?" She spun around to face her friend, the anger and grief all mixed up and fighting for dominance on her face. "I want the time back. I want every party he made me miss because he didn't like how I talked to some guy. I want every painting class I didn't take because he told me it was a stupid hobby. I want every family trip I didn't go on because he didn't want to waste his vacation. I don't want this fucking toaster, Maeve! I want the self-confidence I had when we met. I want to look in the mirror and see myself without his voice echoing in my head!"

Josie scrubbed the tears as they left her eyes, but there were too many to completely erase. "I want him to feel as shitty as I feel every time we fight! I want him to come back to this empty fucking apartment and know I'm never, ever, ever coming back."

She hefted the toaster in one hand. "You know what, I don't want him to have one goddamn thing that isn't his." Her eyes glittered, her jaw clenched, and Josie hurled the toaster to the ground. Maeve jumped as it shattered, but she covered the surprise with a roar of support.

"Damn right!" she yelled. "Fuck him!"

Josie looked at the TV. She cracked her knuckles. "Fuck him," she agreed.

"Oh, uh, hey, Jo, maybe—" Maeve cautioned, but her friend was already marching over to the TV.

"He can buy his own fucking TV!" Josie said.

"So we're taking it? Are we taking it?"

Josie grabbed the edge of the TV in both hands and propped one foot up to pin the base in place. With a tip and a heave, she pulled the TV down, jumping out of its path as it crashed to the ground. It hit the coffee table and the glass front shattered, sending out tiny silver sparks of electricity for a second that luckily didn't catch on anything.

"So we're not taking it." Maeve sighed.

Josie turned to look at her with wide, panicked eyes. "Oh, fuck. What did I just do?"

"It's fine. It's okay. It was your TV!" Maeve pointed out.

"Oh my god. Oh my god," Josie moaned. "He's going to lose his fucking mind!"

"Hey! Hey! It's okay. You're spiralling." Maeve gently took hold of both of Josie's arms and looked deeply into her eyes. "Take a big breath. Okay? In. Good. Out. Yeah, I don't know, I don't think that did it, maybe one more for luck?"

Josie shakily laughed and pushed her friend away. "Shut up."

"It's gonna be fine," Maeve promised quietly. "I know this is all fucking scary and you're so brave it makes my knees weak."

"I'm not brave," Josie said, eyes glittering again. "I'm a fucking mess."

"You're a fucking goddess," Maeve promised. "You are a force of fucking nature, and you are going to find yourself again. Okay? Let's get the hell out of here."

Josie nodded. "Yeah. Yeah, okay." Josie took one look around the apartment, still dazed. Maeve wondered what she was seeing. A year of memories? A year of wasted moments? Or just the destruction she had caused, and how he might react?

"Wait! One more thing." Maeve put down the bag she had picked up, dashed into the kitchen, and came back with a bottle of whisky and a shrug. "I'm tapped out and you're gonna need a drink after this," she pointed out.

Josie laughed and passed a trembling hand over her eyes. "I can't believe I did that," she said, deliberately not looking at the TV. Then she straightened her shoulders and looked at Maeve. Her smile was shaky, but it was there. "I fucking did that."

"Damn right you did."

6

PERI

A thought floats in darkness. *What if? What if I had gone to school for sociology instead of archaeology? Who would I have become?* Blink.

The darkness cracked open around Peri, revealing scenes that floated around them, like apples bobbing on gentle waves. In one scene, Peri sat in a classroom, eager eyes on the professor at the front of the class. Another was Peri at a rally, a sign held high. A group of students at a coffee shop, arguing semantics. "But how you say things matters," one girl insisted. Peri in bed with a woman, their legs wrapped around each other, their hands questing.

Peri reached out to grab a scene-apple, but instead of their fingers wrapping around it, touching it drew them fully into the moment. The world exploded into colour and light around them. They were at a lake-side Peri didn't recognize. Ducks floated on the calm water, and a tree overhead dropped the occasional heart-shaped leaf. Peri was sitting on a bench, sobbing, their whole body vibrating with the force of the sorrow fighting its way out of their chest. A gentle wind blew, turning the tears on their cheeks cold.

Peri recoiled from the raw emotion on their own face, and as their mind stepped back the scene receded, disappearing as the flow of memories came alive around them once more. The little round scenes were still there, new ones constantly appearing in the flow. Peri working an office job, head down, dark circles under their eyes. Peri, dressed conservatively in black pants and a button-up blouse, their hair pulled back into a ponytail, giving quiet testimony in a courtroom. Peri, alone in a house, sitting on a chair and staring into the middle distance, caved in on... herself? No. No, that wasn't Peri, it wasn't them. Staggering away, Peri fought the rush of false memories, opened their mouth to scream—

Blink. A curtain of thick darkness fell, the scenes vanishing behind its steady, comforting weight.

What if? What if I told the woman how I felt?

The darkness cracked once again, but instead of a flow of bobbing scenes, it dumped Peri directly into a what-if world. They were standing in a meadow under a barrage of rain. It came down so hard the flowers and grass were ghostly behind the curtain of water, and everything in the distance was nothing but haze. Peri's clothes clung to their body, but all Peri was aware of was the woman standing with her forehead against Peri's, her eyes closed, drinking in this moment with pain on her face as if she knew the end of time was coming, and this was the only moment they had. Their hands were linked, and Peri could feel her trembling.

This time Peri was torn out of the moment against their will, pulled back into the stream so suddenly it was like they had been dunked in cold water. More scenes floated past. Peri and the woman, grasping for each other's hands as they were torn apart. Peri, awake, in their bedroom, staring out the window as the seasons changed outside. Peri, still and silent, as dust settled on the bedside tables, stratum of time. The bedspread faded, Steven's signature smile yellowing with age. Still Peri sat, as dust settled into the new lines on their face. Blink.

The darkness fell again, curtaining off the scene-apples. Yet it felt somehow less absolute. Tinged with light. *What if?* Peri asked and recognized the voice as their own. "What if I stop being afraid?"

Once again Peri was thrust into scenic time. They stood on a clifftop, the wind in their hair, embodied and present. At their back, waves pounded the bottom of a hundred-foot drop. The sky was wide and depthless, the horizon a smudge. In front of them was an army, jostling soldiers waiting on some command before they rushed. Their weapons looked scavenged—one soldier held a chipped sword, while another tightened and loosened their grip on a pickaxe, and behind them stood a whole line carrying various carpentry tools. Their helmets had only narrow slits for eyes, hiding their faces behind insect-like visages, each different and more monstrous than the last. Sharp mandibles, faceted eyes, delicate hairs along pronounced eye ridges.

At their front, a lone commander stood. They wielded a tall spear made entirely of iron. It was ugly, heavy, workmanlike. Peri tightened their own grip and realized they were carrying a weapon of their own: a blacksmith's hammer, the shaft long and incongruously bright yellow, clearly modern.

Peri turned their attention back to the commander. They raised a hand and the horde surged forward a foot, still held in check but taut with tension, ready to move. But instead of giving the command, the figure reached under their helmet, one-handed, and pulled it off. As she tossed her head to shake her hair free, the mystery woman was revealed, her streaming locks like nothing Peri had seen outside of a shampoo commercial. Peri let a laugh bubble up past the tension in their throat. She was so effortlessly beautiful, this woman—this commander of death and question mark in the fabric of Peri's life.

"How did you make me forget?" Peri asked, surprised at how present they were. So often in dreams they were more the character than the person behind it—more the shadow than the shape casting it. Maybe because this was a dream about Peri's life, they had managed to cling to who they were.

The woman's features tightened, though whether in confusion or anger it was hard to know. The expression barely kissed her brow before it was gone. "Forget the damage you've caused? The lives lost to this war?"

"No." Peri corrected. "Not this dream. How did you make me forget before? What did you mean when you said you were being forced to play too many roles?"

Peri could see the expression this time, and it wasn't confusion, or anger. It was fear. "You can't remember that," the woman whispered. She was standing at least twenty feet away, but Peri heard every word as clearly as if they stood in a whispering gallery.

Peri walked closer, covering about half of the distance to the woman; hesitation made them stop there, though whether from the angry soldiers that made up the dream world or the look on the woman's face, they couldn't have said. "I don't remember. I watched it after."

"What does that mean?" the woman demanded, imperious and cold. She leaned forward, as if wanting to come closer but afraid to lose control over the legion at her back.

"I recorded the dream," Peri said, but the woman darted her head to the left once, not quite a shake but still clearly a questioning negation. Peri was taken aback by the woman's confusion. They'd assumed everyone knew about streaming, but with tech so new and no idea where this woman came from, it was possible she had never heard of it. Or was Peri making a mistake, assuming the woman was real and not just part of the dream's landscape?

Exasperated, Peri ran a hand through their hair, and was surprised to find it cropped short instead of buzzed on one side and long on the other. They grinned at the feel and rubbed their hand back and forth for a second, admiring the more masculine feel, before remembering why they were here. They wanted information. "You know, dream recording. It takes the signals from our dreams and converts them into video files. I didn't remember anything after I reached out my hand, but when I watched the recording, I saw everything you said."

The woman's jaw clenched, her nostrils flaring slightly. It was the only outward sign of fear, but Peri recognized the appearance of someone working hard to contain their emotions. "You have to stop," the woman said, taking two quick steps toward Peri.

In the instant her foot left the ground, the army behind her surged into motion. She turned her head, realizing what she had done, and then suddenly everything was motion, sound, and fury. The woman ran forward, and Peri ran to meet her, the army only steps behind.

"You're putting us all in danger!" the woman shouted over the noise of the army. "Do you understand? You're putting yourself in danger!"

"I don't understand!" Peri yelled back. They collided, their arms wrapping around each other, almost nose to nose. Peri looked into the depths of her brown eyes, trying to memorize every fleck of darker brown, the exact shade of her lashes, the pattern of veins on her lids.

"It's the recording—Peri, it—"

Peri screamed, torn out of the woman's arms by the force of a trowel coming down across their shoulder like a makeshift club. They tumbled to the ground, scrambling to get back the weapon they had dropped, the blank sky nearly blotted out by the sheer number of people standing over them.

"Wait! Please!" Peri reached out for the woman, but her back was to Peri now, her spear a blur as she fought off her own army. Peri curled up, protecting their face as the soldiers raised their weapons, ready to bring them down.

Peri awoke curled up in bed, trying to protect their face from the heavy blows about to rain down. They sat up, trying to get their breathing and heart rate back under control. The dream had been so *real*. They could still feel the dirt under their back, the vibrations of hundreds of feet pounding in time. They could still feel the sting of the cut on their shoulder.

Peri touched their shoulder and gasped as bright pain met the gentle exploration. They looked down, but their shoulder was still covered by their pajama top. They scrambled out of bed and ran for the bathroom, turning on the light and then blinking rapidly to clear stars from their eyes.

When their vision finally cleared, they were greeted by their own eyes, too wide and bright with panic. Their hair, still shaved on one side and curled on the other, was mussed and lanky from sweat. Their shirt proudly declared, "Save the Drama for the Llamas," but this time it didn't make Peri smile. They gingerly peeled it off, eyes trained on their shoulder. They were greeted with a large, thin cut just beginning to bleed, surrounded by the soft pink-red of a new bruise.

7

MAEVE

The smell of frying bacon woke Maeve. Her excitement turned to annoyance when she rolled over and looked at the alarm clock. She groaned and shoved her face into her pillow, then tugged on the oversized shirt she had unearthed from the bottom of her closet last night as it attempted to strangle her.

Deciding she had lost the fight to get back to sleep—and also that she hadn't had bacon in ages, and it smelled amazing—Maeve dragged herself out of bed. She dug a pair of clean underwear out of the cardboard box she was currently using as a laundry hamper and yanked them on while hopping toward her bedroom door.

When she finally came out, she saw that Josie was awake, showered and dressed, and making breakfast.

"I don't have food," Maeve pointed out suspiciously.

"I noticed," Josie said. "You live like a cave troll."

"I have windows," she objected.

"Do those count?" Josie asked, waving her spatula at the tiny windows of Maeve's basement apartment. They were so small she doubted she'd be able to wiggle out of one if there was a fire, and they were covered in thick bars, but they let in enough light to keep Maeve's air fern alive.

"They totally count. They're like—portholes on a ship. It's cool." Maeve rubbed her eyes and wandered into the kitchen. "You shouldn't have bought food," she told Josie, leaning her chin on her friend's shoulder.

Josie turned and kissed her on the head. "Don't worry, it wasn't out of obligation. It was out of necessity."

Maeve scrunched her nose at that. "Mean."

"Do you want bacon or not?" Josie pointedly asked.

"Kind goddess," Maeve said in the exact same tone, and Josie laughed. Maeve walked over to the kitchen table and sat down, yawning. "You going to work?"

"Yeah, I've got clients all day and Sally'll shit a brick if I try to cancel any of them." Josie worked as a registered massage therapist at a big clinic in Yaletown. She hated her boss but loved her clients, and she got to set her own schedule, which was saying something. Not having to work evenings and weekends as a massage therapist was an accomplishment more Herculean than learning the names of all two hundred and six bones in the human body. And Maeve helped her study for that, so she remembered how hard it was.

"How are you not hungover?" Maeve asked. The two friends had made it through the entire remaining bottle of whisky last night while watching bad action movies and reminiscing about all of their worst relationships.

"I drank water," Josie said. It was an ongoing debate—Josie was convinced you didn't get hungover if you just drank enough water. Maeve argued that preparedness couldn't actually protect you from *all* of life's punishments.

"Yeah, yeah. Is that bacon ready?"

"I wish I could say no just to punish you, but actually it is." Josie opened a cupboard, took out an empty roll of paper towel, and gave Maeve a pointed look.

"Takeout napkins," Maeve said, pointing at the appropriate drawer.

Josie took out the napkins, spooned the bacon onto them, and patted the excess oil off. Maeve got up to get her plate as Josie divided the bacon into two piles and added toast to each plate.

"You're a sweet angel from on high," Maeve told her. She

grabbed the cream cheese and headed to the table, where both friends made sandwiches using the same knife.

"I'm done at six-thirty, so I'll be home around seven-thirty."

"I can make dinner. Mom's leftover casserole?"

"Sounds great. Can we talk strategy tonight?"

"There's no hurry. I know you don't want to sleep on my couch forever, but as long as you need," Maeve said for the hundredth time.

"I love you, but my back hates that couch so yeah, I want to figure it out," Josie said with a laugh.

"We could get a two bedroom? We've never actually lived together."

"And I love you and want to keep loving you so I'm thinking maybe we stick with that," Josie told her, the gentleness in her voice making up for the bite of the words.

Maeve almost choked on her sandwich. "Yeah, okay, that's fair."

"How's work going?"

"Slow," Maeve admitted. "It's like... I don't know."

"Tell me."

"It's just hard when so much of it is out of my control, you know? I can't make myself have entertaining dreams, or linear dreams, or whatever the trending topic is this week. And sometimes I feel like... I don't know, it's probably my imagination, but sometimes I feel like the dreams are clawing at me. Like they're trying to drag me back into them and I'm dreaming for longer than I should. All the research says the electrodes are just recording and there's no way it can have any impact on the dreamer, you know? But it just sort of feels—" Maeve laughed and rubbed her eyes. "Like I'm tired and not making any sense," she concluded.

"Don't do that," Josie chided gently. "If you feel something, listen to it. Maybe you should take a break."

"And pay my rent with what, exactly?"

Josie shrugged, acknowledging that. "I don't know, but everyone needs a vacation sometimes." She brightened. "We should do a girls' getaway. Go to a cabin for a weekend and just escape it all."

"That sounds *amazing*," Maeve admitted. "Lemme see how well the latest does, and if I can afford it, I'm down."

"It's a deal," Josie agreed with a smile.

~

In the moonlight, the city looked burnished with silver. Roofs stuck out through the fog like the backs of whales in a calm ocean, appearing and disappearing among the eddies. Maeve crouched on one rooftop, her long slate-grey coat turning her into just another shadow.

"Did they spot us?" a voice whispered behind her. Maeve turned—it was Josie, dressed in a matching long grey coat, her hair pulled back in elaborate braids, backpack bulging with stolen jewels. Maeve's own pockets were full, and when she dipped a hand in, it came out full of chocolate coins wrapped in silver and candy rings glistening like rubies and emeralds. She tucked the treasure back away in case the smell of sugar gave them away.

"I don't know," Maeve whispered back. "But if we don't get this treasure out of the city, the Baron will never be able to rally the child-Kings and depose the Prince."

"And the evil in our land will grow so strong we'll never be able to rip it out, by root or by stem," Josie agreed bitterly. "You don't need to tell me what the stakes are. I lived with the monster for years."

"Then why did you stop to leave that message?" Maeve demanded. "It was foolish!"

Beyond Josie, a shadow moved. It crept toward Josie, who straightened as if she had been filled with new energy. Her face changed, the angles and planes of her cheeks shifting. In the way of dreams Maeve knew it was still Josie, even though she now only bore a superficial resemblance to Maeve's best friend.

"He has to know why we took it," Josie snapped. "He has to know he can't control us, can't command us. We've lived in terror for too long!"

"And you think I wouldn't recognize your work?" a dark voice demanded.

Both women spun. They had been so focused on threats from below that neither had been watching the skies. It hadn't occurred to them that the Prince would be aware of the route they had taken and would follow them here.

Jason sneered, a sword in his hands, his boots light on the rooftop. "You think you're revolutionaries. You're nothing but angry women, pouting and sucking your thumbs when things don't go your way."

"I'll show you angry!" Josie yelled. She pulled her sword from its scabbard and charged. Jason was taken aback and danced a few steps away from her as she lunged and slashed.

"Give up," he snarled. "My men are—" But he had to stop mid-sentence, too taken up by the fight to waste breath on quips.

"Get him, Josie!" Maeve yelled enthusiastically. "Show him that he's nothing but a bully with fear in his heart! He's afraid of you because he can't control you anymore!"

"And you'll never control me again," Josie snarled. She parried a weak thrust and got in under his defences. The slash of her sword opened a thin red line across his chest, and his footing slipped. Jason fell, sliding down the slick tiles, but he managed to catch himself on a fancy crenellation at the edge of the roof.

"Josie," he panted. "Don't do this. You know that I love you."

Josie slid carefully after him, her footing sure despite the treacherous ground. "You love me?" she whispered sweetly.

"Of course I do." He tried to wiggle forward, but she put the tip of her sword against his chest.

"Tell me all the ways you love me," she suggested.

"I—all of them. You know that. Let's forget this silliness. Come home. Help me stop the Baron's uprising, and we can rule together, as we were always meant to."

"You can rule, you mean," she corrected, still sweet, dragging the tip of her sword ever-so-gently down his chest toward his belly button.

"Well, of course, but—"

"And I'll follow your lead. Do as you. Be quiet, dutiful, and meek. Make you look good."

Now he saw the steel in her eyes—and in her hand, as her sword rose. "Josie, no!"

She slashed upward at his hand, and to avoid the blow he let go. His scream was eaten by the fog, and Maeve ran forward to her friend's side.

"Holy shit. You killed him!"

"Cockroaches are hard to stomp out," she said blithely. "He's probably still alive."

Maeve clapped her friend on the back. "Well, whether he is or isn't, I'm proud of you."

Josie grinned. "Thanks. Now let's get this treasure to the Baron before the sand spiders decide they've had enough of negotiating and make a deal with the scorpions instead of the child-kings."

The two friends linked hands for a moment, sharing their strength, and then took off across the rooftops.

~

Sitting at her desk, Maeve cut the five-second chunk of video where Jason fell off the roof and pasted it into a new file over and over to make a GIF. She chuckled again as she watched his eyes widen and his arms desperately pinwheel again and again. This was going to be such a hit.

Jumping back to the main file, she started adjusting the colour balance and fixing a few oddities. She wrinkled her nose when she saw a black blur in the background, just by Josie's feet, at the beginning of the clip. What was that? She expanded the file and saw that the blur was a human shape, crouched in the background. It had been mostly hidden by the nearby chimney, so she hadn't noticed it at first, and she didn't remember it either.

Navigating back through the file, she was surprised to see that the figure was there for the first third of the dream, but disappeared when Josie's appearance shifted. It was almost as if... as if it had entered Josie's character and was the reason for her subtle facial changes. It was odd that Maeve hadn't been aware of it. Dreams didn't have a lot of extraneous details; the mind focused on the events, and anything deemed unnecessary was just left out. It made the experience of watching a dream very different from watching a movie, no matter how narrative the story was. Sometimes entire backgrounds of her dreams were just coloured blurs. In this one, as a perfect example, the sky was pure black, no stars or moon or clouds.

This shadow figure just didn't make sense. If it was a metaphor for possession, why didn't the dream acknowledge that? None of the characters in the dream noticed that Josie's face had shifted. None of them so much as looked at the shadow.

Staring at it was starting to give her the shivers. There was something about it that just felt off. Her reaction was oversized, and she couldn't say where exactly the fear came from. She felt the way she did when she stared at her own face for too long in a dark mirror. There shouldn't be anything scary about it—there just *was*.

Her overactive imagination had been a problem for her in the past, making ghosts out of creaky floors and stalkers from too many identical grey cars on the road. With that in mind, Maeve flicked back over to the window with the GIF and finished her editing, putting the shadow out of her mind.

Afterward, she called Laura, who picked up on the fifth ring. "Maeve. Good. Listen, I had a flash. We sell it to a VR company and get them to turn the missing portion into a choose your own climax thing. So, it's part dream and part game. We're off the beaten path here so there's no guarantee, and I'm guessing you won't get as much for it because they'll have to put in some of their own content and that costs, but I think it could be really innovative."

"Wow. That's... genius." Maeve would never have thought to pitch the dream in that way. Laura really did know the business inside and out. Maeve was still a newcomer, and there were times, like this, when she felt that keenly.

"See, you pay me for something. Okay, talk soon."

"Laura!"

"What?"

"I called you, remember?"

"Oh, did you? What do you want?"

Maeve laughed. Wasn't Laura the one who was supposed to have her shit together? "I've got a great one here. First-person, but Josie pushes her asshole ex-boyfriend off a roof. People are going to love it. You should see the look on his face."

"Who's Josie? Is that someone?"

"Just my friend," Maeve assured her. Dreams featuring celebrities walked a careful legal line. Courts had ruled that dreams weren't subject to laws that restricted the way a person's likeness could be used, but copyright still applied. A dream featuring Laurence Olivier was fine, but a dream where he played Harry Potter couldn't be monetized.

"Good, I love it, it'll be great for your page, draw a bunch of eyes in and maybe we can get you a bit more from whatever VR company I can find. If your monthly views are high, they're more likely to take a risk."

"Awesome. I'll get the promo up today and post it Friday."

"Do Thursday at midnight."

Maeve did the mental calculus. "Like, tonight at midnight?"

"Tonight is Wednesday."

"Yeah, but doesn't the day start at midnight? So, if it's Thursday at midnight—"

"Goodbye, Maeve," Laura said, and disconnected the call. Maeve stuck her tongue out at her watch.

"You're the one who gets mad when I don't listen," she pointed out even though there was no one to hear. "I always say, I listened, I just didn't understand!" For some reason, being right was less satisfying when there was no one to appreciate it. At least she didn't have to get the work done today. Good editing took time—it wasn't as easy as slapping on a backing track and calling it a day.

It was easier now that dreaming was her full-time job, but sometimes Laura seemed to forget that none of this happened by magic. She came from the purist school, and even though she fully embraced the new trends, Maeve didn't think she had really internalized what went into it.

After listening to some music and picking out a great track, Maeve found her attention drifting back to the dream and the strange shadowy figure at the beginning. It could be a bodyguard to the Prince, something she hadn't picked up on. Or one of the various factions Josie had rattled off at the end of the dream.

Or it could be a face-stealing monster waiting for just the right moment to grab you!

Frustrated with herself and embarrassed by her own fear, Maeve closed the program. She knew it was only her imagination, but it felt like the dark image lingered on her screen momentarily before it disappeared...

8

PERI

Peri looked in the mirror again, where four plastic bandages awkwardly covered the worst of the long thin cut. An ugly bruise circled the whole area, already turning from red to dark blue and brown. They kept expecting to find the slash and bruise gone, bandages covering nothing but unbroken skin. But every time, it was still there.

Peri had gone over every inch of their bed, looking for something that might have caused the wound in the night. There were no rocks, pins, or other debris they could find. Juniper had been sleeping in the living room when Peri came out of the bathroom the first time and barely opened one eye before going back to sleep. There was no way the cat had attacked them while they slept. Anyway, Juniper could never have left a bruise like that.

After peering into the mirror to check the wound one last time, they went to the computer. Sure enough, there was a recorded file easily large enough to be the long dream they remembered. They converted it reluctantly and slipped away as soon as possible, relieved that they would have to wait for the file to be ready before they had to confront the dream again. Seeing it happen would confirm the injury. There would be no going back.

Pouring cold water into the tiny champagne glass they kept in the bathroom cabinet, Peri took their regular morning pills, including their daily anti-anxiety meds and a big handful of vitamins. They popped a gummy probiotic and wandered out into their condo. It was late enough that it technically qualified as morning, but much earlier than Peri usually woke up. They walked over to the window, watching the city far below slowly coming to life.

The sunrise was swamped by clouds, which gave off a tinge of gold but largely kept its majesty hidden. A few joggers made their steady way down the quiet streets, and in doorways here and there homeless people slept, not yet having been roused by annoyed store owners or the steady thrum of traffic. Peri thought about leaving the apartment, going down and being in the moment of awakening, but they couldn't rouse enough to actually do it. The ground underfoot felt too unstable.

Peri stood there for almost an hour, observing the changes from the other side of the glass. People went about their business unchanged. Sleepy workers trudged into coffee shops, emerging looking only slightly less sour. Signs were turned from "Closed" to "Open," or activated in neon. The light rose, filling up the space behind the clouds and giving the sky depth.

Their shoulder pulsed, the quiet pain more easily ignored than what the pain stood for. Peri couldn't grasp what was happening—or didn't want to. They had always claimed that dreams held more truth for them than the waking world. Now, when faced with the possibility that dreams *were* truth, their whole psyche shied away. What would this mean for them if it was true? What would it mean for the larger world?

Peri felt fear scrambling in their chest. How could the world look exactly the same when Peri knew, they *knew*, it had shattered? A wound that couldn't exist throbbed on their shoulder, and down below a woman fixed her lipstick in the poor reflection of her cell phone screen. Peri wanted to slam their hands against the glass and scream, "Nothing is the same! *Wake up!*"

But they didn't. No one would have heard them, anyway.

When their legs started to shake from standing too long without moving, Peri reluctantly turned away from the window. Each step excruciatingly slow, they walked over to their computer. They didn't want to watch the dream. That last shot of the dream had been in third-person. The prospect of seeing the blade crashing down across their shoulders was overwhelming. It was easier to think that they were losing their mind. But they could only avoid it for so long.

They hit play, turned the volume up, and watched the dream unfold. It was exactly as they remembered. Peri's internal monologue had been translated as fairly straightforward audio, which was always a plus, and the rush of scenes they had witnessed were all laid out in immaculate detail. The apple-scenes looked like diamonds against the blackness of the inner world, and Peri was almost startled when the first scenic moment began to play out at the lakeshore.

Avoiding this moment had consumed Peri, but now that it was here, they wanted to rush toward it, to rip the Band-Aid off in a single go, to jump off the dock into the deep unknown. Instead, they stuck their hands under their armpits and squeezed, letting it play on. The footage could have important context for the final scene. There might be more here than just what Peri knew to look for.

"What if I told the woman how I felt?" The audio asked, bubbled up from the darkness, and Peri felt an almost overwhelming pressure to look away as, in the dream, the other Peri and the woman linked hands. Was it possible to intrude on yourself, to be an interloper in your own fantasy? It was strange, but that was exactly how it felt.

Finally, just as they had known it would, the point of view pulled back into a third-person playback as the armies rose up and Peri confronted the woman, who fell into their arms.

Peri could easily see the soldiers surrounding them, the raised axes, hammers, and swords. And there was a blow from a war hammer, just as Peri remembered, falling on the back of their shoulder and knocking them to the ground.

They reached up unconsciously to touch the wound. The bruise hurt, a dull throb that insisted, "I am here. I am real." Yet when Peri touched their shoulder, that was real, too, warm and solid under their touch. It shouldn't be possible that something from a dream had hurt them here. Had Peri psychosomatically manifested a wound? They had heard, but never believed, stories of stigmata opening on people's hands, their body's response to their fervour and faith. The placebo effect proved the mind-body connection, and how much more powerful it was than anyone understood, but Peri had never believed it could go that far.

If it did, what did that mean for Peri, who dreamed so deeply and so often? If those dreams started to infringe on the real world, Peri wouldn't be safe anymore. They would have consequences. Brutal, impossible to avoid consequences. It would be the worst of both worlds.

And what about the content of the dream? The woman had been trying to warn Peri, something about the technology that was used to record dreams. That it was dangerous, that much was clear, but why? "You're putting us all in danger! Do you understand? You're putting yourself in danger!" the woman had said, but she had been cut off before she could explain how the recording could bring danger to anyone.

Was she implying that it had some kind of negative effect? She could have been warning Peri about exactly what had happened, the dream bleeding into the waking world. Or was she just afraid of the technology because it was something she didn't understand? And who was "us?" Not she and Peri, surely, since she clarified that Peri was in danger, too. Peri was sure that none of this had come from their own mind. They couldn't continue to pretend that they didn't believe the woman was real. She was out there. She had to be.

For the hundredth time, Peri took a screenshot of the woman and did a reverse image search, but as usual, nothing came up. There was no indication that the woman was real, nothing but the fact of her recurrence, and now this. This strangeness that only happened when she was present. This warning to stay away from the recordings.

Peri saved the file, but hesitated as they went, by rote, to upload it to Zzz+. Putting this video online didn't seem right. Never mind that it was more deeply personal than most of Peri's dreams—they didn't mind that so much. Dreaming felt anonymous, even though it wasn't. As DreamsAway, Peri shared a certain version of who they were, yes, but otherwise they kept so private online that none of their fans knew anything about their waking life. Even their gaming friends only knew them by their first name. *Not that there's much to know.*

No, they hesitated because of the woman. It was clear that whatever was happening, she didn't like that Peri was recording it. Uploading the video felt like a breach of trust. A day ago, Peri couldn't have sworn that the woman was real. They wanted to believe, scanned crowds for her face, pictured what she might be like in their waking life. Did they expect to see her, though? No, not deep in their core. They had doubts. Yet hurting her was unfathomable, an abyss Peri had no desire to fall into.

Resolutely, Peri flicked the window closed and transferred the file into a new folder, which they labelled, "Not Uploaded."

Time passed in a haze. Peri's phone rang, shaking them from their thoughts. Their brother Kyle was calling for a fifth time in the past two weeks, and since Peri had avoided his last four calls, they decided it was probably time to pick up.

"Hey Kyle," they said.

"Oh good, you're alive."

"Ha ha."

"Well, you didn't upload anything, so I wasn't sure," he teased.

Peri uploaded almost every day—it was rare for them not to have a single dream worth posting. But Peri couldn't explain the reason they didn't upload—the mystery of the missing memories, the woman, and the slash across their back.

"What's up?" they asked instead, hoping to deflect back onto Kyle. It was unlikely he was calling just to check on them.

"I can't just call my sister?" Kyle asked cheerfully. Peri made a frustrated sound in their throat, and he quickly said, "Sorry, sorry, my sibling. Right."

"You can. But you don't," Peri snapped, unintentionally letting some of their frustration slip out.

"Sure I do. I just did. Seriously, I was just calling to check in. Mom and Dad haven't heard from you in a while."

"How's my nephew?" Peri asked, pointedly. Kyle knew they were cutting back on contact with their parents, and the fact that he wasn't respecting that was enough to make Peri consider cutting him off, too. They probably would if he wasn't so damn sorry every time he messed up. It was hard to stay mad at him—but even harder to want to spend time talking to him when every conversation felt like a minefield.

Kyle sighed, accepting the graceless conversation change. "Good. They're good. Teddy signed up for dance classes again. Mel's got him doing jazz this time, it's gonna be hilarious. I'll send you the concert if I can."

"That'd be great." A moment of silence stretched out. Peri clenched their jaw and waited, wondering if there was more Kyle wanted to say. When nothing was forthcoming, the awkwardness grew too overwhelming and Peri blurted, "Can we talk later?"

"Got plans?" He sounded hopeful, and Peri's chest hurt. Why couldn't he just love them as they were, instead of constantly hoping that this would be the call where he would learn Peri had a girlfriend, or a new job, or a social life that he approved of? His dashed hopes hurt even more because they came from a place of love, not control. He wanted Peri to be happy. Peri just couldn't make him see that the life they had built was right for them.

"Yeah," Peri lied. "I'm going to an online lecture. Should be cool."

"Ah." Yup, that was disappointment. As far as Kyle was concerned, if it happened online, it wasn't real. He barely answered Peri's long emails and refused to download a messaging program other than the texts on his phone. "Okay, well, have fun. Call me later?"

"Sure. Yeah. Say hi to Mel and the kiddo."

"Bye."

Peri hung up and chucked their phone across the room, aiming for the couch so they could enjoy the thrill of anger without risking any damage. Thank god Kyle lived a whole province and a mountain range away. Peri could just imagine him constantly being in their face if they lived in the same city.

Peri got up and retrieved their vaporizer. They could use a little calm.

After a few tokes, they went and found Juniper, getting in some snuggles and pets before the cat sleepily objected. Next up was rescuing their phone, none the worse for wear after its flight across the apartment. They settled down into the velvety cushions, with their head propped up by a throw pillow decorated with a beautiful watercolour design of Mary Poppins, and scrolled through the notifications on their phone.

They were surprised to see how many comments there were on their videos asking when they were going to upload next. Peri was one of the original dreamers, having picked the tech up while it was still in beta on a whim, and that counted for something. Plus, their dreams were unique. Not many other streamers had such a steady recurring roster of plots and locations, and none dreamed watchable content every night. But it was still odd to realize that people cared. Peri's fans hadn't just noticed Peri's absence—from the posts, it seemed like they were really worried about what had caused the absence. A couple of people said things like, "I don't know you, but if you're gone, you'll leave a huge hole in my life," and, "Please send us a sign. Tell us that you're okay."

After an internal debate, Peri finally decided to upload a video—a loading screen gif with a written apology that just said, "Nothing worth seeing today. Check back soon. Not dead."

It wasn't much, but Peri hoped it was enough to show people that they cared. It was all they had the emotional energy for, though they did copy it to all of the various platforms where they posted their content.

That task accomplished, Peri went back to their computer chair. After some space, they were ready to revisit the video of the fight, examining it over and over, looking for any new detail. But it stayed mercilessly the same. There was no hidden meaning that Peri could find. Over and over the woman urgently gasped, *"It's the recording— Peri, it—"* but no matter what Peri tried, they could not hear the sentence's end. Their sightline lifted as they were hit, so they couldn't try to read her lips to see what she might have said, and the scream obscured the words no matter how many different sound filters Peri applied to the audio.

Over and over they watched it, looking for new details that never came. Juniper came to lay on their lap for a while, and then wandered off—even she was bored of Peri's obsessive analyzing. The sun traced its way down the sky, and Juniper came back, meowing for food. Peri stood up, scrubbing their face and stumbling a little. Their leg cramped and their eyes burned. *So much for the 20-20-20 rule.*

They wandered into the kitchen, portioning out a dish of wet food for Juniper and grabbing a frozen meal they pre-made two weeks before. They tossed it in the microwave and stood in the centre of the room, thoughts roiling, staring into nothing until they were startled out of their reverie by the microwave's rolling series of beeps. It almost sounded like a little song, and sometimes Peri liked to dance along, but tonight they just fetched their burrito, grabbed some vegan sour cream from the fridge, and sat down at the computer to eat.

Navigating away from the video for the moment, they went back and watched earlier streams, looking for hints they might have missed. They weren't sure if they were just reading into it, or if there were signs that the woman might be speaking to Peri after the dreams ended. It seemed like sometimes she hung on, expectantly, as the dream faded away. Other times she made comments that could be veiled references—or could be nothing but the slight nonsense dreams so often held.

Peri wrote them all down anyway, then looked at the list, searching for similarities.

"You look like you know more than you're saying."

"I could tell you things that would blow your mind."

"So, we meet again."

"Today I am. Tomorrow, who knows what I'll be."

It wasn't much to go on. Four lines, drawn from over twenty dreams. Peri knew they could go further, but their eyelids were beginning to droop. They had ignored the alarm that told them bed was waiting hours ago, and they weren't used to staying up late.

Peri took the little notebook with them as they padded around the apartment, getting ready for bed. "You look like you know more than you're saying." Was the woman trying to see if Peri had memories outside of the dream? Or was she just making a cute joke? In that dream, Peri had been at a steampunk convention; they were in the middle of a biscuit duel where Peri had cheated and made their biscuit from cornmeal instead of flour, hardening it for an advantage. And what about, "So, we meet again?" The characters in that dream didn't know each other as far as Peri could tell, but it was a similar storyline to a dream they had recorded nearly a year ago. Was it a throwback to the original dream? Or was the woman pleased to see Peri again—pleased to be in their mindscape? Did she enjoy the adventures they had together? She had been scared of something, no question. Being drawn in too many directions. Was there too much variety to Peri's dreams? Too many roles she was being forced to play?

Peri took out the recording pads, hesitating a moment before attaching them and turning them on. As Peri crawled under their bright comforter, they touched the bright red gem embedded in one of the characters printed on the fabric. Maybe Peri could draw courage from Garnet. She wasn't afraid of anything—or at least, she didn't let that fear stop her. She fought for the people she loved. Peri wanted to do the same.

At the thought, Peri's heartbeat sped up. Was that what they felt for the woman? Did they... Could they... Was it love? Could you love a person you didn't really know? The woman had been in their life for years. In different forms, in different lives and as different people, yes, but always her. The way Peri felt when they thought about her... It made them feel foolish. Exposed and raw. The woman might not even be real, but—yes. Peri loved her. They wanted to turn their dreams into a safe place where the woman could be herself.

Peri shot up in bed, suddenly inspired. What if they could control the dreamscape? Create a neutral world where the woman could appear as herself? For years, Peri had watched as their own gender presentation slowly shifted, coming more in line with who they really were.

They tried lucid dreaming a few years ago, wanting to have more say in how they appeared in their sleep, but they gave it up when the dreams became more real and engaging. They didn't want to be in control of the world—they wanted to experience it first-hand. But now, it seemed like it might be a useful tool again. Peri reached across the bed and snagged their phone, head falling onto the pillow as they curled up on their side.

A lot of the suggestions couldn't be implemented in an evening —one site even suggested launching yourself off small precipices throughout the day to "test reality" and see if you were dreaming, which would make you more likely to engage the same mental muscles as you slept. Another suggested using a dream journal, which Peri found adorably outdated now that dream recording existed. But one technique seemed promising. Peri read it over a few times, then put their phone away to give it a try.

They took a deep breath and thought about the dream where they had been a sentient finger. They built it up in their mind, recreating the planes of the ship, the outfits of the other crew members, even the smell of recycled air. Then, they pictured the moment when the woman announced their true identity, but in their mind, they refuted the claim. "No," they said. "I'm Peri. And I want to know who you are." Out loud, they said, "The next time I'm in this dream, I will know to say those words and know that I'm dreaming. When I hear the words, 'No, I'm Peri, and I want to know who you are,' I'll know that I'm dreaming, and I'll become lucid."

Peri settled back against their pillow, getting comfortable. Over and over, they pictured the scene, their own new reaction, and their intention to become lucid.

They were supposed to keep visualizing it until they fell asleep, but Peri found that they couldn't get relaxed enough to sleep while they were concentrating so hard on remembering. Reluctantly, they put it aside and let their thoughts drift, and gradually sleep drifted over them.

For three nights, Peri went to bed and slipped into a dark void. And for three mornings, they woke up to blankness. Not a single memory. Not a single dream.

There hadn't been one day in the last three years where Peri hadn't dreamed *something*. Even if they didn't remember the whole dream when they woke up, there would be impressions left behind. A haunting refrain, the sound of swaying leaves, the sure knowledge of momentous, if shadowy, happenings. There was always something.

But now, there was only darkness. Even falling asleep felt distant —muddy. Peri couldn't recall the exact moment they drifted off, or what they were thinking of as it happened.

Stumbling out of bed every morning, shivering even in their pajamas, Peri raced to the computer. "NO INPUT RECORDED," a little box noted at the bottom of the screen. The first morning this had happened, they tried to sit down in their chair, but missed and crashed to the floor, breathing hard. They had never seen those words before. No input recorded. No dreams. There had been no dreams.

They couldn't figure out what they had done wrong, how they had caused this shift. Terror infused them at the thought that they might never see the woman again. Was it intentional? The woman had been angry that Peri remembered, angry that the recordings existed. She might have pushed Peri away, disconnecting them somehow from the dreaming world. Or was it Peri's fault? They had experimented with lucid dreaming, trying to control what should be out of their hands. That could have been what caused it. It could all be their fault, all of it.

The days drifted by, and Peri was a passive observer within their gentle buffeting current. Nothing could keep their attention. Nothing could pry them from the spiral their thoughts became. She was gone, and the dreams were gone, and Peri could not find a way through the labyrinth. They missed appointments, forgot to eat meals, spent hours staring blankly at a wall. They ignored panicked notes and social media pokes about their lack of uploads, missed gaming sessions, and disappeared from play-by-post sites. Even Juniper meowing for attention couldn't pull them from the morass of their desperate, clinging thoughts. *What if she's gone? What if I can never get back to her—never dream again?*

On the third morning, as Peri stared at the computer screen, they swayed where they stood. Panic flickered at the edges of numbness like fingers of flame. It devoured the emptiness, leaving screaming terror in its wake. Peri grabbed the neck of their pajamas. Choking. They were choking. They tugged at it, gasping, then finally fought their way out of the clingy T-shirt entirely. They couldn't breathe.

The woman had warned her. *Don't record. Don't use the technology. It's dangerous.* Was that why she had vanished? Was Peri facing the consequences of ignoring that warning?

They curled up on the floor, feeling the cool hardwood against their cheek, struggling to breathe. Peri was all too familiar with the tells of an oncoming panic attack, and their body went into a horrible autopilot to try to protect itself from an invisible threat. Black spots danced at the edge of their vision and grew darker, narrowing their field of vision. Peri thought they might faint, but there was no relief to be found from the waves of panic crashing over them.

For a moment it seemed like the computer desk was collapsing, and Peri threw up their hands to catch it—but no. Nothing was there. They wrapped their arms around their head and waited for the fire to burn out—it was the only thing they could do. But there was so much fear. So much guilt. So much to feed the flames.

9

MAEVE

"Oooh this place looks amazing!"

"That's a scam, Maeve."

"What? Says who?"

Josie leaned over Maeve's shoulder and pointed at the ad on her phone's large folding screen. "I can't show you the property because I'm in Kenya," she read from the ad.

"So? Maybe he's in Kenya." Maeve leaned back against the couch, tilting her head back so that she could see Josie better. "It's half the price of anything else I've seen!"

"Scaaaaaaaam," Josie hollered in her ear.

"Ow." Maeve rubbed her ear with one knuckle and closed the window, going back to the main screen. "Fine, be that way. Crusher of dreams, destroyer of positive vibes."

"Liver in reality. Hopefully liver in an apartment that's actually there when I turn up on day one with all of my stuff."

"People who do rent scams should be drawn and quartered," Maeve muttered. Her phone dinged, a notification momentarily covering the search bar as she tried to navigate to the next ad. "Haha, listen to this one. 'Homeboy has a face I'd love to smack! You get him, girl.'"

Josie snorted. "This is the best catharsis ever. I love your brain."

"It's almost as good as *actually* pushing him off a roof," she agreed. Since she had posted the video two days ago, her views were through the roof. Laura said the buzz had gotten her a few meetings with VR companies, and she was even going to book Maeve on a podcast to talk about the intersections of dreams and reality. It was exactly the launching point her career had been in desperate need of.

"Can you grab me a beer from the fridge?" Maeve asked.

Josie raised an eyebrow. "What am I, your live-in? Get it yourself."

"Pleeeeeeease just get us beer," Maeve whined.

"Abso-lutely not," Josie said. She turned back to her laptop, where she was also scrolling through websites looking for apartments.

"Josie! Just look in the fridge, it was all a clever ploy!" Maeve insisted.

Intrigued enough to get up, Josie raised an eyebrow at her friend and walked into the kitchen. She opened the door and whistled. "Damn, woman, you went *shopping*."

"I've been waiting for you to open that fridge for like two hours! Who drinks tap water?" Maeve complained. Josie grabbed them each a beer and brought one over to Maeve, even though she held out her hands like she was ready to catch a toss.

"We have the cleanest tap water in the world."

"Yeah, but fridge water is cold."

"So is beer," Josie pointed out, and gently tapped hers against Maeve's.

"Cheers." Maeve cracked hers open and went back to scanning her phone.

"You didn't already get paid for the Jason video, did you?"

"No, it's just my regular ad check, but I don't have to be as careful with it since I know the next one is going to be decent. I bought *cheese*, Josie. I haven't had cheese in like three months."

Josie kissed Maeve's head and went back to the dining room table. "You are truly blessed."

"Ooh! This one is only three blocks from here!"

"I must have it!" Josie declared.

Maeve copied the link and dropped it into the messaging app. "How cool would it be if we lived in the same building?" she sighed dreamily.

"Let's kill the guy who lives in the suite upstairs," Josie suggested. "He plays music way too loud on Wednesday nights."

"Plus he's really weird about the garbage. If I try to shove it down to make more room, he accuses me of going through his trash," Maeve muttered.

"*What*. How have you never mentioned this before?"

"I feel like I have." Distracted, Maeve scrolled through a few of her other sites. One of the forums was full of people talking about how DreamsAway, a popular old-school dreamer, hadn't posted last night. Their fans were speculating about whether something had happened to them offline. Maeve couldn't stop a pang of jealousy. She doubted anyone would notice if she didn't post for a stretch. How did DreamsAway do it? How did they have such narrative, vivid dreams *every single night*? It would be so easy to build a following and be a success if you had such a constant stream of great content.

Don't be jealous, Maeve chided herself. *You'll get there someday.*

Across from her, Josie got up to grab her phone from her coat pocket.

"Ew, are you calling them?" Maeve asked.

"Of course I am. A hundred other people are going to email them. If I call, I stand out from the crowd."

Maeve's phone rang, and she screamed and almost dropped it. "Did they hear you?" she whispered. Josie was laughing as her friend picked up the phone, but Maeve's sour face turned the laughter into a question. "Why the hell is Jason calling me?"

"Don't answer it," Josie warned.

Maeve rejected the call. A second later, it rang again. "Asshole," Maeve muttered, and looked at Josie with raised eyebrows.

"Don't tell him I'm here," Josie said.

"Not in a hundred fucking years," Maeve promised. She swiped up to answer the call. "You better have a good reason to be calling me," she said, going aggressive fresh out of the gate.

"You take down that fucking video!" Jason spewed.

Maeve laughed. "Wait, what? *That's* why you're calling?"

"Why did you think I was calling?" he demanded.

"I don't know, I thought you were trying to harass Josie and since you couldn't get through, you figured you'd give me a try."

"If anyone's harassing anyone, it's you. Pushing me off a roof? Seriously? Making me into some big bad villain in your stupid little play?"

"Do I need to explain how dreams work, Jason? I can use teeeeeny tiny words if it helps."

Josie covered her mouth, trying not to laugh, and Maeve grinned at her over the couch.

"It's fucking slander. Take it down!"

"It's actually libel if it's recorded," Maeve offered helpfully. "And in this case, it's neither." She turned on her legalese voice and droned out the caveat she put into every video. "I'm not legally responsible for the content of my dreams. Any resemblance to any person, living or dead, is purely coincidental and not a reflection of the views of the dreamer or any sponsors."

"You think I give a fuck about what a lawyer is gonna say? I'm not telling you to take it down or I'll sue you. I'm telling you to take it down or I'll fucking make you take it down," Jason snarled. "People are talking about this shit. They're laughing at me. Take it down, Maeve."

Maeve tried to keep the smile on her face, not wanting to scare Josie, but she knew it probably looked painted on. She didn't want to admit that Jason was freaking her out. Besides, being scared just made her want to double down. "Grow up. Everyone knows dreams aren't real. No one thinks you're an evil prince."

"No, they think I'm an asshole."

"Well maybe if you weren't?" Maeve suggested.

"What's he saying?" Josie whispered, not wanting to be heard over the phone. Maeve held up a finger; she was almost done with this call.

"I'm not fucking around, Maeve. Take it down."

"You're a fucking bully, Jason, and I'm not afraid of you," Maeve said, pushing the lie through a lump in her throat. "Get over it and don't call me again." She hung up, slamming the two sides of her phone closed and dropping it on the couch.

"What did he say?" Josie asked, louder this time.

"Nothing. He wanted me to take the video down."

"You should," Josie said.

"Fuck him," Maeve promised. "He doesn't scare me."

"He gets... really mad, Maeve. I don't want you dealing with that for me."

"Are you kidding?" Maeve wrapped an arm around Josie, hugging her. "I'm doing it for the cheese."

Josie laughed, though it was clear the humour was pushing past pain on the way to the surface. "If he threatens you..."

"I meant it when I said that he's a bully," Maeve said. "He thinks that he can scare me into doing what he wants, but he's not actually gonna hurt me,"

Josie nodded, reluctantly. "Probably not," she agreed. "But that doesn't mean he can't make your life miserable. He didn't have to lay a finger on me to make things hell," she whispered.

Maeve sat across from her, holding her hand. "If you want me to take it down, it's down. But I can handle whatever that shit-for-brains throws at me, and I don't want him to think he can win."

"What if he slashes your tires, or eggs your house, or something?"

"I don't own a car and this place is a shithole," Maeve pointed out.

"Those were just examples," Josie said, finally laughing in earnest.

"Yeah, I know. And I'm not taking it lightly, I promise. But yeah, if he does something fucked up, great. I can call the cops. Maybe he'll actually get in trouble for something."

Josie sighed. "That would be nice."

"So it's a win-win!" Maeve said with a big smile. She wagged her eyebrows. "Hey. Wanna watch the video again?"

Josie laughed. "I really, really do. But first, I'm calling that listing."

"Sociopath," Maeve told her as she returned to her own phone to keep looking.

~

Maeve's eyes popped open, senses straining, heart pounding. What had woken her? Blearily she looked over at her clock, and groaned when it declared the night to be deep in its cups and morning already sweeping the cigarette butts away. She hopped up, tugging on a T-shirt she had left at the foot of the bed, and quietly slipped out of the alcove that served as her bedroom and into the main room.

Josie was asleep, tilted halfway between her stomach and her side, one hand tucked up under her face. She was short enough that she could stretch out on Maeve's beaten-up old couch. Maeve moved quietly to make sure she didn't wake her up, slipping into the bathroom and closing the door. When she was done, she paused in the threshold, not sure what had stopped her. Was it just having another person in the room that caused a sense of presence, a shiver that whispered down her back and tickled the exposed skin at the back of her legs? Was her imagination doing a five-kilometre run, lapping reality as it headed for the finish line?

Idly she scratched at the sensor on her temple, peeling it off and sticking it back on more firmly. It was almost an autonomic reflex; her thoughts were elsewhere. Had she locked the door? Was there a shadow at the window? Did Josie's breathing sound even and deep, or hitched in fear?

Stop it, Maeve. You're borrowing trouble. Despite the mental words, she padded past Josie, as quiet as possible, and checked the door. *Locked. Obviously.* She knew the more she messed around the more likely she was to wake Josie up, but she couldn't stop herself from walking to the window and standing on her tiptoes to look out. What she could see of the streets through the bars were quiet. Streetlights brought their usual brand of not-quite-darkness to the city, and her view was mostly of car tires parked along the residential street. The front yard was tiny, barely a patch of grass, so her window wasn't far from the sidewalk. Her upstairs neighbours had put the trash out the night before, and it made momentarily alarming shadows. Maeve grinned. *Okay, Maeve. Go to bed before the cans in the recycling bin start moving.*

As she turned away, a noise from outside arrested her movement. She barely stopped a shriek, turning it into an awkward swallow and a burp, as she spun back to face the darkness. Something *was out there.*

A shape moved by the bins, and the noise came again, the slight bang of cans as the bin shifted. Maeve hooked the edges of her fingers on the windowsill and peered out, trying to be invisible as her eyes bored holes into the semi-dark. The shadow moved again... and Maeve almost laughed. It was small and furry. A raccoon, or a cat. Maybe a really big rat. Not an angry ex-boyfriend out to get his revenge.

Maeve let go of the window and walked back toward her bed, telling herself that everything was fine. But she couldn't shake the feeling that there were eyes on her back, watching her as she slipped back into her room.

10

PERI

Peri stood in their dark bedroom, fingers trailing over the cool rubber of the electrode pads. If they did this, there was no telling what they might miss. What if the woman appeared, but made Peri forget again? What if the dream cracked and fragmented, leaving only smudges of thought behind? There would be no record. No way to ever know what they had missed.

They had been reluctant to discuss their current issues with their therapist, Jasmine, and everything that had gone unsaid felt like a popcorn kernel stuck in their gum, an irritating background anxiety that they couldn't entirely push aside. Normally they were an open book with Jasmine—you had to be, for the process to do anything at all—but they couldn't quite admit out loud everything that had been roiling through their head.

How could they, when they couldn't even *think* it without pulling away? *She's real. She's real, and she's out there, and something is wrong.* Even that paled beside the cut on their shoulder, mute evidence that reality as they knew it was shifting. They couldn't tell a therapist, even one they trusted as implicitly as Jasmine, that reality was cracking around them. It made it sound as if *they* were cracking—that they were losing their perception and tether to the real. They felt sure that wasn't what was happening, confident of the evidence of their senses, but they wanted Jasmine's advice. They trusted her.

But with this? That trust simply didn't extend so far. They hadn't been able to hide their distress during their session that morning, so they told Jasmine a version of the truth, skewed to be somewhat more palatable. "I haven't been able to dream for three nights," Peri had said.

"Is something going on to cause that?" Jasmine had asked. She had been wearing her glasses, thick black rims framing dark eyes, and the contrast on her camera made them seem like deep pools of ink.

"I don't know. I don't think... I'm not sure." Peri recalled wrapping their arms tight across their chest, trying not to let the true depth of their terror show. They were pretty sure they had failed.

"What about that is causing you the most anxiety? Lost work? Lack of connection to a place that's normally a safe haven?"

"The second one?" Peri asked.

"Let's talk about that," Jasmine said, gently guiding Peri.

"I just don't know what to do. I feel like I'm standing, holding this precious thing and watching it go up in smoke and I have no idea how to stop it. I have no idea what's causing it pain, what's hurting it, how I can protect it, if—"

"Can I pause you there? You're talking about a sense of responsibility. But that desire to protect, to claim responsibility over something that's not really in your control... That sounds familiar to me."

Peri knew immediately what Jasmine meant. Grasping for control over others, wanting to influence their reactions to situations and events, was something Peri was actively working on. "I'm trying to control the outcome instead of my response to the outcome."

"What does that look like? If you focus on yourself and how this impacts you?"

"I think I don't... *want* to be passive? I don't want to just let this happen. I want to actively figure out how to solve the problem."

"Focusing on yourself and your reactions doesn't mean being passive," Jasmine reminded them gently. "In this case, we're talking about a realm that's inside of you. When something changes in this way, what if you don't try to stop it, but instead think about why it's happening, and whether there's a good reason for it? For instance, what if this is your subconscious trying to give you a break from your respite?"

"Why would I want a break from respite?" Peri asked.

"Because it's false safety," Jasmine suggested, her voice rising slightly in a question. "It isn't real, and it contributes to a pattern of avoidance that we know can be a problem for you. Could this inner upheaval be a sign that aspects of your life have become untenable? You can't avoid them, so you're effectively pushing yourself out of your comfort zone by eliminating the false safety you feel in sleep."

"If this is my mind trying to encourage me to disconnect more from dreams, it's pushing me in the wrong direction," Peri replied bitterly, noticing that Jasmine raised her eyes, inviting them to go on. "I haven't left the condo in days. I haven't even... I haven't talked much. To anyone. I haven't even watched TV or read a book." Time ran into itself each minute endlessly long, each day passing in a blink. Peri still wasn't sure what they had even done minute to minute, hour to hour.

"Maybe you need a change of routine," Jasmine said. "New stimuli to disrupt the cycle you're stuck in. Do something really unexpected. Order takeout just before bed. Go to a mall you've never been to before and get your groceries there. Take your computer to the library and work at a table with other people."

Peri was pretty sure that taking off the recording pads and going to bed wasn't the kind of change Jasmine had meant, but to Peri it was a lot more extreme than signing up for a cooking class. Without the technology, they might not be able to capture every detail of their dreaming life. They wouldn't be able to watch it over the next day, turning soft memories concrete and impermeable. Worse, they wouldn't know if the dream continued past their memories. This was stepping off a cliff with an untested parachute.

Peri's stomach was clenched so tightly acid was pushing back up their throat and every breath was a shallow gulp. If they experienced a dream and didn't remember, it was as if it had never happened. Or would there be something here, something intangible and missing, an ache that they could never identify? If they woke up tomorrow with another blank, they would be haunted by everything that might have filled that space.

But the woman had said the recording was the problem. After the first night, Peri had abandoned the lucid dreaming experiment, hoping that was the problem, but there had been no change. It was time to try something new. Time to change the input.

Peri slammed the nodes back on the bedside table, taking in a long, ragged breath. It hurt to breathe that deep, and Peri felt dizzy from the sudden rush of air. They crawled into bed, breathing deeply a few more times until the natural act no longer felt like an attack. Juniper jumped up on the bed, meowing plaintively, and Peri reached over to scoop her up and snuggle against her.

"Sorry, kiddo," Peri whispered. "I know I haven't been playing with you enough. Tomorrow, you get some epic yarn time. Okay?" They kissed her head and scratched her under her chin until Juniper got tired of the attention and squirmed away. She plopped down at the edge of the bed, just out of reach, and curled up to sleep.

Peri lay back and pulled the comforter up their chin. If this didn't work...

It has to work.

Peri opened their eyes. They were lying in bed, the comforter pulled up to their chin. The darkness was absolute, but as they scanned their surroundings something caught their attention. Despite the darkness, they could see Juniper clearly, sitting hunched on the edge of the bed. Her eyes glowed, reflecting light even though there was nothing in the room that should be able to cast the glow.

"Hey Juniper," Peri whispered. "You okay?"

The cat growled, low and deep and rumbling. Her back arched, fur ruffling as her tail twitched methodically back and forth.

"Juniper?" They drew back a little, clutching the comforter tighter against their chest.

The growl split into two sounds: one continued in that low grumble, but at the same time, another note blended into it, high and angry, somewhere between a hiss and a shriek. Juniper's eyes gleamed brighter, and Peri knew without a shadow of a doubt that whatever that creature was, it was not their cat.

Juniper launched, and Peri screamed.

Peri woke up in bed with a start, eyes wild, breath pounding in their chest. The room was still. Their own heartbeat was frantic, though, and loud enough to rattle the blinds. It was everywhere, speeding up now— racing from one loud beat to the next quieter one, catching Peri up in the stumbling rhythm. *Tha-dump. Tha-tha-dump.* The skipped beat crashed against Peri's chest, and they lifted a hand to press against their sternum.

"Peri?" a voice called. It was faint, coming from outside the bedroom door, but Peri would have recognized it through a thunder-storm, in a crowded auditorium, under the weight of the entire ocean. It was her.

Peri tried to get out of bed, but their sheets wrapped around their legs, pinning them. They thrashed and struggled, and as they did, they realized the heartbeat wasn't coming from their chest. It was so loud because it was coming from outside the window. They struggled harder as the sheets became sticky white web, capturing their hands as they tried to pull it away. They screamed in frustration and rage, and as they did the heartbeat grew so deafening that the glass in the window blew out. Peri tried to lift their hands to protect their face, but they were trapped by strands of silk as strong as steel, no longer sticky but pinning them in place as the glass flew closer.

Peri sat up in bed, gasping, hands flying to protect their face, but there was no glass. No webbing surrounded their legs, and the heart-beat wasn't audible, even in the quiet. Juniper slept peacefully at the foot of the bed, not even stirring as Peri crawled off the tall mattress. Something cracked under their feet, and when they looked down the floor was covered in leaves and twigs. They walked across it gingerly, their bare feet taking on every scratch and tickle.

At the door they paused, looking back at the bed. It seemed a great distance away, the walls of their room stretching out in darkness, a soft halo of light surrounding the bed. They had a feeling that if they tried to return to it, they would be unable to cross the distance.

Knowing that forward was the only way to go, they turned the knob and swung the bedroom door wide open.

On the other side, a hallway stretched into infinite darkness. The walls were made of trees packed together so tightly they might as well have been drywall, and the floor was tiled in huge slabs of marble, rough-hewn and poorly jointed. Peri began to walk, stumbling on the uneven floor. A few steps on, they heard the door slam shut behind them. Spinning around, they saw only the same hallway, disappearing into shadows as it stretched on and on.

Turning back, resolute, they walked on. The lights behind them flickered, turning off one by one, rushing Peri's steps forward. They stopped at the first door they came to and tried the handle—locked. The door was dark red wood, and when Peri touched it, their hand came away bloody. They wiped it on their white nightshirt and hurried on.

The next door was locked, and the next. Behind Peri the lights flared one by one, turning sickly green and turning the corridor into an eerie, haunting portal. Peri rushed ever onward. The woman was here. If they could only find the right door...

When Peri glanced back, the green-tinged light had drawn closer. Peri knew with cold certainty that if it touched them, it would be the end. The end of their search. The end of their life.

Peri ran, barely pausing to check every doorknob, slamming their hands against each door and then moving on to the next, and the next. The sick light kept pace, speeding up as Peri did, hungry and hunting at the edge of their heels.

Peri heard a call, faint but distinct. Not their name, just a sound, but they heard it and their heart soared. There! Not much farther! They could see the door now, a warm golden glow coming through the crack between sill and door. They were running full out now, but as they neared the door they tripped on the uneven floor, scraping their arms as they tumbled down. They were so close they could almost touch the exit, but the darkness closed in, enveloping them.

Peri scrambled out of bed, gasping and shaking, clawing at their face to rip away strands of darkness that clung like satin charged with static electricity. They dropped the pieces to the floor, shaking their hands to be rid of them, then stopped to catch their breath, hands resting against their thighs.

The carpet underfoot was soft and clean. The curtains at the window covered the blinds, unmoving. There was no sign of Juniper, but the door was cracked open. Peri went to the window and yanked the curtains back. Instead of blinds, they were met with bare glass. Beyond the window, a twilight forest extended as far as their eyes could see, branches whipping around in a vicious gale. The dark green forest curved around to the left, revealing a narrow strip of paved road.

On the road, an old car sat, engine running, antique chrome gleaming in bright moonlight.

In the car was the woman. Her long black hair was tied back in a series of elaborate braids and she was wearing a long, slate-grey coat. She waved frantically when she saw Peri, gesturing for them to join her, and to hurry.

Peri let the curtains fall and ran out of the bedroom, into the cabin. As they stepped over the bedroom threshold, something heavy slammed against the front door. They screamed as a second blow knocked the door, and retreated the way they had come before they could see exactly what had invaded their home.

They grabbed a bookcase and tipped it down, dropping it across the door, then ran back to the window. In the car the woman was even more frantic; she beat her hand against the glass, screaming words that Peri couldn't hear. They hauled up on the window, fingers scrambling for purchase, but the wood was old and uneven. The frame caught, rattling as Peri heaved and heaved.

The basso boom against the bedroom door came again. Whatever was out there, it was coming for them. Peri turned back to the window and heaved again. It screamed in protest as it lifted an inch. Two. Peri glanced back as the door rattled and strained against its frame. The bookcase toppled, and something began to shove the door open. Peri turned back to the window and shoved their head through the gap.

They squeezed through, scraping their chest against the rough wood, wiggling their hips to free them. As their hips came free, Peri saw a massive monster break through the narrow gap it had made in the doorway. It roiled like boiling water, bits of viscous matter popping and splattering as it went. Its face was a riot of insects, not forming features except where they gaped into a horrifying mouth full of rows and rows of rotted, yellowed teeth.

Peri looked away before they could see any more, falling to the ground and rolling back up in one smooth motion. Then they were off, running for the car, the wind buffeting them nearly off their feet. The sound of the window shattering behind them was deafening, and instinctively they ducked, protecting their head for a moment before lifting it up again.

When they did, they panicked. The car was gone.

There was no sign of the woman, no sign of the road, even. Nothing but the forest stretched outward on all sides and the sound of the monster behind them. Peri wanted to scream out her name, but they had none to yell—no word they could hold close to their heart. They fell to their knees, sobbing, as the sound of the monster drew nearer. There was nowhere left to run.

Peri woke up sobbing, curled up in bed, knees tucked close to their body. The soft red light of the bedside clock read 4:23 a.m. Everything else was still and quiet. Peri sat up, fumbled for the bedside lamp, and turned it on with some difficulty. They blinked as the harsh yellow light tore through their night vision. Juniper woke enough to chirrup, annoyed by the light and oblivious to their tears.

The room revealed itself slowly, in blotches. There were the curtains, little silver stars reflecting the light. There was Juniper, settling back into sleep, one paw thrown over her face. There were the closet doors, firmly shut, and the bedroom door, just a crack open.

Peri pinched their arm, hard enough to wince. They drew their knees up to their chest and dropped their forehead, shuddering. They must be awake if they were questioning whether they were still in the dream. It never occurred to them when they were asleep, not even when they had repeatedly woken up in the grip of the nightmare.

Peri wiped the tears from their eyes with the back of their arm and swung their legs out of bed. But as they put a foot down, it crunched against something, and they froze.

Afraid to look but terrified not to, Peri ever so slowly moved their foot out of the way. They reached out, carefully, and lifted the object off the ground. It was a leaf, softly curling into a point, bright green in defiance of the autumn weather just outside. Peri ran a finger across its surface, stunned, but it refused to vanish even as the memory of the dream began to lose its edges.

Juniper meowed, and Peri looked up. When they glanced back down, the leaf was still there, slightly bent but stubbornly real. It was *there*.

And Peri was afraid it was only the beginning.

Peri started for the bedroom door, and as they reached for the handle they paused, their hand hovering over it. What if they pulled it back and there was something else on the other side? What if this was just another dream, different only in that they had begun to question it, finally succeeding in lucid dreaming? They looked down at the impossible leaf in their hand and their breath caught. That was the most likely explanation, wasn't it? They were still asleep, still dreaming. Maybe they had never woken up at the end of the finger dream, and all of this was its continuation—the missing memories, the woman's fear and anger, even the lack of dreams that had led Peri to the nightmare. Or it could be worse than that, even more pervasive. They had fallen into a deep coma sometime during university and they were dreaming a whole second life, one where wounds followed you out of dreams and into life, where mysterious women came to life in dreams, where Peri had built something beautiful from the blocks of their imagination.

Peri grabbed the door handle and yanked on it hard, stumbling backward as it moved more easily than they were expecting, cracking open and revealing the night-drenched room beyond. Everything was unfamiliar with shadow, turned unreal by five o'clock. When had Peri ever seen their apartment in just this light? Had their mind conjured this place, this moment? Everything was ordinary, though—everything but the leaf in their hand. They were clutching it hard enough to press its veins into their palm, but it didn't crumble. Was that normal? Peri wasn't sure. When was the last time they held a leaf in their hand and squeezed like it was the lifeline dragging them out of a dark cave and up into the light?

Overwhelmed with the sudden need for air, for space, for openness, Peri ran for the hall. A flash of instinct made them grab their keys on the way out and shove their feet into the slip-on shoes they kept by the front door. Nothing unexpected happened in response. It all seemed real, but it felt off, like Peri was running their fingers the wrong way across velvet. Peri remembered a hated velvet dress they owned as a child, sapphire blue and scratchy at the throat where stiff lace encircled their neck like gloved, choking hands. They had wiped damp palms on the skirt of that dress more times than they could count, hating the way it felt as their hands slid sideways against the weft. They tugged at the neck of their pajama shirt. This one had a pizza print, and Peri scratched at a slice as if it might come loose against their probing fingertips.

Had the walls always been this colour? Had the carpet always made just this noise? Was it always this long a walk to the elevator? Time seemed to stretch out, the hallways stark and bright despite the late hour. Peri floated through them, hands half-outstretched, not quite connecting but yearning to run their fingertips down the walls. At the elevator they reached out, but that was the hand holding the leaf and they couldn't bear to uncurl their fist, didn't want to see that bright flash of green that whispered, *You're dreaming. You're dreaming.*

They hit the button with their left hand instead and jumped in surprise when the doors immediately opened. In that small moment of surprise, Peri had forgotten their purpose, could not remember why they were leaving the building that served as their sanctuary. *I'll know I'm awake if I walk out the doors and the world is there. Then I'll know.*

The lobby was quiet, but the lights blared, loud in their brightness, and Peri squeezed their eyes shut against the brilliance and barreled outside. The sun wasn't up—wouldn't be for hours—though here and there an early commuter already walked the streets, ready to open a coffee shop or heading to their car after a night in someone else's bed. The streetlights cast everything in a golden glow, soft and warm against the barely brightening autumn sky.

Peri shivered. It was cold, and their thin pajamas were no match for the biting wind, as gentle as it was. Were they ever cold in dreams? Did their skin ever pimple into gooseflesh that trickled down both arms? Peri tucked their hands into the opposite armpits, one hand still fisted, the tickle of the leaf tangible against their skin.

They were awake. They had to be awake. It was freezing, and they felt unmoored, adrift in a world that didn't see them, that would never know they were here. They never felt that way in dreams.

Slowly, they unpeeled their arms from across their chest. Shivering, they opened their hand. The leaf was still there, a little worse for wear with Peri's poor treatment of it. It wasn't a figment, caught in a moment and impossible to touch.

"Watch it!" someone yelled, and Peri was yanked backward by a rough hand on their arm as a huge white street cleaning vehicle barreled past, inches from their toes.

Peri gasped, looking over at the stranger who had pulled them out of the path. They had likely only been saved from a blast of dirt, maybe sore toes if the brush had hit them, but it was enough to shock them back to full awareness. They were awake. This was real. The hand on their arm—and the look of disgust on the person's face.

"You high?" the man snapped, rolling his eyes. He walked away without expecting a reply, and Peri swallowed whatever they might have said.

Peri glanced down and realized the leaf had fallen out of their hand. Panicked, they searched the ground, and found the leaf lying not too far away. Picking it up, they closed their fist around it again, breathing heavily.

They were awake, and the leaf was real. That meant...

What? What does it mean? And what the hell do I do next?

11

MAEVE

"Hey Mom, what's up?" Maeve asked, twirling around in her computer chair. It was mid-afternoon, and she was happily answering comments and engaging with the now-infamous Jason post.

He hadn't bothered her since the phone call, and views on the video were skyrocketing. It was the best one she'd had—well, ever, which surprised her a little. It was a good video, but it wasn't *that* good.

"Just calling to say hi. Is now a good time?"

"Yup, I'm just finishing up some work." She flicked her fingers to minimize the screen so she wouldn't get distracted reading comments while her mom talked.

"Oh, honey, I saw that newest video. It was so fun! That Jason sure did get what he deserved."

"Yeah, he's a total creep. Apparently, people at work are teasing him and calling him Prince Humperdinck." Maeve snorted around a mean laugh.

"Are his coworkers all eighty? There isn't a more recent evil prince they could reference?" In the background, soft noises told Maeve that her mother was multitasking. She knew her mom refused to video call because she liked to do things as she talked, and she didn't want the other person to know when they didn't have her full attention.

"Hey, that movie is a classic!" Maeve objected.

"What's that funny little man from Shrek? That would be a good reference."

"Because Shrek *isn't* an outdated reference? You can't even remember his name!"

"I know, but he was so funny."

Maeve shook her head. Her mother was adorable, but she wasn't exactly up on pop culture. "They could go really old school, do Prince John."

"Isn't that a real person?" her mom asked.

Maeve frowned, realizing she had no idea. "I don't know, he's from Robin Hood. Was Robin Hood real?"

"I don't think so. Was he?" Her mom laughed. "I don't know, I think he's one of those folk heroes where they stick a bunch of real people together and make them into one person. Robin Hood, not Prince John. Prince John is definitely a real person."

Maeve laughed and spun around in her chair. "All this goes to show I think Humperdinck is still the most recognizable evil prince, even if it has been a hundred years."

"A hundred years! You do make me feel old, kiddo. Oh, I wanted to tell you, it was the strangest thing! You'll never guess. I had the dream last night."

"You had what dream?"

Her mother paused, dishes rattling in the background as she puttered in the kitchen. "I mean your dream, the dream, the one we're talking about. I had it last night. It was exactly the same, just like I was watching it again. Isn't that delightfully bizarre?"

Maeve sat up straight in her chair. That *was* weird, and it triggered half a memory. Hadn't she seen another comment on the video saying that they had dreamed the dream? She hadn't thought anything of it at the time, but to have two people dream her dream... Well, she wasn't sure that *was* delightful. It gave her an anxious feeling that she couldn't quite place, a bubble of pressure and nerves at the base of her skull. "It's definitely a first for me. Were you Josie, or me?" she asked her mom.

"I told you I was watching it, didn't I?" her mother teased lovingly. Then she was off on another thought. "Oh, how is Josie, honey? Did that place come through?"

Maeve lagged behind her mother's sharp conversational turn. She was still caught up in the idea of other people dreaming her dreams, like she was implanting suggestions in the subconscious minds of her viewers. It wasn't an idea she was thrilled with. What place was her mom talking about? *Oh! The apartment a few blocks over.* "It did! She's going down after work to sign the lease."

"Oh, good for her. That girl works so hard, it's such a shame how it all turned out. I'm so proud of her for getting out of the weeds, though. You take that lesson to heart, Maeve. There's absolutely nothing wrong with being picky. You don't need to be with someone just to be with someone."

"Thanks Mom." Maeve smiled and spun around again. Her mom knew how disheartening Maeve found online dating sometimes, and she was always ready with either a word of encouragement or a push that Maeve was okay as she was, depending on which was needed at the time.

"Do you want to come over for dinner on Friday? Your dad wants to make meatloaf, but I told him I'm not eating meatloaf for six days straight, it's a dinner party dish!"

"I can't. Josie's doing a housewarming on Saturday, so we're going to go thrifting and see if we can fill in some of the holes. She pretty much needs everything."

"Ew, please do not let that girl buy a couch from a thrift store, you know that's how you get bedbugs. Oh! You know what, I think Shannon's son went to college this year, I bet she's got some extra stuff, let me ask her. Oh, and your dad can post on that neighbourhood app he's so obsessed with, I bet we can get a couch from there."

"How is that different from buying from a thrift store? It's still used!" Maeve flicked her fingers and brought up the comments section she had minimized. She wondered if the dream was doing anything strange to anyone else.

"It is not," her mother *tsked*.

"It literally is. You're being classist."

"Oh, fine, sorry! Does Josie like meatloaf?"

Maeve laughed at the three-sixty. "I think so?"

"Good, I'll tell him to make it and we can drop it off on Saturday, you'll want to have dinner before the party, and then if we find anything good, we can bring it."

"Thanks, Mom. I'll tell her."

"Oh, shoot, this is burning, gotta go, love you!" she called, hanging up halfway through the word love.

Maeve laughed and pulled her headphones out, dropping them on the table without turning them off. She shot Josie a message warning her that her parents were on the case of the missing furniture, then turned her attention back to the comment section, not really expecting to find anything out of the ordinary.

Instead, she immediately saw the comment she had been thinking of. *It was like I downloaded it straight into my brain!* the viewer said. Under that was a reply from another viewer. *Wooooah had the same thing! It's a total meme in my head, guys.*

"Weird," Maeve said, her brain scrabbling to reassure her that the viewers were exaggerating when they said the dream had repeated exactly. They'd obviously had a similar dream and were using hyperbolic language. It was weird, but it wasn't creepy. Out of the ordinary, that was all. Not creepy. Nothing to be worried about, nothing at all...

Ding! It was a message from Josie. Maeve flicked over to her messaging program.

Josie
Weirdest thing. Had your dream last night.

Okay, OFFICIALLY WEIRDED OUT!

Was her overactive imagination striking again? She'd been off her game since Jason's angry phone call, imagining threats in every shadow. This was a little weird, but it wasn't weird enough to justify how off-kilter she felt.

It wasn't weird to have dreams based on the media a person was watching. Maeve had dreams all the time that were influenced by the stories she consumed. It was just the language people were using that was throwing her for a loop.

"Exact same." "Like watching it again." "Memetic dream?"

Curious about just how common it was to redream something, Maeve went onto the most popular dreaming forum and hunted for references to strange dreams and shared unconsciousness. She found a post by DreamsAway asking for help with dream phenomena, but when she read more, she saw the popular dreamer was asking about a character who recurred in their dreams, but who they didn't know in real life.

That wasn't something Maeve had heard of. Was it true that every character in a dream was an amalgamation of someone from your real life? Or had scientists disproven that? Maeve couldn't remember. But artists could come up with new faces. Maeve didn't see any reason why dreamers couldn't.

The post was over a year old; it seemed that DreamsAway had never found the mysterious woman they were searching for. Too bad—posts as old as this one got so little traffic they might as well be deleted. Maeve navigated away without looking at the screenshot that was attached to the post. It wasn't the information she needed.

Back on the main page, post after post pointed her to new and interesting aspects of dreams, some that she'd never considered before. But when it came to dreams sprouting up for all of their viewers, she couldn't find anything helpful. Whatever was happening, it seemed like Maeve was the first one to face it.

"Your parents are wild," Josie said, settling onto the new-to-her couch with a plate of meatloaf and a fork. Maeve collapsed into a chair across from her, putting her feet up on the coffee table as she surveyed the apartment.

"They are seriously awesome," she agreed. Her parents had managed to track down a ridiculously nice, barely used couch *and* a double bed with a boxspring. Maeve and Josie had gotten a coffee table and a chair while out thrifting, plus a few floor lamps and an amazing teal retro microwave. Josie was still missing a kitchen table and chairs, and she was using a box of books as an end table in the bedroom, but for a single week's work, the place had come together well. The landlord had agreed to a new coat of paint, so the place smelled a little, but they lit a few scented candles that Maeve found in the back of her junk drawer and opened a window. It was ready enough for a casual housewarming.

Maeve dug into her meatloaf, washing it down with a glass of the sparkling wine she had brought to christen the new digs. "What time did you tell people?" she asked.

"Seven."

She looked at her watch. It was quarter after. "Where's Adya? I was going to get her to help me put streamers up." Adya was always fifteen minutes early for every party. Maeve knew her own penchant for lateness drove their friend up the wall, but she couldn't understand how people were on *time* all the time. Life was unpredictable! Buses never came on time! And dinner never seemed to make itself when she needed it to. Well, except when her parents made it.

"She's going out to dinner first so she's gonna be late. You're stuck actually doing the work you offered to do," Josie teased her.

"Dammit. There goes my clever plan," Maeve mourned as she shovelled the rest of the meatloaf down.

Maeve finished the final touches on the room while Josie got the music set up. They were still arguing playlists when the first guests started to arrive, and it wasn't long before the party was in full swing. The mostly empty apartment forced people to stand up and mingle and it made for a good vibe. The music was low enough to easily talk over while still being loud enough to fill the room with energy.

Enough people had brought extra drinks that Maeve had a good buzz going despite only having contributed one bottle of champagne and a small bottle of scotch, the latter of which she was mixing with someone else's Canada Dry. Maeve had known Josie long enough that few of her friends were actual strangers, but the party was big enough that there were people Maeve didn't know well, and some of them had brought their own friends for company.

At one point Maeve found herself in a corner with a cute guy who only looked vaguely familiar. He was a white guy, a little more muscular than she normally went for, but his glasses undercut any bro energy and his shoulder-length hair made her want to curl her toes happily. On top of that they were arguing the relative merits of

Kraft Dinner over homemade mac and cheese, a subject Maeve could have written an entire essay on.

"But the way the cheese gets all crispy when you bake it in the oven," he pointed out.

"Okay, I'll give you that, but I have the winning card," she promised.

He grinned and put a hand on her shoulder, lightly enough that she could easily step away if the touch was unwanted. She leaned in instead and he relaxed minutely; Maeve found the show of nerves particularly appealing. "Let's hear it," he urged.

"Drunk food. KD is the better drunk food, hands down."

"You've got me there," he agreed, letting his hand fall but stepping a little closer. She matched his energy, grinning up into his deep, almost black eyes.

"Remind me how you know Josie?" she asked.

"We actually met through he-who-shall-not-be-named," he said, and instantly rose in Maeve's estimation. Dropping your asshole friend in favour of his much cooler ex-girlfriend was a baller move. "How 'bout you?"

"We went to school together."

"Oh, cool, are you an RMT too?" he asked.

Maeve waved a hand in negation. "No, this was before either of us knew what we wanted to do, so we were both doing our undergrads because our parents were paying for it. We both signed up for the same Trick or Eat group. You know that thing where you go door-to-door on Halloween and ask for money for the food bank instead of candy? It was amazing, because of course they give you candy since you're doing a good cause. Anyway, she was dressed as a dinosaur, and I was dressed as sexy Jeff Goldblum, and it was best-friendship-at-first sight."

He laughed. "Sexy Jeff Goldblum?"

"An open black shirt and a nude top with a six-pack drawn on it. It was probably my worst costume idea of all time. One person asked me if I was Richard Simmons. And there was no spandex in sight!"

"Oh man, I would kill to see that," he said, wiping tears of laughter out of the corner of one eye. He sniffed and chuckled, getting himself together. "I know what you mean about being forced into school too early. I started in computer science and ended up in library sciences."

"They should give you a year to figure out what you're interested in before you have to pick a faculty!"

"What did you study versus what you actually ended up doing?"

"I took a bunch of useless stuff and managed to cobble together a BA in Communications, but I work as a dreamer now."

"A dreamer? Like those videos people post?" he asked, the same way she would expect someone to react if she said she played online poker for a living.

"Yeah, like those videos." She tried not to show her annoyance, giving him the benefit of the doubt that he might genuinely want to know. It wasn't his fault that too many people reacted this way.

"That's not... really a job, though, right?"

Maeve laughed, though there was an edge to it. It certainly wasn't the first time someone at a party had questioned her entire life as if it was a fun topic of conversation, but she thought she was used to it by now, at least enough that it wouldn't sting. She was surprised by how insistent her voice was when it came out. "There's actually a lot that goes into it. Editing, promotion, building a following. I had to teach myself a lot of the software—"

"Sure, okay. But most of it is just sleeping, right?" He laughed, and she could just hear the unspoken, *"Wish I could do that instead of a real job!"* Or was she hearing what she was afraid to hear, and not what he actually meant?

"I guess you could call that the content creation portion of my day," she said before aggressively trying to change the subject. "So, you said you're a librarian?"

"Sorry, I'm just curious. So that's your passion, or what you do for fun or whatever. But it doesn't pay your rent, does it?"

"It paid for this scotch," Maeve snapped, her good humour gone. She demonstrated by draining the rest of her glass.

He raised his eyebrows. "Huh. Okay. What's that a road to?"

"How do you mean?"

"I mean, your career ambition can't be making little videos people use to kill twenty minutes." The worst part was that he didn't phrase it as a question. He was so *sure* that Maeve must see dreaming as a joke, just like he did.

Fuming, Maeve curled her fingers hard around her glass. "Is that how you feel about movies, too? About books? Creative content offers people important escape and emotional succour from a, let's face it, often pretty shitty world." Her empty hand gestured to encompass the conversation they were having.

"Oh, come on. You know you're not writing *War and Peace*. Dreams aren't art. Everyone has them." He ran a hand through his hair.

That hair should come with a warning, Maeve thought. *Contents do not match sexy exterior.* "Everyone dreams, sure. But just like the so-called hot takes people spew out at parties, not all of them are worth sharing."

His look turned sour as he realized he was the target of that particular jibe. "Well, I can see how you might like the appeal of getting paid to sleep for a living. Personally, I would get bored if that was all I did with my life."

"I'm gonna go refresh this," Maeve said, turning away from his exasperated look and stalking back to the kitchen. She knew she shouldn't let one bad conversation ruin a great night, but the alcohol felt like liquid mercury in her stomach, somehow both heavy and shifting at the same time. She was so sick and tired of entitled jerks who thought it didn't take any talent to dream.

"Sleeping for a living," she snapped, surprised when the words came out of her mouth instead of staying in her head where she had meant them to be. Dreaming *was* a talent. Not one you could develop over time, true, not a skill like art where your practice improved and grew, no. But that made it more special, not less. It was something you had to be born with. Dreams worth sharing were a pure reflection of your imagination. They were beautiful, and important. A book could change the world. A song could. A dream could, too, in the right hands, at the right time and place.

She found her discarded bottle of scotch and drained the last of it, then snagged a beer from a communal pile and drank it way too fast. Who needed entitled guys who didn't get her, anyway? Her job was *cool*. Her brain was cool. People liked her brain. *Bet nobody likes that guy's brain. Bet it's... grey and squishy.* She smirked, finished the beer, and grabbed another one before wandering back out into the party.

Everything was bright and loud, and she danced for a while with some friends, pumping the alcohol through her system and trying to let go of her frustration in the beat. But the music wasn't loud enough to drown out her thoughts, and she felt a bad mood settling over her shoulders with the steady pressure of an ex you just can't dump.

At some point she had finished the second beer, and now there was a red solo cup in her hand. She wandered away from the knot of dancers, drifting past the edges of conversations as she looked for somewhere to settle. She thought she felt eyes on her, but when she glanced around the room, she couldn't find anyone looking her way. The feeling was like oil on her fingers—she couldn't wash it away no matter how much booze she poured down her throat.

She stumbled to the bathroom, relieved to find it empty, and slipped inside. The lock, a slide-bar that fit into place only reluctantly, gave her some problem, but she finally got it. She peed quickly, then splashed water on her face and forced a big breath into her constricted lungs. *You're fine. You're just too hot, that's all.*

She took another breath, easier now, and glanced up into the mirror. But the eyes looking back at her didn't feel right. They weren't quite hers, or they had seen things she hadn't. Shuddering, she ripped her gaze away and made for the door, but in her haste to get out of the bathroom she turned out the light before she could hit the lock. The unfamiliar latch resisted her efforts to pry it open and she felt a presence at her back, eyes on her neck. Was that sound her own breath? Or was there something in the room with her?

Maeve whimpered and closed her eyes, tearing at the lock with both hands. She ripped a strip of skin off her finger but managed to pull the bolt free. Spilling out into the hall, breathing heavily, she looked back over her shoulder. Her own reflection looked back, innocuous now in the warm spill of light. She laughed and pushed a hand through her hair, wiping away a trace of sweat. *Get it together, Maeve. It's a mirror.*

Defying her fear, she stepped back into the bathroom. The eyes in the mirror were her own. But the longer she stared at them, the more she began to wonder if someone was staring back. Something that wasn't just—

A hand on her shoulder made her scream and jump, but it was only a friend, his familiar face laughing. "Are you okay?"

"You scared the shit out of me!"

"Yeah, I had a hunch." He grinned and gestured at the bathroom. "You done?"

"Oh. Yeah. Yeah. Sorry." Maeve stumbled back out, and he went in. She almost told him to be careful of the mirror, but she wasn't quite that drunk.

Maeve moved back into the party, wondering how much she'd had and if maybe the answer was too much. The lights no longer felt bright and free. They were overwhelming, piercing, and she wondered what might be hiding behind their glow, invisible next to their brilliance. Her friends were like people in a music video, not quite here, laughing silently for the sake of a camera.

Maeve ran a hand over her face. *Aaaand we've officially hit that level of drunk. Nope, nope. I gotta go home.* Suddenly she felt cloyingly constrained by the small room and its press of bodies. She needed to get to her own bed, drink a gallon of water, and watch bad TikTok videos until she sobered up enough to sleep. She went to find Josie, pasting a smile on her face that probably wouldn't have fooled anyone if they weren't all as drunk as she was.

"I'mma go pass out!" she hollered, wrapping her arms around the other woman's neck and squeezing tight. It was late enough that Josie didn't object, just kissed Maeve messily on the cheek.

"Text me when you get home so I know you made it safe!" she demanded.

"Yes, mother," Maeve promised, then hugged her once before wandering for the door. She shouted a few other goodbyes at friends as she passed. One couple asked if she wanted to walk to the train together, but she reminded them that she was just down the road. They helped each other find their shoes and coats in the big pile by the door, though, and Maeve was smiling by the time they spilled out into the street and hugged out sloppy goodbyes, laughing more than the situation warranted.

Her good mood lasted all of half a block. The world was tipping slightly around her, not quite spinning but off-kilter, its axis just slightly shifting with each footstep. Every sound felt isolated, too present, the background noise that made up the hum of life silenced. She was too aware of the cold wind and how it bit through her thin jacket, too aware of the way dead leaves rustled past the toes of her banged up boots. The streetlights were too yellow and the sky not dark enough, as if an angry giant had tried to wipe their work away, leaving behind a deep bruise of colour that would not fade.

In the shadows just past the next intersection, something moved. Maeve reminded herself of raccoons, of rats, or all the things that make noises deep in the heart of morning in a city, but despite all of her calm reassurance, the shadow filled her with deep discomfort. Once again, she had that sense of being watched, as if observation were somehow malicious in and of itself. The shadow shifted, and her steps slowed almost to a stop as a canid shape manifested. It was too far away to know if it was a coyote or a dog, though of course, the lizard-whisper in her brain was sure it was a wolf, or some creature of the dark, come to steal her lambs or her children, come to tear down her tent and steal away with the meat still cooking over the fire's quiet embers, to—

"It isn't safe," a voice said. It was liquid and soft, resonant in a way only truly bass voices were, and for a moment it didn't occur to Maeve that it was real, that someone had spoken. When she finally did turn, she didn't quite expect to see anyone there.

But there he was. He was standing closer than a stranger should, but she didn't feel the expected frisson of fear. He was only a few inches taller than her, with a wide strong body, light brown skin with pink undertones, and a short but luxurious beard. His hair inhabited that liminal space between curly and wavy, hanging loosely around his ears. He was wearing a dark grey hoodie, which blended perfectly into the shadows and explained why Maeve hadn't noticed his approach. Maeve noted that he was also heart-stoppingly, jaw-droppingly gorgeous; a moment later she chided herself for the thought, wondering if that was why his sudden appearance and ominous words had yet to cause her any fear at all.

"It isn't safe?" she asked, a direct echo of his words.

"You have to get out of here. You have to wake up," he told her.

Maeve laughed nervously. "I thought I was the drunk one," she said, taking a cautious step away from him. She glanced back at the street, then did a double-take when she saw that the dog was gone. She looked for it, heart pounding, but it had completely disappeared. "Did you see that?" she asked.

"You think you understand what's happening, but you have no idea," he insisted.

"Okay. Sure. I'm gonna go," she said, and took off at a fast walk. She glanced behind, but the guy wasn't following her, just watching as she left, a frustrated look on his face. She sighed in relief and turned the corner. The three blocks between Josie's apartment and her own suddenly left immense. Another block, another turn, and she would be home. But the streets felt unfamiliar, and for a moment she was completely disoriented. Was this even the right street? Was she on her way home?

She looked behind her again and saw someone walking toward her. The figure was tall and slim, wearing a long black coat, but even though it wasn't that far away, she couldn't make out any of its features. She picked up her pace, telling herself she was being silly and not caring. She no longer felt drunk—was it possible fear had sobered her up? Or was it an illusion, a temporary flush of reason brought on by adrenalin?

Another glance showed the figure had sped up, and her heart began to race. She moved quickly, almost running, but it didn't seem like the end of the block was coming any closer. She should be there by now! She looked at the houses as she passed but none were familiar landmarks, and she felt the weight of panic as she broke into a full-on run.

Behind her the figure was running, too, but not quite keeping pace, falling just a little behind. She grinned, attention turning back to the path in front of her, but too late; she saw the city street ended in a jagged cliff. She screamed, arms pinwheeling as she tried to stop her forward momentum, but it was too little, too late. The world tilted and she was falling, falling into the dark.

Maeve woke up in bed, hair plastered to her face, stomach churning with the sick burn of alcohol. She threw off the sheets, which were twisted around her legs, and made it to the bathroom with just enough time to empty the contents of her stomach. The burn brought tears to her eyes, and she crouched over the toilet, gasping and crying, as she tried to orient herself. What the hell had just happened? Where was she?

She flushed, rinsed her mouth, and splashed water on her face. She drank a little water from her cupped hand, wincing as it washed down her raw throat. She was still wearing her clothes from the party the night before. The sun was up, but she had no idea where her watch was. Her head was pounding, which didn't help. She was at the party, then someone had warned her, told her to wake up. Was that part of the dream? Had the party even happened? When did her memories end and the dream begin?

She scratched her face and realized that she was wearing her dream-recording equipment. She must have put it on last night by rote. Peeling off the sensors, she stalked back over to her bed. Her watch was on the dresser next to her phone, which was sitting just next to the charging dock instead of on it. *Of course.* She moved her phone so that it would charge and checked the watch. She had two concerned text messages from Josie, one asking if she was home, the other berating her for passing out without saying she was home safe. She sent a quick message back just to say she was alive, dropped her watch onto the charger, and went to take a shower.

She was undressed with the water running before she remembered the recording pads. In the nude she dashed out of the bathroom and over to her computer, tapping it awake. There were two files waiting, so she set them to transfer, then ran just as quickly back into the bathroom and hopped over the lip of the tub and into the shower. The scalding spray brought her mostly back to life, though the headache refused to leave, and her throat was still scratchy from throwing up.

After towelling off and tossing on a bathrobe, she called Josie through her watch as she chugged orange juice and made waffles.

"You're up early!" Josie said.

"Fuck, you sound cheerful," Maeve complained.

Josie laughed. "I told you to drink water!"

"What time did I leave last night?" Maeve asked.

"I don't know. After midnight. How come?" On the other end of the line, Josie yawned, which made Maeve yawn, too.

"I had this dream, and I thought... I don't remember getting home except that I *dreamed* I walked home, and I remember that. It's fucking creepy." Maeve pulled a plate out of the cupboard and slapped it down, wincing as it hit too hard.

"How do you know it was a dream and not what happened?"

"Because it was an actual nightmare. This dude was telling me to be careful and then someone's chasing me and then I wake up and I'm in bed with all my recording stuff on. And no shoes."

"Shit, seriously? That is next-level spooky."

"You're telling me." Grabbing supplies out of the fridge, Maeve cut off a hunk of butter and stuck it in the microwave to soften it up. "That's literally never happened before. I mean, I know I was drunk, but like..."

"I guess you blacked out and then the dream started from where you remember last?" Josie suggested.

"Yeah, probably. But there was some weird stuff at the party, so how much of that was the dream and how much was real?"

"Weird like what?"

Maeve scraped a finger down from her inner eye and past her nose. "I don't know. Stupid stuff. Getting scared of my own reflection."

"I don't know what to say. That's definitely messed up."

"Yeah." The toaster popped loud in the sudden quiet. "I'm gonna go shove some food in my face and sober up. You want help cleaning up later?"

"No, I'm good. Sophie ended up crashing so she's helping me now, we're basically done."

"Okay, cool. Say hi for me."

"Yeah, will do. Bye."

"Bye." Maeve tapped her watch to disconnect the call. As she spread the butter on her waffles, she glanced over at the computer. The progress bar was slowly moving across the screen. Whatever happened last night, she would have to wait a little longer for answers.

12

PERI

Peri's fingers hovered over the keyboard, hesitating. They made a throwaway account so it wouldn't be linked back to their usual online presence, but it still felt strange to put any of this out into the world. What kind of three-wolf-howling conspiracy theorist asked the question, "Have your dreams ever followed you into the waking world?"

Scanning the post once more, Peri corrected a few minor typos before admitting there was no more putting it off. Either they hit enter or they didn't. Either they admitted to the leaf and the cut on their shoulder, or they kept this brewing terror quiet, tucked into an ever-expanding part of their chest that would one day completely consume them, utterly erasing the line between sleeping and waking and leaving them trapped in a shadow world from which there was no escape. *When you put it like that...*

Peri double-tapped a finger against the desk and sent the post live. Knowing they were likely to sit there hitting refresh and obsessing, they navigated away from the site entirely, checking their socials for something to do. A few people had reached out about their continuing lack of updates, and there was a TikTok video their brother Kyle had sent them that normally would have made them laugh, but it wasn't quite funny enough to pierce the fog that had descended over their life.

Pulling up an alcohol delivery service, Peri hesitated. Drinking wasn't something Peri did often; they weren't social enough for it, frankly, and they didn't like the way being drunk made them feel. The gentle high of weed was a safer choice; high, they were still who they were, just loosened. Expanded. Drunk, they were unpredictable. Weed and alcohol were both known for leading to dreamless sleep. Peri never had a problem with cannabis, but they remembered getting blackout drunk for their nineteenth birthday, and how dead to the world they had been. That was before they started remembering their dreams every night like clockwork, but it was all they had to go on.

But right now, they craved the quiet. A night without dreams, without questions. A chance to sleep and experience no other world behind their eyelids. Recently, that same scenario was their idea of hell; a single dreamless night had sent them spiralling into chaos. Now that they were on the other side of that panic, they questioned everything they knew. That fathomless void had become a refuge.

Before they could second-guess the choice, Peri ordered a bottle of tequila. The liquor store didn't sell mixes, so they processed the payment, then opened their regular grocery store app to order a bottle of margarita mix. The delivery charge was more than the margarita mix, and Peri wrinkled their nose in frustration. Never mind—they would grab a bottle from the corner store. They could be there and back long before the other delivery arrived.

Peri got up, heading for the front door, but as they neared it their steps slowed. The last time they left the condo, reality had felt like it was bleeding away around them. Everything had been jumbled, hollow, and uncertain. More than that, their last foray outside had blurred the lines between waking and dreaming so profoundly that it was becoming harder to separate the two. What if they opened that door and there was a winter forest on the other side? What if this place was the dream, a haven they had built in the maelstrom of unfinished phantasms?

Then again, reality had warped inside the condo, too. That was where they found the leaf. Where the bloody bandages were still stuffed into the bottom of their bathroom garbage. With that in mind, it seemed foolish to try to delineate between the outside and inside. Angrily, they stuffed their feet into the slip-on shoes and shrugged into a jacket, too light for the cold weather but the first thing their hand landed on.

They reached for the handle, but hesitated. A wave of dizziness passed over them as they contemplated the outside world. It didn't matter that logic dictated their apartment was more dangerous than the outside world, given it was where they had gotten the still smarting wound on their shoulder. Peri felt safe in their home. Contained. Out there the world was unpredictable, uncertain. They could step in front of a car. Walk off the boardwalk into the ocean. Cause such a scene that strangers, afraid for their lives, called the police. At least here, they were safe from the censure of strangers. At least here there was no one but Juniper to judge their strange behaviour.

Peri took off the jacket, letting it fall to the ground rather than hanging it back up. It made a stark though small pile on the otherwise spotless floor, and after a second Peri changed their mind, picking it up and carefully stowing it away in its place. They took off the shoes, too, putting them back on their plastic mat by the door. *The delivery fee isn't even that high.* And they could order a few other staples to offset the unnecessary cost. There really wasn't any *need* to go outside.

It wasn't avoidance. It was just practicality.

～

Peri woke up late the next morning, head pounding and mouth dry. The tequila had done its job last night, obliterating any dreams they might have had, and they had only vague memories of rewatching old episodes of *Steven Universe* and crying at all the good parts. Now, they were paying the price for the night of peace.

They groaned and rolled over, throwing an arm across their face before peering out from under it at the clock. They never used an alarm in the morning—a longer period of sleep just meant more dreams, which was good for their income—but they were shocked to see that it was past eleven. As soon as they stirred, Juniper dashed into the room, meowing plaintively before launching onto the bed. She was in Peri's lap in an instant, knocking her face against Peri's and demanding attention.

Peri gave Juniper her requested cuddles, then dragged their body out of bed to give Juniper what she *really* wanted, which was her breakfast. Unable to think of food themselves, they crashed down onto the couch, dragging a blanket over their head and moaning dramatically. This had been a terrible idea. Yes, they had gotten the dreamless sleep they craved, but the cost was an entire wasted morning.

It took Peri a while to get up and go through their morning routine at a fraction of their normal speed. Breakfast still sounded like a risky proposition, so they stuck to a handful of nuts and some orange juice, which they used to wash down a few painkillers while they waited for their computer to wake up from sleep.

The first thing they did was check their message boards. There were a handful of responses to their post about liminal dreams, but none of them particularly useful. One person claimed to see dead relatives in their dreams all the time, and another asked if Peri was referencing a movie about a screenwriter who discovers the super-power to bring elements of his dreams into the real world. A few people talked about false awakening, describing thinking they were awake only to wake up once again, which Peri already knew was a common feature in nightmares. Several asked Peri for proof of what they were describing, but Peri pointed out that, out of context, a photo of a leaf and a bruised shoulder wasn't really proof of anything.

Still, the fact of the leaf's existence felt important to Peri. And since avoiding dreams had gotten them nowhere, maybe it was time to get a bit more proactive. They needed to take a risk and invite a few other people into the secret. Or at least start collecting data.

They ended up taking a picture of the leaf and posting it on the message board before uploading it to one of their Discord group chats, too.

What kind of leaf is this?

Noodles
Elm?

> **Elma**
> Alder?

> **Greg**
> That is a Plutonic leaf, my friend.

Elma suggested they try out a new escape room, but Peri couldn't summon the energy for more conversation.

> Too hungover.

> **Noodles**
> Peri? Drinking? I thought you were sober.

> Just no social life. Lol.

> **Greg**
> Anyone seen that viral dream about the prince?

> Not me. 😢

Peri was notorious for being a dreamer who didn't watch a lot of dreams. Their friends teased them about it. It wasn't that Peri didn't like dreams—they watched other streamers now and then. It was just that their own dreams were more alluring, and there were only so many hours in the day.

Peri and their friends chatted back and forth a bit, but by the time everyone else had downloaded the new escape room game and activated it, the chat went quiet.

Peri spent a few hours online, browsing websites about dreams and looking for anything that might explain the woman and her warnings, but there was nothing. They even sat down with the electrodes and a magnifying glass and looked for anything out of the ordinary, but there was no evidence that the technology did anything other than it said it did—not that Peri would have known exactly what to look for, anyway. A transmitter didn't look different to the uneducated eye than a recorder, and theoretically signals went both ways. But that didn't explain the nightmare, where Peri had seen the woman despite no longer wearing the recording device.

By lunch, Peri was starving and in the mood for carbs, so they slathered sauce and vegan cheese onto thick rye bread and fried it in margarine, dipping it into ketchup as they ate. Juniper came to investigate but had no interest in the knock-off cheese and ended up curling up beside Peri on the couch instead, cleaning herself while Peri polished off the large sandwich.

Peri tried to read a book, but their thoughts kept drifting. The dreamless sleep the night before had felt good in the moment, but the hangover sapped all their energy. They couldn't keep this up indefinitely—and they weren't sure they wanted to. They weren't ready to give up on finding the woman. That meant returning, sooner or later, to the land of dreams. But every time they contemplated going to sleep, panic took hold. They couldn't quite get a full breath, and they felt a panic attack hovering, an angry monster waiting to dig in its claws.

Later, as they browsed apps on their phone, Peri noticed an email from a casting agent they had ignored the week before. Peri was consistently headhunted by casting agents who wanted to cash in on Peri's following to help boost their sales for indie movies, and normally Peri responded with a no that was just polite enough that they kept getting the emails despite having no interest in the opportunities. But now Peri stopped and considered it.

They didn't want to upload any videos, not with this mystery hovering over them. The woman said the technology was dangerous, and even though Peri had no reason to believe the woman was real... they did.

But real life went on. Bills had to be paid, and sitting in this apartment stewing over their own perceptions and what was and wasn't real was obviously not helping. Jasmine would shriek with delight if Peri said they had taken an *actual job*, one that got them out of the house and forced them to interact with other people— normal people. People who watched reality TV shows and went on dates and had feuds with their best friends over petty things and then made up over mimosas at brunch the next morning.

That was exactly what Peri needed. They needed to clear the fog and get their head on straight so they could start to sort what was real from what wasn't. They needed an excuse to walk out that door that they wouldn't be able to reason away. They needed a shock to their system, something completely new and different, an experience that wouldn't remind them of anything. They never dreamed about being a movie star—it wasn't the kind of fantasy that appealed at all. Maybe if they could imbue their waking life with more reality, it would be able to stand on its own against the dreams, and sleeping would be safe again.

Peri picked up their phone and dialled. It rang three times before a cheerful voice answered, "Tina Macklan's office!"

"Hi, can I speak to Tina, please?" Peri said.

"This is Tina. What can I do for you?"

"Oh, sorry, um. Hi. Yeah. Um... you emailed me about a—" Peri panicked. They hadn't actually *read* the email and had no idea what the role was. "An acting thing?" Peri finished lamely.

"Oh, great! What's your name?" Tina asked.

"Right. Uh. Peri. Briggs?" they added, hating that it sounded like a question.

There was a short pause, presumably as Tina checked her email or notes. "Oh my gosh, you're DreamsAway! Hi! Thank you so much for getting back to me."

"Yeah, of course. Um. I'd love to hear a bit more about the project."

"I think you'll really love this. It's a music video for this absolutely beautiful up-and-coming singer-songwriter. She wants to do this dream theme for the video, since the song is all about dreams, so she's really excited about the idea of working with a dreamer with such a huge fan base and just, you know, such a great pedigree. It's actually so amazing that you called, because since we hadn't heard from you, we decided to go in a different direction, but the dreamer we were supposed to work with dropped out and we've been absolutely scrambling to find a replacement. So, it's a little tight notice, we're shooting on Tuesday, but they only need you for two days and the pay is $500 a day, and it would be a really great safe space for you to spread your wings and try out something new, you know? You haven't done any acting before, right?"

"That's right, um. Is that okay? I mean, I don't really have any—"

"Oh, honey, you'll be totally fine. It's very chill, and there aren't any lines, and that's really the hardest part of acting, you know, all that memorization! I would just love to tell them that you're interested, and maybe we can arrange a call with you and the director to go over details before you make a decision?"

Peri took a deep breath and jumped before they could change their mind. "Great. Let's do it."

"Ah! I am so excited, oh my gosh. Yes! I am going to call him *right now* and get you two on the phone together this afternoon, because I know they're anxious to get this locked down. This is so great! Can I ask what changed your mind?"

"Sorry?"

"Oh, just that I've sent you a few of these casting calls, and we usually don't hear much back. Are you a fan of Kelsey?"

"Kelsey?"

Tina laughed. "The singer."

"Oh." Peri closed their eyes, fighting a wave of embarrassment that threatened to knock them right out of their chair. "No—I mean, I don't know—I'm not familiar. Um. With her. No, I just... I need a change of pace. This seems like a great first step to try it out and see if maybe... acting would be the right fit for me," Peri finished breathlessly.

"That's great, Peri. That's so great. I love it. Okay! I'm gonna go and you're gonna get a call in a few minutes from Nate, that's the director, Nate, okay? I might be on that call too. We'll see what he wants to do. Talk soon!"

"Okay, great. Bye." Peri hung up and flung the phone to the other side of the couch like it was a hot potato. They pressed their hands against their eyes and groaned loudly.

Movement on the couch made them open their eyes. Juniper came up to investigate the noise, and Peri leaned forward and pressed their face into the cat's long, thick fur. "What have I done?" Peri mumbled out loud.

Of course, there was no answer.

13

MAEVE

The views on Maeve's last video were through the roof, which was great, but the strange comments continued to roll in. *That's like nothing I've ever seen before!* one user said. *Holy shit did you dream after this?* another asked. Scrolling through, Maeve saw there were hundreds of comments along the same lines, talking about how much the dream had stuck with them, and how they had dreamed about it after watching it.

For the life of her, Maeve couldn't figure out why. Sure, the story was fun, and everyone loved a little revenge now and then, but there wasn't anything about the dream that was particularly unique. It was just a cute little scene of a woman tossing her ex off a roof. It wasn't even third person. Why was it inspiring so much redreaming? What about it did people feel drawn to?

Her fantasy dream had been picked up by Envisage VR, so Maeve hadn't been able to post it, but she wouldn't have been surprised if *it* had been a big hit. But this one? It just didn't make any sense.

Maeve was drawn away from her deep dive into the comments when her computer beeped gently, letting her know the rendering of her latest dream was finally finished. Her hand was shaking enough that gesture navigation kept sending her to the wrong tab, so she grabbed her little-used mouse and clicked over to the right screen. She breathed air out of her nose in a big rush, and then opened the first file.

The dream opened partway through her walk, when she noticed the streetlights turning the world eerie and unreal. There was nothing recorded before she left the party, so everything she remembered from there—including the eerie feeling in the bathroom—must have happened. Or at least, in her drunken state she had perceived it as happening. That didn't mean anyone had been watching her necessarily, but... There had to be a reason she had been so on edge, didn't there? Some instinct told her she wasn't safe, urged her to get away from that party and find her way home.

Maeve leaned in closer and watched as the dream played out exactly as she remembered, from the shadowy canine to the handsome stranger and his fruitless warning. The figure that stalked her was no easier to see on the recording than it had been in the dream, as if a thick pane of old, warped glass obscured it. Even through a computer screen, it made goosebumps flush down Maeve's arms.

What did it mean that the dream showed her walking home? Had she been so blacked out from the booze that her body was on autopilot, walking her home, while her mind slipped into dreams? If that was the case, there shouldn't be a recording of it, though. She couldn't have put the electrodes on to record until she got home.

Was the dream, then, a sort of memory? A reflection of what had happened to her while she stumbled, half in and half out of consciousness? There was no way to know, and that scared her more than anything had in a long time. The boundaries between the waking and sleeping worlds had always been concrete. If that started to change, what did it mean for her?

She debated whether she should upload the video. Nightmares generally did well if they were lucid because most of them weren't. She remembered one nightmare where she had been *utterly* terrified of a cat, for no reason at all.

Something about the dark figure that stalked her through the dream wouldn't let her go, and despite the sick feeling in her stomach she rewound the footage and played it over and over. There was something about that shape that was so... familiar.

Maeve gasped as she grabbed the mouse and clicked back over to her last uploaded video. Scrolling back up through the comments, she hit play. There, in the back of the scene, was the dark figure she had noticed earlier. And it was *exactly the same profile* as the thing chasing her in the second dream. She quickly moved back and forth between the screens, just to be sure, and confirmed her suspicion. It was a little clearer in the more recent video, but there was no question that it was the same person—or thing.

Maeve x'ed out of both windows and shoved away from her desk. She had never seen a recurring element in her dreams like that. She knew there were other dreamers who had characters that returned from dream to dream—sometimes they were almost celebrities in their own rights. But Maeve's dreams were straightforward representations of her own life. The people in them were almost always her friends and family. This strange black shadow, it just didn't fit.

Her fans would probably go wild for it, so even though her stomach was still churning, and she had only just dramatically shoved herself away from her desk, she reluctantly dragged her wheely chair back into place and reopened the file. She uploaded it quickly, adding the appropriate tags and putting together a campaign hinting at the Easter egg in the video. It felt a little odd to be turning her nightmare into a fun surprise her fans could find, but doing anything else felt like giving the creepy figure too much power.

Was it absolutely terrifying that she had somehow slipped from lucidity to sleep with no hint of it? Yes, of course it was. Did that mean she didn't want to get paid for her trouble? *Obviously not!*

It was hours before Maeve surfaced from her work, her head pounding and eyes burning from staring at the screen. She got up and poured a huge glass of orange juice, chugging it in her kitchen, then tossed some chicken into the air fryer with a few frozen French fries.

She was chewing on a carrot when her phone rang, and she tapped her watch to answer since her phone was still in the bedroom. "Yello?"

"Is this Maeve Kessler?"

"Yesssss." Maeve narrowed her eyes and drew out the word. She was already lifting a hand and getting ready to disconnect the call, assuming he was probably a telemarketer.

"This is Detective Lee. I'm hoping you don't mind coming down to the station and answering a few questions."

"What? About what?"

"You were at a party last night with Josie Aranda?" He made it sound like a question, not a statement, so she answered it that way.

"Yeah, I was."

"We just have a few questions, and we'd prefer to chat in person if you're okay with that."

"You have questions about the party?" she asked, her mind totally blank. Had something happened? Had she been asleep and done something she didn't remember? Had someone done something to *her*? Josie would have noticed if anything remarkable had happened, though, and she hadn't said anything when they talked this morning.

"And if you wouldn't mind bringing your phone, if you took any photos or video, that would be great," he said. "We'd really appreciate it if you could come down now. Does that work for you?"

"I—I guess."

"Great. We're at the main station on Cambie, you know where that is?"

"Uh—yeah, yeah. I'm on transit so it'll be half an hour at least."

"No problem at all. Just ask for Detective Ouyang at the front desk, and we'll see you soon."

"Okay, thanks." Maeve hung up and then immediately tapped her screen again. "Call Josie," she said. The phone rang through to voicemail. Maeve was already on the move, going to her bedroom to put on some semi-respectable clothes. She grabbed her phone on the way and sent a text to Josie asking if she was okay and detailing the call, then stuffed herself into a pair of nice black pants.

A moss-green blouse she hadn't worn in at least three years was hopelessly wrinkled from being crammed in the back of her dresser, but it was presentable enough. The pants didn't have pockets, but it was cold enough for a jacket anyway, so she tossed her phone into her jacket pocket, grabbed her purse, and was out the door in less than five minutes.

She was close enough to walk to the SkyTrain, but she was on the wrong line from the police station, so she only rode a few stops and then transferred to the B-line down Broadway. It was packed at the best of times, but on a nice Sunday afternoon in the fall it was an absolute mess. She ended up crammed against the bendy wall that joined the two long sections of the bus, bracing herself on the back of someone's seat because she couldn't reach the handles, all the way to Main Street. A crowd of people got off there, which would have been more helpful if her stop wasn't five minutes away by that point. She moved closer to the door so it would be easier to get off, though, and joined the throng of people moving off the bus with no trouble. From there it was only a few blocks down to the police station.

She'd only been once, to do a criminal record check for some summer job. It was a large brick-and-glass building that didn't tower so much as squat on the corner of a fairly quiet street just a block away from a major intersection.

Even though she knew she'd done nothing wrong, Maeve shivered and hesitated on the threshold. It had been a long time since she had believed that institutions like these catered mainly to justice. Even though she was a young white woman and thus insulated from the worst the police had to offer, not knowing why she had been called down was doing a number on her head. And stomach, which was already sour from the hangover.

Maeve realized she had left the chicken and fries in the air fryer —thank god it shut down when the timer went off, or she would have burned the whole house down. Of course, now she was thinking about food, and she was absolutely fucking starving.

Sighing, Maeve pulled the big front door open and went in. It was quieter than she expected, with a small waiting area and a big desk behind glass. She went up and gave her name, and the woman directed her to the sixth floor and pointed the way to the elevators. A few people were going about their business, a mix of uniformed officers and people she assumed were civilians. She wiped her palms on her thighs as she hit the button for the sixth floor, then got into the elevator. She had to squeeze past a few people on her way out.

The sixth floor was much busier than the entryway. It was a mostly open-plan office similar to police stations that she'd seen on

TV, with people moving around holding files, but without the sullen cuffed people sitting at desks discussing their cases. She didn't see anyone who looked like they were under arrest, and she wondered if that happened somewhere else.

Again, there was a very small waiting area with a handful of chairs and a desk, this one with a woman in uniform behind it. She approached and gave her name and the detective she was here to see. The uniformed offcer showed her to a small meeting room that wouldn't have been out of place in any office. It smelled like someone's lunch, soy sauce and spices, which made Maeve feel a little more at ease. How bad could it be if people ate their lunches here? It wasn't exactly an interrogation room.

"Coffee or tea?" the woman asked, and it took Maeve longer than it should have to process the question.

"Oh, uh. No, thanks," she said, sliding down into a chair that let her see the door.

It wasn't long before two people came into the room. One she assumed was Detective Lee, and he quickly confirmed that as he reached out and shook her hand. He was in his thirties or early forties, with buzzed black hair and a stiff, military bearing. The other person he introduced as Detective Reid. She was older than him by at least a decade, and her pantsuit looked out of date by a similar number of years, but her smile was warm as she took a seat across from Maeve.

"Thanks for coming down so quickly," Reid said to break the ice.

"Sure. Sorry. Can I ask what's going on?" she asked, laughing with more nervousness than she intended.

"Jason Geddes was murdered last night," Lee said, as if he was describing the weather.

Maeve's entire brain went blank, white noise fuzzing at the edges of consciousness. She sat there for longer than she probably should have, trying to process the overwhelming rush of emotions and feelings that just crashed over her. Jason was *dead*? No, not dead. *Murdered*. Jason was a giant asshole, and Maeve couldn't admit to true grief at hearing the news, but she was still shocked, and scared. She knew this was probably a privileged position, but people simply didn't get murdered in her life. It wasn't a thing that happened—not to people she knew.

"Jason is *dead*?" was all she could think to say. Then the words caught up to her. "Oh my god, you don't think I did it, do you? It was just a dream!"

The detectives exchanged a look that was probably supposed to be subtle, but clearly said, *Shit what is she talking about? Should we know what she's talking about?* "What was a dream?" Reid asked.

"I'm a dreamer. And I had a dream a few nights ago that Josie pushed Jason off a roof."

"Off a roof?" Lee asked, his voice hard.

"Yeah, but it was just a dream. He was, like, an evil prince, you know? It was this, like, totally silly stupid thing."

"Can you show it to us?" Reid asked.

"Oh, uh, yeah, of course." Maeve took out her phone and opened her channel, hit play, then pushed the phone across the table. She fiddled nervously as the detectives watched the video, taking notes the whole time.

"Had Mr. Geddes seen this?" Lee asked.

Maeve swallowed and wiped her hands across her thighs before taking back the proffered phone. "I mean... yeah. He told me to take it down."

"And what did you tell him?" Reid asked.

"...No?" Maeve said. *Obviously.*

"I imagine he wasn't too happy about that."

"Not really, no. He yelled a bit, and I told him to go to hell and that was that. He just called me the one time."

"How would you characterize your relationship with Mr. Geddes?" Reid was clearly taking the lead on this, but Maeve didn't quite turn her entire attention to the other woman. Lee was watching her too thoughtfully.

"I don't know. Fine? He was Josie's boyfriend, and I didn't like him very much, but like... we hung out sometimes with her there. He was angry all the time and possessive. But you don't tell your friends to break up with people, you know? Cuz then if they don't, or if they get back together, suddenly you're the bad guy." She laughed nervously, wishing she was done talking but not quite able to stop herself. "I was happy they broke up, but not like—*murder* happy." As soon as the words left her mouth, Maeve regretted it. It felt way too cavalier.

"Josie told us the two of you were at a party last night?"

"Yeah. Uh—I went over at like, five or something, and my parents dropped off some furniture. We ate meatloaf and set everything up, and then I drank a whole lot, so I don't remember exactly what time I left but Josie said it was after midnight."

"You spoke to Josie today?" Lee broke in.

"Yeah, this morning."

"Do you have any photos from the party?" he asked.

"Yes!" Maeve was always good about taking photos early in the night, though she wasn't sure how many shots she had once she started drinking. She grabbed the phone again, opened her camera app, and slid it over. "Uh, Hayley's really into photography and she left pretty late, so she probably has more. I can give you her number."

"That would be great." Reid slid over a piece of paper and a pen.

"Oh, I'll—need the phone," Maeve said with a laugh.

A little of the ice in her chest melted when Reid laughed too. "Oh, right. Why don't you email those photos and the number to me?" Reid traded the pen and paper for a business card with her name and email on it.

"Sure, yeah." Maeve took a deep breath, trying to stay calm as she reclaimed her phone and sent Reid an email, attaching the photos and a contact card. "Um, is it okay if I ask when Jason died?" she asked.

There was no way Josie had killed anyone, not even that utter creep, but Maeve knew the girlfriend was always the prime suspect —especially the ex.

"We're not going to reveal that until we have a timeline figured out. It helps us ascertain alibis," Reid explained.

"Oh, right. Okay. But Josie isn't a suspect, is she? Because of the party?"

"Josie is our *prime* suspect," Reid said.

"What?!" Maeve couldn't stop her voice from rising, and both of her hands fell flat against the table, louder than she intended. "That's insane! She was with me all night, and she would never do something like that!"

"The alibi is compelling," Reid agreed, "and the photos certainly help her case. But we have surveillance footage that puts someone matching her description squarely at the scene."

"That's impossible. I swear to you, it's impossible. Josie is the nicest person you could ever meet in your entire life. She's not a murderer."

Reid leaned in, voice surprisingly gentle as she said, "I've never had a single person sit in that chair and tell me that a person they care about is capable of murder."

"I'd like to ask you more about this dream," Lee interrupted as he finished downloading the photos and handed her back the phone.

"Why? Am I a suspect?" Maeve asked dryly. Her eyes widened when the cops just looked at each other. "Oh, shit, am I a suspect?"

"At this stage of the investigation we're mostly gathering information," Reid said. She most definitely did *not* say, "No, Maeve, you are not a murder suspect."

"Oh my god." Maeve squeezed her eyes shut and then opened them again. "Shit. Okay. Yeah. Ask me anything. I'm an open book."

Lee asked her some basic questions about her history as a dreamer, how the technology worked, and who had seen the video. He was shocked when she told him the number of views, and made her bring the video up again to show it to him.

"So, when you said Jason asked you to take this down, he must have known people were watching it."

Maeve shrugged, uncomfortable, aware that every word she said made it look more likely that Jason might have had a reason to want to hurt Maeve, which was in turn a motive for her hurting him first. "Yeah. People at work were teasing him, I guess. But I have a full legal disclaimer that says the people in the videos are products of my imagination. It isn't *him*, it's just a dream I had that someone who looked like him was in. You don't own your likeness in dreams."

"Jason doesn't strike me as the kind of person who would care what the law had to say about it," Reid pointedly said.

"No. I guess not."

"Did he threaten you?"

Maeve shrugged. "A little."

"How do you threaten someone a little?" Lee asked.

"You know, like... 'Take that down or you'll regret it!'" Maeve said in a poor approximation of Jason's voice. "Like, no actual threats or anything. Jason was a bully. He thought he could rant and pound his chest and people would just cave. I wasn't worried he would actually do something to me. I even told Josie—" Maeve stopped, biting her lip and regretting bringing Josie into it.

"Josie knew he had threatened you?" Reid said.

"...She was there when he called. But I told her, if he did actually follow through that was a good thing because then I could call the cops on him. I wasn't worried, and she knew that."

"Did that scare her? That you weren't taking the threat seriously?" Reid suggested.

"No. She knew I was right. It wasn't a real threat."

"You're sure about that?" Lee pressed.

"I'm sure," Maeve insisted, fudging the truth in an effort to prove Josie's innocence. "Josie was glad to be rid of him, but she wasn't scared. He was out of her life. She was moving on."

They went over it a few more times after that, checking for inaccuracies in her story, and got her to write down contact information for a few friends who might have taken pictures and could verify what time she left, or knew what time the party wound down. Finally, they shook her hand, gave her their card, and told her that they would be in touch if they had any questions.

"I don't think you need legal counsel at this time," Reid said, "but let us know if you won't be in easy contact for any reason, or if you have any upcoming trips planned."

"Is that the nice way of saying 'don't leave town'?" Maeve asked.

"Yes. It is," Reid said. This time, her smile was less reassuring.

"Is Josie still here?" Maeve asked as Reid and Lee both stood up, scraping their chairs across the rough carpet.

"I think they're releasing her pretty soon. You can wait downstairs for her if you want to."

"Great. Thanks." Maeve followed them out of the room, then took the elevator back to the lobby. She checked her phone and found a few panicked texts from friends who had also been contacted by the detectives, so she found a seat and answered them as best she could. All the while, her thoughts were churning. What did it mean that Jason had died in her dream, and it happened for real a few days later?

Nothing, she told herself angrily. It was a coincidence. It didn't mean anything. *He probably got stabbed by some angry investor.*

But no—if that were the case, Josie wouldn't be the prime suspect. She was in the crosshairs because someone matching her description was spotted near the crime scene. Of course, that didn't mean much. Eyewitness reports were notoriously unreliable. Plus, what did "seen in the area" really mean? This was Vancouver. Tall Southeast Asian women were hardly in short supply.

Maeve curled her arms protectively around her body. She felt like every person who walked past was staring at her, wondering why she was there, what crime she had committed. Was this Maeve's fault? Her dream couldn't be to blame. Someone who saw the video could have decided it made Josie look guilty. They could have taken advantage of that to commit murder. But why Jason? Or was Josie herself the target?

The cops hadn't known about the video, that much was clear. And Lee had been particularly focused on the fact that Jason fell off a roof in the dream. Was there a connection there? Had his death involved a roof in real life, too? So many people were talking about having the dream, it could be that someone had heard about it. Someone with a weak grip on reality might have believed the dream was a memory, or a prophecy, and killed Jason because they thought they had to. Or was that farfetched?

Half an hour later, Maeve was still morosely going over and over the same information and the same questions, with no concrete theories. She could have sat there all day, but Josie appeared out of the elevator, looking absolutely shell-shocked. Maeve's heart crumpled at the sight. *Please don't let it be my fault. I can't have hurt her like this.*

She leaped to her feet and crossed the distance between them in two heartbeats. "Josie!"

"Maeve? Oh my god, Maeve, they think—"

"I know." Maeve crushed Josie into a hug, hating the way her friend was shaking, shock and tears dancing across the surface of her skin. "It's gonna be okay. You're gonna be okay."

They stood like that for a long time, not moving, not saying a word, just waiting for time to start moving again.

14

PERI

Peri couldn't believe how quickly everything moved. Half an hour after they hung up from the first call, they were on another with Nate, and before the end of the day they had a signed contract and a call time for Tuesday morning. The script was simple: Peri was a mystical creature who dispensed dreams from a tower in the sky, and the singer lived out fantasies in each of those dreams.

Peri just had to float around, look mysterious, and drop plastic globes out a window. Then there was a final scene where the singer —*Kelsey, that was it*—entered the tower and smashed all the globes while Peri cowered. Peri read it through four times, which seemed excessive, and felt pretty confident even they could get it right.

Their determination to get out into the world didn't stretch to leaving their condo before then, however. Peri did everything they could to stay awake, collapsed into bed reluctantly, and woke up to an alarm early each morning. Exhaustion and alcohol kept Peri's dreams at bay for the next few nights but left them feeling disjointed and out of sorts. The sense that dreams were leaking into the waking world hovered at the edge of their foggy perception, and they couldn't concentrate on anything.

They skipped their therapy session, claiming a sore throat, and ignored the memes their brother sent every couple of days. They spent their days watching comfort TV they had seen a hundred times before, stirring only to feed the cat and eat a bite of whatever they could find that didn't require cooking.

Every time they thought about leaving the condo, they were hit with that same sense of dread. The world outside was unpredictable. Random. Who knew what was real and what was their imagination? How could they keep safe if they couldn't tell what around them might fade away as soon as they put a hand on it? Anyway, they were leaving on Tuesday. That was soon enough. No need to face the uncomfortable until then.

It soon became a mantra. *I'm leaving on Tuesday. I'll get some exercise on Tuesday. I'll cook a real meal when I get home on Tuesday.* The days in between bled into each other, time stretching and contracting. What was Tuesday? Was it a state Peri would ever reach? Could it lift the horrible weight that settled across their shoulders? *Tuesday. Tuesday. Tuesday.*

When Peri's alarm went off earlier than a dairy farmer's on the morning of, it hit them like breaking the sound barrier, all chaos and fury and deep, restless nausea. Peri rolled out of bed, hitting the floor with a desperate groan as they fumbled for the phone to turn off the persistent alert. Their head pounded and they lay on the ground, panting, the silence a pressure against their eardrums, demanding to be let in. They had to try three times before they could summon the energy to rise, and they deeply regretted the booze that gave them a dreamless, though hardly restful, sleep.

Stumbling into the shower, Peri let the water scour the long night away. Fear was not as easily let go of. They stood under the spray, shaking, alert, and terrified of what lay ahead. *Tuesday.* No longer a safe space in a nebulous future, a thing they would deal with when they reached it. *Tuesday.* They couldn't pretend that they were ready, that they hadn't been hiding, not when they were shaking so badly that they dropped their body wash bottle three times, almost cracking their head on the shower dials as they bent over to pick it up the final time. *Tuesday.* Today they would walk up to that front door and push through.

They had to. They were under contract.

Still, Peri lingered on every task. They changed their mind about their outfit three times, even though the production would be providing clothes for Peri to wear on set. They checked their email and socials, watered their one lucky bamboo, and gave Juniper extra kibble to make up for the fact that there would be no wet dinner tonight. But finally, there was no more delaying. It was only Peri, the long hallway, and the imposing door at the end of it.

"Don't miss me while I'm gone!" Peri called brightly to Juniper, trying to fill the silence with normal things. "I know it's early and you're confused about what I'm even doing awake, but you'll hardly notice that I'm gone. You'll be asleep all day anyway." Peri shrugged on their coat and squirmed their arms into the small back-pack they used to carry their wallet and other supplies. It currently held an e-reader, a granola bar, and some Kleenex. Last on were their runners, which they crammed their feet into and then wiggled to adjust rather than unlacing anything.

Their keys hung on the hook by the door, and they took them down and grabbed the front door key, shaking the rest out of the way.

"Okay. I'm off." Juniper slept on the couch and didn't look up, even at the sound of jingling keys. Peri turned back to the door. This was it. They just had to open the door and walk out. It was Tuesday, and it was time to face the world.

They should probably grab a water bottle. Who knows what they had on set.

Peri hurried back to the kitchen, grabbed a reusable water bottle, and filled it up from the fridge. They stuck it in the side pocket of their backpack and went back to the door, veering off to scratch Juniper under the chin.

"Are you going to miss me?" they asked, and they were rewarded when Juniper purred and rolled onto her side, exposing her belly. Peri petted her gently, luxuriating in the soft fur. They closed their eyes and took a long, slow, steadying breath. "Okay," they whispered. "You can do this. You do this all the time. You just have to open the door."

Peri tried to kiss Juniper, who batted them in the face. They were laughing as they turned back to the door and started the slow walk toward it. *Just turn the handle. That's all you have to do.* Peri put a hand on the handle and closed their eyes.

They were still standing there a moment later when their phone beeped, informing them that their ride was only a few blocks away. Peri took the phone out and swiped the notification away. They had no choice. They had to go. The car was almost here. Plus, people were waiting for them on set. They couldn't let them all down. They would never live through the shame.

Squaring their shoulders, Peri grabbed the handle, turned, and yanked open the door. They darted out into the hall and froze there, letting the door slam shut behind them. Their breath was too loud in their ears, but the hallway outside their room was surprisingly mundane. There were no windows in this part of the hall, so it looked the same day or night, but it lacked the other-worldly lurch Peri remembered from the last time they had been here.

Slowly and carefully, Peri walked down the hall. Their steps were swallowed by the soft carpet. Occasionally, the muffled sound of people at their lives drifted through the doors that Peri passed, reminding them uncomfortably of the long hallway in their dream. But it wasn't long before they reached the elevator, escaping the memories as the doors crashed shut on the too-familiar view.

A short ride and they were in the lobby and then out on the street, breathing fresh air as if they had just burst up from the ocean floor and feeling almost as dizzy as a diver with decompression sickness.

They straightened up and looked around with a weak smile. They had done it. It was Tuesday, and they had made it back to the world.

～

The ride to the studio managed to calm their nerves somewhat, and Peri arrived feeling almost human. The music video was filming in the back of what looked like a recording studio, where a huge open space with double-height ceilings had been converted into a tempo-rary film set. It looked like they had been at it for a while already; everyone was running around looking official, with headsets on and walkie-talkies strapped to the belts of their functional cargo pants. A few beautiful women in gauzy clothes chatted lazily in stark contrast to the crew, who looked like they were already three hours behind on a day that had just started.

There was a sign-in table right by the door, which Peri made a beeline for. The woman there checked Peri in and directed them to the green room, which was the staging area for the actors. It wasn't green and it was barely a room; several chairs were set in a rough circle with a coffee maker and a tea kettle on a little table against the one wall. A few people were already sitting down, reading magazines or surfing on their phones. They were friendly, though, and exchanged the basic greetings all strangers exchange: what's your name, what's your job, how was traffic.

Peri wasn't sitting for very long when a frantic but friendly woman popped over and scanned their faces. "Peri?" she asked as her gaze settled.

"That's me."

"Oh, thank god. We're ready for you in costume," she said. "You can leave your bag here."

Peri hesitated, not sure about leaving their wallet on the floor with a bunch of strangers in an unsupervised room, but the woman was already moving away, and they didn't want to get left behind. After a moment, they stashed it under a chair and hurried to catch up. The costume department had an actual room, just across the hall from the staging area for the cast, and two other women looked up and smiled but didn't stop what they were doing as Peri came in.

"Okay, we've got a great costume for you, I think you'll love it," the woman said. She went over to a colourful rack that was full of costumes of every style—the costumes were elaborate and varied, with the premise of the video being jumping around between dreams—and pulled one out.

Peri took it and held it up. It was a beautiful shimmery grey robe, but they weren't entirely sure what they were supposed to put it over. "This is gorgeous. But, um... It's kind of sheer?"

"Oh, god, sorry, obviously you won't be wearing just that!" the woman said with a laugh. "You'll have underwear, obviously." She grabbed another hanger off the rack and held it out. It was a bra and underwear set, fairly full coverage, but lacey and white.

Peri shook their head, mutely horrified, words not catching up with their initial physical reaction. The woman saw Peri's reaction and froze for half a second, then plowed bravely forward. "Obviously, if you're not comfortable with that, we can adapt." She was thinking as she talked, her eyes flickering slightly as she scanned her memory. "Hey Alice, do we have that powder blue miniskirt from the mermaid scene?"

"Uh—yup," Alice said, getting up and going to grab the item in question.

"Um. Sorry, it's not that just, it's just... Um... It's that those are... women's underwear," Peri stammered out, wanting to crawl into a corner and die. Their awkward gesture ended with them clutching both hands together as if to stop from talking any more.

The woman, who had never given her name, looked at Peri in mute horror, but Peri was relieved when she finally spoke, and it was clear that the horror was self-directed. "Oh my god, I am *so* sorry. Nobody said—shit. Fuck. I'm so sorry. We will fix it. I promise. We've got you." She grinned, and Peri felt relieved tears welling.

"Thanks," they whispered, hating that their voice cracked a little. Peri always braced themselves for the worst when their gender came up against people's expectations. Hell, their parents had been their first example of this, refusing to acknowledge their pronouns or their new name when Peri came out in college.

Shaking the unpleasant thoughts from their head, Peri watched Alice and the costume lady as they disappeared into the clothes in a flurry of conversation and debate while Peri sank into a nearby chair, shivering. *There's no point in panicking now. She was totally chill. It's over. You're all good.*

Long minutes passed, punctuated by the sound of a sewing machine, before the woman returned, looking breathless and incredibly pleased with herself. "How's this?" she asked. She was holding up loose powder blue shorts that would probably hit midway down Peri's thigh, with a lot of flowing bits coming off that made it look almost like a cloud. Peri took it in amazement. She was pretty sure it was the miniskirt that had been referenced earlier, but somehow the costumer had completely transformed it into an appropriate, gender-neutral garment.

"This is great!" Peri gave her a warm smile that burned off the last of the anxiety that had been shadowing their eyes.

"Yes! Okay, great. For the top, I'm thinking we go for a kind of

Peter Pan look, it's going to be under the robe so you won't see it that clearly, but I want to use this fabric and sort of wrap it around and then shred the edges, what do you think?" She held up a bolt of sapphire-blue fabric, and Peri nodded.

"Love it."

"Awesome, okay. If you can put that on and strip down, I'm gonna pin this right on you." She paused for a second. "Is that okay?"

Peri smiled and nodded. The costumer turned away, so Peri had some privacy to pull off their jeans and put on the shorts. They pulled off their T-shirt, feeling a little self-conscious. *These are professionals. They don't care what you've got—which isn't much.* Peri chuckled. They didn't wear a binder most of the time; they were naturally slim and small-breasted, and the testosterone they took made them even more flat-chested. Some of the time they even liked the small swell of their breasts, though they wished they could summon the appendages and dismiss them at will.

The woman turned back, and Peri stood patiently while they were wrapped in fabric. Once that was done, the costumer called Alice, who was clearly her assistant, over to help with the process of tearing the edges to give it a wild look. The gauzy robe went over top, and by the time the hood came up Peri really did feel like a powerful creature of dream, far beyond the petty wants and desires of mortals. They twirled once and the costumer clapped.

"Yes! Okay, I'm going to grab Nate and get this signed off, you can head to hair and makeup," the costumer said, then disappeared before Peri could ask where that was. Luckily, Alice saw their bewildered expression and laughed.

"Sorry, it's always a little wild on set," she said. "I can take you."

"Thanks." Peri meant to be a little more effusive than that, but talking to strangers hadn't suddenly gotten easier just because they were genuinely grateful, so they settled for a warm smile before following Alice out of the room and across the large studio. Hair and makeup were set up in the large accessible washroom, which felt problematic to Peri, but not enough that they were comfortable saying anything. It was another team of two young women, both fashionable enough that Peri felt almost uncomfortable.

"Hey! I've got your Dream Giver for you," Alice told the ladies.

"They're nonbinary, so if you can make sure the makeup reflects the look, that would be great."

Peri nearly melted in relief at not having to have that conversation and took a seat feeling calmer than they had since they arrived. The women introduced themselves briefly and then ignored Peri as the two had a conversation that literally went over Peri's head about how to use makeup to full effect while staying away from gender norms. They finally decided to stick to their original vision but scrapped the lipstick. The heaps of eye makeup that drifted off to the sides and down Peri's cheeks took half an hour to do but created a distinctly otherworldly vibe that was powerful and alluring. The director appeared around halfway through the process, said a quick hello, told Peri they looked great, and disappeared immediately. Clearly, he was busy, and Peri didn't mind at all.

After makeup, it was time for hair. Peri was already starting to feel fidgety—they weren't much for primping on a regular day and had never spent this long doing anything to their appearance—but they did their best to be patient and still as the woman dived in, chatting amicably about her side gig as a props assistant. The woman braided the long side of Peri's hair back in small, tight lines. She left it loose at the back, and Peri was delighted to see that the effect was martial and powerful.

It was back to the green room from there, where a different set of actors were now lounging around, chatting about this and that. They said hello when Peri sat, but made no particular effort to include them in conversation, which Peri was fine with. As the minutes dragged on, Peri grew increasingly nervous. What if it turned out they were terrible at acting? What if they made the wrong kind of face, or looked in the wrong place? At least they didn't have to worry about forgetting their lines, since they had none.

With the mad rush everywhere and a pool of silence surrounding them, Peri felt the disconnected feeling of the last few days creeping back. This environment was so unfamiliar that there was nothing they could cling to and say, *At least this is normal. At least this is real.*

Peri stood, moving out of the holding area and looking around. They found a cardboard box and jumped off it, testing to see if they felt the landing. It was one of the reality tests they had read about when they were researching lucid dreaming. When their feet hit the ground with a normal thump, their overly quick heartbeat slowed a little. They were awake. They had to be awake.

"Peri?" a voice asked. Peri turned sharply to see a young man with a walkie-talkie who had appeared at their side. "They're ready for you."

"Oh. Yeah. Great." Peri wiped nervous hands on their costume and followed him.

"Cast walking," he said into his walkie, leading them through the hubbub and onto the main set.

There was a wall with a window in it to act as the outside of the tower, held up by wood scaffolding that was presumably too low for the camera to see. On the other side of the window, a small area had been converted into the dreamer's lair, with a single wall and no ceiling. It was gorgeous, but unsettlingly so—everything was just this side of real looking, so Peri felt further off-kilter. The lights were too bright, making the large room swelteringly hot, and the ceiling was high up and pitch black, making everything cavernous and exposed. The floor was black, too, and Peri felt like they were walking through... well, a dream, which was the last thing they wanted.

The director waved Peri over and situated them in the middle of the room. "Okay, we're going to start with the scene where you're tossing dreams out the window, okay? This is from the perspective of inside the room. You're magical, but you're not evil. You're unknowable. Unfathomable. You don't have human under-standing or sensibility, okay? So, I want you to embrace that, give me sort of haughty, sort of curious. You're a scientist. You want to see what humans will do with the dreams you dispense. Okay? Great."

He didn't wait for Peri to answer or ask questions, just disap-peared behind the cameras. Another man approached, once again not introducing himself, and directed Peri on exactly where to stand. A third showed them how to handle the dream props. They were plastic balls painted to look like an ethereal fog was parting to reveal tiny dioramas tucked inside. Peri wondered if they could take one home after the shoot—they were pretty cool.

Another assistant crouched on the other side of the window to catch the balls as Peri released them.

"Okay!" Nate shouted. "Let's do a rehearsal. Peri, I want you to pick up that dream and walk it toward the window."

Peri took a deep breath and unconsciously held it. They picked up the dream, moving their head a little as if they were examining it, and then walked toward the window.

"Good! Slow the walk down. Better, yeah. Can you glide? Like, make your steps less obvious? Yes! That's good. Okay, now release the dream like it's a bird that you're letting fly. Don't toss it, just gently. Okay, that was good!"

Peri remembered to breathe again and smiled down at the assistant who had neatly caught the ball. "Not too bad?" they asked.

"Perfect," the man assured them. He hopped up and ran the ball back to its original place, then returned to his as Nate came over to talk to Peri.

"That was great, Peri. You had the gliding walk by the end, I think. Let's do it one more time, but this time I want to see a little more unknowable-ness in your face. Try to think about nothing but make it look like you're concentrating. Okay?"

"Okay," Peri said, even though they had absolutely no idea how to accomplish that. Think about nothing while concentrating? What did that even mean? Peri returned to set, adjusted the placement of their feet after being told they weren't quite on their mark, and tried to settle their face into something sort of distant. They imagined they were looking out over a misty kingdom, surveying a land that they might one day inherit, but only if they could stop their uncle from usurping the throne...

"Okay, go for it!" Nate said.

Once again Peri picked up a ball, glided across the floor, and released it out the window.

"Great! Okay, we're going to do that again but with the cameras rolling. Ready?"

"Ready," Peri agreed. They were grinning. This was going to be easier than they thought.

It was a little disconcerting to see how close the camera got to their face at the beginning of the shot, but Peri was pleased by how calm they stayed as the camera rolled. Someone called action, and a digital clapboard recorded the scene and take number. They picked up the dream, carefully walked across the room, and dropped it into the hidden assistant's waiting hands. They were expecting the director to yell cut, but instead he said, "Okay, that was perfect, Peri!"

Peri straightened, proud and pleased with their work. That had been easier than they expected!

"Let's do it again!" Nate yelled.

Peri watched, confused, as everyone around them scurried to reset the cameras and props. *If it was perfect, why do we have to do it again?*

≈

That thought echoed through Peri's head several times over the next hour. They did the same scene *eight* times, with Nate making small adjustments to the angle or giving them more and more difficult to follow directions ("Like a swan!"). The lights blasted down on Peri, turning everything outside of the set hazy and indistinct and creating a false separation between them and the rest of the set.

When the camera was rolling, you could hear a pin drop. The rest of the time voices raised almost aggressively high, as if to let out the energy they kept balled up every time they were recording. Peri's top hadn't felt tight when they were first wrapping it up, but it grew more and more constricting, until it felt like someone had wrapped huge hands around Peri's chest and were slowly squeezing.

Finally, after "One more for good luck," Nate called a wrap on the scene. "Let's set up for scene sixteen," he called to the people around him. "And can we make sure Kelsey is ready?"

"Do I—" Peri hesitated when it was clear Nate wasn't listening to them, but the woman who had been counting scenes was looking their way. "Do I have time to go to the bathroom?"

"Yeah, of course," the woman said, and Peri gratefully fled the set.

They were hoping the feeling of dissociation would fade once they were off the black floor and away from its cardboard accoutrements, but the feeling only grew. Everywhere around them people were in motion: talking, laughing, building something, destroying something. But they weren't a part of any of it. The robe swished around their feet as they walked, making a sound that was too much like a heartbeat for Peri's comfort.

Not wanting to ask for directions, they did a full circuit of the room twice before they found the bathrooms, tucked away in a corner near the back entrance. A sign pointed the way, but when they reached the door there was no washroom sign on it. And something about the dark redwood twigged something in Peri's mind. Something about the hallway—the light spilling out from under the door, the way the dark cherry wood glistened...

Peri reached out a trembling hand and pressed it flat against the door's surface. It was damp, and as they pulled their hand back, they saw a faint outline left on the wood. And their hand, when they held it up, was crimson and etched in blood.

Peri screamed, stumbling back from the door. They tripped on the unfamiliar length of the robe and crashed to the ground, scrambling to get back, to get away from the door.

"Are you okay?" someone asked, dashing to Peri's side.

Trying to draw a breath against the knot of terror in their throat, Peri looked up at the bathroom entrance—and saw a plain grey door, with a little cartoon man painted on the front. No sign of a handprint. No crimson wood. Against the brightness of the room they were in, there wasn't even a visible line of light spilling out from underneath.

"I—I—tripped," Peri gasped.

The woman laughed and offered her hand to help Peri up. Peri reached out—and saw in horror that their hand was bright red, covered in blood that was now patchy from having been brushed against the ground.

"Do you see that?" Peri gasped. Their eyes were so wide they knew they must look crazed, and the woman rocked back from the crouched position she had taken to help Peri up.

"Do I see... what?"

"My hand!" Peri screamed. "Is it red? Is my hand red?" Peri was on their knees, shoving the palm of their hand under the terrified woman's nose.

"What? Yes?" the woman asked.

Peri closed their eyes, trying not to fall apart, trying not to sob right there on the floor. "Oh, god. No. No."

"It's okay. Did you—cut yourself or something?"

"No. I have to—I have to go," Peri gasped. They were on their feet and running out of the room before the woman could ask them anything else.

Peri sprinted with no direction, no thought in their head other than getting away. They didn't get far before they had to slow to a walk, panic and physical exertion teaming up to rob their breath. They wiped their bloody hand against their robe, watching in alarm as it left a mark against the soft, grey fabric. *It's real. The damn door vanished and it still left something real behind.*

There was no question now. Peri hadn't imagined that the leaf was an incursion of the dream into the waking world. The leaf could have tracked in from outside, but the blood on their hand couldn't have come from anywhere but the phantom door, and the other woman had seen it as clearly as Peri had. Tears welled in their eyes as they took in several short, sharp, gasping breaths.

It was all real. The woman in her dreams, the danger of the recording devices, everything. And it was utterly *terrifying.*

Peri patted their pockets in a daze, intending to grab their phone and call a ride, only to remember that their phone—and their wallet and keys—were still back in the studio. Peri stopped and pressed their hands against their eyes, swearing quietly and unimaginatively under their breath. They weren't sure they could stand going back in there, but they couldn't get back inside without their keys. And they had made a commitment to the video—they couldn't just walk away.

But if the dreams were somehow leaching out of their mind and into the waking world, was it dangerous to be around other people? Something truly terrifying could come through, like the monster from their nightmare. Peri imagined that terrifying visage opening wide, spewing out bugs that devoured Alice and Nate and the entire set.

Worse was the idea that these breaks in reality were only real to Peri. Had anyone else seen the red door? Or could they only see the blood, the result of Peri interacting with the dream? If something bled through while they were on set, Peri would look like they were having a psychotic episode. There would be cops, paramedics, an involuntary stay at St. Paul's Hospital. With Peri's mental health history, an involuntary commitment order was a real possibility.

Going back was terrifying... but they couldn't just stand out here. They had no way to get home, and being out on the street wasn't any safer than being on set. They were exposed.

Peri hesitated, wishing lightning would strike them down and make a choice unnecessary, but eventually necessity won out over caution. They had to get their backpack before they could go home, and they couldn't very well walk back inside and just... leave. There was no real choice. They had to finish the shoot.

There was only one scene left to film. Peri would go back in, get through it, and get home before anything happened. If they saw anything that didn't look real, they would ignore it, avoid it, and deny it. They could do this. They just had to push through. They had to stop letting fear dictate their choices.

They did a quick circle breathing exercise and headed in. There was a knot of people talking inside, looking panicked, and when they saw Peri there were several relieved faces.

"Oh, thank god! We thought you left!" the guy with the walkie-talkie snapped.

"What happened to your robe?" Alice gasped in horror.

"I'm so sorry—" Peri thought fast and was surprised at how easily a lie came to their lips. "I guess I had a nosebleed and didn't realize. I couldn't figure out where the blood came from and it totally freaked me out. I just went outside to get some air, but I didn't realize I got it on the costume. I'm really sorry."

The lie seemed to mollify everyone, and they burst into motion to solve the problem. Someone got Peri an ice pack for the back of their neck, Alice grabbed some stain remover and went to work on the robe, and the walkie-talkie guy hurried Peri back to set to rehearse the next scene.

Getting through the rest of the day was a challenge that left Peri with a blinding headache and muscles so tense even their vape pen couldn't help. Though Peri had a newfound sense of determination, they couldn't stop from jumping at every shadow, and people noticed. The director snapped at them for ruining shots more than once, and Kelsey, the sweet-natured singer whose video it was, quietly offered Peri some coke to 'settle their nerves,' which Peri declined as politely as possible.

In some ways, though, Peri's distraction was good for the shoot. The creature they were playing was supposed to be otherworldly, and the unfocused way that Peri was watching the world certainly added to a sense that they weren't fully in the flesh. It was a small miracle that the shoot involved no lines, because Peri barely managed to stumble through the basic blocking they did have.

The team shot for nearly eleven hours to make up for their slow pace, and Peri was due back the next morning for at least another half day. Peri collapsed into the back seat of their rideshare and only managed to stay awake through a heady combination of nerves and terror. They weren't sure if falling asleep would make the dreams more likely to encroach into the waking world, and they weren't about to find out in the back of someone else's car.

Peri got home and opened their door with relief, nearly tripping over Juniper, who was meowing in excited alarm and weaving in and around their feet. Peri was almost never out this late, and the poor cat was beside herself. Peri petted her until she calmed down a little, then led her into the kitchen without turning any lights on and fed her a scoop of wet food, to Juniper's delight.

Seeing the half-empty bottle of tequila still sitting on the counter, Peri picked it up and hefted it. Avoiding dreaming hadn't stopped phantasms from leaching out into the daylight world. If anything, it had made the breakdown between dream and reality worse. Peri's strategy needed to change. As much as they wanted to run and just keep running, it wasn't working. Avoidance wasn't getting them out of this. It was time to face their fear head on. That meant taking control of their dreams once again. Peri had no idea how they would do that, but the first step was opening up to dreams again.

Still scared but determined to find a path forward, Peri opened the tequila and poured the rest of the bottle down the drain.

Peri got ready for bed and climbed under the covers, but they were so keyed up that sleep was hard to find. They tossed and turned for hours, watching the clock count down and calculating how many hours of sleep they could conceivably get before their alarm woke them up for work. *If I fall asleep right now, I'll still get six hours. If I fall asleep right* now, *I'll still get five and half hours...*

When Peri finally did fall asleep, it was fitful and restless. They barely dipped into dreams, and when they woke, they remembered only the barest fragments of colour and shape. Their newly awakened determination ignited again as they reflected on the shreds of their fitful dreaming. If they had found the woman again, they had no recollection. But they would do whatever it took to get back to her.

15

MAEVE

Maeve walked into her suite, looked around, took five steps over to the couch, and collapsed face-first down onto it with a loud and heartfelt groan.

She had taken Josie home and gotten her settled before getting the whole story, which was pretty much exactly what she thought it would be. Josie spent the whole night at the party. She had no idea what happened to Jason, or who could have wanted him dead. He was an asshole, but he wasn't the kind of asshole who collected murderous enemies. Someone filling his jockstrap with itching powder? Sure. Someone murdering him in cold blood? It made no sense at all.

Maeve hesitantly brought up her dream, and the strange way the cops had reacted to him being pushed off a roof in the dream, but Josie didn't think anything of it. She was less than willing to entertain any conversation about the circling, dizzy loop that Maeve's mind was on, and almost bit her head off when she brought up the weird figure in the back of both that dream and her later nightmare. Maeve quickly backed off, frustrated but not angry, understanding how upset Josie was.

After a few cups of undrunk tea and a whole lot of tears, Josie's mother burst in the front door and took over. She was a stout Filipina woman who practised corporate law in Phoenix, Arizona. She jumped on a plane as soon as Josie called her, still in the back of the police car on the way to the station; with some good timing on flights, she arrived in town just seven hours later.

Feeling a little like an unnecessary appendage, Maeve had given out a bunch of hugs and kisses and then left the small family to it. It was getting late, she hadn't eaten anything all day, and she was still hungover and exhausted from her poor sleep. More importantly, she couldn't shake the feeling that whatever was going on, it was linked to her dream in some way. She had dreamed Jason was dead, and now he was. Not just dead—murdered. She was having a hard time explaining that away as a process of her overactive imagination. Thinking about it only frustrated her, though. She had no answers for how a dream could be to blame for a person's death. It left her feeling irritable and guilty, jumping at shadows.

Getting up from the couch, Maeve staggered over to the kitchen and tossed some water on to boil, then went and booted up her computer. Or tried to—it was already on, and she ended up turning it off by mistake and then having to wait for it to power down so she could turn it back on. Grumbling, she tapped the screen a few times as if that would make it wake up faster, which of course it didn't. Finally, it was on, and she watched her original copy of her nightmare video again. The figure in the background was no easier to see this time. She wondered if it was Jason, but the height and build were totally off. *Anyway, how could Jason get into my dream? And what would that even mean?* Maeve shook off the odd thought.

Maeve opened the original, unedited dream file of Jason's so-called murder and watched it carefully. Once again, it provided no further insight. There was the shadow, watching from the edge of her perception. There was Jason, looking remarkably similar to how he did in real time, except for the fantasy-inspired outfit he was wearing. It was eerie seeing him there, knowing he wasn't alive anymore. Like the dream had captured a piece of him, pinned like a butterfly and made him dance. Would he have trouble moving on? Would peace be hard to find, when this little fragment was stuck here?

She shuddered at the line of thinking. *Get it together, Maeve.*

There was enough going on without the added fear of restless spirits. She wasn't sure she even believed in souls, or an afterlife. She wasn't religious, not really, but she believed there was some kind of spiritual aspect to the world. Maybe that was just energy, energy that lived beyond death, that impacted the world. Maybe there was a pattern, a Creator of some kind. But where Jason was now—and what dreams were really a reflection of—she had no idea.

Maeve generally scoffed at the idea that dreams reflected some deeper meaning or reality. Her dreams were ridiculous, and they weren't based on anything but the media she happened to be consuming at the time. They weren't portents of the future or glimpses into some shared collective consciousness. They were just the brain processing random bits of unprocessed information.

Probably.

The sound of the pot lid clattering brought Maeve back to the present. She tossed in a box of white cheddar Kraft Dinner and gave it a stir. She quickly cleaned out the air fryer, then tossed in a chicken breast seasoned with some salt and pepper and some baby carrots. As she cooked, she let her thoughts drift back to the videos. If she could figure out what about them was out of the ordinary, maybe she could start to narrow in on why her instincts were screaming that the dreams were, somehow, to blame for all this.

So what did she know? In the dream with Jason, a dark figure was watching from the shadows. Then, at the party, she felt a presence like someone was watching her. After blacking out, she had a nightmare where a handsome stranger warned her to wake up, and she didn't recognize his face from anywhere. A dark figure then chased her home. At the same time that she was dreaming her nightmare, someone in the real world killed Jason—she didn't know exactly how. A woman who looked similar to Josie had been nearby and may or may not have been involved.

What did all of those threads have in common? Dreams acting in unexpected ways. Could there be clues in other, earlier dreams? Had this all started with Jason, or did it go back further?

She cranked the dial on the air fryer for twelve minutes and drifted back to her computer, where she opened the last dream she had before everything went strange: the narrative dream in the castle. She played the unedited copy and watched it carefully, looking for anything out of place. Were there any people out of place? Dark shadows concealing watching figures?

She was three minutes in when she saw something. If she'd been holding a plate, she probably would have dropped it in her lap. The guy from her nightmare—the handsome stranger who had warned her about the danger—was in the dream. He didn't seem to have a character, which is probably why Maeve hadn't recognized him. He was just standing around in the background of a lot of the scenes, wearing clothing appropriate to the setting and watching the action with an amused tilt of his sensuous lips. *Ugh, you did not just think the word sensuous, Maeve.*

She barely heard the alarm when it went off, finally pushing herself up and out of her chair when she remembered that, unlike the air fryer, the pasta wouldn't turn itself off. She kept glancing back over her shoulder as she chopped up the carrots and chicken and stirred it into the pasta. She grabbed the pot, a large spoon, and a fabric trivet, then stomped back over to the computer and went back to it, mindlessly eating out of the messy, makeshift bowl.

She didn't have to reopen the nightmare file to know that it was the same person. His face was seared into her mind, and she was sure he was no one she knew from the real world. She had thought it was strange enough when the shadowy figure appeared in two dreams in a row, but this man had been in two and she hadn't even remembered him.

Only two?

Nervous, Maeve started opening old unedited video files and scanning through them. There was the bar she had been thrown out of before the slugs appeared. And in the background, just behind the bouncer? The handsome stranger with a smile on his face. Horrified, Maeve went further and further back. The man appeared often, though not always. Usually, he was in the background, just watching without interacting. Occasionally he played a role: he was a tutor in one steamy Victorian dream and a swashbuckling pirate to her cyberpunk assassin in another. She had no idea how she hadn't made the connection, except that his roles were so minor, and he was often just on the periphery of her vision. Half of the time he didn't even make it to the edited versions of the dream, the ones she posted. Which explained why fans hadn't noticed, either.

Capturing a still shot from one of the dreams where he was more prominent, she did a reverse image search. Nothing came up except for a few look-alike actors or models, none of whom were exactly right.

"Who are you?" Maeve demanded, knowing there would be no answer. "What do you *mean*?" She was glad when the screen didn't answer; by then, she half-expected that it would.

Maeve went to bed early that night, after a quick check-in with Josie by text and her mom by phone. Of course, her mother was absolutely freaking out and kept asking for Maeve's assurance that she wasn't a suspect. She had to stretch the truth a little bit to promise that she was barely on their radar, but she didn't feel any guilt over the lie. She was pretty confident that the footage of someone who looked like Josie committing the crime ruled her out.

Idly, she wondered if Ms. Aranda knew enough about Josie's relationship to want Jason dead, and then immediately felt guilty over the stray thought. She'd only met Josie's mother a few times, and she was a strict woman who didn't open up easily, but that was no reason to suspect that she was a murderer.

"I've never had a single person sit in that chair and tell me that a person they care about is capable of murder," Maeve remembered Reid saying. She shivered. There was no way Josie could have done something like that and lied to her face about it afterward.

Was there?

Guilt immediately washed over her. She knew Josie as well as she knew herself. Maeve believed that anyone could be pushed to murder if they were defending their own life, but she didn't believe Josie would lie to her. There was no way that Josie was involved in Jason's death, even peripherally.

It was no surprise that Maeve's dreams that night were turbulent. She didn't remember any of it after she woke up, and there were so many tiny files on her computer that Maeve knew none of them would be worth posting. Short files meant she had been dropping in and out of REM sleep, and there wouldn't be any coherent narratives in the soup of her thoughts. She trashed the files without bothering to convert them.

She couldn't bring herself to get much work done, so she spent the morning lazing around in the giant sweatshirt she had stolen from an ex and watching bad TV. By lunch, she was feeling guilty enough about playing hooky that she checked her messages and answered her emails. Most of them were from friends who had read about Jason's death in the papers and wanted to know what happened. There weren't many details yet; the cops were keeping it under wraps while they completed their investigation, according to the article. It just said that Jason had died under "suspicious circumstances" and that the cops were asking anyone who might have been nearby to contact the department.

There was an email from Laura about recording lines for the interactive portion of the VR project, and something about 3D modelling her hands, which she glossed over and agreed to without much thought. It would pay her bills for the next several months, and with the ad revenue she was getting from the—her mind skipped over *murder dream* and stuck in the words *Josie dream*—she would even have enough for that trip with Josie. *If Josie still wants to go after all of this is over.*

She wondered if the video had seen an uptick once the news of Jason's death hit the internet, and she clicked over to Zzz+. As the video loaded, her eyes widened, though whether in delight or horror she couldn't say. She had to look at the number twice to process what it even was; there were just too many digits. Nineteen million? *Nineteen million views?!* She couldn't figure out what that meant in a dollar amount. Sixty thousand? Seventy? She had never seen a payout like that, not ever. Her video with the highest views had been seen almost a million times, but that was over a two-year period. This happened *overnight*. And the number was going up, slowly, even as she watched.

Her eyes were naturally drawn to the comment section, but what she saw there drained her joy like a bad haircut.

Watched this ystrdy and last night had exactly the same dream except it was my ex pushed off a building! Maybe he'll die too, lol, one post read.

Can't wait to kill off my ex in a dream, ha! another user said.

But it got worse from there.

Maeve scanned down the comments, barely breathing. Some people talked about a creepy feeling of being watched that lingered after they closed the video; others wanted to know how she had made the dream feel so lifelike. Hundreds talked about having their own version of the dream, or the feeling of the dream following them into the waking world. And over and over people tagged their friends. *Gotta see this,* one read. *Whole new thing!* said another, and *So cool!*

Maeve got up and paced back and forth in front of her computer, her breath coming in little gasps. When she tried to calm herself down and breathe deeply, she felt like she couldn't get enough air. Her vision swam with black dots, and she sucked in a desperate breath. Was this what a panic attack felt like? She grabbed the back of the chair and blinked rapidly, fighting to get back to a normal breathing cadence. Were you supposed to breathe in longer than out? She couldn't remember.

Maeve scrambled back into her chair and logged into the creator portal, her mouse hovering over the delete button. As her breathing evened out, she stared again at the number of views. She couldn't give up income like that, not when she had no idea what was truly happening with the video. Plus, deleting it might make her look guiltier in the eyes of the police. Really, common sense said she should keep the video up. The killer might even post a comment that would lead the police to his—or her—capture. *Whatever's going on, the video isn't the cause of it. It can't be.*

There was some kind of connection, though. She couldn't deny it. There was the man she kept seeing, and her strange experience at the party. They were pieces to a puzzle that Maeve didn't have enough information to solve. But whether or not the dream was somehow to blame for what had happened, the damage was done. Jason was dead, and taking down the video wouldn't bring him back.

Maeve turned off her computer screen before she could do something drastic and stalked into the bedroom. She just needed a distraction, that was all. She would take a shower and then go over to Josie's and see if there was anything she could do to help. Maybe bring some pho or something.

After all, she could afford it.

16

PERI

Peri got home late in the afternoon on Wednesday, absolutely wrung out and wondering why anyone in their right mind wanted to be an actor. The work was fun, but the days were gruelling, and there was way too much talking to strangers for Peri's comfort. They had chatted with strangers in the green. They had chatted with hair and makeup. They had chatted with PAs and DPs and several other acronyms that they didn't know the meaning of. No one had really taken the time to explain—well, anything—and Peri had constantly felt one step behind and one step removed. The bonus, they supposed, was that they didn't have time to think about any of their lurking troubles.

They nearly collapsed on the floor as they came in, gathering Juniper up into an enthusiastic cuddle that the cat happily returned. They sat like that for long enough that their butt started to hurt, but they didn't move until Juniper decided she'd had enough and squirmed out of Peri's arms. Only then did Peri get up. They put away their jacket and tucked their shoes back onto the mat by the door, then grabbed their backpack and took out the e-reader and water bottle, stowing each in their proper place.

Grabbing their phone, Peri connected to the wireless speakers in the kitchen and living room and chose a quiet, woman-with-her-guitar playlist. They were determined to sleep well and deeply, and they were going to start early. Relaxing but exhausting, that was the goal. First up, dinner. Peri put out a cat soup snack for Juniper, then grabbed their laptop and clicked through their recipes. They pulled up the ingredient list for seitan and got to work. It was a simple recipe but took a lot of time.

While it boiled for an hour, Peri changed into workout clothes and went through a basic dance routine on YouTube. The music was from the latest Pixar movie, and Juniper came and watched, baffled as always by Peri's occasional desire to leap around the living room. They only worked out a few times a month, way less than they knew they should, but they always meant to do it more.

They had time for a quick shower before the seitan was finished, and they put on their fuzziest slippers and softest bathrobe. Heading back to the kitchen just as the timer went off, Peri drained the seitan, chopped it into fine pieces, then blended some vegetables and tossed the slurry into a frying pan. They added coconut milk, tomato paste, more spices, the chopped seitan, and some chunky broccoli, and set it to medium-high heat. They fed Juniper dinner while the mixture cooked, then took their own meal and dished it into a shallow bowl.

With a serving of naan on the side, Peri took their dinner over to the couch and turned on the TV. They ate while watching comfort movies they had seen a hundred times before; *Serenity* first, then *Encanto*. They had a bowl of ice cream during the second film, which they tried to feed to Juniper, but she wasn't buying cashew milk as a good dairy alternative and walked away in disgust.

By ten o'clock their eyes were drooping, and they decided it was late enough to start getting ready for bed. They took their anti-anxiety meds, then grabbed their testosterone kit and readied an injection. They usually took their weekly dose on Sunday, but they always noticed that they slept more deeply on nights when they were dosing. Testosterone helped sleepers stay in the REM cycle, which meant less bouncing in and out of the dream state. Peri regularly increased or decreased their T, wanting to achieve an androgynous look without growing facial hair, so they weren't worried about one extra dose. They would take a little less on Sunday and it would even out in the wash. They injected the T into the fatty part of their thigh, which hurt a lot less than the muscle injections that used to be common, then tossed the used syringe in a medical waste container and washed their hands.

Peri was in bed by twenty after, lights off and Juniper curled up on their feet. They were worried sleep might be elusive again—that they might crave it too badly—but their dual strategies of action and relaxation had done their job. Peri was asleep within five minutes.

Peri came back to awareness standing on the deck of their child-hood home. Looking down, they saw that they were wearing their brother's clothes, T-shirt proudly displaying Spider-Man swinging across the city, canvas shorts riding high on their thighs. They seemed to be their adult self despite the clothes, but when they peeked into their underwear they grinned. "Oh, hello there," they said, and were pleased to hear their voice dipping at least a quarter-octave lower than usual. In the waking world, Peri strove for androgyny because it was the closest they could get to fluctuating fully between male and female as they would have liked. Some days they highlighted femme charac-teristics and other days they highlighted masc characteristics, depending on the situation and how they felt.

In dreams, on the other hand, Peri could experience being physi-cally and completely male or female, each a reflection of their heart and soul in the moment. It was a truer reflection of their gender, but one that was largely impossible in the waking world. Not every gender-neutral person felt that way, of course. It was Peri's truth, and dreams were the place where it manifested best.

Climbing up onto the top of the deck's plexiglass railing, Peri spread their arms wide and felt a warm summer breeze play across the small hairs on their arms. This was a flying dream, one they had dreamed dozens of times when they were a child. *Huh*, Peri thought. *I'm dreaming. I know who I am—I wonder what else I can do here?*

"Don't fall," a soft voice whispered behind them.

Dexterous despite the narrow surface, Peri turned. On the deck below them, arms wrapped protectively across her chest, stood the woman Peri had seen in so many dreams. She was largely unchanged, dressed today in the same kind of homemade dress that Peri's grand-mother had often made for them as a child.

Peri reached out a hand. Hesitant, the woman took it, and Peri pulled her up into their strong arms. A hand across her back kept her steady, and she planted both hands against Peri's broad chest, though the expression in her eyes had more fear to it than Peri was comfortable with. After a moment, they realized the fear was not of them, but for them.

"Are you safe?" the woman asked.

"I think so. I took off the device, like you asked me to. But..." Here Peri hesitated. They didn't want to ruin this moment. They wanted to ask her about herself, learn her name, what she loved, what she hated, who she *was*. They didn't want to waste time with practical questions— but they couldn't stop clinging to the rational, even now. "Elements from the dreams have started leaching into the waking world."

"You say that as if it shouldn't be possible." The woman laughed, tilting her head toward Peri and half-closing her eyes. "As if the waking world is real and this is just an illusion."

"If this is real, tell me!" Peri insisted. Then considered their next words carefully. "Or... show me."

The woman looked up at that, eyes sparkling. For a moment she studied the shape of Peri's face, the hesitant quiver of their lips. But then the humour drifted away, replaced by clouds of worry once more. "I don't know how long I have."

"What do you mean?"

"There are too many signals," she says, voice rising slightly in alarm. "Too much noise. I'm being drawn in a hundred directions, turned into moments that are no part of me. I'm having trouble... clinging to myself. Finding myself at all. I think I'm losing pieces, but I don't know, I don't understand! I've been trying to reach you, but I couldn't."

"You were there. In that nightmare."

She nodded, breath coming a little ragged, eyes wild. "I saw you trying to come to me, but something had its claws in me, and I was dragged away." She looked up at Peri, sustained eye contact pushing her terror through to Peri, as if to make them understand. "I don't want to be anyone's monster."

"You said it was the technology. The recording device?"

"I don't understand everything," the woman admitted. She pressed her face against Peri's chest and Peri held her closer. "But there are some dreams that cling to me, drag me around with them. I should be able to leave, slip easily from one to the next, but I can't. Someone dreamed about the device, and then another, and I thought they must be something real, in your world. Something I don't understand."

Your world. Peri heard the words and knew them for truth. They tightened their grip unconsciously. "Who are you?" Peri asked.

"This is my home," the woman said, lifting her face and pointing awkwardly with one hand, her arm mostly held in place by their tight embrace. Peri knew instinctively that she meant the dream itself, and not the place it represented in the waking world.

"You're... a dream?" Peri asked.

The woman wrinkled her forehead. "No. That's not—it's hard to explain. You make these places. But we live here. You are the creators, but you know nothing of what you build. Most of us don't even consider you beings, did you know that?" Then quickly, as if to forestall objections, she went on, "But I know that isn't true. I've seen you. I've watched you, and I've seen the wonder in your eyes at the worlds you create. It's magic, isn't it? You have magic in your veins, and you bring it to life so carelessly."

"No one has ever called me magic before," Peri whispered.

"You are incredible." The woman brought her hands up, touched Peri lightly on the sides of their face, as if to hold them there. "Can you hold me here?"

"How?"

"I don't know. You call to me. Just—keep calling?"

"I couldn't stop if I wanted to," Peri promised. "Every atom of my being calls to you. Even when I'm awake, when the world I'm building isn't there, I think of you. I remember you. I wish you could be there always."

"I wish that too," the woman says. "I want to be myself again."

"How can I help?" Peri asked.

"Just this. Hold me and let me be myself for a little while."

Peri brought their chin down to rest on the top of the woman's head. Her hair tickled their nose, but they didn't mind. They tipped backward, off the railing, and the woman gasped in momentary fright— then laughed as Peri swooped up, away from the ground. This was a flying dream, and Peri was in control of it.

Together they climbed higher, up into the blue skies. Clouds drifted here and there, soft as cotton candy and twice as sweet against their lips. It clung to their eyelashes as they moved through it. Soon the city was spread out below them, lazy in summer, the people tiny dots moving against the shimmering steel landscape. Peri tilted sideways, so they could both see the calm expanse unfolding.

"How long does this dream last?" the woman asked.

"As long as I can make it," Peri promised.

They drifted on, neither speaking, the warmth of the sun above a soothing lull, the breeze a promise of things to come. They drifted on, safe in each other's arms.

17

MAEVE

Being a suspect in a violent murder investigation turned out to be nothing like Maeve had expected. Over the next few days, life just sort of... continued as it always did. Josie's mother hired a great lawyer, who agreed to represent Josie and offered Maeve some legal counselling on how to talk to the press about the case, ostensibly to help protect Josie but more likely because Ms. Aranda also felt sorry for Maeve and wanted to make sure she didn't do anything stupid.

But other than meeting with the lawyer a few times, there was nothing much for Maeve to do. There were no more calls from the police, though a few reporters did manage to track her down. Two of them asked her about the video, one going so far as to question whether her dream had been inspired by a desire to see Jason hurt. Thanks to the lawyer's coaching, she had a bland response prepared, and her quote didn't even end up making the papers.

Fielding well-meaning calls from friends and family was a little harder, though there weren't an overwhelming number of those, either. Her mother had gone into full-blown overprotective mode, trying to have her over for dinner every second night, and Maeve had given up trying to put her off. The company was nice, and since she hadn't had any captivating dreams the last few nights, she didn't have a lot of work to do editing or putting together promos. She was a bundle of nerves, and kept reminding herself that it was a good thing that there were no cops knocking down her door. But the odd combination of stress and what should have been relaxation was eating away at her. She had acid reflux for the first time ever and was chowing down on Tums like they were candy. They tasted pretty good, surprisingly, but it was still annoying.

She was sitting cross-legged on her couch, wearing a blanket over her head and watching a documentary about a man who was wrongfully accused of murder and got out thirty years later, when her phone rang with a call from an unknown number. Debating the pros and cons, she decided to answer. "Maeve here."

"Hi, is this Maeve Kessler?"

No, it's a completely different Maeve, pretty weird coincidence, right? "That's me."

"Hi, Maeve. My name is Claudine Atazadeh. I'm a reporter for Global TV and I was hoping I could ask you a few questions."

Maeve muted the TV. "Sure, I'm happy to answer any questions that aren't a violation of my or my friends' privacy," she said. The lawyer had said that response would put the reporter on the defensive and assure them that she wasn't going to give them any tabloid-style dirt.

"Are you aware that Jason Geddes was pushed off a roof?" the reporter asked.

Maeve felt her brain short-circuit. Her mouth moved but no sound came out. *I'm having a stroke. This is what a stroke feels like. What did she say?*

"Hello?" the reporter asked.

"He—what?" Maeve managed.

"I've spoken to a source at the coroner's office, and they've confirmed it. The police are trying to keep it under wraps, but I think it's an issue of public safety and that people should know. Do you have a comment?"

"Are you sure?" Maeve demanded.

"I'm sure," the woman confirmed.

"Jesus fucking Christ," was all Maeve could manage.

"Do you have a statement you'd like to make?" the reporter repeated.

"I. Um. No? I don't—I mean, I'm totally—sorry, I just need to process that information. They didn't say anything to me. You'd think they would have said something to me, right?"

"So, the police didn't tell you how he was killed."

"No. They said they couldn't."

"Do you think someone saw your video and copycatted it?"

"God, I hope not," Maeve said, and then thought that probably wasn't the smartest thing to say. "Look, I'm sorry, I know you're just doing your job but I'm kind of reeling so I'm just going to hang up now."

On the other end of the phone the woman was saying something, but Maeve couldn't hear what it was; she had already pulled the phone away from her ear. She let her hand fall to her side and stared at the TV, where silent people talked about the failure of the courts to protect an innocent man.

Jason had been pushed off a roof. Her worst fears were manifesting. She had tried to tell herself that Lee's odd hesitation when she mentioned the details of the dream was nothing, but she had *known* it couldn't be. All that work telling herself that she was overreacting. All that insistence that the dream couldn't be the reason Jason had died. Telling herself, over and over, that she wasn't to blame.

But she was. The dream she created, the dream she had chosen to post, had been used as some sick template to murder a man.

Maeve scrubbed her cheeks, hiccupping around sobs. *It doesn't mean it's your fault*, she thought as her breath hitched and caught between sobs. It was only a dream. Whoever killed Jason had made that choice, regardless of whether they were motivated by Maeve's video.

It explained why the cops had been keeping the details under wraps, though. They probably didn't want people to start copycatting the murder. Unless... What if people already had?

Adrenalin spinning through her veins and pushing the tears away, Maeve picked up her laptop from where she had abandoned it on the coffee table and pulled up the news. She typed in, "Man pushed off roof," and saw with horror that there was more than one recent article. She clicked through them, her pulse buzzing as her wild eyes tracked over words. One man dead in Chicago. Another dead in London. Another in Montreal. Port Douglas. Akaroa. All in the last week.

There were others, too, from earlier in the year, but the cluster of events this week felt too staggering to be coincidence. Maeve sat back, crushed. People around the world were dying, being pushed or falling off roofs, just like Jason. Just like her dream. That had to mean her dream was at the heart of it all. If her dream was contagious, the implications were staggering... but could she be sure there was a solid connection between her dream and these deaths? She had to know more. If this was her fault, she would do everything she could to make it right. But she couldn't quite make herself believe any of this was real, even with so much evidence laid out in front of her.

It just didn't make *sense*. The world didn't operate under these laws. It was so improbable she wasn't sure anyone would believe her, even if she had rock solid evidence to present to them. She didn't believe it herself. She considered going onto the forums and asking for advice, but what would she ask? She had no idea how to talk about any of this. She needed more data points.

Leaning back over the keyboard, Maeve jotted down the victims' names and the towns they were from, then did some cross-referencing to try and find common usernames they used online. She managed to track down three of them. Then, she logged into her Zzz+ account and did a search through the comments for those usernames.

Watched this video seventeen times, one read. *Can't get it out of my head!*

You all really dreaming this? Totally wanna dream too. I'm gonna be the prinze, lolz, the second said.

Why can't I stop watching this! It's on a loop in my brain, I swear to god! the third said.

Panicked, Maeve navigated back and forth between the victims' usernames and the three comments, thoughts tumbling in blind panic. All three comments were dated the day before the victims' deaths.

This can't be real. This can't be happening. It has to be a coincidence. Maeve pushed away from the keyboard, shaken. Maybe she hadn't done as good a job playing detective as she thought. And people died falling from roofs all the time. More than she would have thought before she put "man pushed off roof" into her search.

She had to answer these questions, or she would completely lose it. Maeve went back to the original articles and wrote down every-thing she could find that seemed relevant, then went back to her search program to double-check her work. As she was diving into the second victim's social media accounts, her hand froze over the mouse. Could the cops look at her history? Would all of this research implicate her in Jason's death?

Scrambling, Maeve grabbed the laptop and cleared her browser history, then cleared her cookies and cache just to be safe. She navi-gated back to the video, hesitated, and then clicked on the edit func-tion. Her mouse hovered over it for a moment. Was she being insane? Dreams couldn't influence people to conjure a murder into existence. The people in her dreams couldn't step out of her computer and commit murder on their own, either.

And yet... if she ignored the evidence of her own eyes, she risked being complicit with everything bad that happened after this point. She felt conviction settle heavily in her bones.

Maeve closed her eyes and took a deep breath, trying to think over the evidence as logically as she could. There were four deaths, all people being pushed off roofs. The most direct explanation was that a serial killer had seen her dream and copied it. Except... No. The cities were too far-flung. One person would never have been able to get from one to the other quickly enough.

The least logical explanation was that the dream was *causing* the murders. There had to be a theory that was less fanciful than a murder video but not so easily disproved as a serial killer. A dream so vivid it inspired people to murder, made them want to deal with the bullies in their own life just as they had seen dream-Josie take on her own bully? But the people watching the video weren't commit-ting murder. They were dying.

Then there was the feeling she had at the party that she was being watched, which lingered in her dream that night. The most logical explanation was that she had been drunk and scared, and that fear bled into her dream. The least logical explanation? That some element from the dream had influenced the real world—that she had seen something from her nightmare while she was still awake, thanks to the mind-bending effect of alcohol.

Last, but not least, there was the man who had warned her about the danger, the man who had been in her dreams for months without her knowing. She had never noticed him before, despite editing the dreams and watching them over and over. That was disturbing, and she had no idea what it signified.

No logical reason answered her questing thoughts. She could not come up with anything but the illogical answer: that something in her dreams was aware. And it wasn't friendly.

Maeve opened her eyes, trembling and cold. Whether she believed the most logical answers or the least, the facts were clear: the video was at the heart of this. Removing the video was the only thing she could do. She worried the police would find it suspicious, but even that wasn't enough to stay her hand. The video had to be destroyed.

She wished she could call Josie and talk it over with her. That was what she always did before she was about to make an impulsive decision. But there was no way she could lay any of this on Josie. Her friend was going through way too much already. She would have to trust her instincts and hope for the best.

Maeve deleted the video from all three of her feeds. She scoured her social media and deleted every post she'd made about it: every promo image, every gif, every teaser. She even got up, went to her desktop computer, and moved the raw files onto her backup hard drive. That way she could turn them over to the police if she had to, but she wouldn't be tempted to reupload them in a moment of weakness. She stuck the external drive in her bottom desk drawer and leaned back against her chair, breathing like she had just finished a marathon.

It was done. Now if only it was over.

~

A few hours later, Maeve was back at her marathon of true crime when her phone rang. She answered through her watch without checking to see who it was first, out of habit, and then winced when she saw the caller ID.

"Laura!" Fake enthusiasm dripped through her voice. "Heeey."

"Seems like there's a problem with your feed," Laura said without preamble. "I'm seeing a bunch of angry comments that your Jason video is gone from all of your feeds."

"Right. Yeah. Well—I deleted them."

"Did the cops make you? Fuckers! They have absolutely no legal standing—give me the number, I'll call and straighten it out, we'll have you up and running by dinner."

"No, uh." Maeve rubbed her eye, wishing she could disappear into the couch. Or go back in time and not answer the phone call. "It was just me."

"What? Why?"

Maeve debated lying, but she had no reason not to tell the truth. She doubted Laura would be on her side, but she didn't have to be. "People have been saying they watched the video and then had the dream and then... someone in their life got pushed off a roof?"

There was a pause. "What are you saying? That makes no sense."

"I know. It's weird, it's, uh—" Maeve rubbed the back of her neck awkwardly. "But I took it down."

"Maeve, don't be ridiculous. No one is watching a video and then pushing someone off a roof."

"They literally are."

"Listen, okay? This is classic impostor syndrome. You're just afraid of success! You're reading into all this stuff that has nothing to do with you and it's freaking you out. And no wonder! You're under a huge amount of stress. Can anyone blame you if you're taking it hard? Someone you know died. You need to process it, okay? Tell you what. Put the video back up and then go for a spa day. You can afford it!"

"You want me to get a facial? People are dead!" The familiar thrill of anger pulsed through her, and Maeve sat up straighter on the couch.

"People die every day. It's not your fault when someone has a heart attack raking leaves. And it's not your fault when someone gets pushed off a roof! You didn't make it happen. That's not how this works."

Maeve shook her head, adamant. "What if it is? What if the rules are changing, and we don't understand it?"

"Maeve! Please! Get a grip. This is your *career* on the line," Laura snapped.

"You can't bully me into putting the video back up!" Maeve snapped back. She was proud of herself. She never stood up to Laura, trusting her to make decisions about her career even if they felt wrong. That was going to change.

"I'm not bullying you. I'm talking sense into you! I negotiated your contract on the VR project based on the popularity of that video. You can't just—"

"I did just." Feeling better than she had in days, Maeve lay down on the couch. "Besides, that contract is signed, there's nothing they can do about it."

Laura's voice was clearly coming through gritted teeth. "And what about the next contract, the next deal? There won't *be* one if you turn into some loose cannon that no one can rely on!"

"There'll be more dreams. But this one is gone and there's no unpopping the balloon."

"You're going to give me a stroke. I'm fifty-two years old. You want a death on your conscience? It'll be mine." Laura hung up without waiting for Maeve to answer.

Maeve starfished on the couch, both exhausted and relieved. The last two years had been full of constant pressure to do what was right for her career, to perform, to get that next deal, to make that next video. Now that there was something more important to prioritize, Maeve was flooded with relief.

A bubble of laughter burst out of her, loud in the silence of her tiny suite. Laura might be right. This might have been the wrong move for her career. But it was the right move for *her*, and for the first time in a while, that mattered more to her.

The first person she wanted to call was Josie—she'd been wanting to call her all day. But Josie had her own stuff to deal with, and Maeve doubted more conspiracy theories about the video were the distraction her friend needed right now—or that they would be well received. Instead, she got up and got dressed. She had promised to have dinner with her parents, and though she'd been dreading it all day, she suddenly craved the warmth of their laughter. At the last minute she packed an overnight bag with fresh underwear for the next morning and a toothbrush. Maybe she would crash on the spare bed. It might be silly, but it seemed like bad dreams couldn't follow her back to her childhood home.

And she was growing more and more afraid of her dreams.

18

PERI

With a deep breath, Peri opened their eyes. The guided meditation left them feeling calm and loose-limbed. They blew out the candle burning in front of them and climbed to their feet to turn on the lights, almost tripping over the grey bundle that was Juniper watching their strange behaviour with querying judgment.

Peri had spent the last several days immersed in lucid dreaming techniques. If they could gain more control over the dreams, like they had during the lucid flying dream they had shared with the woman, they might be able to create a permanent safe haven, some-where the woman could rest from other dream signals even when Peri wasn't there.

Their previous foray into this subject focused on clickbait posts like, "How to Lucid Dream In Just Five Minutes!" and "Lucid Dreaming 10 Easy Steps!" Now, they moved on to scholarly articles about the psychology of lucid dreaming. One article argued that those in a lucid state engaged multiple parts of their brains, creating a network that was more powerful than the sum of its parts. Another compared lucid dreaming to the state of psychosis in that both could be accompanied by dissociative tendencies, which Peri stressed about for the next several days before storing it away in an anxiety drawer in their bed to take out at some inopportune moment in the near future.

First up was "reality testing," which Peri had already done a little of. The theory was that by making an action habitual, you would start doing it in your dreams, but that, since it was a dream, the test would fail, and you would realize you were sleeping. Peri had chosen to press their extended index finger against the palm of their other hand to see if they could push it right through. They did this every hour or so throughout the day.

For the last two nights they had used the "way back to bed" technique, which just meant they set an alarm for five hours after they went to bed, got up and did Mensa mind puzzles for twenty minutes, and then went back to sleep. It was supposed to make your mind active in the hopes that you would stay aware once you fell back asleep. It did seem to produce more dreams in the second half of the night, which Peri considered a win even if they hadn't fully unlocked the lucid aspect.

They had attempted to return to a previous dream after waking up, which was successful and had even seemed to lend more lucidity to the experience. But Peri wasn't convinced they had fully fallen asleep, rather than drifting and daydreaming. Where was the line? How deep did they need to go before *she* would be there?

They were currently trying a technique where they attempted to meditate and enter a hypnagogic state just before falling asleep. It was definitely relaxing, but they were fairly sure they lacked the discipline to truly shut off their mind while also trying to be creative and create a world to enter. They couldn't label it a failure until they went to sleep, but they weren't hopeful it would yield results.

They had gotten a few glimpses of the woman, but so far only in the context of the early, traditional dream. By the time Peri grabbed lucidity the woman was gone; or perhaps trying to force lucidity drove her away. There had been no conversations with her after flying together in that beautiful dream.

Peri wished they had recorded it so that they could revisit it whenever they wanted, but the woman's warnings and fear were too palpable. They had to settle for their memories for now.

Their phone rang, and when Peri glanced at the screen they saw it was the buzzer downstairs. Excited, they buzzed the delivery person into the elevator. They ran to the door and bounced up and down on the balls of their feet, waiting. They only had one package on the way. This had to be it.

Peri opened the door just as the man approached, accepted the package with a smile, then shut and locked the door before running into the kitchen to open the cardboard box. Inside was another cardboard box, cushioned by brown paper and proudly declaring that the device within would unlock all of Peri's wildest lucid dreams.

When their research brought up the idea of wearable lucid dreaming devices, Peri was hesitant. The device was simple: a headband with two electrodes that rested on either temple. The electrodes released a gentle electrical charge that was supposed to stimulate brain activity and help drop the wearer into a lucid state. It tracked the user's sleep cycle and only delivered stimulation during the dreaming phase, thereby not interrupting the more delicate rest cycle of sleep.

Proponents swore by the devices, while critics dismissed them as a complicated placebo. The technology had been around for almost a decade in its most basic form, but there weren't a lot of peer-reviewed studies detailing its efficacy. It was unrelated to dream-recording tech, which had come about as a result of accessibility research into reading and translating brain waves.

On top of that, the device couldn't be used in conjunction with the recording tech because the electrical signal it put out created too much interference. That incompatibility meant that when dreaming skyrocketed into public awareness, lucid dreaming wearables had stayed decidedly niche. Peri had found this company because a dreamer they followed claimed using it every second night helped train their brain to lucid dream more easily on the nights they weren't using it. Peri was eager to try anything, and this was low on the scale of how drastic they were willing to go.

After a quiet afternoon and evening, Peri got ready for bed with more excitement than they had felt in a long time. They settled in and picked up the device. It was a sort of headband, open at one end, with two large plastic nodes that settled against either temple.

They got the device in place, then lay staring up at the ceiling for a while. The weight against their forehead wasn't substantial, but it was distracting. Peri wasn't a delicate or light sleeper, but it took some effort to relax into their pillow and forget about the alien pressure on their temples. Finally, when they closed their eyes and let their breath steady, it wasn't long before the world slipped away to be replaced by something far more enchanting.

Peri was standing in a field of cornflowers whose texture reminded them of thick oil paint. The scene was very like a movie they had once seen where Robin Williams wandered through a world styled after his wife's paintings. Experimentally, they reached out and ran a hand across a blossom. Sure enough, the tiny petals came away on their hand, and when they closed their fist, it opened to a smear of colour across their palm.

Peri realized with a start that they were inhabiting no character. There was no story propelling them through the dreamscape. They weren't a pirate prince, sitting in this meadow awaiting a lost love. They weren't a shepherd, wiling away the hours under the cloud-brushed sky. They were just Peri, dreaming an oil-painting dream, inspired by a movie they saw a decade ago. Peri poked the palm of their hand with their finger just to be sure—and their finger slid minutely into their hand.

It worked! The lucid dreaming device worked! Delighted, Peri concentrated on their surroundings. As if a giant brush had dipped into paint and was now adding a new layer, all of the flowers around them turned scarlet. Next Peri concentrated on their own body. They wiped away the last of their small breasts and slimmed their hips to boyishness. They changed their clothing from the black pants and white shirt that the dream had put on them to a paint-splattered jumpsuit. A brush appeared in their hand.

Momentarily distracted from their goal, Peri began to play. It had been so long since they had done something for the sheer joy of it, and they found that their joy infected the world around them. The flowers were soon a riot of colour, strange alien shapes rising above the meadow, petals flaring and alive. The sun received a laughing smile and was soon singing an off-tune wordless melody to which all of the flowers bobbed and danced. Peri was covered in paint, a streak across their nose and another matting their eyelashes on the right side, but they didn't mind.

They had never felt so free.

After rearranging the flowers a few more times and building a little cottage in the distance, Peri walked up the hill to the building they had just created. The closer they got, the more details appeared, until they were standing in front of a beautifully wrought English summer cottage straight out of *Pride and Prejudice*. Or that one where they moaned about being poor because they only had the two servants. Peri admired the roses climbing up the trellis by the door, the broken pottery sitting as a decoration in the garden. Everything was so crisp and tangible despite being rendered in broad brushstrokes.

Peri looked at the door. They took a calming breath, closed their eyes, and opened them again. "Okay, here's how this is going to go," Peri told the door. "I am going to open you, and you aren't going to lead into the cottage. You are going to lead me to a place outside of this. A place beyond my mind. You are going to find a mind that shines like diamonds, that is warm as a summer fire. You are going to find a beacon in the sea and guide me to the lighthouse."

Peri closed their eyes and reached forward. They found the round doorknob, which turned easily. Without opening their eyes, Peri took a long, confident step over the threshold. They opened their eyes...

And were immediately battered by howling wind and torrential rain. They raised both hands against the gale, squinting to take in some of their surroundings. The cottage was gone, as was the quaint painted effect. The world around them was darker, less detailed. They were on the deck of a sailboat, in the middle of the worst storm Peri had ever seen. The sky was a mass of roiling clouds and the occasional lightning flash, and the rain hit almost horizontally thanks to the strength of the tempest. Almost invisible through the storm, Peri could see the faint beacon of a distant lighthouse.

At the bow of the ship, an unfamiliar woman struggled with a rope leading up the mainmast; Peri didn't know much about boats, but it seemed that she was trying to lower the sail.

Closer to Peri, a man in a grey raincoat was watching her work. There was something about him that seemed to set him apart from the dream, but Peri wasn't sure what it was. A solidity, maybe. He didn't seem as vague and poorly defined as the rest of the dreamscape. A moment after Peri noticed him, the man tensed, sensing something, and turned their way. They made eye contact, and it was clear that whatever he had felt, he hadn't been expecting Peri. He looked over Peri's shoulder and they followed his gaze, glimpsing the door to the meadow that was still ajar behind them—a rectangle of light in an otherwise dismal world.

Peri only glanced away for a moment, but by the time they looked back he was in their face, his wide frame menacing despite the fact that Peri was at least three inches taller than he was.

"Who the hell are you?" Though he was clearly yelling, his words were half-stolen by the storm's rage, and Peri had to fill in the blanks by reading his lips.

"Is this your dream?" Peri asked, but they could tell their voice wasn't carrying. They tried again, yelling and pitching their voice lower, and he seemed to understand. He looked angry enough, at any rate.

"You shouldn't be here! How the hell did you even—?" Once more he glanced at the doorway behind them. Peri checked it reflexively, relieved to see it was still there.

This dream didn't feel like one of theirs. It wasn't crisp enough, and Peri had no particular affinity for sailing. This felt like the nightmare of someone who had once been trapped in a storm. Peri laughed even as the wind whipped their face and the man loomed angrily over them. It had *worked*. They were in someone else's dream. They had left the boundaries of their own mind for wholly uncharted territory.

They had hoped the door would lead them to the woman. It seemed to have taken Peri literally instead, bringing them to a lighthouse in the sea. Or had it? Was it possible she was here, somewhere, just waiting to be found?

19

MAEVE

Whether her childhood bed had somehow wrapped its worn comforter around her shoulders and protected her, Maeve didn't know. All she knew was that she slept deeply—and if she dreamed, she woke with no memory of it. Her father made her pancakes in the morning, the way he used to do on Sunday mornings when her mom slept in, and Maeve finally allowed herself to relax.

Being at home was easy, but the world didn't disappear the way she wanted it to. When she finally got back to her own apartment a little before lunch, she was exactly where she had been the day before, just twenty-four hours later.

She spent the day as busily as she could, answering messages and trying to put out the fires that deleting her video had lit. She filled in the holes in her promo schedule with some older popular videos, using a 'best of' angle to appease new fans who might not have seen her earlier stuff, then spent two hours going through her closet and getting rid of clothes she never wore or that didn't fit her. The purging was soothing—she wasn't a very organized person, but every couple of years the spirit hit her, and it felt good to be tackling something that was totally under her control.

She bagged up the stuff she didn't want and scheduled a pickup from a charity organization, dropping the bags in her tiny storage room until then. She was craving something healthy but didn't have anything in the house, so she ordered a chicken noodle soup and a big salad from a place down the street and ate in front of the TV.

The evening went by easily. She did some crafts, read a cheesy romance novel, and watched a few more episodes of her true crime show. It was nearly midnight before she decided it was time to sleep. She checked to make sure the door was closed, brushed her teeth, and then pulled off her clothes and crawled into bed. Just before her eyes drifted shut, she remembered to attach her dreaming nodes, and then she was out.

The bomb whistled as it fell, a trail of white pointing down to where devastation would be wrought only moments later. Maeve ducked as it fell on the building to her left. Chunks of concrete and fragments of shattering glass rained down, barely missing her as she crouched low against the side of the building.

"We'll never get through!" Seamus hollered.

"You just need to have faith!" Maeve yelled back. The noise of the bombs and the fighting around them was deafening, but Seamus was only a few feet behind her. He was still wearing his school uniform, the shirt torn to reveal some of his muscled chest.

"I have faith. In you," he said.

"And I have faith in them. Faith enough to spare," she promised. She grabbed his hand, and he squeezed it tight, though he looked no more convinced than he had a moment before. "We just need to get a little closer. We must be ready to move."

He nodded grimly, and the two of them moved again. Darting from cover to cover, they took shelter behind blasted-out cars and towering doorways. Every few seconds another bomb fell; some were dangerously close, while others could be heard whistling as they fell upon nearby streets.

Soon they reached the edge of a wide, open roadway. Just on the other side was a large, boxy building with a huge antenna tower reaching into the sky. It alone was unscathed. Neither bombs nor bullets marred the perfect black stone of its facade.

"There it is," Maeve breathed. Her eyes widened. They had done it. They had come this far.

"Do you really think—" Seamus started, but stopped again as he looked up. Maeve followed his gaze. The bombs had stopped falling, and for a moment, the city was wreathed in smoke and a perfect, icy stillness.

"They did it!" Maeve shouted. "They took out the targeting defence system! I told you they could do it!"

"We better move!"

Maeve nodded. There was no time for celebration. They had a job to do. Looking both ways, the pair took off across the street. Maeve braced for the sudden impact of bullets, but it seemed no snipers guarded the doors. They made it across the street and into the shadow of the building.

"This is it," Maeve told him, stopping him in the doorway. "If we can get in there and send the signal, the Zixians will come and wipe the Calidoori out. Earth will be free."

"And if we fail—"

"You don't have to tell me the stakes," Maeve interrupted. She held up her arm; the ugly scar from her escape from the implantation centre was stark against her pale skin.

"I know," Seamus apologized. "I just..."

He wrapped an arm around her waist and pulled her close, waiting for a signal that it was welcome before dipping his head down and smashing his lips against hers in a hungry, desperate kiss. She touched his hair, his face, felt like the sweat and grit of their desperate run for survival and knew this was the other half of her, the answer to the questions she had been asking all of her life. And there was a good chance they wouldn't both make it out alive.

He pulled back and they looked at each other. There was so much to say, but no time to say any of it. She nodded instead, and he nodded back. And that was it. No time for more.

Maeve pulled the door open and prepared to face the monsters.

The inside of the building was cool and dark. She entered cautiously, Seamus close upon her heels. As her eyes adjusted to the shadows, she expected to see the towering carapaces of the Calidoori soldiers, or even the deadlier but stupider monsters they used as foot soldiers. Instead, all was still and dark. Slowly, the room began to come into focus, shadows transforming into recognizable shapes: a desk, a large ergonomic chair, a set of shelves.

One shadow to her right remained dark and difficult to see. She turned toward it, hand tightening on the small knife that was her only weapon. The shape launched toward her, but it didn't turn into a monster—or not the kind she had been expecting, anyway. It was a person, still wreathed in shadow and difficult to see. She was so taken aback that she failed to get out of the way fast enough; the humanoid figure managed to knock her down, the knife skittering from her hand and rattling across the floor. Maeve rolled away and disengaged, rising cautiously to her feet.

"You did this to me!" the shadowy figure screamed. Maeve was shocked to hear a woman's voice, powerful and resonant but clearly human, with a local accent rounding out her vowels.

"Maeve!" Seamus yelled. He tossed her his knife, and she caught it in mid-air and twisted back around in one smooth motion, putting the slim shard of metal between her and her attacker.

"Listen, lady. I don't know who you are—"

"You did this," the woman snarled. "And you're going to pay."

She launched herself at Maeve with a guttural roar. Maeve slashed with the knife, barely keeping the other woman back. "I'm just trying to save the whole goddamn human race!" Maeve hollered. "Maybe we don't have to do this right now?"

The woman didn't seem to hear. Even at this distance her face was shadowed, as though the dim light couldn't reflect off her features. It was as if she had been cut and pasted into this world from a film reel with less ambient lighting; nothing here touched the darkness that shrouded her. The woman ducked low, but Maeve spun around and past her, over to the controls.

Maeve hit the necessary buttons to send the signal. That was it. She had done it! She had—

All the air dashed out of Maeve's lungs as a bony shoulder connected with her solar plexus. She went down, the woman squarely on top of her.

"You're too late," Maeve panted, struggling to get her knife arm free. "I've already—".

Her face exploded in sharp lines of stinging pain as the woman's fingernails raked across her flesh. Grimacing with effort, Maeve wrestled her knife up between them. The woman snarled, face bestial and full of fury even through the shadows that obscured her exact features.

She grabbed Maeve's hand and knocked it to the side, pinning her down with shocking strength.

Maeve had done it—she had sent the signal! If the woman wasn't here to stop her, what *did* she want? She said she wanted Maeve to pay. It seemed like that debt would be settled in blood—or her very breath.

20

PERI

The man on the boat cleared the gap between him and Peri effortlessly. There was nowhere to go except back through the doorway, and Peri wasn't yet willing to flee. They held their ground instead, wishing they had a sword or a staff or some other weapon. They had no idea who this man was or whether he was dangerous. He looked more than powerful enough to overwhelm them physically, though that wasn't saying much. Peri was slim to the point of fragility.

"How did you get here?" the man demanded again. "How did you open that door?"

"I just... opened it," Peri said. "The way you open every door."

"It shouldn't be possible," he said, but the words were low enough the storm almost stole them, and Peri had the feeling the mumble wasn't directed at them. His next words were, though, and they were heavy with anger. "You are playing with forces you don't understand! You're like a child rampaging through a field of chrysalids, destroying everything in your path with a laugh!"

"Then tell me!" Peri yelled back, refusing to be intimidated. "Tell me the truth!"

There was a scream, guttural and enraged, and both Peri and the man looked around for the source of the noise. Peri recognized it immediately. They ran to the side of the boat, looking for her in the storm, but there was nothing but wind and rain and waves that ate the horizon.

A second scream followed, this one higher pitched, more frustrated. A different voice, clearly. Peri looked back over at the man, intending to question him on what was happening, but saw to their fascination that he was opening some kind of doorway in the air. It hadn't occurred to Peri to consider how their own doorway had appeared in this scene, but now that they thought of it, their breath caught. Had it been just like this for him, observing them? They hadn't seen how the man had created the new doorway, but it manifested in the air like he was opening the door of an advent calendar, neatly splitting the sky and boat. He stepped through before it was fully open and vanished through to the other side.

Peri raced after him, but by the time they had cleared the ten feet or so that separated them from the man's vanishing point, no trace of the door remained. Peri waved their hands through the air, frustrated and angry, but whatever method he had used was invisible to them.

Peri ran over to their own door and leaped through. They appeared back in the sunlit world they had created. The comparative silence echoed and buzzed in their ears after the rage of the storm, and even the warm breeze made them shiver as they stood in their wet clothes. Peri grabbed the door and yanked it closed, blinking away impressions of sunlight that were burning behind their eyelids.

Thinking hard of her, of only her, of her hair and her lips and her desperation, Peri opened the door and stepped through again.

They looked around in dismay. They were standing in the middle of the country cottage the door clearly led to. Normally they would have been delighted by the porcelain place settings at the little table and by the small library across from the fireplace with a comfortable sitting chair arranged to catch the best light from the window. But they barely took any of it in. Instead, they stepped out, closed the door, and tried again.

Only the cottage.

Peri screamed, adding their own frustration and rage to the world, wondering if somewhere their voice was echoing, too. If the woman of their dreams could hear it, wherever she was. If she could follow it to its source.

One thing was clear. Wherever the strange man had gone, Peri didn't yet have the skills to follow. But they would learn—they would learn, and they wouldn't be kept from finding their way back to her.

21

MAEVE

There was nowhere to go, no path to escape. This woman was determined to kill her, and Maeve was starting to fear that she would succeed. As much as she twisted and writhed, she could not dislodge the shadowy woman. "Get! Off! Me!" Maeve grunted.

Suddenly the pressure on her chest was gone. The woman sailed through the air, and as Maeve watched in wide-eyed terror, the still-shadowed figure vanished through a— a— Maeve's mind stuttered and halted, not able to comprehend what she was seeing. It was like someone had cut a hole in the air itself, a perfect rectangle leading to a space even darker than the one they were in. The woman went through it and disappeared, and someone stepped up and waved his arm, sealing the space up as if it had never been.

He turned toward her, and Maeve's forehead crinkled in concentration. There was something so familiar about him, about his curly brown hair and the warmth of his dark eyes. But she couldn't place him no matter how hard she tried.

"Are you all right? Did she hurt you?" the man asked with surprising care. He knelt in front of her as if to help her up, but when he saw the scratches on her face, he became distracted. Reaching out, he moved to touch her, but she jerked back. She had no idea who this man was, but she wasn't about to let him paw her face just because he saved her life.

"What the hell just happened?" she demanded.

"I can't always be here," he told her. "I was lucky I happened to be close and listening. You have to be careful."

You have to wake up. Maeve was struck by the memory of those words, as clear as if he was speaking them now. She felt the twisting confusion of fear, not knowing where the memory came from or what it meant, but at the same time the words made her feel... calm. Safe. When had he said them to her? On a street, she somehow knew, in a place so different from this one—in a time unalike as well.

"I know you," Maeve said, frustrated, trying to sort her memories into buckets that made sense.

"Time to wake up," he decided, and he gave her a gentle shove.

Maeve came awake surprisingly gradually, given the shove that had belched her out of the dream. Groggy and out of sync, she turned over and snuggled into her pillow, enjoying the softness of the sheets against her arms and shoulders. When the dream started to come back to her, she remembered small details first, then all of it crashed over her like a tidal wave. She sat up, rubbing the sleep from her eyes, and took a moment to process what the hell had happened.

She had been deep in the dream, in the persona of some freedom fighter, and she had been attacked by— Was it the shadow from her other dreams? A woman, definitely, and one she had no memory of seeing before. It had to be the same figure, she was sure of it. And that voice! She had been so *angry*. She said it was Maeve's fault... but what was "it"?

The woman also told Maeve to leave, told that she shouldn't be "there." But those interactions had all happened within Maeve's own mind. How could she leave her own mind? It wasn't fair that someone could hate her—could want to hurt her so passionately— when she hadn't done anything wrong. Or had never been told how to avoid whatever it was that she was doing.

The man in the grey coat, at least, had clearly had her best interest at heart. He had come to save her, knocking the woman out of the dream before doing the same to Maeve. That could mean the woman was a person, dreaming just like Maeve was dreaming. It could be that there was someone out there with technology that Maeve knew nothing about, something that let real people walk into the dreams of others. Maeve shuddered to think that technology might let a stranger enter someone else's mind without permission. The consequences of that were staggering. How could you ever protect yourself? Maeve had no idea what she would do to keep herself safe from the woman in the future.

And if the woman was a dreamer like Maeve, what did that make her rescuer? She hadn't remembered him, not at first, but eventually, Maeve's actual memories had intruded upon her dream-self's reality. It had all been flooding back when he shoved her and woke her up.

Maeve got up and made her slow way into the living room, grabbing a baggy T-shirt on the way to ward off the chill. She sat down and opened her computer, where the dream files were sitting, waiting to be processed. She frowned, looking at the file—and as she did, the skin on her cheek pulled painfully.

"What the hell?" She touched her cheek and found it sore to the touch. Picking up a picture frame sitting by the computer, she used the glass as a makeshift mirror to investigate the source of the discomfort.

Four deep scratches stood out in stark red against her pale cheek.

Maeve swallowed. She reached up and trailed her fingers across the scratches. She could feel them, sharp lines of stinging pain. She lined her fingers up with the scratches, but they were a little too close together to be self-inflicted; anyway, her nails showed no signs of blood or skin beneath them, which indicated that she wasn't going around mauling her own face in her sleep.

What the hell was happening? What were these dreams, and who were the people in them? The stranger, the woman... They felt real, in some way she couldn't explain but just *knew*. She was dipping her toes into something terrifying, and whatever it was, she no longer thought she was wrong to wonder if Jason's murder had something to do with it.

Her eyes travelled back to the computer screen as she thought. When they focused, she saw the files sitting there, waiting to be rendered. "Fuck that," she whispered, her voice raw with emotion. With a few flicks and a tap of her fingers, Maeve deleted the dream file. Whatever was in there, she was going to do her best to protect the world from it.

"Shit, shit, shit, wait." She scrambled for the recycle bin, but in her haste the gesture controls misread her click and she emptied it. "Dammit!" Maeve dropped her head into her hands and then recoiled at the feeling on her raw cheek. Why had she done that? She should have at least watched it over again! She might have missed an important detail or forgotten something that she thought was clear.

Had the woman said, "This is your fault"? Or had it been more like," This is on you"? What if there was nuance that Maeve was missing? Then again, watching her last dream had done horrible things to her fans. She had no reason to believe that *she* was immune from those same negative effects. Maybe deleting it had been the right thing to do. It had been smart. She was taking the cautious path.

Maeve got up and started to pace her tiny main room, thinking furiously. Whatever was happening in her dreams, she had to learn more about it. But how? There were only two people who seemed to know what was happening, and she could only get at them in her dreams. What she needed was a way to stay in the dream world for longer. A way to really connect and get the answers she needed. She needed...

Oh, fuck. Am I really doing this?

22

PERI

Peri woke slowly from a deep sleep, groggy and disoriented when they didn't see the sweet English cottage around them. As they took in the familiar shape of their bed and the room beyond, they wondered if they were still dreaming. Then they heard it: a banging on their door.

Throwing off their comforter, Peri nearly tripped getting out of bed, and had to take a moment to brace against the mattress. They were physically drained despite just having woken from a night of sleep. *A really long night,* Peri realized when they saw the clock by the side of the bed. It was after eleven.

Peri hurried through the condo, nearly tripping over Juniper, who threaded through their feet in anticipation of their delayed breakfast. Peri picked her up so she wouldn't try to dash into the hallway when they opened the door. Juniper was uncharacteristically squirmy and unhappy as Peri pressed her against their chest.

Awkward with the struggling cat, Peri unlocked the door and opened it.

They weren't awake enough to be expecting anyone, and it didn't occur to them until they swung the door open that no one had buzzed up. So, they were surprised on two counts to see a stranger standing in front of them. The man was in his fifties, wearing jeans and a button-up shirt that were worn but clean. He gave Peri such a shocked look that Peri glanced down, not sure what to expect.

They were soaking wet from head to toe. There was even a trail of water dripping down the hall. No wonder Juniper was so angry! Peri put her down and gave her a little shove away from the door, apologizing mentally, then held their arms over their chest, self-conscious.

"Can I help you?" they asked.

"Sorry to bother you. Your brother called the building. He said he was worried that you weren't picking up your phone and asked if we could check on you."

"Are you kidding me?" Peri demanded, and immediately regretted the outburst. It was Kyle they were angry at, not the building manager.

The man shifted from one foot to the other. "Um. Should I... not do that in the future?"

Peri winced, his kindness adding lemon juice to the wound of their guilt. "I'm sorry, but no, thank you. I'm a private person, and my family worries for no reason. I'll talk to them. Sorry. Thank you, sorry," Peri said, closing the door before he could get a response out.

They were fuming, guilty and awkward anxiety just fuelling their anger. *What the hell was Kyle thinking!* They hunted for their phone, which they found on a counter in the kitchen where they had probably put it down while they were making dinner. Picking it up, they started a video call with Kyle. They wanted him to see the fury on their face.

He answered quickly. "Peri! Thank god. I thought you were dead."

"Where do you get off calling my *building manager* to knock on my door?" Peri demanded.

"Did you not hear the part where I thought you were dead?" Kyle answered, laughing, completely disregarding the anger radiating off Peri in waves.

"You don't know anything about my life, Kyle! I might have been out of town at a conference. I might have been camping for the weekend." He started to laugh, but Peri plowed on, not letting him interrupt. "I might have been doing a lucid dreaming technique that requires meditation and concentration. I don't tell you my plans! Vanishing on you doesn't mean I've vanished from anybody else!"

Kyle's face got really close, peering at the screen. "Jesus, Per. You look like shit."

Peri could see their reflection in the small box at the bottom of the screen. There were deep shadows under their eyes—they hadn't been sleeping well since they started to work on lucid dreaming techniques during their nightly ritual. But it was none of his business, even if it was true.

Peri turned off the camera. "Better?"

"Come on, you know I didn't mean it that way. I'm not allowed to be worried about you?" Kyle asked in his usual wheedling tone.

"No! You're not!" Peri knew they sounded childish and petulant, but they were so *tired*. They couldn't think past the fog of anger. It was a hand pressing on their chest, a monster breathing in their air, urging them on.

"That's bullshit. You're my sis—bling. You haven't posted in forever, you don't answer my calls. I'm supposed to worry!"

Kyle's concern rankled. It was so hollow. *Supposed to worry?* That was nothing but obligation. He was checking off the box labelled "Keep In Touch With Family," while dodging the complications that came from actually being in Peri's corner. Kyle wanted so badly for everything in his life to be simple and ordered. He had never been able to handle that Peri was messy. Or that their family was so much to blame for that.

"How about this?" Peri suggested bitterly. "How about I promise never to answer your calls again and then you don't have to worry when I don't?"

"That's a bit extreme."

Peri closed their eyes, fighting back tears. They had to get off this call before they took it somewhere they had no intention of going; the last thing they needed was to dredge up old wounds. *Where were you when I actually needed you? You didn't do anything when Mom and Dad slammed the closet door on me. You didn't stand up for me because you were too afraid of "making it awkward."*

"Look, I'm tired, okay? You woke me up and I'm grumpy and I

don't want to deal with this. Let's just leave it before we things we can't take back."

"Are you—" he started to ask, but Peri had already hit the button to disconnect the call.

Crumpling to the floor, Peri pressed their palms against their eyes in a vain effort to stem the flood of tears. Kyle had no idea what was going on in their life. He never did. Peri remembered a night, decades ago, when Kyle had woken them up late at night. He had led the way out the window of the cabin they were staying in with their family and onto the roof. Outside, he'd put his sweater over Peri's shoulders and pointed out the few constellations he could remember, in cautious whispers that carried easily in the silence.

The night had been so dark and the sky so full of stars. Staring up at that glittering expanse, their eyes steeped in the sheen of childhood, it was impossible not to believe in magic. There was no way the world could contain such beauty and not the wonder that went with it.

They had sat out there together, barely speaking, just staring up at the sky, for a long time. It was the last time Peri could remember being in sync with their brother.

Was that his fault? Was it theirs? It was so easy to blame Kyle for letting them down, for not standing up for them with their parents. But the truth was, they had never been close to their brother. They weren't close to anyone, not in the ways that counted. Here they were, immersed in a story the likes of which they could never have imagined, could never even have dreamed, and there was no one they trusted enough to tell.

Peri sniffed and wiped away the last of their tears. They had always been a solitary person. They didn't have a lot of friends, and they were happy that way—genuinely. But they knew that over the last few years, they had let even those few friendships slip away. Their life in dreams had been so compelling that they had forgotten how to nurture their waking life. Now, they were truly alone, and solitude didn't seem as compelling as it once did. They were desperate to reach out, even for a sympathetic ear, but there was no one whose reception they could be certain of.

And testing the waters with someone they weren't entirely sure of? That could be disastrous. Peri knew how it would all sound. They had been in therapy since coming out and breaking off contact with their parents, when their anxiety and depression had spiralled. If anyone didn't believe Peri, it would be painfully easy to put them under involuntary observations. Their therapist Jasmine, Kyle, even their friends on Discord were threats.

Peri knew they had taken their fear and anger out on Kyle, and it wasn't really fair. He tried, in his own way. He continued to reach out even when Peri never reciprocated. The only reason they had a relationship at all was because he was persistent, cheerful, and unbending. He was as stubborn as Peri in his own way, and he deserved better from a sibling.

It wasn't his fault Peri's world was collapsing. But it was up to Peri to do something about it. If they couldn't talk to anyone in their life about what was happening... maybe they could talk to people who *weren't* in their life. Maybe they could find a way to take back a little of the control they were missing, re-establish their equilibrium.

After feeding Juniper and taking a long, hot shower, Peri felt a little more human. They texted Kyle an anemic apology, saying they were stressed about a project and just needed a little space. They changed their sheets, which smelled of salt and were still damp from the night's dream, and then got set up in front of their computer.

They opened recording software and gave their image a critical look, but eventually decided it didn't really matter how they looked.

Taking a deep breath, Peri turned on the camera.

"Hello. My name is Peri Briggs. You might know me as Dreams-Away, my streaming handle. I've been recording my dreams for nearly four years and was one of the early adopters of the technology. Dreams have always been very special to me. Some people think of dreams as a poor reflection of the waking world, but I've always known that they're more. Dreams are powerful. They're a glimpse into another world, one as real and tangible as ours." Here Peri paused. They pressed their lips together and dragged their teeth briefly across the folded edge, wondering how to phrase what they had to say.

"Lately, I've been experiencing side effects of the technology that we all use to record dreams. I've been approached by concerned parties who have told me that the technology is dangerous. It has side effects that we don't yet understand. It's doing something to the dreams. Not just recording them. Something about being witnessed, being logged, changes the nature of the dreams. I don't have proof to offer aside from anecdotes. I know I'm making a wild claim and asking you to make a change based on faith. But that's what I'm doing, I guess. Taking a leap of faith.

"I'm asking you to stop recording your dreams. Pay attention to them. Pay attention to what changes when you don't record them. And ask yourself if you notice a difference. Be a critical consumer, and demand further answers. This technology is supposed to be harmless. But it was developed with a one-sided understanding— how to record brain signals and translate them to images. We've gotten good at identifying more complexity in the signal output, but we still don't understand what a dream *is*. Until we better understand what we're touching when we enter that state, we cannot in good conscience continue to use this product.

"Thank you."

Peri turned off the recording and let out a deep sigh. There. It was done. There wasn't a lot to it, and they weren't sure if anyone would be convinced by something so tenuous, especially when it came to changing their habits or abandoning a lucrative source of income. But if people even stopped just for a night or two, maybe it would give the woman the breathing room she needed to find Peri and tell them the rest of the story. Maybe it would help, a little bit.

Peri uploaded the video. Then they went back through all of their old footage, deleting any of the dreams that featured the woman from both their streaming pages and their archives. It would seriously impact their royalties, and Peri wasn't sure how long they could keep paying a mortgage with what remained, but they would figure that side of things out in good time. For now, they would do anything they could to help.

Anything.

23

MAEVE

Shoving her hands deeper into her pockets against the fall chill, Maeve looked around the park and mentally kicked herself for agreeing to meet in such an isolated spot. It was her first drug deal, though, and she hadn't really thought it through. She'd tried magic mushrooms and MDMA a few times, but she'd always been able to find a friend to hook her up. This time, she had to go a little further outside of her social circle.

Blank had only been on the market for a few years, though from what Maeve knew it was a blend of the active ingredients from various psychoactive herbs that had been used to connect with the beyond for thousands of years. As usual, the capitalist-industrial complex had taken sacred medicine and turned it into something moderately addictive and mildly dangerous by distilling those oneirogens into pill form. From what Maeve knew, it was possible to overdose on them, but unlikely. The addictive quality was mostly psychological, as the dream state it evoked was deeply restful and incredibly engaging. People found a world they wanted more than the real one, a world with no consequences and no permanence.

She could understand the appeal.

It seemed like the perfect answer to her dilemma of how to

connect more fully with her dreams. On Blank, she might be able to stay present long enough to shake someone until answers fell out.

The only problem was none of her friends were into it.

It hadn't been safe to take street drugs in Vancouver for years after the fentanyl crisis started in 2015. It was mixed into everything, from party drugs like MDMA to harder hits like meth, cocaine, and heroin. Thousands of people died from accidental overdoses. With the legalization of weed in 2018, a lot of people in Maeve's circles just sort of lost interest in anything else. The occasional person would show up to a party with shrooms, and in her university days people tried all kinds of weird things like salvia and ayahuasca, but for the most part, they stuck to legal substances like weed and alcohol and left the rest of it alone.

Blank was new enough that it was popular for the novelty, but more cautious users avoided it not knowing what the long-term effects might be. Most of what she had researched in anticipation of making this purchase had just been anecdotal. She knew she was taking a risk, but at the same time, she was pretty sure she could handle it. If she could get through the process of buying it.

She'd managed to find Jason's friend, Douchebag McGee, on socials. She'd asked him for his hookup, and he'd eagerly given her a phone number to text and the name, "Duke." He'd also started messaging her dumb memes, which was apparently the price she had to pay for making it sound like she cared about anything other than his Blank dealer. *That's the last time I try to be polite to someone I've nicknamed Douchebag McGee.* She'd reluctantly texted 'Duke,' and arranged to buy the smallest number of pills that seemed reasonable.

So here she was in Central Park at 2:30 p.m. on a Tuesday afternoon, waiting for a guy in a blue jacket and red shoes to approach her. She wasn't sure if it was paranoid to be worried that the police were following her, but just in case, she'd gotten off a stop early on the train and walked back to the park, taking quiet side streets to make sure no one would follow her. She had the cash in her pocket so she wouldn't have to go into her purse to get her wallet, and she was pacing back and forth and checking her watch every few seconds in case she missed a text or time suddenly jumped eight minutes forward.

She saw him coming down the wide paved path. He wasn't what she was expecting, although she wasn't entirely sure what she *was* expecting. He was younger than her by a few years, clean-cut, wearing faded pink jean shorts despite the cool afternoon. He had on a nice, short-sleeved printed button-up, the blue jacket he had described in his text, and a pair of red sneakers that made candy apples look dull. He clocked her checking him out and zeroed in on her with a friendly smile.

"Maeve?" he asked.

"Yeah. Hi."

"Nice to meet you. Duke." He offered a hand and she took it, blowing out a nervous breath. "First time?" he asked with a chuckle, and she felt her cheeks get a little warm.

"I made it that obvious?"

He grinned. "I can tell. People have that look, you know? Watching the shadows thinking an undercover cop is gonna jump out of the bushes."

Given that was *exactly* what Maeve had been picturing, she couldn't quite make herself laugh. Of course, he had no way of knowing that she was on a watchlist for an active murder investigation. *It's not paranoia if they're really out to get you.* "No, yeah. I know it's fine."

"It's all good. Look, there are kids playing in that park." He nodded his chin, and Maeve turned to look. Sure enough, there was a play structure not that far away, and a few kids were climbing around on it, watchful parents keeping an eye. It made her feel significantly worse, not better. She didn't want kids who were just trying to play and live their lives to witness a drug deal. And she *really* didn't want any of them noticing her and saying anything to a helpful nearby police officer...

"Should we... like... go somewhere else?"

He laughed. "It's not like we're shooting up. We're just having a conversation, making a transaction. It's only a matter of time before it's all legal, anyway. You know they're doing tests on therapeutic use of acid in treating PTSD? More effective than any current medication and half as addictive."

"Yeah, I heard about that, it's pretty cool."

"And this stuff is *way* less intense than acid. It's actually pretty fun stuff. You had it before?"

"Uh, no."

"Cool, cool. Make sure you take it before bed, like, be tired already, you know, or you'll totally mess with your circadian rhythms, and it'll be absolute hell trying to get back on a schedule. It takes about half an hour to hit, but don't stress if it takes longer, everyone's bodies are different, you know? Whatever you do, don't decide it isn't working and take a second one, okay? Trust me. It's working!" He laughed, and this time Maeve found herself joining him.

"Yeah, I've done that with edibles," she said. "*Not* fun."

"Right? Every rookie's first mistake," he agreed. "The first time I tried edibles I got so paranoid I thought my friends were aliens in skin suits and the only way to make sure they left Earth without conquering us was to convince them we were so dumb we wouldn't be worth the effort of enslaving. Shaved both my eyebrows off."

Maeve barked out a surprised laugh, embarrassed at how sudden and sharp it was. The last of her nerves faded, and she gave him a genuine smile. "I'll make sure to avoid razors."

He laughed. "Don't worry, you'll be out like a light. Make sure your roomies don't draw penises on your face, though."

"Noted."

"So, you got ten pills here, ten bucks a pop, but since it's your first time I'm giving a discount, so it's eighty all in, yeah?"

"Yeah." Maeve glanced from side to side. "Do I just... hand it to you?"

"Not like that, you look like you're buying drugs," he teased. "How would you hand over money if you were paying your friend back for the delicious tea he bought you?" He pulled his backpack around and took out a canister of Tetley tea.

"That's some pretty fancy tea," Maeve teased back. "What is it, shat out of a monkey?" She took the money out and handed it over as casually as she could, and he slipped it into his backpack and zipped it up in one smooth motion. Maeve dropped the tea canister into her purse and zipped it closed.

"Why would it being shat out of a monkey make tea *more expensive*?" Duke demanded.

"It's a coffee thing. The most expensive coffee beans in the world are eaten by some animal and then pooped out. Monkeys or lemurs or something."

"No. What. Actually?"

"True fact," Maeve swore.

Duke laughed. "Fuck. And people think the stuff *I* sell is messed up."

Maeve grinned, and he nodded his head.

"You let me know how it goes, keep in touch. Have fun with it."

"Thanks. I will." Maeve hiked her purse up higher, and they each went in opposite directions down the path. At the end Maeve glanced back over her shoulder, but Duke was long gone. *Huh. So that's a drug deal.*

That night before bed, Maeve made sure she was prepared. She didn't have anything to drink for three hours before sleeping to avoid any unfortunate accidents in a pee-mergency should she fail to wake up—she'd heard some bed-wetting stories that weren't pleasant. She put on a T-shirt and an old pair of pajama pants in case she wandered out of the apartment or did anything strange while she was out of it. Another story featured someone who woke up mid-trip—still groggy and half-dreaming—because she had driven a tractor through the side of a barn.

Maeve considered calling a friend and asking them to watch her sleep, but all of her friends these days had day jobs. She couldn't think of anyone who would want to miss a night's sleep just to give her some peace of mind except for Josie, and she had enough going on that Maeve didn't feel like she could impose.

She could have waited until the weekend and had any number of people willing to help her, but she was anxious to get it over with. She had too many questions, and she was too afraid to spend the whole week thinking about them. If she did, she might start to wonder if she was losing her damn mind. If any of this was real. If *she* had killed Jason, and all of this was a paranoid delusion she had built up in her mind because she couldn't bear to face the truth.

Maeve settled down to sleep. She was expecting a smooth transition, but she was still amazed at how seamlessly sleep stole over her. One minute she was lying in bed, trying to decide if she felt anything yet...

And the next, she was standing on a cobblestone street, feeling the rough edges of the wide, flat stones through the thin leather soles of her slippers. All around her the market was alive with activity—to her left Charmaine was grilling roast rabbit and onions on sticks over a small fire, the grease dripping into a tray to be sold later to Mrs. Arbuckle, who made the most amazing pies in the city. Next to Charmaine, a young woman had crisp red haw berries for sale, also on a stick and drizzled in barley sugar.

Maeve took a deep breath. Festival day smelled different than any other day. It wasn't just the cookies in the shape of the princess that people only baked today, or the glue from the many lanterns that people were constructing as they sat outside their houses and talked, watching their children idly as they ran around playing games and shouting. If she had been pressed, she would have said it was the smell of joy, but she knew that was silly. Could joy be said to have a smell, though, it would be the smell of today.

"Maeve! Are you ready?" Alyse popped up beside her. Slight and dark-skinned, Alyse had a smile almost as wide as her very narrow hips. She was wearing a simple but elegant green dress slashed with blue at the sleeves and skirt. Her thick hair was braided through with blue ribbons for the occasion, and Maeve winced, imagining Alyse's mother's strong hands and how long her best friend must have been sitting, squirming in her chair, to have it done.

"We won't be chosen," Maeve said as she linked her elbow through Alyse's. Despite her words, she was wearing her second-best dress, blue linen that she had painstakingly embroidered with suns, moons, and of course, stars. The stars trailed down her full skirts and swirled around her hem in bright yellow and cheerful white. If only they could have been silver, she would truly have looked like the sky brought down to Earth, but silver thread was beyond the means of anyone who lived in the village. Only the nobles in the castle looking down at them could have such a thing.

"We might be chosen," Alyse reminded her. The touch of her fingers against Maeve's arm was warm, roughened by the calluses on the tips of her fingers from all the sewing and baking she did. "Someone has to be!"

Giggling, the two girls raced through the crowded market toward the stage that was set up in a corner of the town square. The square itself was strung with decorations, silver stars in a sparkling line; small fires in narrow, tall containers gave extra sparkle to the gilded finish. The square was already packed with other young women hoping to be chosen as the Star Queen, to sit at the head of the festival and take the place of the missing princess. Maeve doubted she would ever be chosen for such a great honour.

But it was always nice to dream...

On the platform, the prince was already smiling at the crowd, handing out favours to the children who clustered at his feet. Small candies, pennies, and here or there a wooden tree or carved star. His long hair was pulled back in a simple club at the nape of his neck, and he was wearing tight, royal blue pants tucked into tall black boots. His coat was open, showing off a black vest with buttons shaped like stars. Each button was connected by a delicate gold chain, and he shimmered almost as brilliantly as his smile.

Maeve watched him, daydreaming. If only she could catch his eye from across the vast space. He would take a deep breath, as if amazed to find a woman of such beauty and grace in the ranks of those he had never paid attention to before, leap down from the platform in a single motion, his curly black hair coming loose from its ties and fluttering in the burst of motion. Walk across the huge space, the puzzled crowd making room for him as he moved ever closer...

"Maeve," Alyse gasped. "Maeve!"

She blinked, trying to clear the fantasy and return to reality—but the prince was truly coming toward her! She grabbed Alyse back. It wasn't —could it be?

He moved closer, and there was no question it was her that his eyes were fixed upon. The band began to play a slow waltz, and as the prince came to a stop in front of her, he held out his hand in invitation.

"I know you," Maeve said."

"You shouldn't," the man chided. He took her hand and began to turn her in a slow and gentle dance. Around her, the people began to fade away, the square falling silent except for the gentle music still carried on the air and the steady murmur of wind in the nearby trees.

Maeve stared, enraptured. "I do know you," she said as a deluge of real memories came flooding into her mind. The dream she was inside of was so real, so tangible, that for a moment she felt the memories of the real world fighting with the dream memories. Was she a dreamer from another world at all, or just a girl in a marketplace who dreamed of being more than she was? Who did embroidery and wanted to be the Star Queen, to watch the lanterns fill the sky tonight and create their own magical universe right here, in this place.

The real Maeve won, clawing her false memories aside like an imprisoning cocoon to emerge, gasping and lucid, at the front of her mind.

"You shouldn't be able to remember me," the man said. Then, almost to himself, he muttered, "What the hell is happening lately?"

"I took some drugs," Maeve admitted. She squeezed his hand, felt the warmth of his skin, the smoothness of his nails. "I feel everything about you. You're real."

"I was already real," he snapped, but even as he did, he pulled her closer, spinning her. She didn't know the moves to this dance, but he made it easy to follow; she wasn't sure if it was because he was such a confident lead, or if it was because the dream version of herself hadn't entirely evaporated when she took control. Was it still there, feeding her memories and bits of reaction?

Silver stars began falling from the sky, filling the air with shimmering light that made everything even more ethereal.

"Who are you?" Maeve asked as he spun her through the reflective shower.

"This is my realm. You're just a visitor. You may create the—the scenery—but you don't live here. You shouldn't be able to draw me to you so easily. Something has changed. Something dangerous. And you're putting yourself right in its path."

"I'm not afraid," Maeve said, with a defiant tilt to her chin.

"Why the hell not?" he asked, dipping her so that her wavy hair fell loose behind her. He pulled her back up, looking deep into her eyes, but she wasn't sure how to answer.

For a moment they just danced, slow circles that kept each other mostly in the other's arms. "Maybe I don't know enough to be frightened," she finally admitted, quiet.

He held her close. "I know just enough to know that I should be."

She put her face against his jacket. She could feel the rough wool, smell his scent—a spicy oaken smell, definitely cologne—and hear the faint beating of his heart. The music seemed to have grown more distant, and the rain of stars had slowed. When she looked up, the sky was full of light, suffused with it. More stars than she had ever seen—had ever imagined. Each one was a subtly different colour, and they trembled slightly, their light inconsistent and fragile.

"Tell me, then," Maeve pressed. "Let me find a way to help. Don't push me away. That woman said that I did something to her. What was it? What did I do?"

"It's the technology. The recording devices. They're creating... echoes. They're affecting her somehow, but I don't understand it." His voice was low and urgent, and Maeve felt a tremor of fear. This was the first time he had referenced anything from her world. More so than the scratches on her cheek, more so than the infectious dream, this seemed proof that whatever was happening was happening both here and in the waking world.

Could he be telling the truth? And if it was the recording device, why did it affect the woman and not him? "If you don't understand it, how do you know what's happening? And what's changed?"

Something out of the corner of his eye caught the man's attention. As he glanced to the left, Maeve followed the motion and saw a shadowy shape descending on them like an avenging spirit. It was the woman from Maeve's last dream, the one who had attacked her. Maeve couldn't see how she had arrived; one second there was nothing and the next the woman was on them, hands outstretched in rictus claws, face an obscured mask of rage.

Maeve had just enough time to scream and then the man was pushing her away—

Maeve awoke in her bed, heart pounding, groggy and disoriented, caught in a twisted mess of blankets. She lay there for a long time, drifting in and out of consciousness, lost in the drugs but never quite able to fall back into dreams. And in her thoughts the dream circled endlessly, the stars as bright and crisp as if they were a true memory.

～

By eleven, Maeve was conscious enough to drag herself out of bed and take the longest shower of her life. It relieved some of the grogginess that lingered from her long, deep sleep, but her thoughts circled like a bird on a wire, never able to move far from her shocking discovery. She had done it. She had *actually* done it. The Blank had given her control and lucidity during her dream and kept it fresh and bright in her mind after waking. She could still see the stars twinkling above. She could still hear the musicians, the sweet deep clarion calls of fingers on strings. And she had made contact with the dream beings! For better *and* for worse.

If only the woman hadn't shown up and interrupted her, Maeve might have learned something more concrete. At least she knew that the dream-recording equipment was to blame for whatever was happening. If she could only figure out what it was doing, or how. She couldn't stop recording her dreams indefinitely—she was barely making rent as it was. She needed answers fast. Maeve itched to pick up the Blank and dive back into slumber, but she doubted that would be good for her body.

Making an entire pot of coffee was her next order of business, then; she poured it into the biggest mug she owned and used the rest to make coffee oatmeal. As she lifted the first spoon of oatmeal up to eat, she caught a surprising smell: like roasted meat cooking over an open fire.

Maeve shook her head, confused, trying to pinpoint where the smell was coming from. It was the fried rabbit from her dream the night before! Which made no sense, because she had never *smelled* rabbit before, so how would she even know what it smelled like? Not that her oatmeal necessarily smelled like rabbit—it just smelled like how she imagined it would smell while she was dreaming.

Leaning down, Maeve took another sniff. Nothing but coffee and the faint undercurrent of the oatmeal it was soaked into. A nervous nibble proved it was as mundane as the smell implied. She ate it reluctantly, expecting at any moment for it to morph in front of her. Blessedly, it stayed inert and oatmealy.

Returning to the main room, Maeve grabbed the emerald-green micro plush blanket off her bed and wrapped it around her shoulders, seeking comfort in its warmth. As she settled it over her shoulders, something scratched the back of her neck. She stuck her hand down between her neck and the blanket, feeling for what she assumed was the tag. Instead, her finger met something sharp. She shrieked, a bit ashamed of how immediately and violently she threw off the blanket. *Bug bug bug bug!* As she whipped it around, a shock of silver rained down across her floor. She bent over and picked one up, stunned.

It was a small silver star.

Oh, god, it had happened. She was still dreaming. The Blank had been so powerful that she was trapped in a cycle of dreaming, tricked into believing she had woken up, and any moment now she would open her eyes and wake up in bed and still not be sure that she was awake and—

Get it together, woman! You're not asleep. She pinched herself and waited expectantly, holding her breath in case anything changed. Nothing did, but she wasn't sure what that meant. *The pain was supposed to wake you up.* Did that mean this was real? She bent down and picked one of the tiny stars up. It certainly *felt* real.

Maeve tracked down her cell phone, which she'd never set to charge the night before, and took a picture of the star. She sent it to one of her group message threads with the caption, *What is this?*

An answer came pretty much immediately.

Matt
Confetti?

Josie
A shooting star!

Hayley
Is this a meme or something?

> Found it in my bed this morning. I'm sweating stars, lol.

Matt
You're just ready to be a trivia staaaaaaaaar.

It was a reference to the group's plans to go to bar trivia later that night. Maeve sat on the couch, her phone beside her, and turned the star over in her hands. It was larger and heavier than confetti, about the size of a fingernail accessory, but three-dimensional, not flat. She rubbed her thumb over it, feeling the smooth coldness of the metal and wondering if it might be real silver.

If I can never record another video, at least I can pay my rent with the weird dream stuff that appears in my bedroom, she thought bitterly.

She dropped down on the couch with an exaggerated sigh. Maybe she wouldn't go to trivia. How could she go through the motions and act like everything was normal when the rules of reality were actively changing around her? She had no idea what to do next. She needed time to *think*.

From somewhere underneath her, Maeve's phone pinged minutely. She arched her back, feeling around for it, and extracted it with no small effort. The message was from Josie. *Not sure about trivia tonight.*

Maeve immediately called, knowing that Josie would be easier to persuade over the phone. Her best friend answered with voice only. "I'm at work," she said, laughing.

"You're obviously not with a client or you couldn't be texting me," Maeve pointed out.

"I have fifteen minutes between clients. I'm doing paperwork."

"This'll be so quick. You need to get out of your apartment! I promise to shut any talk about anything *at all* down. All topics off limits other than trivia and beer."

There was a long, pregnant pause. "I'm just kinda wiped," Josie said.

Maeve was a huge proponent of respecting when people were low on spoons, but Josie hadn't been out or seen anyone since Jason's death. Maeve knew that, like her, Josie thrived on social interactions. Trivia was a great, lowkey activity where she could soak up some quality time with friends without being forced into any awkward conversations.

"I get it," Maeve said, "and I will absolutely respect it if you just aren't feeling it, but hear me out. I think you'll feel good once you're out. Trivia means you can focus on being a genius and no one will expect you to be witty or bubbly or *on*. It'll help."

"You think?" Josie asked, doubtful but coming around.

"I know. I'll meet you at your office and we can bus down

together and if you need to leave we can go early okay I love you byeeeee!" Maeve yelled, and hung up before Josie could object.

She dropped her phone on the table and sat up, but the first thing she saw were the stars, still sprinkled all over her floor. She couldn't deal with it right now. She needed space from the dream. She had no idea what to do with the information that the technology she had used for years was the cause of dangerous and imminent threats. She needed a plan for how to move forward. Since she didn't have one... she needed to turn her brain off for a few hours and pretend this whole thing was someone else's problem.

Embracing avoidance wholeheartedly, Maeve logged onto her computer and dealt with the least real thing she could think of: her social media presence. She fielded a flurry of angry emails and messages about the video being down. People were speculating that there was a cover-up going on, and some intrepid internet explorers had learned of Jason's case and were claiming the police had taken the video down to stop copycats. She didn't respond to any of it, just deleted any violent comments and let the rest of them speculate at will.

The worst part was that the speculation was only wrong on a technicality. The police *hadn't* forced her to take the video down, but they might as well have. The video *was* to blame for copycat murders. She felt the sharp stab of guilt and shoved it away, angry. It wasn't like she could control what she dreamed. There had been no way for her to know! She wasn't culpable. Not legally, not morally.

The thought didn't help, but Maeve moved on, posting an update that everything was quiet, and approved some initial image files from the VR company.

A little after six, she changed into clothes that were more outdoor appropriate and went to meet Josie at her office. As Maeve made her way there, she kept thinking she heard voices shouting for her attention. But whenever she turned to look and find the source of the sound, there was no one there. It didn't take long before she started to recognize the voices as the hawkers who had been selling their wares in the marketplace. Hawkers who didn't exist, from a city she didn't live in, from a dream that would not let her go.

She forced a smile on her face for Josie's sake, and by the time the two of them got to trivia, her nerves were fried from pretending so hard at normalcy. To her surprise, the noises faded as soon as she stepped through the door, chased away by the sound of real people enjoying themselves. She sank into a chair, relieved, and after a few rounds of drinks had been shared and several rounds of trivia answered, Maeve even managed to relax and enjoy herself.

Maeve was thrilled that Josie also seemed to be relaxing as the night went on. She had dark circles under her eyes and her attention wandered to the door every time it opened, but she smiled at Matt's antics, contributed answers now and then, and even fought good-naturedly with Hayley over minutiae around one of the questions. Maeve had warned everyone not to talk about Jason, and the friends kept the conversation light and easy.

It was turning into a fun night when they got to the music round and things went sideways. The host played a clip of music and Maeve crinkled her nose, confused. "Since when do they do classical for these things?" she asked.

"I'm sorry, how is Taylor Swift classical?" Matt demanded.

Maeve scoffed. "That wasn't Taylor Swift."

"It was definitely 'Love Story'," Josie said, giving her a look that gently questioned her sanity.

At that moment the host played the clip again, and Maeve whipped her head around to stare at the sound system. The song was *nothing* like the clip she had just heard. Her friends were right—it was Taylor Swift, no question. And with sinking dread, Maeve realized where she had heard the other song, the one she had mistaken the music for. *Shit.*

Maeve felt panic gripping the front of her shirt, and she downed the rest of her beer to cover the awkward moment. What was happening to her? The stars were one thing, but it was clear now that elements of the dream were *seeping* somehow into the world around her. Was it because of the Blank? Had it done something to her? It could be lingering in her system, blurring the lines between sleeping and conscious thought. She'd heard of people who got acid flashbacks days or even years later—or had that been disproven? She couldn't remember, and she couldn't look it up. Cell phones were aggressively banned during trivia.

Whatever was happening, she couldn't let it take over. She

promised Josie a night away from her problems, and Maeve wouldn't be the one to ruin that. She would refuse to acknowledge anything out of place, refuse to even *think* about it. The dream couldn't intrude if she didn't let it.

The strategy was semi-successful. She thought Josie could tell something was a little off, but her friend didn't call her out, and she made it through the rest of the night on a buzzing high of adrenalin, anxiety, and alcohol. Their team, Ms. Quizzle's Magic School Bus, came in second, and Matt offered rides to Maeve and Josie, who both lived near him. Matt easily made up for Maeve's unusual quiet with an exuberant monologue about a new band he was obsessed with, and Josie was smiling when they dropped her off. Maeve breathed a sigh of relief and sank back into the front seat, which she'd claimed after Josie vacated it.

Matt pulled back out onto the quiet suburban streets. It was only nine-thirty, but there were no other cars on the back roads between Josie's house and her own. Ornamental cherry trees choked the streetlights, creating pools of shadow and light, and Matt's headlights were bright between them.

"She's gonna be okay," Matt said, breaking the silence that had fallen between them.

"I know." Maeve smiled over at him. "Thanks for being cool tonight."

"Am I ever not cool?"

"Want me to make a list?" Maeve teased. She held up a hand and started ticking things off. "Every time you talk about dogs. That summer you were into crypto. When—"

"Hey, look, we're here," Matt interrupted. He pulled to a stop in front of the house where Maeve rented the basement. It looked homey, even in the semi-dark. A thread of blue LED lights stayed on year-round and gave her enough light to see the path to the back of the house even when she'd forgotten to turn the motion-activated side light on.

Maeve thanked Matt and left, hurrying around the house like there was a zombie on her tail. She got inside and locked the door immediately, turning all the lights on around her. She was confronted immediately by the stars that she never cleaned up off the floor.

Stars and sounds. Music and mayhem. Waking up with scratches on her face had been scary, but this was a whole other kind of unsettling. Strange noises only she could hear? Scents that seemed to come and go? She wanted to blame it all on the drugs, but there was no way to know for sure. She had contaminated her own evidence.

Without a second thought, Maeve marched into the bathroom, grabbed the Blank, and flushed it down the toilet. She watched them go with a deep sense of satisfaction. It had been a mistake to try them, even if the results had been incredible. She wouldn't give that dream back for all the sanity in the world, but she wanted to be able to trust her perceptions. She wanted to know the ways in which the world was shifting under her feet, so that she could steady herself and control her fall, if she had to. If she could.

24

PERI

Peri blinked and came back to consciousness as the guided meditation ended. They were exhausted. They had been sleeping twelve or thirteen hours a day but still felt constantly wrung out, as if the mental strain of developing their lucid dreaming was robbing their sleep of its restorative properties. They weren't sure how much more of this they could take, but they had yet to fight their way back to the woman, and after their previous success, there was no way they were going to give up.

So far, they had managed to come to awareness a few times mid-dream, but every time it woke them up. They were getting good at falling back to sleep and returning to the same dream, but so far none of them had been particularly lucid.

Turning off the app on their phone, Peri sat down in front of the computer and clicked open their email program.

"What?" they roared. The email that had upset them was from Zzz+, notifying them that their video had been taken down because it had been reported for breaking community guidelines.

"This may include harassment, libel, hate speech, violence, or other activity not allowed on our platform. Your video has been removed while we investigate the claim. This process will take anywhere from 2 to 6 weeks. You will receive an email from the team if we have any follow-up questions. Thank you for using Zzz+!" The email was so cheerful Peri wanted to scream, but they were held back by the knowledge that a scream of the decibel they wanted to loose would probably bring concerned neighbours down on their head.

The email was from a no-reply address, so they couldn't even write back and demand to know who had reported it and for what. They had no choice but to wait for the verdict with something resembling patience.

Peri navigated back into their inbox, where they found a similar email from YouTube—and another that immediately drew their attention. The title read, "Notice of Delivery of Cease and Desist." The sender was none other than DreamR, the first and most famous of the dream-recording companies. A few of the big tech companies, Google and Valve among them, had released their own versions a couple of years ago, but they hadn't managed to steal much of the market share from DreamR.

Peri opened the email and scanned the legalese. It was a boiler-plate cease and desist letter claiming that Peri's video telling people not to use the technology was defamatory. "There is no evidence that our technology has any negative side effects," and, "We have contacted the platforms where your video was posted and had them remove it." A bunch of threats followed about what would happen if Peri continued to advocate against the technology without any evidence to back up their claims, which, according to the DreamR legal team, Peri clearly didn't have.

The problem was, they were right. What Peri had was the word of a woman in her dreams, and they had a feeling that wouldn't hold up in court. They didn't have the skill to examine the device to prove that it was emitting any sort of energy or field. Besides, there was a chance it wasn't. In quantum physics, it was possible to alter the state of energy just by observing it. Or something like that— Peri's understanding of the phenomenon didn't even stretch as far as what it was called, and they weren't entirely sure they were remembering correctly.

But Peri wasn't about to give up.

If convincing people not to use this technology was the only way to protect the woman in her dreams, Peri was damn well going to find a way to do it.

Peri found a copy of their video and uploaded it to a service that allowed you to set up password-locked content. Then, they posted on every forum they could find, telling people that their video had been taken down, that they received a gag order, and that it was clear that the powers that be wanted to shut them up. Shameless, they used every conspiracy hook they could think of. The title of most of their posts was, "They don't want you to know the truth about Dreaming!" They invited people to private message them for a link to the video and included redacted screencaps of the cease and desist to prove they were legitimate. They even shared it with their Discord friends, who expressed concern about Peri but promised to share it where they could.

It wasn't enough, but at least it was a start.

Peri sat hunched over a microfiche machine in the basement of an old library, scrolling through articles about a strange rash of murders. The murders took place exactly one hundred years previously, and each victim had been found missing their heart. Peri was debating whether the murders could be connected to the recent deaths of two of their classmates when they remembered that they hadn't been in school for years. They had no classmates—because this was just a dream.

Peri leaned back in the old plastic chair with a grin. They had done it—they had woken up inside the dream, without waking up in the waking world. The last time that Peri had done that, there had been no story to escape from. It felt like more of a victory this time knowing they hadn't wasted much time walking the path the dream had set for them.

Standing up, Peri looked over the library. It was no place they had ever been, but it did remind them of more than a few movies and TV shows they had watched. They were standing in front of one of three computers in a bank. Beyond the computers, wheeled wooden stacks filled the space from wall to wall. Most of them were open, and Peri could see rows of textbooks and leather-bound tomes, none of which looked more modern than the 1950s. No novels or Reader's Digests in sight.

Curious about what they could do, Peri tried to summon an ice cream sundae into being. Nothing happened. It seemed like their ability to twist and warp the paint dream had been a product of the dream itself, not the lucid dreaming. They recalled that in the past, the few times they had been lucid in a dream, their ability to influence the dream had usually come in the form of shaping the plot, often to avoid a nightmare or anxiety dream.

Peri considered the plot of the dream they were in, then considered what might fit—a librarian immediately came to mind. Peri pictured a classic librarian from the kind of media that had inspired the dream: a woman in her 40s, hair in a bun, wearing a cardigan over a button-up blouse. She would have glasses on a string around her neck and look either like sour grapes or someone's loving mother, depending on whether she was there to shush the main characters or provide the valuable intel they had needed all along.

As Peri built the librarian in their mind, they concentrated not only on what she looked like, but on the reason they needed her. They couldn't solve the murders on their own. There had to be some clue, some hint they were missing, that only a trained librarian could solve. She would come down the stairs so quietly Peri wouldn't hear them until she spoke up, right from behind their shoulder.

"Can I help you?"

Even though they were expecting it, hoping for it, Peri couldn't stop a shriek as they spun around. The woman standing in front of them was exactly as they had pictured, down to the colour of her cardigan and the way it draped across her shoulders instead of being worn over her arms.

"I did it!" Peri hollered. They tossed their arms around the librarian, then immediately regretted it and stepped back from the hug, feeling sheepish even though the woman was a figment of their imagination.

"Please be quiet," the librarian shushed. "What are you researching?"

"It doesn't matter." Peri ran over to the stacks and looked them up and down. Last time, they had managed to step into another dream by creating a doorway. It hadn't worked a second time, but they were pretty sure they just needed to practice the skill. And what better place to find a doorway into another world than a library?

Peri closed their eyes and thought. They needed to picture a city street they had never been to but could see in their mind's eye. And since it was currently night in Vancouver, it had to be south of them so that the city's citizens would also be asleep. Hmmmm. Somewhere in South America, maybe? Buenos Aires wasn't too far east; it would do. They had just read *Bad Times in Buenos Aires*, and the author had done a great job of making the 'Paris of the south' come alive. Peri pictured the tall, crumbling stone buildings; the wide avenues with overgrown trees that cracked the concrete; the mass of humanity rushing to and from various destinations. At the heart of it all, they pictured a lonely man just wanting to be seen.

With their eyes still closed, Peri grabbed the wheel nearest to them and turned the stacks until there was a gap big enough to fit through. They took a step forward and opened their eyes to a whole new world: downtown Buenos Aires on a rainy evening, shadows lengthening between buildings.

It was both like and unlike what they had pictured. The streets weren't as crumbling as they had imagined, and there were plenty of modern touches amid the stonework of the previous century. To one side of Peri, a McDonald's sign lit up a six-story stone building with beautiful arched windows. The mass of people was much like Peri had imagined, but it was entirely made up of couples: young men and women, arm-in-arm, laughing and shrieking as they ran or walked quickly in every direction. The cars on the street were decades out of date, and they all had flat tires, but they were somehow still moving at a steady clip. Music played from a handful of different sources, the resultant cacophony practically a physical assault.

Peri found the dreamer they had envisioned, though he looked nothing like Peri had pictured. He was crouching on the sidewalk, his arms thrown over his head, whimpering every time one of the pedestrians slammed into him. He was in his late middle age, whereas Peri had pictured someone young, and he was wearing a colourful printed shirt that caught the eye.

Fighting their way to his side, Peri touched his arm. He looked up with a tear-streaked face, and whatever he was expecting to see, it clearly wasn't Peri. He said something, stunned, but it was in Spanish —or at least, Peri's brain interpreted it as Spanish. They had learned French in school, so they spoke a few words, and the languages shared a little here and there, but otherwise Peri was lost. So were they in a dream of a Spanish speaker? Or was Peri's brain just filling in sounds that sounded like Spanish?

"Do you speak English?" Peri asked him gently. If this was a real person, he was going to be confused as heck in the morning!

"Yes," he said, in hesitant but lightly accented English.

"What's the Spanish word for forbearance?" Peri asked. It was a word they didn't know, and there was no way they subconsciously knew but couldn't remember. He would tell them, and in the morning, they could look it up. If the word was real, they would know for a fact that they were stepping through dreams, connecting to other people sleeping around them.

"I have no idea," he said with a laugh. "Who are you?" He stood, gazing at Peri in a rapturous way that made them more than a little uncomfortable.

"Right. Simple enough you know it, but obscure enough I would have no idea. Uh... where were you born? Were you born in Buenos Aires?"

"No. I was born in Desaguadero."

"Perfect! I've never heard of it. Can you tell me something about it?"

"It was a stop on the Camino Real del Oeste?" he said, but he was unsure enough that it made it sound like a question.

"Desaguadero. Camino Real del Oeste," Peri repeated. They said each phrase three times, to make sure they would remember both when they woke. "Thank you."

"Thank *you*," the man said. He caught their hands before they could dodge out of the way, squeezing tightly. "I am not alone. You are here."

Peri squirmed, uncomfortable with the fervent contact. "Uh. Yeah. I'm here. I have to go, but... I was here."

He nodded. Dropping one of their hands, he brought the other one to his lips and kissed it. He said something in Spanish that they didn't understand, tears of gratitude in his eyes.

Peri squeezed his hand. "The path out is there," they told him. They pointed, and sure enough the mass of people shifted, and Peri could see a path leading away from downtown to a beautiful ocean view.

The man sighed in relief. He turned that way, offering Peri an air kiss over his shoulder. Peri smiled and nodded, then turned away, repeating the words a few more times before walking back through the portal and into the library.

Once there, Peri grabbed the wheel and closed the stacks, sealing it up. The librarian was still there, reading the microfiches so intently that she didn't even look over at Peri. No doubt she was learning the key that would unlock the mysterious murders. Peri smiled—another time, they probably would have gotten absolutely sucked into a dream like this. Now they just wanted to wake up so they could check and see if the information they had was real.

One great way to ensure you woke up in a dream was to fall, so Peri made their way up through the library to the second floor. As they went, they repeated, "There's roof access from a little door in the children's section." They found the children's section easily enough—it was decorated with a papier-mâché castle that covered the wall above the bookshelves, and comfortable cushions were stuffed into every corner. Peri ran a hand across the books, but they couldn't read any of the titles; it was just a blur of colour.

Peri found a door marked No Access—Roof just past the carpeted area, exactly where they had imagined it would be. It wasn't locked, and they climbed the small flight of stairs and stepped out onto the damp concrete.

The view was incredible—the city that stretched out in front of them was nowhere from the waking world, but somehow familiar and soothing at the same time. It had the feeling of Victorian London, but cleaner, with more green space. Trees grew everywhere and they were all alive with flowers, a riot of pink and white and purple. The scent on the wind was complex: spring blossoms and petrichor mixed with gasoline and manure from the cars and horses on the road, a unique blend unlike anything Peri had smelled in the waking world. They spread their arms with a smile, taking a deep breath of the perfumed air.

"Are you going flying?" a voice asked, just as they were about to tip forward into the unknown.

Peri spun in delight, taking a few awkward steps to keep from tumbling backward off the roof. "You found me!"

The woman was a few feet away, wearing a soft green silk dress that looked modern, but with the slashed cream underskirt of a medieval gown. The bodice was cut straight across and bound her chest tightly, and the skirts swished prettily as she walked closer. Her hair was pulled away from her face but fell straight and long down her back, and she was smiling with her whole body. With relief—with joy.

Peri crossed the space separating them from the woman in a heartbeat. The magnetism that propelled them was met in equal force by her strong embrace, and they fell into each other as though it were the only right thing in the whole messed up, dream-bending world. Peri instinctively felt the rightness of it. The feel of the woman in their arms, the warmth and presence of her, solidified their determination to hold on forever.

When Peri finally pulled away, their face passed within an inch of hers and their eyes met. Peri was overwhelmed by a swampy mire of panic. They pulled back, but their sharp motion was arrested by the woman's hand on their arm.

"What's wrong?" she asked.

"I thought you might... um—" Peri laughed nervously. They pulled their arm through the woman's grip but stopped when their hands met and their fingers intertwined. Peri whispered the words, not making eye contact. "I thought you might kiss me."

"It's okay," the woman said gently. "I've been here with you for years, Peri. You're just getting to know me, but I know all of you."

Peri looked up at her, hating that there were tears in their eyes. "You do?"

"I do."

"And you don't... mind?"

"I will take all of you," the woman whispered, and Peri couldn't stop a shiver of fear. "All of you, as you are."

"Tell me what you need. Anything," Peri pleaded.

"You've found a way to control the dreams. To alter the narrative. That's what I need."

"You're trapped by the narrative of dreams?"

"We walk in them," she agreed, "we don't control them."

"I can show you," Peri started, but the woman cut her off.

"Share it with me. Give me some of what you have, and I will give you some of the dream. Maybe this way, we can find a middle path."

"Of course," Peri agreed, not entirely sure what they were agreeing to. "Just tell me what to do."

"Like this." The woman held up her hands and Peri matched her, placing their palms against hers like a mirror. "Close your eyes and think of the world beyond. The way it is solid, unchangeable. Your place in it. How you decide, every morning, what your day will be, but only in the context of what already is. Think of the weight of air on your skin, of time on your being. Breathe in. Breathe out."

Cold pressure spread from the woman's fingers, and Peri gasped in pain as the feeling shot up their arms. It felt like an icy snake constricting even as it wove ever closer to their heart. It stopped just as it reached their torso, and the tingling spread out and evened. Peri opened their eyes. The woman let her hands fall and Peri did the same, moving experimentally to see how it felt. Their skin was pins and needles, and cold when they brought a hand up to their cheek.

"Did it work?" Peri asked, surprised to find their voice a quiet rasp.

"I don't know," the woman admitted. "I've never tried anything like this before." She stepped closer, not touching Peri but entering their personal space, catching their eyes and not letting go. "Time to find out," she said. With a wink, she dropped backward and disappeared— falling through the roof like a ghost.

Peri yelled, startled. They fell to their knees and scrabbled around the stone surface looking for a way through, but there was no sign of where the woman had gone. Shaken, Peri wrapped their arms tight across their chest and squeezed. Their arms were still tingling, still cold, and Peri wondered what they had given up.

And if there would ever be a way to get it back.

25

MAEVE

Maeve was on a mission to be present for her best friend. The photos from the event had come back, and thanks to Hayley's enthusiastic photography there was proof that Josie had been home all night. The cops still considered her a person of interest—maybe she had hired someone else to commit the crime—but there was no danger of charges coming down any time soon. Josie's mom had left that morning, with a promise to come back if there were any changes.

"I've got bagels. I've got wine. And I've got a list of movies in my head that won't make us think about anything at all," Maeve declared as Josie swung open her door. Maeve and Josie had made plans the week before to get together as soon as Ms. Aranda was gone. As much as Maeve liked Ms. Aranda, the woman was a little intimidating, and it was hard to lounge in front of a TV and watch bad murder documentaries under her disapproving eye.

Josie raised one eyebrow and stepped back to let her in. "I wasn't sure you would remember."

"What? Why wouldn't I remember?" Maeve came inside and kicked off her shoes.

It was true that Maeve and Josie hadn't been seeing as much of each other as they usually did these last few weeks—partly because Maeve didn't want to get in the way, and partly because she was distracted by her investigations into the dreaming world. Since her foray into Blank, she had gone five nights with no clear dreams and no answers. She spent her days recycling old dreams to keep her streams active and researching everything she could find about the dream beings—which so far was a whole lot of nothing.

But she was a little offended by the idea that she would forget a plan they had *just* made.

Josie didn't say anything, just walked over to the couch and sat down. Maeve followed, laying out the fresh bagels and wine on the coffee table, then heading into the kitchen to grab a couple of glasses. Josie didn't have any wine glasses yet, so Maeve took two mugs with her. Josie had cracked the wine by the time Maeve was on the couch next to her, and she poured as Maeve held out one mug and then the other. They clinked before drinking, the toast silent, and then settled back into the couch.

Josie toyed with her handle for a moment. "Have you been busy?"

"Yeah," Maeve said, not realizing how fervent she sounded until the word came out. "Uh, things have been... kind of a lot."

"For me, too," Josie pointed out.

"I know," Maeve said. "That's why I was trying to give you some space."

"I didn't really want space."

Shit. "I'm so sorry, Joze. I didn't want to crowd you with your mom here, and I know how much you hate it when people hover and when you don't have any space. Plus, my stuff is... kind of weird?" Maeve rubbed her ear, awkward and unsure. "I've actually been fucking *dying* to get your take on it, but I didn't want to, like... make it all about me."

"Okay, that sounds way more interesting than me wallowing in my shit. What's going on?" Josie demanded.

Maeve hesitated.

"Seriously. I need a distraction," she quipped.

"I don't know if this is really a distraction," Maeve hedged, but finally she laid it all out: the strange copycat murders, the way people claimed to be sharing her dream, and the warning she had gotten that she needed to run from danger. She even told Josie about the dream leaching into the real world—about the scratches that she couldn't have given herself and the smells and sounds she heard at trivia night. Finally, she pulled one of the little stars out of her pocket and passed it over to her friend. That and the scratches were the best evidence she had that she wasn't just going insane.

Josie listened calmly at first, and then with more and more questions and interjections as Maeve went on. She had a hard time believing the sounds weren't just the result of the drugs until Maeve pulled out the star, and then she took it so hesitantly it was clear she half-expected it to vanish when she tried to touch it. But it stayed there, stubbornly real, as she held it up to the light to examine it more closely.

"Fuck," she finally said, letting her hand fall and looking across the couch at Maeve.

"I know."

"I mean—fuck."

"This is why I was having a hard time figuring out how to tell you!" Maeve took a big gulp of her wine and crashed back against the cushions; she had been leaning forward, eager in her recitation. "At first it all just seemed like conjecture and suspicion, and I thought I was probably just being paranoid and weird because I was scared about what happened, you know? But then the guy. And the dream. And then... that." She waved at the star. "It's not in my head. I don't get what it is, I don't understand it, but I know that much. It's not just me."

"You need to take that video down," Josie fervently said.

"Oh, it's down."

"So... What do we do now?"

"You believe me?" Maeve's voice cracked a little at the end, and Josie reached out to squeeze her hand.

"Of course I believe you." As Josie rubbed her eyes, she added, "No one would make up a story with this many holes and question marks."

Maeve laughed. "Yeah. Good point."

"We have to tell the cops... right?"

"Tell them *what*?" Maeve asked. "That I found a star that I dreamed about? They're never gonna believe me. I barely believe me."

"Not that," Josie agreed. "But the copycats? The comments on the video?"

"Fuck. Maybe I shouldn't have taken it down," Maeve muttered.

"No. You definitely, definitely should have." Josie's eyes were wide and insistent.

"I guess I just tell them about the other cases, and that all of them commented on my video?"

"Yeah, I think so."

"Okay." Maeve took out her phone and scanned through her call history.

"Now? You're doing it now?"

"Should I not?"

"I—I guess. Yeah. Okay."

Josie watched with her arms wrapped around her knees as Maeve called. For some reason, when it was important she always reverted to the phone rather than using her watch. Something about the solid presence against her ear, maybe.

The detective picked up on the second ring. Maeve laid out what she knew about the copycat killings: that all three she had looked up had been people who posted on her video, saying they had experienced the exact same dream. She explained that she had taken it down because she was afraid of inciting anyone to violence. She told him that someone techier than her could probably still access all of the deleted comments if they had the original URL, and since she kept all of her URLs in a posting spreadsheet, she could send it to him.

It was clear that he hadn't heard anything about potential copycat killings, or at least hadn't made the connection, and he was interested in what she had to say. He grilled her a little and was clearly frustrated that evidence was going to be more difficult to uncover now that the video was deleted. But there really wasn't much more to say, and much to Maeve's relief, he didn't seem interested in making her more of a suspect for her decision. Eventually he thanked her for the tip and wished her goodnight.

She hung up and drained the rest of her wine, collapsing against the arm of the couch and letting her body hang over it, upside-down. "So, it's done."

"There must be a way to find out. You said there was a guy in your dreams. Maybe he's another streamer?"

"Maybe. I did a reverse image search and couldn't find him, though."

"Show me?"

Maeve lifted her body back to a sitting position and scrolled through her phone until she found the image. She showed it to Josie.

"Hm." Josie shook her head.

"I can't be the only person this is happening to," Maeve huffed. "I've got to find other streamers and see if I can get them talking."

Josie sat up and cracked her knuckles. "Okay. How do we get the word out?"

"You're such a nerd." Maeve hugged her, laughing, then stayed snuggled up against her friend as she thought. "I need to ask around about something strange without making it sound like I've downloaded 'Conspiracies 101' onto my Spotify and fallen asleep listening to it."

Josie snorted, her chuckle trailing off as she thought it through. "Post something simple," she suggested. "'My dreams aren't acting like they normally do. Has anyone else noticed odd, recurring people in their dreams?'"

Maeve took Josie's laptop and tapped her watch against the sensor on the keyboard, signing into her own account. "Should I post it on the forums?"

"No, go direct. It'll feel less like conspiracy baiting if you're just asking casually, one on one," Josie suggested. "While you do that, I'll check the forums again. See if I can find anything you missed about dreams with similar themes."

"You know you're the actual best?" Maeve asked.

"I do," Josie assured her with a smile.

They turned on the TV for background noise, picking a sitcom they'd seen before, and got to work. Maeve sent out almost a hundred messages to other dreamers. Some she knew from the web of comments and shares that she had inevitably built up over her career; others were just names she had seen now and then, people who were tangentially familiar.

Then there was nothing to do but wait. Maeve and Josie hung out for a few hours, then Maeve went home and crashed. She had a stress dream about being lost in a sprawling big-box store, but she couldn't remember who it was she was searching for.

The first thing she did in the morning was roll over and check her phone. There were about sixty answers to her hundred or so messages, and she combed through them eagerly. As she jumped from message to message, her adrenalin slowly died. Most of the responses were dismissive, assuming it was some marketing ploy they weren't interested in. Others laughed it off, and she wasn't sure if they knew more and weren't willing to say anything, or if they really hadn't had any strange dreams.

One message, though, seemed promising. It was from Dreams-Away, who Maeve remembered had been hunting for recurring people in their dreams.

DreamsAway
I really thought I was the only one. Almost gave up looking. When can you talk?

Now works?

Maeve added her contact card to the message. She hoped this wasn't a red herring, just more about their mystery woman. There was a long pause, and then Maeve's phone rang. She took a deep breath, held the phone up, and answered.

26

PERI

Peri glanced over at the clock. It read 11:04, and they had no idea if that was a.m. or p.m. until they checked the curtains and saw sunlight peeking through. Ever since what the woman in their dreams had done—whatever it was she had done—Peri had felt... disconnected. Distracted.

The faint buzz of energy in their arms never quite gone away, though they were no longer as numb as they had been when Peri first woke up. Peri thought they had given the woman some of their connection to the waking world, a way to be more herself when the current of dream threatened to toss her around. But that left Peri adrift. It was their own connection they had sacrificed, and they had no idea if it would ever return.

TV held no interest. Books could barely keep their attention for more than a few pages. They hadn't been on Discord in days, hadn't spoken to any of their friends. Juniper still managed to rouse them now and then, but only for a few minutes, and then Peri would wander back to their bed. Looking up the town from their encounter with the Argentinian gentleman had provided a momentary flash of excitement—this was proof they had walked into a real person's dream! —but even that had only lasted a short while. There was nothing concrete for them to do with the knowledge—no one to tell —and the excitement faded like mist at sunrise.

The days were growing shorter and shorter as Peri spent more and more time asleep. With the lucid dreaming techniques they were slowly perfecting, the world of dreams was becoming more and more open to them. Whatever the woman had done, Peri could now step easily from dream to dream, exploring the minds of strangers. Each mind was a new world. Peri couldn't believe how differently other people interpreted the world, how everything from the colours of a city to the tenor of a voice was subtly different when seen through another's eyes.

Some dreams were entirely abstract, strange and dangerous voids where the rules Peri knew didn't apply. In one, Peri had become a series of interconnected colours, each splash of bright pigment a part of who they were that flexed and fought to be a whole. They had drifted there for hours until the person woke up and ejected Peri back into their own dreamscape. In another, Peri had watched, mesmerized, as faces and objects blurred and shifted in and out of reality, a heaving morass of half-finished thoughts and impressions that almost, but didn't quite, form a picture.

They hadn't yet learned how to control dreams in major ways. They could make subtle changes, like adding the librarian or creating doors, but they had to work within the established rules of the dreamer. It was as if the narrative were train tracks running through each dreamer's mind. They could create new tracks and redirect the train onto them, but they couldn't make the boxcar fly.

They were convinced that if they could learn how to do that, how to upend the rules the dream operated under, they could free the woman from whatever trapped her. Peri hadn't seen her in the last few nights, but they knew it was only a matter of time before they found her again. And when they did, they would be strong enough to help her. They would do anything to ease the pain and fear she felt, to give her solace from the storm that she was trapped in.

Peri knew exactly what Jasmine would say to that—that Peri should care equally about their own well-being. That they couldn't help anyone if they were too exhausted to function. With that in mind, Peri had set careful rules to ensure that they cared for their body while they worked at improving their mind. They showered at least every second day. They ate one healthy meal every time they woke up, and they spent at least eight hours awake before returning to bed. They avoided another session with Jasmine, since they couldn't figure out how to lie their way around their current situation, but they kept her lessons in mind, and tried to maintain some kind of connection to the waking world. They had even texted Kyle a few times.

It was the motions they had to go through, but more and more those things felt extraneous, as if those empty motions were the dream, and Peri was just killing time, waiting for real life to begin again. As more days crept by without the woman appearing again, Peri grew more and more frustrated that they hadn't asked her more questions when they had the chance. There was so much they still needed to know!

They understood very little of the dream world, and how the creatures in it operated. Did they exist on another plane as well? What happened to them if they were in a dream and the dreamer woke up? When Peri had been in a dream and the dreamer woke, Peri had been knocked back into their own mind. But Peri had no idea if the dream people had their own lives, their own personalities, outside of what the dreams made them. Peri didn't even know if they were human, if they lived in the waking world or only dreams, if they had a whole society or existed as solitary beings. So many unanswered questions! Peri could have drunk the answers like wine, bathed in them like milk.

Still in bed, Peri felt blindly for their phone and dragged it over from the side table, snuggling into their pillows. They checked their email but didn't answer any of them, then scrolled through their other social media platform, opening everything but leaving all of it on read.

They were just about to close the whole window when a message caught their eye.

> **Maevericious**
> Hey—hope this doesn't come too out of the blue,
> but I'm wondering if you've had any weird dreams
> lately. Stuff that's just out of the ordinary, maybe
> with recurring people from dream to dream? I'd
> love to chat about it if you have.

Peri immediately sat up in bed, hunching over the phone. They had been searching for someone else who might be experiencing what they had, but there had been absolutely no responses on the forums. And now, out of the blue, someone messaged them directly asking about that very thing? Was it too good to be true? *Maevericious*. Peri didn't recognize the username, but that didn't mean much. They weren't as tied to the community as they should be.

> I really thought I was the only one. Almost gave up
> looking. When can you talk?

Peri was nervous and thrilled and hesitant, feeling the most alive they had felt in weeks. In months, maybe.

> **Maevericious**
> Now works?

Peri reached out to tap the video button, then hesitated. What if it was just someone pranking them? What if someone from DreamR had found out they were still circulating their video, and this was a ruse to serve them notice or something?

But what if it wasn't? What if for once, finally... Peri wasn't alone?

Before they could change their mind, Peri hit the little video camera. Their face appeared, shadowy in the dark bedroom, and they quickly flicked the bedside lamp on so they didn't look like quite as much of a hacker from a bad nineties movie. A second later, Maevericious appeared on the screen, her screen name and pronouns under the video. She was a beautiful woman around the same age as Peri, with a beaming smile that lit up her soft round face. Her thick brown curls filled most of the screen that her face didn't, and she was wearing subtle makeup and huge rainbow earrings.

"Hey!" Her eyes took Peri in, but whatever she thought didn't so much as twitch her smile off her face. "Thanks so much for talking to me. My name is Maeve."

"Hi, yeah, I'm Peri, so you've seen people? Recurring people—strangers, more specifically?" Peri asked, ignoring the socially acceptable preamble that was no doubt expected of them.

Maeve didn't seem to mind. Her eyes brightened even further, if that was possible, the smile on her lips splashing warmth over her whole face. "Yes! You have too? I've asked so many people and no one has."

"I was starting to think I might be the only one," Peri agreed with a shaky laugh.

"Is it a guy? Sort of short, curly hair?"

Peri started to shake their head, and then their eyes widened. "Wait. Latino guy? Or maybe Middle Eastern? Built like a bouncer?"

"Oh my god! Yes!" Maeve practically bounced up and down in her excitement. "Holy shit. I can't believe this. You've actually seen him. He's real. He's like... fully real. Fuck. Hold on, I'm sending you a screenshot." Her face disappeared momentarily in a dizzying blur of the ceiling, and Peri's phone beeped as an image came through. They switched windows to check it. It looked like a dream screenshot, or maybe a photo that had been run through a filter. It was definitely the man from the boat dream, the one who had run off after the woman's yell and left Peri alone.

Excited, Peri went into their own files and found a good shot of their mystery woman to send through. "That's definitely him! I'm sending you a picture, too. Have you seen her?"

Maeve stared at the photo, eyes as wide as a cartoon princess. "That's her! Oh, oh, that's her! When I've seen her in the dreams, she's always been wrapped in shadows like they're part of her, I didn't think I'd ever seen her face but—I *have!* There was this weird blip in the dream where Josie's face shifted. She looked like herself, and then she didn't. She looked like *this.*"

Peri couldn't believe what they were hearing. After all this time, all these years of searching, they finally had it. They had proof that she was *real.* She existed somewhere in the world, independent of

Peri. She was no ghost, no shadow. Peri wasn't in love with a facet of their own mind. They were in love with *her*.

"She's real," Peri breathed, but hard on the heels of their joy came sinking, creeping dread. It poisoned their happiness like an oil slick on water, not killing it but choking the surface, making it hard to wade through. "She attacked you. I don't understand why."

"The man that we've both seen, he tried to explain it to me. He said the dream-recording technology is making echoes, or something. It's doing something to the woman, but he doesn't understand what. It sounded like it wasn't impacting him, or at least not yet."

Peri sank back against the pillow propped against their headboard, dazed from the whiplash of emotions. It was all real. Answers were within their grasp, and they weren't facing any of it alone. "She said the same thing to me. That she was trapped."

"Tell me everything," Maeve urged. Her enthusiasm brought Peri back to life, a rush of energy tingling down their arms and into their toes.

Peri shared what they could, holding very little back but still cautious, afraid to open up entirely. When Maeve took her turn, she seemed like an open book; her recitation was full of hand gestures, laughter, and dramatic flourishes. After they compared notes, it turned out there wasn't a lot that one of them knew that the other didn't.

These people, whatever they were, lived at least partially in the land of dreams. The technology had begun to negatively impact them. Lucid dreaming, either on Blank or with the help of technology, seemed to offer dreamers like Peri and Maeve more control and helped them interact with and remember the dream people.

Then there was the woman. She had attacked Maeve multiple times. She seemed dangerous, almost unhinged, so different from the woman Peri knew. But then... how well did Peri really know her, versus the version of herself that she showed in Peri's dreams?

If the recording technology was harming her, she was just trying to defend herself. It was true that Maeve didn't mean to cause harm, but Peri couldn't blame the woman for fighting back. She was doing what she had to do. That fit with the woman Peri knew. Strong, fierce, unafraid, and unapologetic.

"And there are these... murders," Maeve said, almost reluctantly. The blood drained from Peris's face as Maeve described the murders that had been copycatted all across the country. All across the world. All people who had seen Maeve's video and been killed soon after.

Peri thought of the leaves, of the blood on their hands. Was this a more extreme version of the same? Elements of Peri's dreams leached into the real world, but they didn't take over. Except the one time. In the nightmare Peri had seen a door made of blood, and then the door had appeared in the real world. If Peri had stepped through it, who knows what might have happened.

The same thing could be happening to these people. They dreamed the dream and woke up on a roof in a precarious position. They fell, and the dream itself was what killed them.

"I've seen elements from the dream intruding into real life," Peri admitted.

"Me too. I've heard a snatch of song, seen a small star thing."

"I'm going back into the dream tonight," Peri decided. "Maybe with what I know, I can convince her to tell me more. To tell me how I can help her."

"You don't think..." Maeve hesitated. "If she is the same person..."

"I don't know," Peri admitted. "The woman I know is kind. Fierce, but not cruel. If she's going after you, it *must* be for a reason we don't understand. Maybe I can get through to her, convince her that we can find another way."

"Be careful," Maeve stressed. "I wish I could go with you."

"I'll be okay," Peri said. "Thanks for this."

"Well, will you call me tomorrow morning and tell me what you find?" Maeve asked.

Caught off-guard, Peri answered in the affirmative before they could stop. "Oh—uh, yeah I guess."

"Great! I'm gonna order one of those lucid dreaming thingies. I won't be much help until then, I don't think, but let me know if I can do anything. Anything at all."

"I will. Thanks." Peri felt weak with relief. Maeve was a stranger, a face on the other end of a video screen, but she was *real*. Here, at last, was someone who understood what Peri was going through.

She was someone to bounce ideas off of, someone to remind Peri of what was real and what wasn't.

But it was more than that. Maeve was like Peri in ways that few of Peri's friends were. She was drawn to the dreams and felt a connection to that world. Peri could see it in the way she spoke of the dreams. The longing on her face was a reflection of Peri's own longing, that drive to reach for something intangible that pushed Peri to live a life so different from what others thought that Peri should want.

Just talking to Maeve, just knowing she was there, made Peri feel a surge of hope. Whatever was happening, they could handle it now. They were ready to face whatever came next.

"Oh, Peri! What time zone are you?"

"Pacific."

"Me too! I'm in Vancouver."

Peri shivered. They glanced at their window, where the Vancouver skyline spread out and showed the ocean beyond. "That's a weird coincidence."

"You too?" Maeve asked. She looked sort of terrified and delighted at the same time. "Okay. Yeah. Spooky. Though, not any spookier than the rest of this stuff, I guess." She laughed, the sound full-throated and warm. "Well, good luck. And call me tomorrow. Promise."

"I promise," Peri agreed. They hung up before Maeve could ask anything else of them.

Peri fell back into bed, dragging their pillow down and snuggling into it, thinking. If the woman was after Maeve, there was something they were missing. Maeve assumed that a dream creature was committing these murders, but it could be the dream itself, leeching out just like the leaves and door had leached into Peri's life.

Or it could be the narrative of the dream itself, forcing the woman to reenact it. If that was true, it may be true that the woman had killed people, but it wasn't her fault. Peri had to find a way to help her break the cycle. If they could do that, maybe she could find a way to be free. And it would be Peri who saved her.

~

Peri went to bed early that night. As they lay awake waiting for sleep to take them, they thought about the woman, trying to fix her in their mind. Her eyes, dark and intense. Her quick wit that had a comeback to every one of Peri's thoughts. Her need, a churning river that Peri was caught up in.

Peri became aware again in a fluorescent-lit late-night diner with stained carpets and uncomfortable vinyl booths. They were with a group of friends from college, arguing over what to order. It was a loud, messy thrum of humanity. Through the floor-to-ceiling windows Peri could see a city street, night-yellow from streetlamps, shimmering in a mist of rain.

As if thinking of the rain had drawn them there, Peri looked down to see that they were standing, feet on asphalt, in the centre of the road, the diner glowing like a TV screen just to their right. It was cold, the rain the kind that seeped through your clothes, limned your eyelashes so the whole world turned to rainbows. Where is she? Peri turned and she was there, right behind her, abrupt and present. Peri gasped, taking a step back, and then relaxed as they took her in. She was wearing a long camel trench coat and bright red fedora, Carmen Sandiago meets Dick Tracey, her lips a splash of violent red in a shadowed face.

"You called?" she teased.

"You could hear me," Peri said, amazed, but as they had the thought there was a crash of thunder overhead, and they held up their arms uselessly to protect against a sudden torrential downpour. It fell in thick curtains they could hardly see through or hear over, and the cold shock of it might have been enough to wake them if they hadn't been clinging so tightly to the dream.

"Is that you?" the woman asked in amazement.

"Is what me?" Peri yelled back.

"You're doing this!" The woman laughed, gesturing at the world around them, amazed and delighted.

Peri looked up at the sky. Were they doing it? They hadn't intended to, not like the dream with the paintbrush. Peri lurched, clutching for purchase that wasn't there as the world shifted under their feet. Suddenly they were in that painted meadow, Peri on their knees in the smudged wildflowers, yellow and green and blue and white crushed under their hands. They looked up, alarmed, but the woman had made the trip with them. She was still dressed for the rain, but even as Peri had the thought, her clothes transformed into smears of paint, bright white and blue that somehow moved with her, shifting seamlessly as she knelt beside Peri.

"Take a deep breath," she counselled, cupping Peri's cheek so just the tips of her fingers traced against their skin. "Clear your mind."

Peri felt more than saw the shift this time, and looked around to see that they were in a void, blackness around them, though still wearing the paint they had collected in the previous dream. Peri smiled. They hadn't meant to think it, but it was true. There was nothing in the world but her.

"Better?" the woman asked, drawing Peri to their feet.

"How am I doing this?" Peri asked.

"When you gave some of your essence to me, I had to make room for it. I gave you my connection to the dream in return," she explained.

Peri was amazed. "I'm... like you?" they asked. Suddenly the world was a carnival mirror, copies of both of them stretching out into infinity in every direction, and Peri was wearing the same clothes as the woman, hugging the same mature curves. They panicked, trying to turn away, and smashed face-first into a mirror. Spinning around, they hit another. "No! Where are you? What's happening?"

"Calm." The woman's voice came from everywhere and nowhere. Her tone was meant to be soothing, but it echoed, building on itself and becoming alien and cold. There were hundreds of her, thousands, and Peri had never felt more disconnected from her.

"I'm losing you!"

"You aren't. I'm right here." Suddenly she was, her arms around Peri's shoulders, her chest pressed against Peri's back.

Hyperventilating, Peri pressed back against her, struggling to breathe.

"Hush. It's all right. You're all right," the woman murmured.

"I can't control it," Peri gasped. Their panic seemed to be making it worse: they were cycling through locations now, the world shifting under their feet, sometimes destabilizing enough that Peri had to brace against the woman to stay upright. From day to night, from forest to castle to undersea conclave, all places Peri and the woman had met over the years—over the dreams.

"Peri, listen to me." The woman turned Peri around, and hungrily Peri clung to her shoulders, stared into her eyes. It helped somewhat to block out the world around them, to focus on one thing. "It wasn't enough. What you gave me, it helped. I can feel it beginning to work, can feel the bonds the echoes have over me weakening, but I'm still trapped. Do you understand? I'm trapped."

Peri shrieked as vines snaked up and caught the woman, pinning her arms to her body. There were thorns on the vines, and the woman snarled in pain as they tore tiny furrows in her skin.

"Stop it, stop it!" Peri shouted, horrified at what their power was manifesting. They grabbed the vines and tore them free, ignoring their bleeding palms as first one vine, then another, fell to the ground and vanished. The woman sagged and fell into Peri's arms.

"You have to help me," she begged. Her hat had tumbled off, her hair loose around her shoulders. She looked up at Peri with desperation, tears in the corners of her eyes, and Peri knew in that moment that they didn't care what she had done. They would protect her no matter what.

"It's Maeve's dream, isn't it. Everyone who watches it and dreams their own version creates an echo, and that echo pulls you in."

Weakly, she nodded. "I don't have the strength to fight it. I'm afraid of what's happening—of what's already happened."

"The people—the people who've died," Peri asked, without being brave enough to put the actual question into words.

"They were part of the dream, just like I was," she said with a helpless shrug. "When I fight to escape, sometimes... the walls crack. What happens in the dream bleeds out. Not enough to let me out. Never enough to set me free." She closed her eyes on the tears that filled them. "Will you not help me?"

"What can I do?" Peri asked. "We can't stop people from dreaming the dream. Only time will do that."

"I need more of what you gave," she said, and her hungry hands were on Peri's face, around their neck. "I can be free, Peri, I know it, I can break the connection the dream has over me. But I need more."

"You can have everything," Peri offered. "I... I love you."

The woman's eyes were pained, haunted, warm, loving. They were everything. "I would be lost without you," she promised, her voice a caress as she drew Peri close. They felt that painful chill spread through their body, and as it closed a cool hand over their heart, the woman whispered, "I can only be because of you."

~

For a time, Peri drifted. The sun seemed to rise and set, or maybe lights turned on and off. They didn't believe they had ever closed their eyes in a dream, but now they seemed not quite aware of anything. Their whole body was pins and needles, a stranger's body they could perhaps move if they cared to try. They didn't. She was gone, and they were a tiny cloud in an endless galaxy, particles of star stuff touched by cosmic rays. They listened to the sound of the universe, felt its vibration in their bones. They were everything, and also just this tiny cloud—a speck of nothing in the grandness. It made them feel, surprisingly, safe. There was freedom in insignificance, freedom in knowing everything would continue on without you.

And yet...

Was Peri lost? Were they happy drifting out there, alone? Or was there something they were supposed to do? Somewhere they were needed?

The song of the universe vibrated, shifted. It sounded familiar. Almost like a voice, from a throat, saying a word that Peri knew. "Peri. Peri."

Shocked into awareness, Peri's eyes flew open. Everything was spinning, wild and formless. The stars were a wash of light above them, and pressure was building all around. Peri was falling—falling through the atmosphere toward a wide expanse of farmland rushing up to meet them. Peri's impact, though painless, tossed dirt and plants into the air and left a crater a mile wide around them. They lay there for a moment, reflecting that though they had fallen many times in dreams, they had never landed before. Everything felt wrong. The shape of things, the pressure of it. It was a dream like none they had known before, a dream that stapled itself to their skin and almost, but not quite, hurt every time they tried to shift or move.

"Peri," the exasperated voice said, and Peri turned to see their mother standing in the crater, hands on hips. She looked just like she had when Peri was a child, towering over them, bigger than the sky. "What have I told you about daydreaming? You're wasting everyone's time! You think you're so special? You think you deserve to cause a disruption everywhere you are? Why can't you just be normal?"

"No," Peri mumbled, scrambling to their feet. "You don't—" The words stuck in the back of their throat. They coughed, trying to dislodge the words, and felt their teeth vibrate as their tongue knocked against them. They were loose, all of them, and in horror Peri started to spit them out, their hands filling with teeth as they coughed and choked.

"That's disgusting!" their mother shrieked. "You stop that! Stop that right now! Put on your church dress immediately!"

Peri looked down. They were wearing a soft yellow dress with little white flowers on it and black patent leather shoes. "No!" Peri snarled. "You don't control me anymore!"

Peri slashed a hand through the air and saw the shock on their mother's face as she split diagonally in two, bloodless but still viscerally violent. "I don't understand why you're so angry," she begged, tears in her eyes, as her torso slid off her legs and tipped to the side. "I love you, sweetheart. I'll always love you."

Peri spun away and pushed, escaping the crater and their mother. Instead of making a door it was like carving through Play-Doh, and they stepped out of a ragged hole shaking bits of reality out from between their fingers. In front of them, nuns in full riot gear poured out of a Lynx flat-bed truck, hundreds of them, screaming prayers like condemnations as they raced toward a group of university students holding signs that read, "Enough is enough!" and, "Say no to communion wine!"

Peri shook their head and kept running, pushing through again, stumbling out into another scene of chaos. People dressed for Coachella in bright rompers and gold-foil makeup ran screaming as giant pterodactyls swooped down, picking people up one at a time and tossing them into the sky to be torn apart by their waiting flock mates. Throwing up their arms to shield against falling blood, Peri kept running. This time they barreled through realities like the Kool-Aid Man, and they could almost feel the breeze they left behind as they ran through the hall of a luxury space-liner, a huge black hole visible through the glass viewscreens.

From there they hit a wall of water and had to swim through a dinner party in an opulent mansion, ball gowns floating in the saltwater that filled the room. Their fingers clawed for purchase, but they found nothing. Pulled through by the current, they were suddenly falling, caught up in a tornado that carried them through the sky. Diving and rolling in the eye of the dervish, they screamed and wrapped their arms around their head.

"Enough! You are in control. Return to your own mind. To your own dream." They grit their teeth and opened their eyes. Below them, elevator doors opened like a portal and they fell in. They hit the floor, which immediately became the wall as the elevator reoriented around them. It was a wood-panelled elevator, fancy but old-fashioned, with mirrors on the walls and Muzak playing quietly over the speakers.

Gasping, soaked, and windswept, they hit the button for the ground floor and waited. As they finally caught their breath, the elevator dinged and the doors opened... on a scene from hell. In the literal, demons dipping people into vats of fire as bat-winged demons raced overhead, hell.

"No! Absolutely not!" Peri roared and mashed the button to close the doors. A demon caught sight of them and started winging closer, but the panels closed just before it could reach them. Peri heard the impact, and sank to the ground, panting. "You are in your own dream," they whispered. "You are in your own mind. You can make this place anything you want it to be. Create a haven. Create a place to rest. Breathe."

Peri pictured softness. A world made of clouds, with no sharp edges or loud noises. Stillness, a white expanse that was both empty and completely full. An entire world where nothing rushed, where no one waited. They could feel it coming together, clay under the urgent fingers of their lucid mind. It felt like they were building something real, a place deep within their own mind where they would be safe.

"This place is waiting for you," they murmured as they crafted cumulonimbus skyscrapers and smoothed out vast cirrostratus high-ways. "You can get there."

Opening their eyes Peri stood up, trembling like a colt on new legs, and hit the top button on the elevator. They felt the lurch of motion and put out a hand for steadiness as the elevator returned to the ascent. A moment later, the doors opened and Peri staggered out, looking around. They were in a modern city, except everything that should have been steel or concrete was made of clouds. Panes of glass glittered in cloud-shaped skyscrapers. Square cloud garbage cans sat by cloud-shaped bus stops advertising the latest in cloud-seeding technology.

No one walked the streets. No cars drove. A faint breeze stopped it from feeling stagnant and smelled of lemons and vanilla.

Peri collapsed to the ground, also made of clouds, and lay sprawled there, panting. They closed their eyes and let the soft clouds cradle their aching, bruised body. They felt like they had been in an actual riot. And a tornado.

With a start they realized they were still wearing the hated yellow dress, and they scrunched up their face and sent it away. The breeze hit their naked skin, but they didn't care. They were free.

A booming knock echoed through the air, disturbing Peri's peace. When it sounded again, Peri realized it was coming from the elevator doors. "Oh, no," they sighed. Had they not gotten away? Was this world not the refuge it felt like?

It took real effort to stand, to walk over to the elevator. As they went, they covered their nakedness with leather armour over a silk robe. They would be ready for anything. "Bring it," they snarled, getting psyched up, and hit the down button.

"What the hell are you doing?" a voice demanded as the doors cracked open, and then a man stepped through the doors. He was familiar—and entirely unwelcome.

"You." Peri sighed and fell back against a nearby cloud wall. It held them at a slight angle, free from gravity. "What do you want this time?"

"Do you have any idea how much damage you just caused? Tearing through people's subconsciouses like that shouldn't even be possible!" The man was clearly furious, but when he had stepped through the door his clothes all changed into clouds. It was hard to take a man seriously when he was wearing a little cloud diaper and a big cloud cape, with cloud boots and a cloud scabbard at his side.

Peri resisted the urge to giggle. They were so sleepy. What did he want? "Every time I see you it's a lecture. You've never even told me your name."

"That's what you're worried about? Not unravelling the fabric of the universe? Not rewriting the laws of physics? My name?"

Peri shrugged. "Names mean something to us, you know. Maybe they don't to you." They trailed their fingers through the clouds of the wall. How was it they could lean against it without falling through, but still disturb it with such a soft gesture?

"They don't," he snapped, though Peri wasn't sure if he was telling the truth or just annoyed with their line of questioning.

"I didn't wake up," Peri said, and he blinked in confusion at the sudden change in subject. "I fell, but I didn't wake up."

"You want to wake up?" he demanded. "Fine! But this time, don't come back!"

He shoved Peri sideways, knocking them to the ground. Peri hit the clouds and bounced gently, rolling twice before coming to a stop. They lay there for a moment and stared up at him, unsure which of them was more stunned.

"Did you—" Peri asked.

"Why the hell—" he started at the same time, stopping when Peri trailed off.

"I'm not awake," Peri pointed out.

"Yeah, thanks, I can see that." The words dripped with sarcasm.

Peri sat up, touching their arms. They were still cold, numb, from whatever the woman had taken from them. An unwelcome realization slowly began to take hold, one that Peri wished—longed with every fibre of their being—to shove away and declare to be slanderous lies.

"Oh, shit," they finally mumbled. They looked up at the man, eyes wide, horror consuming them. "I think I may have made an awful mistake."

27

MAEVE

In the moonlight, the city looked burnished with silver. Roofs stuck out through the fog like the backs of whales in a calm ocean, appearing and disappearing among the eddies. Not far away, Maeve could see two figures crouched on a rooftop.

"Did they spot us?" one of them whispered.

"I don't know," the second voice whispered back. "But if we don't get this treasure out of the city, the Baron will never be able to rally the child-Kings and depose the Prince."

"And the evil in our land will grow so strong we'll never be able to rip it out, by root or by stem," the first voice agreed bitterly. "You don't need to tell me what the stakes are. I lived with the monster for years."

Maeve crept forward, tightening her grip on her sword with a grin. The two women were arguing, and their voices easily covered the sound of her footsteps as she made her way across the roof toward them. With the covering fog, they wouldn't see her until she was right on them.

"He has to know why we took it. He has to know he can't control us —can't command us," the woman snapped. "We've lived in terror for too long!"

"And you think I wouldn't recognize your work?" Maeve demanded as she strode out of the fog bank.

Both women spun. One of them was tall, with long hair and dark eyes. The other—the other was Maeve!

The realization jolted Maeve out of the narrative of the dream. Panicked, she looked down at herself. She was dressed as the prince from her dream. And that meant... "Oh, no, no, no. Hell no!"

"I'll show you my work!!" the other woman yelled. She looked at lot like Josie: tall, with straight black hair, dark eyes, and a commanding sort of beauty. She was racially ambiguous: her eyes were slightly tilted but had thick eyelid creases, and her skin was a shade of light brown that could have been a tan or could have been melanin. She was, without a doubt, the woman who had stepped in and taken over Josie's role in the dream. As Maeve stuttered, the woman pulled her sword from its scabbard and charged.

Maeve scrambled to stay out of her way as the other woman lunged and slashed. "Stop trying to stab me!" she screamed. "It's a dream! It's a dream, you're caught in a dream!"

Doubt and anger warred on the woman's face. Beside her, the dream version of Maeve didn't seem to be aware that the dream had shifted.

"Get him, Josie!" Dream-Maeve yelled enthusiastically. "Show him that he's nothing but a bully with fear in his heart! He's afraid of you because he can't control you anymore!"

"It didn't work," the dream woman wailed. "It wasn't enough! I took it *all* and it still isn't enough!" With a raw, throat-burning scream, she came at Maeve, slashing the sword wildly through the air. Her anger made her form sloppy, and that was all that saved Maeve as she parried the blow. The impact vibrated fiercely up her arm.

"Would you stop trying to kill me!" Maeve screamed. If dream-Jason had been a poor swordfighter, Maeve was even worse. She had full-on dropped her sword during the first assault, and she was instead scrambling around the roof, trying not to fall or be stabbed as the woman doggedly pursued her. The only thing that saved Maeve was the slick footing. Neither of them was doing well, but running away was easier than aiming and stabbing when you were sliding around a gabled roof.

"Wake up wake up wake up," Maeve begged herself as the

Wren Handman

woman's sword slashed her upper arm, cutting into her fancy brocade coat and drawing a thin line of blood.

The woman grinned. "Wake up... Now isn't that an interesting idea. What if we *both* wake up?"

The world lurched. "What?" Maeve looked down at the ground below—and saw the backyard of her own house. The fog was gone, as were the fantastical city streets. She was in Vancouver, in fall weather that felt too real against her naked skin. She chirped in panic and tried to cover up. She was completely nude, with no sword to defend herself, standing on the roof of the fucking house! "Holy shit, you did it. You're in the real world!"

The woman looked like she'd eaten a lemon. "Your world is a cardboard farce. I hope never to step foot in it again." She advanced, sword slashing, and Maeve abandoned decorum to scramble further up the roof with a shriek as she took several glancing cuts to her arms.

"Why are you still trying to kill me!" she yelled, terrified.

"It's the only way I can think of to be free of the dream," the woman explained. She sounded almost apologetic. There was very little remorse, like she was telling Maeve she wouldn't be able to attend her birthday party. "If you die, the dream ends."

"Come *on*! That can't be the only way." Maeve glanced right and left, but there was nowhere to go. She was trapped. She turned around, panting hard.

The woman shrugged. "It's the only way I know. I *am* sorry." Her face hardened and she brought the sword up again. "But I won't be your puppet anymore."

There had to be a way to break the narrative without Maeve dying! She just had to figure it out. She had to think, which was hard to do with a sword flying at her. She tripped, scrambling for purchase as she slid a few feet down and toward the edge. Her bare heels caught in the gutter, and she watched in horror as the woman reared up in front of her. She looked down at Maeve dispassionately, and slowly brought the sword up and back.

"I'm sorry!" Maeve screamed. The woman paused, the sword still drawn back, ready to be plunged into Maeve's stomach.

"You're what?"

"I'm sorry," Maeve panted. She turned slightly on her side,

careful not to fall from her precarious position but wanting to make eye contact. "I will never try to control you again." She thought about the words of the dream, about what Josie had wanted from Jason, and tried to weave that together with what the woman needed from her. There was no way that Maeve's death was the only way to stop the flow of the dream. If she could change the dream's narrative, maybe she could free the woman that way. The woman's desperation to be free was a clear reflection of Josie's desire to be free from Jason. Maeve could use that.

"You were right—I was a bully. I took over when I should have listened. I made a mess and left it for other people to clean up. That was wrong. It wasn't fair to you, and I see that now. I'll step back. It's your turn to rule—it's your right. I'll follow your lead. You decide. You shape the future. Create the world you want to see, and I will live in it happily, and be grateful for the chance to watch what you come up with. I swear it."

The woman listened to Maeve's speech, stunned. The anger faded from her face, slowly, replaced by something like awe. "You mean this?" she asked.

"I do," Maeve promised. "We don't have to be trapped by the past. You can create something new."

The woman opened her mouth, but Maeve never got a chance to hear what she was going to say. Like smoke hit by a rough wind, the woman's shape shifted and then scattered, dispersing into the night air. Her sword clanged to the roof, alarmingly real, and Maeve let herself fall onto her back, panting. She had done it! She changed the narrative of the dream and released the woman from the loop she was trapped in. Holy shit.

And now she was stuck on a roof... naked.

"Help?" Maeve called, tentatively. "Help! Someone! I'm—uh—on the roof!"

It was going to be a long night.

~

As it turned out, having to call the fire department because you were stranded on your roof naked triggered a whole lot of questions. Maeve had managed to wake her neighbours after what felt like an hour of screaming and banging on the roof, though it was actually less than ten minutes. Unfortunately, they didn't have a ladder that was anywhere near long enough to reach her, and since it was about four a.m., they couldn't exactly phone up a friend and borrow one.

911 was the only solution, and a very confused fire department rolled up about twenty minutes later. By then Maeve's legs were jelly, and she was terrified she was going to lose her toehold on the gutter and fall off the roof before they could get to her. Luckily, they moved fast once they arrived, and being carried naked off the roof in the arms of a hot firefighter significantly improved her night.

They wrapped her in a silver emergency blanket and sat her down on her front steps, where a less-attractive but higher-ranked firefighter proceeded to grill her about how exactly the hell she had gotten onto the roof in the first place. Oh, and where the fucking sword had come from. Even after twenty minutes of prep-time, a plausible lie failed to materialize in her brain, so she just shrugged and told them she had no idea. She had been fast asleep in her basement suite and had woken up on the roof, as naked as when she climbed between the sheets.

Sleepwalking didn't exactly explain how she scaled a two-story building with no ladder, but it took the onus out off her to explain the mystery. She wasn't sure the guy she was talking to believed her, but since she hadn't committed a crime there wasn't much he could do. He gave her a disbelieving look and kept asking the same three or four questions until he finally gave up and told her that she could go back to bed.

Not having been involved with any crimes came with the added bonus of keeping the dream sword. Maeve didn't necessarily want a memento from the woman who attacked her, but it was easier to say she was a theatre nerd with a prop sword than to claim it didn't belong to her. She shucked it over her shoulder and took it with her.

Maeve was tired, but she had no intention of going back to sleep —maybe ever. Back in her apartment, she sent Peri a quick note, warning them that she had been attacked by the woman from the dream and that she thought she might have solved the problem. She wasn't surprised that Peri didn't answer—it wasn't even six by the time the firetruck left—but she wanted the message to be there as soon as Peri woke up. Who knows what Peri had faced—or was facing.

Maeve showered until the hot water ran out, silently apologizing to her neighbours in case any of them were still up, too, and then made a pot of coffee and waited for the world to wake up. She checked her phone obsessively, but there were no messages from Peri. At seven, she messaged Josie and told her to call as soon as she was up, and then went back to pacing her house and generally killing time.

Josie finally called at seven-thirty, bleary-voiced with sleep, and Maeve unloaded everything on her in a rush. She slashed the sword for emphasis every time she described something exciting, its weight still a shock in her hand. Josie desperately wanted to call in sick, but she hated to leave her clients in pain, and Maeve assured her there was nothing to be done. Instead, they made plans to get together after work and go over everything that had happened.

Around ten she decided it was late enough to call Peri, but there was no answer. She paced around the apartment, wishing she had something to occupy her time, and finally gave up and went out. She killed the day shopping for things she didn't need and wasn't sure that she could afford, given that her income was dependent on technology that was no longer safe.

Unless what she had done was enough to solve the problem. She hoped that it had been. After all, the woman had vanished. But could she be sure it was over? She'd been recording her dreams for two years without any dream creatures getting caught up in a narrative and trying to murder her. Something had to have changed. Something had to have started all of this.

Would there come a point where she could turn the technology on again? She had to believe there was. She had a Communications degree, and some experience working for nonprofits, but she couldn't go back to that life. Not when she'd finally experienced what it meant to be a creator, to fill that artistic drive to leave something of herself in the world. It was everything she had always known it would be, a fire that lit answering sparks deep in her soul. She couldn't stop. She had to find a way forward.

She called Peri three more times, getting more and more worried that there was no answer. Peri had been intending to confront the woman, and instead she had ended up on Maeve's roof, trying to kill her. The woman might have done something to Peri, angry that they hadn't taken her side. Maeve knew Peri was in Vancouver, but nothing else. She had no way to track Peri or the woman down.

By dinnertime there was still no word from Peri, and Josie came over with takeout, eager to hear everything. She picked up the sword in awe, swishing it around just like Maeve had, and over the evening she kept returning to it, picking it up and hefting its weight as if expecting it to disappear at any moment.

Josie helped Maeve look up DreamsAway to see if Peri had ever posted more about where they lived, but they were a ghost online. They kept their life private, and Maeve couldn't find any way to contact them outside of the phone number they already had.

"Maybe they're just a flaky person," Josie suggested, almost hopeful.

Maeve sighed and nodded. It was possible, but she had a bad feeling about it just the same. While it was true that she didn't know Peri, she had seen how excited the other dreamer was to have someone to talk to, to bounce ideas back and forth with. If Peri wasn't answering, there had to be a reason.

Eventually, the friends had to admit defeat. They weren't going to find Peri, and there was nothing more to do. They put on a bad movie, and instead of watching it, gorged themselves on junk food and talked. Josie was grieving Jason and struggling with how to handle grief over a man she had left, a man she had been glad to leave. Her emotions were complex and thorny, and Maeve mostly listened quietly while Josie thought out loud.

The realization that Jason had been killed because of a dream—by a dream—helped Josie process his death. She had been scared, thinking there was someone out there who wanted him dead, maybe someone she knew, someone who might come after her, too.

Josie went home early, since she had work the next day, and Maeve went to bed not long after. She was absolutely wrung out, but nerves made it hard to get to sleep. She had no idea what she would find on the other side. She had no Blank to ensure that her dream would be lucid, and the device she had ordered wouldn't arrive for weeks. The only reason she had managed to snap to consciousness inside the dream the night before was because of the shock of seeing her own face. If it hadn't been for that, she would be dead—just like all of those other people.

It was clear to Maeve that the woman, trapped in the narrative of the original Jason dream, had been reliving the dream over and over in other people's sleeping minds. For some of those people, for some reason, the dream crossed over into reality, just like it had for Maeve. The woman had killed them, throwing them off the roof, because that was what the dream demanded. With Maeve she had made a choice, but all those others... the poor woman's hand had been forced.

Maeve couldn't imagine what that would feel like. Trapped in a vicious cycle, watching yourself commit crime after crime... She had sympathy for the woman, even if Maeve had almost become her victim.

With those thoughts circling endless in her mind, exhaustion eventually won out over fear, and Maeve drifted off.

She woke up in her parents' car, the one she had learned to drive in. She was driving down the highway, on her way to school. The traffic was light, and she smiled as she switched lanes. The road took a bit of a dip, and she pressed her foot against the brake to slow down... but nothing happened. If anything, the car started to speed up. Panicked, she smashed her foot against the brake. She swerved around the road, trying to avoid other cars as the wheel under her shuddered and moved of its own accord. The car was absolutely out of control!

A hand reached over and yanked on her emergency brake. The car spun in a circle, and with a screech of tires came to a safe stop on the shoulder of the road. Panting, Maeve turned to take in the passenger she hadn't noticed until now. He was incredibly handsome, and his broad frame filled the small car's narrow seat. His knees were practically at his chin even though he wasn't a tall man.

"You need to slow down," he chided her.

"Thanks," she gasped. "I don't know what happened."

"I need your help," he said. "It's Peri."

"Peri?" she asked. The name rang a bell. Was it someone from her classes? Someone she knew through her parents?

The man reached over and squeezed her hand. "You don't know them," he assured her, "but I think they're in trouble."

I know Peri, Maeve thought. As her internal monologue snapped out of sync with her physical body, she felt a jarring jolt like a record scratch. She *did* know Peri, but forcing the words out felt like fighting upstream against a powerful current. "Peri is a streamer. They were supposed to call last night, but they never did."

Maeve gasped in relief as the block fell and memory returned, and right on its heels came fear for Peri. They had promised to call but hadn't, and now this man was here to warn her about them. That couldn't be good.

"It is never what I expect with you," he said, taking her hand with a smile.

"I'll take that as a compliment."

"It is," he promised, and even though he wasn't a prince anymore she was struck by his smile, by its warmth. He had so much charisma, and she was pretty sure he had no idea, which made it all the more appealing.

There was time for that later, though. "What's happening with Peri?"

"Right," he said. "You need to go and wake them up."

Maeve sat up in bed, the words *wake them up* echoing in her mind. She was pretty sure there had been more to the dream, but she couldn't remember it. Frustrated, she sat up in bed. Running a hand through her hair, Maeve tried to mentally cling to the last fragments of the dream. She knew she was supposed to go wake Peri up, but how was she supposed to find them? Vancouver was a big city, and that was assuming Peri didn't live in Burnaby or Surrey and just *called* it Vancouver, which a lot of people did.

Maeve got out of bed and turned on the lights. As she pulled off her shirt to change into real clothes, she caught sight of something on her arm, and grinned.

It was an address written in felt pen. Apparently, the man in her dream had known exactly where to send her.

28

PERI

The world was soft and smooth, nothing but even, white light. Peri reached out and trailed a hand through the gentle clouds, absently noting the way the water vapour puffed away at the slight motion and yet cradled them in a smooth, sensationless embrace. They were floating, half in and half out of the city street, lazily stroking their arms away from their torso and back to keep up their gentle forward motion.

Had there been someone here, not long ago? Peri thought so, but they couldn't remember. Something had happened. They had been trying to do something, trying to get somewhere. None of it seemed important now.

But there was something, wasn't there? Another life, a distant one that Peri had once been so invested in. They remembered the sunset over water. A warm, soft cat purring in their lap. The taste of cinnamon and nutmeg.

Or was that all a dream?

They were so tired. Why couldn't they sleep? There was something they had to do, somewhere they had to get to. Someone? A flash of dark eyes. A laugh, so rich and full. Perfect arched lips, with a small brown freckle above the right cusp.

Peri sat up, startled, their heart beating faster. Who was she? She had something to do with this place, or with Peri. She was important. Was she part of what Peri had been supposed to do? No, that couldn't be it. Peri had been sleeping, that was all. They had been sleeping, and now it was time to wake up.

Peri clenched their fists... but when nothing happened, they forgot what they were trying to do. They relaxed, lying back down among the clouds. What had they been thinking? They couldn't remember. It couldn't have been that important. It was peaceful here. The clouds rocked them, and Peri wondered what would happen if they let go of the voice in their head and the beating in their chest. If they drifted away...

A voice in the back of their mind whispered that they had to wake up. That if they didn't, it would be too late. Peri didn't listen. They just wanted to rest here, for a little while...

29

MAEVE

It was a little after midnight when Maeve locked her door behind her and jumped into the waiting car. It was too late to take the SkyTrain, which stopped running early on weeknights, and she wanted to get there as quickly as she could. She had no idea what would be waiting for her at Peri's. All she could remember from the dream was the man's imperative: "Wake them up."

If Peri was trapped in a dream, what the hell did that even mean? Maeve had no idea how to wake someone up from a magical sleep. Well, other than the obvious, but that brought up issues of consent, and anyway it was a fairytale thing and probably didn't apply here.

She couldn't stop worrying that this was somehow her fault. She thought she had changed the narrative and freed the woman, but what if there had been unintended consequences? Could she have sent the woman back to Peri? If that was the case, there were probably equal odds that Peri was in danger or that they just didn't *want* to be woken up. The way they had talked about the woman was obviously romantic. There was attraction there, deep and committed. But if Peri was caught up in some lover's tryst, the man surely wouldn't have sent Maeve to the rescue. He had to know that something was wrong.

The trip turned out to be short. The address was in Yaletown, and it was late enough that traffic over the bridge into downtown was light. The carshare pulled up in front of one of those towering skyscrapers that dotted the skyline, glimpses of dark ocean visible in the far distance. Maeve ran up to the door and found Peri's apartment number in the electronic listings, then buzzed. There was no answer. She hesitated. There was no doorman she could prevail on to let her in, and no way to get to Peri's apartment without getting through the front door.

She tried calling a few random apartments, but it was late, and no one answered. On the fourth try, someone picked up. She told them she was trying to get into 1207 but the buzzer wasn't working, and the grumbling voice on the other end told her to fuck off—but then buzzed her in. She wasn't sure if it was an accident or a prime example of Canadian politeness at work, but she wasn't about to question her luck. She yanked open the door and ran to the elevators.

At Peri's door, Maeve pulled out the bobby pins she had in her pocket. She straightened them both out and stuck them in the lock, shaking them around.

Nothing happened.

Maeve frowned. She wasn't entirely sure what she was trying to do, but the people on TV made it look so easy. She tried again, fishing around inside the lock. She could feel differences in pressure depending on how she moved them, but she had no idea if she was getting closer or further away from opening the lock.

Swearing, Maeve slammed her hand against the door handle. It vibrated, and Maeve hesitated. If she made too much noise, some angry neighbour might call the cops on her. But how else was she going to get inside? Maeve picked up the welcome mat, hoping for a hidden key, but there was nothing. She knocked briefly but as hard as she could. She heard a plaintive meow from the other side, but no other answer.

Guess we're doing this the hard way. Maeve glanced around, thinking. She grabbed her scarf and wrapped it around the door handle.

Looking both ways to make sure no one was coming, she took a deep breath, took aim, and kicked the handle, sideways, as hard as she could. Three more kicks, louder than she liked, and the doorknob was cracked and hanging at an odd angle. With a screwdriver she had brought, Maeve reached through the hole and shoved at the deadbolt until it shifted and unlocked.

Maeve opened the door and was immediately assaulted by a very unhappy grey cat. It wove around her legs, complaining loudly, and darted away when she tried to pick it up. She pushed the door shut and locked it to keep it closed, then turned on a light and looked around. She whistled as she took in the condo. Peri's place was *nice*. Way nicer than hers. They had tasteful artwork on the walls, matching furniture, and a view of the city that took her breath away.

Turning on lights as she went, Maeve found the bedroom. "Um, Peri? I'm not a stalker and please don't freak out but I guess I'm here to rescue you?" Maeve called out. She turned on the light there, too, revealing an adorably nerdy bedroom with one clearly occupied bed. In sleep, Peri looked even younger than they had on camera, and it made all of Maeve's considerable protective instincts flare to life. She may not know Peri well, but she would be damned if she was going to let anything happen to them.

She hurried over to the bed and winced as she was hit with an unpleasant smell. Peri had wet the bed. Maeve's heart started beating faster. Something was very wrong. She approached cautiously, taking in Peri's sleeping form, but there was no obvious harm or ailment—aside from not waking up, that is. No signs of trauma, no whimpering nightmare.

Maeve reached over and carefully removed a metal and plastic band from Peri's forehead. She examined it critically. It was the same lucid dreaming device she had ordered, the one Peri had recommended. Could it be the reason Peri hadn't woken up?

Setting it aside, she gave Peri a quick, sharp shake. "Peri! Wake up!" When the first shake didn't do anything, Maeve tried again, and her voice rose to a yell. "Peri! It's Maeve! You have to wake up! You have to wake up!"

She wasn't sure what reaction she was hoping for, but it definitely wasn't the complete lack she got. Maeve stepped back, trying to formulate a plan of action, and almost stepped on the cat, which had come over to investigate this strange woman in its apartment.

"Okay. You need food and water. Let's fix that and maybe we'll have an idea," Maeve told the cat. She took a detour to take off her shoes and leave them by the front door, then went into the kitchen and found matching food and water bowls by the fridge, both empty. Maeve filled the water from the tap and then hunted for kibble. She couldn't find any, but she found a tin of wet food and gave the cat that instead. It scarfed the food down happily, and even let Maeve pet it a little bit.

"Let's think this through. Peri is stuck in dreams," Maeve mused out loud, directing her thoughts to the cat. "We have to get them to wake up. If we can't get them to wake up in the real world... The lucid dreaming thing!"

Maeve leaped to her feet and raced back into the bedroom. The lucid dreaming tech was where she had left it, beside the bed. Maeve put it on, settling the electrodes against her temple and adjusting the strap at the back into it settled comfortably. Then she climbed onto the bed beside Peri and lay down beside them, their arms touching.

"Sorry," she murmured to the sleeping figure beside her. "I know this is a bit weird, but hopefully it works."

Maeve closed her eyes and took ten deep breaths. She thought that being in a stranger's bed about to do something potentially dangerous would mean falling asleep would be next to impossible. But it was late, and she was exhausted. In less than ten minutes she found the edges of the world growing misty and dark...

Maeve was standing in a white, snowy wood. The forest around her was covered in ice, and every leaf and twig glittered like jewels. The air was so cold and crisp it burned her lungs, and the sky overhead was the kind of blue that made her eyes water.

Maeve turned in a slow circle, marvelling that this incredible landscape had come from her. She was dreaming it, bringing every crystalline sparkle to life with her mind. It was all part of her. She laughed, throwing her arms wide and spinning again. It had worked! She was in the dream *and* she was lucid and aware. Halfway there.

Now she just had to find Peri, or hope that Peri could find her.

"Peri?!" she screamed. "It's Maeve! I'm here to rescue you!" Her voice echoed across the empty winter landscape. There was no other sound. Not a single bird, not a winter hare, not even the wind, which should have turned the twinkling ice into a symphony. Would the silence be enough to carry her voice through to Peri? And what the hell would she do if it wasn't?

30

PERI

What would it be like to be a cloud? To let go of body, let go of self, and drift away? Would it hurt, to know what you were giving up? Or would you never know, and in never knowing, never mind?

Their little finger twinged. Was that a voice, calling their name? So strange. Did they even have a name? Did they exist at all outside of this moment?

Peri, they thought. The voice had called them Peri. The thought sent an answering spark racing through their mind. Their eyelashes fluttered. They had eyes to open, eyes that could see the world. A world of clouds, white and formless and void. Two strange lumps were sticking out of the clouds. Birds?

Peri sat up and the lumps moved. Toes. It was their toes, sticking up out of the clouds. Sitting—they had a body, didn't they? A torso, legs. *Peri*. They were Peri. That name belonged to them, defined the shape of them. Peri was a person.

Gradually, piece by piece, Peri reconstructed a sense of self. Peri owned a cat. Peri loved learning about new things, hated meeting new people. Peri read books and watched movies. They wanted to escape from reality. *No, not escape. Run toward it.* Peri hated being cold, because they always felt cold when they were depressed. Peri loved hot showers, would sit sometimes in the bath and let the shower drive all care away. Peri sometimes felt like a man and sometimes like a woman, and wished they could be both at once sometimes or neither, too, when the mood struck. Peri didn't like being touched casually, felt touch should mean something, longed for someone to curl up beside them and do nothing but hold their hand.

Peri was asleep. Peri was dreaming—but they were ready to wake up.

"Peri! It's Maeve!" the voice called. Peri sat up, shell-shocked and shivering. They were asleep, in their own dream—and someone was calling.

31

MAEVE

Maeve walked through the forest, heading for higher ground and calling Peri's name all the while. Maybe she could find something in the dream that related to Peri, and call them that way?

"Maeve?"

Maeve screamed, turning so quickly she fell in a puff of snow. Peri had appeared behind her, completely silently and from absolutely nowhere. They looked haunted. Their pale skin was even paler than when Maeve had seen them last, and there were dark circles under their eyes. There were hollows in their cheeks and shadows across their clavicle.

"Peri, thank god. Are you okay? I tried to wake you up, but I couldn't." Maeve climbed up from the snow, brushing it off her back. It was surprisingly warm and grainy, like sand.

Maeve expected one of Peri's subtle telltale smiles, but to her horror, Peri's eyes filled with tears. "She left me... She took it, and she left me there."

They started to cry, and in a flash Maeve was at their side. She reached out and enfolded Peri in a hug—Peri jumped at the contact, but then relaxed into her arms before Maeve could change her mind and pull away.

"She just... left." Peri sounded like they hadn't spoken in days. Their voice caught and stumbled coming out of their throat.

"I'm so sorry," Maeve whispered, with just enough anger in her voice to show Peri there was no pity there. She leaned her chin against Peri's hair and held them, silent, as Peri let the tears fall. After a long moment, Peri pulled away. "I can't wake you up," Maeve repeated. "I'm in your apartment but nothing is working."

"How did you get in?" Peri asked, then slashed their hand through the air, negating the question. Their eyes were large and haunted, and there was no force to their voice, like they might drift away in a sharp wind. "Never mind. It's my connection to the waking world. I'm losing myself, Maeve, I... The woman used it to fuel herself, to get out. My mind is forgetting that my body exists. We need to do something, something to stimulate that connection."

"I don't think slapping you is going to do the trick," Maeve admitted. She didn't voice her first, silly thought about a kiss.

"I've got an idea," Peri said.

Maeve looked around in wonder as the snow around them melted away. The sun came out in full force, and within moments the forest was in the height of summer. Birds sang, the wind whispered, and the sun caked moisture out of the ground. Maeve brushed a hand over her forehead; it came away damp with sweat.

"Did *you* do that?" she asked, amazed.

There was the smile Maeve was already growing to like, a sweet soft upturn at the corner of Peri's mouth. "I'm learning," they admitted. "I'll stay here and get it as hot as I can."

"What do I do?" Maeve asked.

Peri laid out the plan, but Maeve could hear the hesitation under their confident words. This was uncharted territory, but Maeve thought it could work.

"I'll see you on the other side," she promised, and pushed herself awake.

Maeve woke up beside Peri, the dream crisp and clear in her mind. She took off the lucid dreaming device and immediately sprang into action.

First, she ran into the bathroom and filled it with cold water. Then she went to the kitchen and filled a big popcorn bowl with ice from the fancy ice maker in the fridge. She dumped that into the tub, then went back for seconds. The bowl half-filled before a red light flashed on; she guessed it needed time before it could make more. It would have to be enough.

Back in the bedroom, Maeve awkwardly hauled Peri out of bed, grateful that Peri slept in pajamas. Maeve wasn't exactly strong, but Peri was light, and the bathroom wasn't far. Maeve was most worried about getting Peri into the tub without accidentally dunking them under the water.

Eventually she stepped in herself, howling at the cold, and then dragged Peri in after her so that she could hold Peri's head up. The tub wasn't big enough for them both to be submerged, but she sat on the edge with Peri's head in her lap and let the rest of their body fall into the water.

Peri's theory was simple. The contrast between the extreme cold of the ice bath and the extreme heat of the dream would shatter the connection the dream had over Peri, vaulting them back into the real world.

Maeve held on tight and splashed ice water over Peri's core. "Wake up," she urged Peri's sleeping form. "Wake up, wake up, wake—"

Peri gasped like the dead being resurrected and thrashed in Maeve's arms, knocking their forehead painfully against her nose. She held on for dear life, terrified that she would slip, and Peri would end up with a mouthful of ice water.

"I've got you!" Maeve shouted. "You're safe, you're okay, I've got you! I've got you!"

Panting, Peri grabbed onto Maeve's hands where she held them under the arms. They clung on for dear life as their thrashing calmed and their breath slowly returned to normal.

"I've got you," Maeve said one last time, shivering and wet and thoroughly thrilled. "I'm here, and I've got you."

32

PERI

Peri sat in the shower, shivering, as they cleaned away the missing day. They couldn't stop questioning whether the woman had known the consequences of what she asked for—that Peri wouldn't be able to wake up from the dreaming world. They could have died. *Juniper* could have died! If Maeve hadn't found them...

They couldn't quite let go of what they felt—it was a habit of love that they knew would be hard to break—but Peri felt anger rising to overwhelm it. She had been so—so selfish! She took everything Peri had to give, everything, without care of consequence. She saved herself by dooming Peri.

The hardest part was that Peri wasn't sure they could blame her for it.

Peri towelled off and headed into the bedroom to change, where they discovered to their horror that they had wet the bed. The mattress protector had done its job, and the mattress was fine, but everything needed washing. Peri put everything into the laundry, then found Maeve in the kitchen making a vegan grilled cheese. Juniper was still stuffing her face at her feet. The clock read 2:00, and Peri had to look outside to see that it was the dead of night.

"I figured you'd be starving," Maeve said. "I hope it's okay I just sort of... dived in."

"Yeah, of course. And thank you. For all of it."

"How did it happen? That guy from the dreams showed up and told me you were in trouble. He gave me your address." She held her arm up. She had taken her jacket off, and now she shoved back the sleeve of her long-sleeved purple shirt to show Peri's address stamped on her forearm like a tattoo. "Also, I broke your door," she added, sheepish.

"I don't know where to start," Peri admitted. Their legs were wobbly from being in bed that long. They sat down at the kitchen table while Maeve cooked. "She—the woman, the one from my dreams—she told me that she needed my help to fight the narrative. She thought she could break free if I could help her boost her connection to the waking world. I didn't know it would lock me in."

"Shit. Oh, shit. Shit!" Maeve said, as if coming to a startling set of realizations in quick succession. "You made her manifest! That's how she showed up at my house! She made part of my dream real. I was back in the rooftop dream I told you about, only this time I was the prince. She said that she thought killing me would break the narrative and set her free."

"She tried to kill you?!" Peri gasped.

"Stabbing was involved." Maeve pulled her overshirt off, momentarily barring a splash of her stomach and causing Peri to shift uncomfortably on their seat. Maeve dropped the shirt and held out her arms, displaying a series of shallow but long slashes. "She told me it was the only way she knew to be free. It was like —she was sorry for it, you know? But not sorry enough not to do it."

"What happened to her?" Peri asked.

Maeve slid the cooked sandwich out of the frying pan and onto a plate, handing it to Peri. "I apologized."

"I'm lost."

"Sorry." Maeve laughed. "She said she needed to be free of the narrative. So, I thought, what if I changed the narrative of this particular story so she stops killing people? I apologized, the way Jason's character should have—oh, that's the guy who got pushed off the roof—anyway, it seemed to work? She vanished and I was awake on my roof, naked as a newborn. So that was fun. Hot firemen were involved."

Maeve poured two glasses of water, already at home in Peri's kitchen, and shooed them over to the kitchen table to eat. Peri's mind was churning, but they were starving. They dug into the sandwich and took a few generous bites before answering.

"I could have gotten you killed."

"Hey—that's on her, not you. You just wanted to help her." Maeve shrugged. "Plus, I'm alive, so no use crying over milk that didn't even spill, just, you know, wobbled a bit." She made the 'so-so' motion with her hand as she said wobble.

They sat in silence for a little while as Peri finished their sandwich. They were pleased to see that Maeve gave them space to process—so many people were afraid of silence. Peri needed the time to think. The confirmation that the woman was capable of murder was chilling. It sounded like Maeve had in some way been responsible for trapping the woman, given that she was stuck in the narrative in a dream of Maeve's creation, but Maeve hadn't done any of it intentionally. There was no justification to hurt her—*to kill her. Say what it is.*

The truth that Peri didn't want to admit was that they could forgive the woman for her violence. An animal caught in a trap would chew off its own leg to be free. But the woman had said that she knew Peri completely. She had known that Peri would give whatever she asked and not demand answers. Had she known how much danger she was putting Peri in? Had she taken that energy knowing that Peri would become trapped, unable to wake? Peri wasn't sure they could bear that.

Now that the woman was free, maybe she would be more honest about her motivations. If, that is, she was free at all...

"You said that you freed the woman from the narrative of the dream, and that released her," Peri said.

"Yeah?"

"But there are still tons of people out there who've seen the dream. What if one of them dreams it again?"

Maeve shook her head. "I'm not sure. I don't know exactly how the woman and the dreams are connected."

"She was in your original dream, right? She took Josie's place,"

Peri said. "Somehow, every time someone watched that video and was inspired to have the same dream, the woman was pulled into their dream. She was being dragged from one end of the planet to another like a leaf in a raging river."

"Oh, shit. She told you that?" Maeve asked. When Peri nodded, she frowned and drummed her fingers on the table. "Why now, though? I've been streaming for two years. Why hasn't it happened before?"

"The woman told me that she knew me well. I've been dreaming her for years, and recording her hasn't done her any harm. So it isn't that. Maybe this is the first time she was in one of your dreams? It could be that something about the intersection of her, your dream, and the technology caused the problem."

"So the only way to free her is to—what? Wait until every person who saw the dream forgets it?"

"Unless we can find some way to isolate her from the dreams. Create a narrative buffer that's stronger than the narrative that pulls her out, maybe?"

"We can't be dreaming all the time," Maeve pointed out. "What's she going to do when we're awake?"

Peri blew out a frustrated breath. "I don't know," they admitted. "But we have all the pieces. We need to confront them both, *together*." Together they had a better chance of finding an outcome that didn't end in anyone's death.

Maeve nodded. "I'm down. We confront them together. How do we do that, though? You heard me calling to you—will you be able to come to me again? And how do we find the woman?"

"The first part is easy. After I started using the lucid dreaming tech, I found a way to punch through into other people's dreams. I haven't tried bringing someone else with me, but there's no reason to think I won't be able to."

Maeve looked impressed—and shocked, too. "Are you serious? Are you sure?"

"Yeah. I went to Argentina, imagined my way into a stranger's dream. I asked him for details about his hometown, somewhere I'd never heard of, and then looked it up when I woke up. It was all real."

"Holy shit." Maeve's eyes were wide and distant; then, like a light switch turning on, she suddenly lit up with laughter. "You'd think I'd stop being amazed at everything by now."

"I get it. It's enough mystery for a lifetime," Peri said.

"You'll have to wake me up. Out of the narrative, I mean. I can't lucid dream on my own without Blank. Every time I've done it, something that didn't fit the narrative has shaken me out—like seeing that guy."

Peri thought about the tingle in their arms, the coldness in the tips of their fingers. "You can use my lucid dreaming wearable again, if you want. I don't think I need it anymore."

"Well, that was ominous," Maeve teased, and Peri found a smile on their lips, having snuck there without their awareness. "So, I usually save this for the second date, but I guess let's go to bed?"

As it happened, Peri set Maeve up to sleep on the couch, not in their bed. There was plenty of room, but Maeve was a stranger, and Peri panicked just thinking about her that close to them. Luckily, she wasn't offended, and even offered to help Peri put new sheets on—an offer Peri declined. She had already done too much, and Peri didn't like to feel like an inconvenience. They often worried they would miss a subtle social cue that someone was offering to help but didn't really want to give that help.

Peri gave Maeve a couple of warm blankets and the lucid dream headband, helping her get the dual pads centred over her temples, then went into the bedroom. Juniper immediately followed, afraid to be more than a few feet away from them. They climbed into bed, surprised at how tired they were despite having been asleep for a whole day.

It was shockingly easy to fall asleep—dangerously so. Peri just concentrated on the tingle in their arms, and before long they were plummeting into dreaming.

Peri was standing on the stage of their high school auditorium. Classmates they barely remembered were getting ready for a talent competition, but Peri ignored them and marched for the stage door. Maeve. They opened the door and walked through.

The door let them out into a hedge maze. Maeve was standing

among the moon-dark leaves wearing a form-fitting scarlet evening gown with a huge silky train, and her grin when she saw Peri made them swallow a nervous laugh. She was stunning in red, and the way her dress hugged her was scandalous, even though it wasn't revealing that much skin.

"It worked!" she crowed. She covered the space between them in a heartbeat but didn't hug Peri—she might have noticed the tiny step backward they took. "I've been wandering through this maze forever. At least ten minutes. Can I change my clothes? Well, I guess we're not going to be getting into a fight. Hopefully not. Unless... Maybe I should change my clothes. Do you just think about it?" As she spoke, her dress shifted, twisted, and she was wearing a linen suit accentuated with leather pieces that rode the line between armour and decoration.

"You probably still have to work within the narrative," Peri explained. "Those changes are easier than shifting toward something that shouldn't exist within the dream."

"Gotcha. So, if I want a weapon, I should go for a sword." She held her hand out, and a sword appeared in it, as long as her arm and wickedly sharp. She was so surprised she almost dropped it and had to scramble to get her grip back.

"Here." Peri held out a scabbard, and Maeve gratefully took it and sheathed the sword, buckling it around her waist.

"Okay. Lead the way." Maeve held out her hand and Peri took it. They led Maeve around a corner in the maze, where a large wooden door revealed itself in the next arch. Peri opened it and stepped through, concentrating hard on both bringing Maeve with her and finding the woman.

As Peri crossed the threshold, they felt that tingle in their hands grow stronger. Their grip on Maeve tightened involuntarily, and the cold crept up past the first knuckle of every finger. Then they were through, Maeve still at their side, the world around them shifting from night to day. A crowd of Troll dolls was doing a musical number in front of a waterfall; Peri couldn't tell which of them was the dreamer, or if there even was one. It could be a third-person dream.

"There," Maeve whispered, pointing. In the woods, just beyond the circle of warm sunlight, a dark figure stood watching the dance. She hadn't noticed Peri and Maeve yet, all her attention focused on the sweet display in front of her. *This is what she does with her freedom?* Peri marvelled. *Take in a show?*

Together, Peri and Maeve crept under the protection of the trees. It was harder to move silently there than it had been in the meadow, and their pace slowed down to a crawl as they flanked her. They split up just enough to come at her from two sides, then as one they stepped forward enough that she could see them. She spun, as if ready to flee, but saw that they were on either side of her.

She could still easily have taken off into the middle of the Trolls, but when she saw Peri, guilt flashed across her face and the coiled energy of her tense muscles stilled somewhat. She was still on the balls of her feet, ready to move at any minute, but she waited to see what Peri would do.

The problem was, Peri had no idea what to say.

Maeve, on the other hand, knew exactly what to say. "Do you know that you almost killed Peri? I had to break into their apartment just to wake them up. They were in a coma or something."

The woman didn't so much as glance at Maeve, her whole attention on Peri. Her guilt shifted minutely to something close to regret. "I didn't intend that," she said.

"But you knew it might happen," Maeve challenged.

The woman answered Maeve without taking her eyes off Peri. "It's never been done before, not that I know of. I was working blind—going on hope. I'm sorry that happened to you." She flicked her eyes briefly to Maeve. "And you seem fine."

"Gee, that's a great apology." Maeve's hands twisted on the hilt of her sword, but she didn't draw it.

"Maeve thought she might have freed you—that it was the reason you disappeared."

The woman shook her head. "She ejected me from *that* dream, but I can still feel the pull. All the other dreamers, waiting to dream me again. It hurts me." Her eyes were huge, liquid with pain, begging to be understood. Peri couldn't look away. "You see why I had to do what I did, don't you?"

"Not really," Maeve snapped. "Killing me wouldn't even have worked. You get that, don't you? All that blood on your hands wouldn't have set you free. It's not me keeping the dream alive. It's everyone else who watched it."

Snarling, the woman turned her full attention to Maeve for the first time. Peri felt adrift as cold crept up their arms and chased across their chest. They longed to draw her attention back but fought the urge. Was the regret she showed enough to sway Peri to her side? Regret wasn't love.

"It would have been worth it, even so," the woman snarled at Maeve. "You're dangerous. The dream that lured me in came from you. Who knows how much more damage you might cause." The taut energy of her balance shifted, ever-so-slightly, as if she was considering once again launching herself at Maeve.

"Killing me here won't kill me," Maeve reminded her.

Was that true? Peri wasn't sure what the rules were anymore. An injury in a dream had certainly followed them out into the waking world. That didn't necessarily mean death could do the same, or even that there was consistency to the rules of this place, but it was enough to make Peri cautious.

The woman licked her upper teeth lightly, considering. "Why are you here?" she purred. The question took them both by surprise.

"I have the same question." A fourth voice had all three spinning on their heels to face this potential new threat. But as he stepped out from behind a tree, Peri saw a familiar sight—the man Maeve had spoken of so flatteringly. Maeve perked up as he appeared and threaded her way through the trees toward him.

"You found us," she said with delight.

"I've been keeping an eye." He took in Maeve's sliced-up arms in alarm. "Or I thought I had—when did this happen?" He reached out, surprisingly tender despite his bulk, and ran his fingers down her arm where the skin was unmarked.

"Funny story, that," she said dryly. She looked over at the woman. "Your friend crossed into the real world and tried to shish kebab me."

The dream woman crossed her arms and raised a lazy eyebrow. Her expression screamed, *So what if I did?* But she didn't say a word.

"You—what? No, that's impossible. How?" the man spluttered.

She ground her teeth and didn't say anything, but betrayed herself with a glance at Peri. The man followed the look and appraised Peri, calculating. Whatever he saw, he didn't like, and Peri unconsciously wrapped their arms protectively across their chest.

"So, I had a day," Maeve said. "And I'm pretty sure I knocked her ass right out of the dream she was stuck in."

"Again... How?" the man asked, laughing a little at his own incredulity.

"I changed the flow of the dream so the characters forgave each other." Maeve shrugged, but the man shook his head and refused to let her dismiss what she had done.

"That's incredible. You were smart to think of it—I never would have."

Maeve didn't quite blush, but her grin was a little bit pleased and a little bit embarrassed. "Thanks."

"Why you?" Peri asked. Their voice felt startling after the long silence. "Why did Maeve's dream trap you, and no one else?"

"I have no idea," the woman said.

"Liar," the man countered. The woman glared at him, and there was a moment of standoff as they made eye contact before the woman, grumbling, looked away. The man turned his attention to Peri, apparently having somehow won the right to speak. "She was hooked because of you."

"Peri didn't do anything," the woman snapped. "And you have a theory. That's not the same as knowledge."

"Fill us in?" Maeve gently prompted.

"We drift from dream to dream," the man explained. "Our society is a loose thing compared to yours, but we do have common lore. Ours says that staying in the mind of one dreamer too long is unwise. She ignored the lore. She grew attached to you," he said, directing that last to Peri, "and began to spend every night in your dreams."

Peri was stunned. Attached to them? Breaking the rules just to see them? Had Peri been wrong? Had it not been one-sided after all? Desperation had made the woman do things—terrible things—but it hadn't been selfishness alone that made her seek Peri out.

"But if she was stalking Peri, why did she get trapped in *my* dreams?" Maeve asked.

"Some dreams are close to each other, in the way that we understand geography. It's complex and follows rules that have nothing to do with the world as you know it. Suffice it to say that you and Peri dream side by side. Your dreams have an odd quality. A power, a charge."

"A pull," the woman corrected bitterly.

"Because she spent so long in your dreams, the pull caught her. I've been studying the phenomenon. It's why you've seen me in your dreams, observing, for some time now."

"That's a little hypocritical," Maeve pointed out. "To tell her she's being an ass to be up in Peri's dreams, but then do the same to mine?"

"A little," he agreed with a smile. "But I was taking risks with caution. She stepped directly into the flow of your narrative. I don't do that. I keep to the background of the dream and avoid your direct attention. I did, at least, until you became aware of me. And since then, you haven't been recording, so I haven't been in any danger."

"But that means... I can't record safely. Ever again?" Maeve staggered back, as if the realization was a physical fist around her heart.

"Some of your dreams are more potent than others. But if one of us is in one of your dreams, taking part in the narrative, I don't think they're safe to record."

"What about the way dreams have been leaching into the waking world?" Peri asked the woman. "It was always after a dream with you."

She shrugged elegantly. "I was struggling to escape. It made the walls between realities... unfortunately delicate."

"You should have told me," the man chided.

"As if you would have helped?" the woman snapped. "You have no loyalty to me! You tell them everything and act as if I'm the perpetrator of my own agony, when she is the one to blame! You would expend no energy on my saving! I'm trapped, and as long as people remember the dream, I won't be safe."

"I can keep you safe," Peri whispered. The idea had been forming as the others spoke, and they knew with quiet and grim surety that they could do it. In fact... they already had. "I can create a world outside of our dreams. A pocket narrative, running alongside us, where you'll be protected from Maeve's influence. You can stay there, live in that dream, for a year or two. People have short memories."

They both looked shocked. "That's impossible," the woman said. "How could you do a thing like that?"

"That place you created—the place in the clouds," the man said. "I couldn't get in until you opened the doors for me."

Peri nodded. "It was easy, and I think I could anchor it so that it doesn't rest within my sleeping mind. It would be there even when I'm awake." They turned to the woman. "I can build something like that for you, but it won't be a place I can visit. If I do that, it'll weaken the narrative you craft. It might make the walls permeable."

"I won't see you again," the woman stated.

"No," Peri said. "No, I don't think so."

She nodded. "It is as it must be, then."

Peri felt her rejection like a sharp knife. They knew it was the only solution, and the one they were offering, but they had hoped that it wouldn't be such an easy decision to come to. That giving them up would hurt her, at least a little.

"Are you sure?" the man asked, urgent and yet gentle.

"I think I'll find it interesting to write my own story," she answered, "with no dreamer in sight. Tell the others I'll see them soon?"

"I will," he promised. He walked forward and embraced her, oddly tender and yet somehow formal, their bodies held apart but their foreheads touching, their hands light on each other's shoulders. They stayed that way for a moment, and then he and Maeve stepped aside to give Peri some privacy.

Peri hesitated. "You... really came to see me?" they asked. "To be with me in my dreams?"

"I did," the woman said. "Your dreams are brave. You have a thirst for life that matches my own. I enjoyed the lives I lived with you."

Peri felt their eyes fill with tears. "Then why risk it all by taking so much of my connection to the world? Why not explain to me what you really needed, what I might be giving up?"

"You didn't ask," the woman pointed out.

"No." Peri was bitter. "I would have given you anything."

"You should hold yourself more precious," the woman chided. "It isn't up to me to do it for you."

"It should be. If you care for someone," Peri argued.

"Perhaps we both failed, then." The woman shrugged. "I'm sorry for that, at least. Does that count for anything?"

"I suppose," Peri said, although they weren't sure that it did, in the end. "Are you ready?"

"You are kind to do this, when I did less for you."

Peri shrugged. There was nothing to say to that, not really, and it was time. They closed their eyes and fixed a place in their mind. It was nowhere and everywhere; a blank canvas, waiting to be written on. It would conform to the will of the dreamer, would become whatever she wanted it to be. A world that Peri would find right there. Through the elevator doors.

Peri stepped around a large tree. There, hidden from sight, the doors to the elevator stood as if they had been there all long. They were silver, surrounded by a simple frame with a round light above the doors. In the panel the up button glowed, and as they watched the light above the door turned on. It was accompanied by a sweet, low chime.

The woman stepped up beside Peri, their shoulders almost touching. "And so you make a world for me, as you always have."

"And you leave me in my own, as you always would have," Peri whispered.

The woman nodded. She turned to Peri and held out her hands. Hesitantly, Peri copied her. They closed their eyes and felt a flood of warmth shoot up their arms, shattering the invisible vines that had wrapped cold tendrils around them. Peri opened their eyes to the sight of the woman's back, walking toward the door. She opened it and disappeared inside, never once looking back.

Peri watched them go, still feeling the quiet, almost familiar tingle in the tips of their fingers, side by side now with the warmth they remembered. They had it all... everything but her.

33

MAEVE

Maeve stepped aside with the man, giving Peri and the woman space to say goodbye. They didn't go far, but kept their voices pitched low out of politeness.

"Is it over, then?" Maeve asked. She meant the dreaming, the life in the waking world she built for herself, but he misunderstood.

"It doesn't have to be. There's still a mystery to be solved."

"The mystery of me?" Maeve asked, forcing a small smile.

"I hope you don't mind," the man said, bashful and kind. It was almost enough for Maeve to forget her worries. Almost.

"If you keep visiting me?" Maeve asked.

"There are answers there, if we can learn to find them," he agreed. "And maybe we can even find a way to protect my people from it. To insulate us from whatever your technology does, from whatever you do, from whatever Peri has become."

"That's a lot of things you need protecting from," Maeve said. Then she smiled brightly. "Good thing you've got me on your side." Suddenly, it occurred to her. "I don't know your name."

He laughed. "We don't have names. It's such a human desire to catalogue everything."

"Says the guy who couldn't help but document my dreaming," Maeve teased. "Would it be okay if I called you... something?"

"Call me anything," he said, and winked.

$$\sim$$

Maeve woke up late in the afternoon to Peri politely calling her name and the smell of eggs. At least, she thought it wás eggs until she eagerly joined Peri for breakfast and shovelled a forkful into her mouth. She couldn't figure out what she was eating until she remembered all the vegan food in Peri's fridge. Right. This was probably tofu masquerading as eggs. Once she'd identified it, she found it wasn't too bad, and she polished off her plate.

Peri had clearly been awake for a few hours; they had cleaned up the remnants of the snack Maeve made the night before, and they were on their laptop, typing away on some chat program. The two dreamers didn't talk much, but Maeve helped clean up the dishes and promised to stop by later and see how Peri was.

Outside, Maeve sent Josie an SOS and asked when her last appointment of the day was; her schedule was different every day. Then she let her steps carry her mindlessly toward the SkyTrain. She couldn't believe how much had happened in such a short time. Everything was a blur since she had woken up on the roof, naked, with a sword in her hand and a newfound fragility in her heart.

It seemed impossible that any of this was real. That this was what her life had become. Peri had a magical dream creature living in their head. Maeve's dreams were traps, black holes that lured these creatures in. And the dream technology that Maeve loved so much? It created echoes of those black holes, copies that could snap shut on the unwary and cause untold damage.

She couldn't believe that she might never record another dream. There *had* to be a way for her to do what she loved safely. Dreaming had given her something she had always been reaching for. It was her path to creative expression, her one chance to *make* something. It filled the hole she had always felt at her core, that desperate need to be something more than what she was.

She couldn't imagine going back to her life before all this. Working for a non-profit for shit pay where most of her work involved answering phones wasn't the life she wanted for herself. She wanted *more*. What a cliché. Every gifted kid whose parents thought they could change the world felt that same urge. They had been promised that they would be extraordinary, and when they weren't, their self-image collapsed like a house of cards.

When Maeve had felt the cards flutter and doubt settle in, she had done something about it. She had quit her job and taken the hard path forward, determined not to let apathy win. And it had been working! Well, it had mostly been working. She was on the path to where she wanted to be, she felt that in her bones. She couldn't go back to the version of herself from two years ago, pasting a happy face on her bone-tingling fear. She couldn't. She would suffocate. She would scream.

By the time Maeve got to Josie's office, she had worked herself into a state. She had an hour to kill before Josie was done, so she sat on the curb outside and dropped her head onto her knees. She tried to think about anything else. What did it feel like for Peri, having someone living in a dream they made? Could Peri sense her? Maeve wasn't sure she could handle it.

She took out her phone and answered some messages, told her mom a highly edited version of her day, and then played word games online until Josie came out. Maeve turned and waved, waiting until Josie was close enough to talk easily.

"You'll never believe the night I had," she said. Where should she even start? With the call for help? The outcome of it? With everything she and Peri had learned from the dream creatures? "I —" Her voice stuttered and scratched. She found her breath coming in short, hard gasps, and realized she was fighting off tears. What was wrong with her? She was fine. She could talk about it. "I guess... a lot—"

Then she was crying, deep sobs that shook her from her core up through her throat. Josie was at her side in a flash and holding her, and she let all her fear rush through and out. That she would have to give it up. That she would never be this version of herself she knew she could be. That it was over.

She cried until her head hurt and Josie's shirt was absolutely soaked with tears. "Fuck," she said when she could say anything at all.

Josie gave her a tissue to blow her nose and dragged her to the nearest coffee shop. It was a little past six, so the daytime rush was done and the place was quiet. The smell of roasting beans filled the air, tinged just a little with fresh baked goods. It was a comforting mix, and Maeve blew her nose again to take it in. She grabbed a seat in a corner while Josie got them both coffee and brought it over.

"Start from the beginning," Josie advised. "Did knocking that bitch back into her own lane not work?"

Maeve talked Josie through it quickly. She tried not to leave anything out, and she was surprised at how crisp all her memories of the events were. Even the conversations that happened in dreams were easy for her to pull up in her mind.

When she was done, a stunned Josie sat back, taking it all in. "Wow." Josie grabbed the little crescent moon pendant of her necklace and played with it, skating it up and down the length of the chain. "Holy shit."

"Yeah. I feel like I should apologize to you."

"What?" Josie tilted her head like a bird. "For what?"

Maeve shrugged. She had both her hands wrapped around the tall ceramic mug of coffee. Her nails were jagged in a few places. They were forever breaking, and she always forgot to file them. "If I'd taken that dream down like Jason wanted me to..."

"Maeve. Oh, no, babe, you can't take that on!" Josie leaned forward and forced one of Maeve's hands away from the cup so she could hold it. "Thinking your dreams could hurt someone would have been unbalanced. You can't seriously expect yourself to have known."

Maeve sniffled a little and leaned back, hugging herself for comfort more than warmth. "It's just that... all of these people were killed, and it was because of something that my dreams are, something that makes them inherently different from everyone else's. What if it's because I wanted it too bad? Maybe that's what makes my dreams so toxic."

"They're not toxic," Josie snapped. "They're beautiful. You said yourself that guy wants to study them, even after everything that happened."

"I guess," Maeve agreed, wiping away the fresh tears that had sprung up as Josie talked. It felt so good to talk about it, to expose those dark fears to the light so they could be banished. "Fuck. I was trying to apologize, and it became all about me. I meant, you know, this all hits you too. How are you? Does any of this make anything better? Or worse?"

Josie considered that carefully. She squeezed Maeve's hand before she let it go, so her friend would know she wasn't mad, and then ran her index finger through a drop of condensation on the table, clearing it away.

"I'll be okay," she finally decided. "I'm glad that it's over. It was hard, not knowing what had happened or why. I feel like I've been part of it all but also on the periphery, you know? Cut off from what's actually happening? That's been hard for me. I kept checking my phone every five seconds, wondering if anything had happened, if you'd learned anything new."

"That must have really sucked," Maeve agreed. It had been hard enough being part of it all. She couldn't imagine just watching from the sidelines.

"You did a good job keeping me informed," Josie assured her, then added a little dig. "Once you got around to telling me, anyway."

Maeve laughed. "Did I apologize enough for that? I can buy you a doughnut."

"I think we both deserve doughnuts."

Maeve got up, ignoring Josie's assertations that she had only been joking, and went over to the counter. The woman behind the counter smiled and gave Maeve one of those gentle looks you give someone having a bad day; obviously, her eyes were red from crying. They were all out of most of their baked goods, so Maeve came back with an oatmeal cookie and a croissant, looking apologetic, and gave Josie the first pick.

Josie took the cookie with a shake of her head. "Do you really think all of this means you won't be able to record your dreams anymore?" She broke the cookie apart into little pieces before popping one into her mouth.

Maeve sat down heavily. "I don't know. I won't take the risk of anyone being hurt like that again. But... the dream guy told me the woman entered the narrative of my dream too forcefully, and that's why she got stuck. And remember how your face in the dream changed into hers? It was damn obvious, in hindsight anyway, once we understood what it meant."

"So you think it would be easy to check recordings over and make sure there were no dream beings in them before you posted anything," Josie filled in.

"Yeah, exactly. That should be safe. That's what I keep telling myself. But how do I know what I don't know? So many people died because I had no idea what I was messing with. It all feels precarious. There's this huge unknown on top of this thing that I really love, that used to be something that made me feel safe. It feels I lost something." Maeve put a hand to her chest, the knuckles curled in to tap her sternum.

Josie scooted her chair closer and hugged Maeve with one arm, and her friend leaned in and accepted the comfort. "You've always got me, kid."

"I know." Maeve nuzzled Josie's cheek. "And you've always got me."

Outside the window, the sun was setting. The Northshore mountains were visible in the distance, and the lights of the ski lift glittered like a jewel at the fork of two crests. The sunset was softened by clouds, and outside traffic rumbled past, oblivious to the drama unfolding in all of the windows that dotted the street.

Josie sighed dramatically and kissed the top of Maeve's head. "Gosh, we sure are adorable."

Maeve laughed—and didn't stop for a long time.

34

PERI

Finally alone again, Peri fed Juniper and got the condo in order. They had only been away from it all for a day and a half, so it was really more about re-establishing control than it was about actual cleaning. Peri knew that, but couldn't stop from organizing drawers that were already organized, cleaning surfaces that were completely clean, and redrawing their budget in case the times stayed lean.

As they worked, they kept pausing mid-effort or mid-thought, listening to a half-heard noise or feeling a faint breeze and wondering... was that her? Could Peri feel her? They were sure they couldn't, not really. The lines between dream and reality had been cracked by the woman's efforts to escape the trap of Maeve's dreams. With that over, there was no reason for the waking and dreaming worlds to collide. Peri was on one side of a strong barrier, and the woman was on the other.

But every football from the condo upstairs, every horn honked outside their window, still felt like a quiet call—one Peri knew they shouldn't answer.

They didn't know much about love. They had only had a few short relationships, and nothing that lasted. But they knew enough to know that what they felt for the woman wasn't healthy. She asked and took and never gave back. They were too inclined to put others first, to push their own needs aside as unimportant. It was exactly what they had done with their parents, until Peri reached the breaking point and exploded.

Peri hated that Kyle refused to see how awful their parents were, but the truth was, some of the blame for how bad things had gotten was on their own shoulders. They had never spoken up or asked their parents to do better. They never said how any of it made them feel. They couldn't say why, exactly, they had been so silent. Maybe they were scared of the consequences of speaking up. Maybe they were convinced it was pointless, that their parents wouldn't care. If it wouldn't help, what was the point of trying?

That wasn't to say their parents hadn't been wrong. They had been inflexible, bigoted, and oblivious. They hadn't understood Peri's relationship to their gender and had refused to try. When Peri came out, they wouldn't use their new name, consistently dead-naming their child instead. Peri knew they had been right to cut them off, to put their own mental health first. They didn't question that.

But they were starting to see how they had contributed to that situation. How they had given their parents licence to be shocked and offended when Peri finally snapped, because it came entirely out of left field for them. Their parents hadn't known how much their actions hurt. How their stance ground glass into a wound Peri was just learning how to heal. If Peri had expressed that, had found a way, maybe things would be different.

Picking up their phone, Peri emailed Jasmine and asked for an appointment the next day. They weren't entirely sure how they were going to talk about what had happened, but they needed to unpack everything with someone who could help them navigate the maze.

In the end, they weren't sure if they had stood up to the woman, or if circumstances had just conspired to make standing up to her unnecessary. They didn't want to think of what might have happened if push came to shove, and the woman refused to give back Peri's connection to the waking world. If they would have had the strength to demand it.

On the other hand, they were excited. They had kept the power the woman had given them to explore the minds of the whole slumbering world. It was something that no human, as far as Peri knew, had ever had before. There was an entire new world waiting for them. That could be a problem. It could end up being even more enticing than the dreaming world had been before. They would need to navigate that, find ways to stay connected to their waking life. But after having almost lost that connection, they had a feeling it wouldn't be so hard.

The first thing they had done after waking up, while Maeve was still sleeping, was reconnect with all of their friends on Discord. It had been easy to fall back into those relationships, and it had felt *good*. Peri had a newfound understanding of everything their life gave them. The solidity and truth that only existed when their eyes were open.

When my eyes are open. I like that, Peri thought, and smiled.

Around eight that night, there was a knock at their door. Peri went over and unlocked it, opening it with a little difficulty due to the broken handle. They were surprised to see Maeve standing there, holding a huge paper bag.

"I don't know what you like so I got some of everything," she said, holding up what was clearly food.

"What? Why?" Peri asked.

"You were just in a coma, and I accidentally killed people with my brain," Maeve teased. "I thought you might want to hang out."

"Hang out." Peri couldn't remember the last time they hung out with anyone in person. Had they even had friends over to the condo? There had been virtual movie nights and boardgames with their friends on Discord, but that was it.

"We survived bewildering magical nonsense—and there's gonna be more of it," Maeve pointed out. "I think it goes without saying that we're friends now."

Peri didn't know what to say, but a surprised laugh slipped out and said it all for them. They took a step back, their door wide open.

And just like that, Maeve walked inside.

acknowledgments

When my brother was a kid, he and his best friend became convinced that they were sharing dreams. Every day they would get together and talk about the adventures they'd had the night before, seamlessly agreeing that, yes, that had absolutely happened in *their* dream, too. I was desperately jealous—and utterly in awe. Thank you, Misha, for filling my young life with magic (even when it wasn't real).

Thank you to the Parliament House team for believing in *my* magic and taking a chance on this quiet, weird little book. Special thanks to Malorie for your incredible content edits, and to Alexandra for your enthusiasm and help along the way.

Thank you to my family for your unwavering love and support, and to all the friends who read early drafts and gave me feedback, especially my mom and Kali.

Thank you to the Vancouver Genre Writers group, who gave me advice on building newsletter lists, chatted endlessly about naming monsters, joined my ARC team, and just generally provided a welcoming community.

And of course, thank you to you, my readers. I would love to claim that I write solely for myself, but the truth is I write to send the stories out in the world. I am so grateful that you have found this one, and I hope it resonates.

about the author

Wren Handman is a novelist, fiction writer, and screenwriter. She has published seven novels, for both adult and teen audiences, including I Walk Alone (Parliament House Press) and Havoc & Happiness (Wandering Roots Press). Wren was the lead writer for award-winning sitcom The Switch, her TV pilot Doomball won entry to the Telus Storyhive Web Series program, and her feature Home(less) was awarded funding from the Harold Greenberg Fund. Wren has a bachelor's degree in Creative Writing from the University of Victoria, where she graduated with honours, and a master's degree from the University of British Columbia, in the prestigious joint program in Theatre and Creative Writing.

WRENHANDMAN.COM